Lifers

Jane Harvey-Berrick

HARVEY
BERRICK
PUBLISHING

First published in Great Britain in 2014
ISBN 9780957496187

Harvey Berrick Publishing

Cover design by Hang Le / byhangle.com
Cover photographs: iStock by Getty Images

DEDICATION

This book is dedicated to Dina and Steve.
For letting love win.

ACKNOWLEDGMENTS

Thank you to all the early readers who were so generous with their comments. Including my gal pal team Kirsten, Lisa, Sheena, Dina, Audrey, Barbara, Cori, Shirley, Trina, MJ Fryer, Kelsey, Kandace, Sophie Callahan and the redoubtable Dorota. To my ARC readers: Brittany Topping, Bella Bookaholic, Emma Dach-Harris, Michelle Ocha, Sarah Bookhooked, Kim, Jackie Fiorentini, Thessa Marj-Laj, Carol Sales, M. Robinson and Charmaine Stephens.

To fellow writers A. Meredith Walters, Devon Hartford, Jasinda and Jack Wilder, and G.E. Griffin for their support and friendship.

To Hang Le for her enthusiasm, fabulous cover design and chapter headings – and for her never ending creativity.

To the book bloggers who have been so supportive, especially Maryse, Aestas, Smitten, and Totally Booked.

To the fb friends who have become real friends, especially Ellen Totten, Ana Carvalheiro, Ana Kristina Rabacca, Karen Wright, MJ Fryer, Showdog, Bruninha, Vip and Toni Mehta, Reese Call, Miranda Bing, Angie Lynch, Feifei Le, Erin Spencer, Nikki Groom, Netzel, Soraya Naomi, Christopher Lindsay, Nuw Writer, Stacy Hgg, Liliana Li, Ani Surnois, Alex FF, Sarah Tree, Lorraine Hatt, Vicki Jackieshopper, Lelyana Taufik, Laura McCarthy Benson, Paola Cortes, Wendy Onefitgily, Steph, Mary Dunne and well, so many more of you.

To Ian Hamilton, for information on car engines.

To the very patient Lori Sabin, for editing this book.

To Kelsey's son (who ought to remain nameless to protect the innocent, but let's call him Shaun Burns), thanks for Mobi work.

Further conversion work by Polgarus Studios.

To Aud, again, for her fab-u-lous trailer video; and to Bruninha, for her Seb & Caro trailers in Portuguese!

Thanks, too, to the wonderful but crazy Stalking Angels. Love ya loads.

And, as always, I must thank my hardy fanfic readers, without whom this book would not exist.

Prologue

And Cain said to the Lord, "My punishment is greater than I can bear."

Chapter 1 – Adjudge

Torrey

The morning rush was nearly finished. I knew from my experience of two days at the Busy Bee Family Diner that it would be quiet until lunchtime.

I stared out at the main road where not a single car or truck bothered to stop, and watched dust devils spin in the lazy summer breeze. That was about as exciting as it got. What a freakin' dump.

Waiting tables wasn't exactly my dream job, and not where I thought I'd be at 24 years of age with an expensive college degree several years behind me. In fact, I was shocked to find myself back waitressing, the kind of work I'd done when I was a teenager. But I liked to eat, and I couldn't face crawling back to my dad to ask for a donation to the Torrey Delaney Life Achievement Award (Pending). He'd only chew me out again for walking away from my own apartment *and* a good job.

Yeah, well, when you've slept with your boss and then he dumps you and treats you like shit, no job is worth hanging onto, in my opinion. And I'd thought about it *a lot*.

All of my friends were clambering up their career ladders; they all had a plan. Something. I couldn't face sleeping on couches and seeing pity in their eyes, while they put on their business suits and pumps, and headed out to their well paid jobs.

All I knew was that I had to leave Boston—start fresh somewhere else. Besides, Dad had just gotten remarried to a silicone-tit slut only a few years older than I was. Neither of them wanted me around. The feeling was mutual.

So I'd ended up calling Mom for the first time in six years and taking up her offer of a room in Smallbutt, Nowheresville, on the gulf coast of Texas.

Oh, she'd been happy to help, and thanked God that her prodigal daughter was returning to her at last. Yeah, well, some dreams are born to be shattered. Her idea of cozy nights reading Bible stories together and spending some quality mom/daughter time didn't really match up with me going out drinking till all hours and being dropped off at the Rectory before dawn by a guy in a truck.

Yup, I was the talk of the town. At least I thought I was.

I'd been lucky that the Busy Bee's owners were short-staffed, otherwise I'd have had to drive the 40 plus miles to Freeport, or 35 miles to Corpus Christi for a job. Of course, tip money would *probably* be better in the city, but that was a lot of gas money to lay out every day, never mind the time wasted driving back and forth. People sure weren't overly generous here, unless it was with advice I didn't want to hear.

I pulled out my phone and started texting one of the hook ups that I thought might be worth a second go. He'd been an okay ride for a country boy, and was a halfway decent distraction.

Doreen threw me an angry look. That was nothing new. My theory was that she'd been born with a broom handle up her ass. Or maybe just thirty years of waiting tables had left her as dried up and frustrated as a landed largemouth bass. Well, the expression was certainly the same.

I'd just pressed 'send' on my text when the old fashioned bell jangled above the door, and I glanced up. Now *that* was a long, cold drink of water on a hot day. Tall, over six foot, ripped, and with sandy-blond hair that was just a bit too long, tats running down both arms to his elbows, cheekbones you could file your nails on, and lips that were just perfect for biting.

I jutted out one hip, a move that I knew made my ass look great. The only problem was the guy seemed more interested in staring at his shoe than looking at me. Huh, maybe he wasn't into girls. I didn't think my gaydar was malfunctioning, but you never know.

I suddenly realized that all conversation had stopped and that each one of the redneck customers was staring at the newcomer. Yeah, I thought he was cute, but I didn't think that was why the Vardry brothers, Chuck and Mo, were staring daggers at him, or why the two teenagers in the corner looked like their eyeballs were about to explode.

The hottie twitched uncomfortably, as if he could feel their glares bouncing off of his broad shoulders.

It seemed weird that Mr. Fine and Fuckable, a guy with all that lickable muscle, was acting so shy.

"What can I get for you, handsome?" I asked, ignoring Doreen's hiss of annoyance.

"Uh, could I get a black coffee to go?" he asked hesitantly, still not making eye contact with me or anyone else.

I couldn't see what color eyes he had, but his lashes were far too long and pretty for a guy. Life could be so unfair.

"Sure! I'll just get that for you, hon."

"No," Doreen barked.

My eyebrows rose as I stared at my coworker, her vinegar face purple with anger.

The guy hunched his shoulders even more and didn't argue the point. He ducked his head and left the shop.

"What the hell was that?" I said, turning and staring in amazement.

"Just putting out the garbage," Doreen said nastily, and went

4

into the kitchen to stir her cauldron some more.

I didn't know what the hell was going on, but I wouldn't have treated a stray dog like that. I poured some coffee into one of the paper cups we used for take-out, and headed after him.

I was just in time to see the guy climbing into a battered pickup truck.

"Hey!"

He stared at me, and for a fraction of a second our eyes met—beautiful, soulful brown irises. They were so deep, I could have swam a few laps in those eyes.

I realized I hadn't spoken again and that he was still staring at me.

"You left without your coffee."

I gave him my best smile, but he'd already dropped his gaze.

I held out the paper cup to him, but for a moment I thought he wasn't going to take it.

Then his hand reached through the truck's window. I noticed he had the word 'love' tattooed across the back of his wrist. I wondered if he had 'hate' on the other side.

He took the coffee from me without a word, not even a thank you—I really hated that. Then he just started his truck and drove away

"What a jerk!"

I shook my head, more determined than ever to get out of this one-horse town where the horse had died.

Doreen had built up quite a head of steam by the time I walked back in.

"What on God's green earth do you think you were doing, serving that boy coffee, running after him like a bitch in heat?"

My mouth dropped open in surprise. I knew Doreen was a dried up old fatass, but she hadn't been blatantly rude to me before.

"What's wrong with this town?" I shot back. "A guy comes in for a coffee, all shy and polite, and you just treat him like trash!"

"Don't you back sass me, Miss High-and-Mighty! Your

momma might be the preacher-lady, but you're no better than you ought to be!"

"What does that even mean?" I yelled.

"You just quit your job, young lady!" spluttered Doreen, red in the face.

"Fine, whatever. I didn't like stinking of bacon grease every day anyhow."

I dipped my hand into the tips jar and shoved the change into my pocket.

"I'll consider it severance pay," I smirked at the old witch.

"You put that back!"

"And you really should remember to wash your hands after using the ladies' room," I called over my shoulder, throwing my apron onto the nearest table.

The bell jangled cheerfully as I slammed the café door behind me.

Seeing as I was currently unemployed—and probably unemployable as far as Buttfuck was concerned—I decided to spend the rest of the day working on my tan at the beach which was only a ten minute drive away.

I climbed into my beloved Pontiac Firebird, stroking the paintwork as I buckled up. It was more than 20 years old, and one of the last third generation models to roll off of the production line at Van Nuys. Bright red, it reminded me of a fire engine, made 13 miles to the gallon on a good day, and I loved it.

Maybe I gunned the engine more than a little, before I tore out of that small town in a cloud of dust.

I drove a few miles along the shore before I found an empty sweep of beach at Matagorda Bay.

The white sand stretched for miles in both directions, fringed by wiry grass. There was no one around and not even marks left by tires to show that anyone had been here.

Abandoning the car at the side of the dirt road, I felt the sun hot overhead as the light fractured the deep blue of the ocean. I left the windows down, sure that no one was going to hotwire my car this far from nowhere. I hiked the short distance down to the shore, wishing I had more than a three-day old bottle of tap water in the car for refreshment. But wishing wasn't having, so I dropped my ass onto the sand, pulled off my t-shirt and bra, then shimmied out of my jeans and panties.

I hated tan lines.

I must have been asleep for nearly two hours because the sun had shifted when I opened my eyes again. Somewhere in the pile of clothes, my phone had buzzed, shaking me out of a weird dream where Doreen was trying to make me go fishing for bass.

I peered at the screen: I had two messages—wow, I must have really been out for a while because the first one was from an hour ago and I hadn't heard it.

The good news was that my hook up—Clancy—was free and eager. I'd suggested meeting at a bar in the next town over. It was more of a guys' beer drinking joint than the kind of place I'd usually go, but I wasn't planning on spending too much time there before taking Clancy for a ride in the back of his truck. I just hoped he was as good as I remembered. Although, to be fair, the details were a little hazy.

The bad news was that Mom had heard I'd been fired from the Busy Bee after a record two-and-a-half days. Guess good news traveled fast in a small town.

I had no idea how she could stand it.

My mom was a good person, I think. At least she tried to be. She wasn't a huge hypocrite like some preachers I'd heard about, and she had as big an aversion to polyester suits as I did, but we still didn't exactly see eye to eye either.

I had a pretty average, middle class life for the first 13 years of my existence. Then Mom had found God, or maybe God had found Mom, I'm not quite sure. Because she decided that she had a calling—and it wasn't being a wife and mother. She had a mission to spread the Word of God.

Ironically, that ended up with Mom and Dad getting divorced. He didn't much like playing second fiddle to a guy who was bigger than he was, so to speak. And I didn't like being the child who was always waiting around for a mom who seemed to think that everyone else's problems were more important than her own daughter's.

Looking back, maybe we were being selfish, but I thought my mom could have looked in the same mirror and seen that, too.

Anyway, as soon as she finished her training at the Seminary, she got her first job down in the deep south. It was a world away from big city Boston, and I can only guess what the adjustment was like for her, being a woman and a liberal.

Then she moved to Texas and from what she told me, her church had been all but empty for the first six months, people preferring to hear their preaching from a man, not a woman who was also a Yankee.

In the end, her persistence paid off. I'd been here two, long, dreary weeks, and I had to admit I had a grudging respect for her. Hell, I'd never last in this state, let alone this town. And I didn't intend to try.

My mind wandered back to the hottie in the coffee shop. I wondered what crime he'd committed to be the local pariah. Maybe he'd fucked the sheriff's daughter. Nah, I'd met her in the diner once. She must have fallen out of the ugly tree and hit every branch on the way down. Besides, she was so uptight, he'd have needed a crowbar to get those legs apart.

Still, whatever he'd done, it kept the heat off of me. Not that I cared what they called me, but I didn't want to make things any harder for my mom. Damn, probably too late to worry about that now. Maybe I really was a lost cause.

I decided I'd have to try and find a new job tomorrow. What a drag.

I walked down to the water to wash off sand that had found its way into some interesting crevices. It just so happened that a couple of fishermen copped an eyeful as I cleaned up.

"Hey, sexy lady! You're a sight for sore eyes!"

"You probably jerk off so much you're already going blind," I shot back.

His friend was laughing his ass off while he thumped him on the back; my contribution to the fun was to flip them off.

I think they decided to try their luck, because they looked like they were planning on beaching their boat. I pulled on my jeans over damp legs, and got my arms in my t-shirt before they made it ashore.

I burned out of there so fast they were probably breathing my exhaust fumes for the next hour.

Mom was out when I got back, which was no surprise. She was hardly ever around, day or night. God's work kept her busy. I wondered what His health benefits were like. Did she get dental?

I took a shower and contemplated what to wear. I hadn't unpacked any of my city clothes so I didn't have a huge amount of stuff to choose from, but more than enough for Clancy. Although my ass looked at its best in skinny jeans, a skirt provided easier access for what I had in mind. I hoped Clancy would appreciate the sacrifice I was making on his behalf.

I chose a short denim skirt and a blue tank top that wasn't too slutty. I teamed it with a jean jacket, made sure I had condoms in my purse, and headed out.

I didn't bother leaving a note—I didn't want to set a precedent.

As I drove out to the bar, I realized I was getting low on gas again and since I'd quit the only job I'd had for a while, my bank balance was less of a balance and more of a sliding scale toward zero.

I still had the handful of change in tips that I'd scored from the diner. I pulled over to the side of the road and counted out the coins: nine dollars and a few cents. That wasn't going to buy a whole lot of gas.

I sighed and shoved the money back into my change purse. I wondered if Dad would be good for a couple of grand. Maybe if he was still blissed out from his honeymoon with his bimbette he might spring for some cash. It was worth the cost of a phone call.

It went straight to voicemail. Perfect. At least he hadn't blocked my number.

"Hey, Dad, it's me. Just wondering how you are and whether you and, um, Ginger had a great time in St. Thomas. I bet it was awesome. Yeah, so, the reason I'm calling—turns out it's not so easy to get work around here as a paralegal, or as anything really, and I was wondering if you could loan me a thousand, maybe two, just to tide me over until I get a job. I'm going to head up to Freetown tomorrow, so … anyway, hope you're both well and, um, thanks, Dad."

Yeah, that should do it. Just enough humble pie mixed with fake sincerity. With a bit of luck, he would put two K straight into my bank account without either of us having to speak to each other.

Feeling better about the state of the world, I used my credit card to fill up the tank. At least I wouldn't be paying for drinks tonight. Clancy had better be good for the beers if he wanted to get laid.

He was already there when I arrived. I liked that he was eager, but was less happy that he seemed well on his way to being toasted. I hadn't driven this far for a guy who couldn't get it up.

"There she is!" he slurred, to no one in particular. "Prettiest little cowgirl in the state."

I rolled my eyes as I sat on his lap.

"Cowgirl? Seriously? Do I look like the kind of woman who wears plaid shirts and a Stetson?"

He laughed uproariously and fastened his hands around my hips.

"You're funny, pretty girl."

Great. I think he'd forgotten my name. I mean, jeez, he had it on his cell phone. It couldn't be that hard to remember.

He waved at the waitress, and she brought us over a couple of beers. There wasn't much conversation, mostly Clancy just trying to feel me up. Perhaps he hadn't heard the concept of a sure thing.

He was good looking in a generic sort of way. Medium height, medium build, nice teeth. You know, just *nice*. I couldn't help comparing him with the coffee shop guy—Clancy definitely came up wanting.

I decided I'd get the evening's entertainment out of the way and head back home. I was feeling tired and a little out of it.

"Come on, fella," I said, pulling on his arm. "Come and show me some action."

I snagged the two bottles of beer for later and watched, irritated, as he stood up and swayed. He was a lot more drunk than I'd thought. This day just wasn't getting any better.

I hustled him outside and after fumbling his keys from his pocket, I managed to get him into the back of his truck. He sprawled out on the seat and pointed to his zipper.

"Get suckin', baby."

Oh hell no! I wasn't doing all the work here without getting something out of it. I pulled open his pants but didn't bother going any further—he'd already passed out.

Sighing with frustration, I started to climb out of the truck. Then I had another thought. I wrestled with his drunken ass, and managed to pull his wallet out of his back pocket. I was pretty sure that he'd lose his money if I left him like this, and I didn't want to be the one getting the blame if it got stolen. Asshole would probably assume it was me and call the police.

I shoved his wallet into the split lining at the back of the driver's seat and sent him a text telling him where it was and to never, ever call me again. Then I deleted his number.

Mom's car was in the driveway when I got home, but the lights were off so she must have gone to bed. I was relieved. I didn't feel like any mother/daughter bonding or discussion of my lifestyle choices right now.

I took another quick shower, my third of the day, and dropped into bed, cursing the heat and lack of a decent air conditioning unit. Well, it probably wasn't the unit—more likely the fact that Mom had set it too high to save money. Texas in the summer was a bitch.

Frustrated and pissed at Clancy's lack of, well, anything, I used my five-fingered friend to get myself off and wondered if I'd have a chance of better quality hook ups in a bigger town.

Something to look forward to.

Jordan

I knew who she was as soon as I saw her. Even though no one talked to me, I'd heard the gossip. She was the preacher lady's daughter—the wild one.

I was glad for the coffee though. Usually, I took a thermos when I headed out for work, but I'd forgotten it today and I really needed my caffeine fix. It was surprising how you could become addicted to that stuff so quick.

I fucking hated that I was her charity case. I was so tired of it. But I wasn't in a position to do anything about it either. And that made me pissed.

I had to admit she was something to look at though. She had a sweet, heart-shaped face, framed by this mane of curly brown-gold hair that hung down to the middle of her back. A man could lose himself for days in hair like that and not even care. And damn if her body wasn't something, too, with curves in all the right places.

It was a long time since I'd had a woman—eight, long years—and I couldn't see the drought coming to an end any time soon. So a woman like that got me imagining all kinds of things.

Her momma seemed like a nice lady. She tried real hard to get people to accept me. I could have told her she'd be on a losing streak betting on that hand. I was born in this small town, and I was certain that no one wanted me around here. Truth be told, I didn't want to be here either. Even so, it was way better than where I'd been. I had to stay for another four months, maybe more, then I was out of here. I'd be shaking this small town dust from my shoes and never looking back. I didn't know where I was going to go—anywhere but here sounded good. And not one damn person was going to miss me.

I parked outside the Rectory like I'd been told, and the Reverend Meredith Williams came out as soon as she heard my truck. Usually she met me wherever she'd found me work for the day, but this morning she'd asked me to come to her home. She said her yard needed fixing up and would take a few weeks to sort out. I didn't really care what I did.

"Good morning, Jordan. How are you this lovely summer day?"

"Fine, thank you, ma'am. You want me to start on the backyard today?"

"Actually, Jordan, I was wondering if you could do me one more favor. Hector Kees called and it turns out his car has broken down again, and you know he takes the three Soper sisters to church on Sunday. Your mom told me that you had a way with engines, so I wondered if you could take a look?"

"Um, sure. But will he want me to be fixin' his car?"

She got a determined look on her face.

"Don't you worry about, Hector. Leave him to me. You just worry about his car."

I wasn't happy with her 'favor' but I couldn't say no either. I followed her in my truck, bumping down the dusty, pot-holed road. Not that I needed directions—I could have found my way around in the dark with my eyes closed.

Hector's place was on the edge of town, near the bay. I used to drive out here with Mikey to get high or get wasted. It was kind of our place. We even had a pact not to take girls there.

I didn't really like being here again, but I didn't have a choice.

I stayed in my truck while the Reverend had a very heated discussion with ole Hector. I didn't want to hear what names he was calling me, so I turned on the radio and sat listening to an

Evanescence track that was playing—'Bring Me to Life'. The irony wasn't lost on me, and I flipped over to a Texas country channel instead.

I'd missed out on a lot of music over the last eight years. Since then, I'd spent most of my down time at my folks' house listening to the radio while I worked out in the converted garage. Saved Dad and Momma from having to look at my face, too.

Eventually, the shouting subsided and Hector stomped back into his crappy little wooden house. The preacher-lady waved at me to come on down. She was smiling, but it wasn't a real smile—it was one that she'd pasted on just to encourage me.

She dangled the keys to Hector's car and dropped them into my hand.

"Sorry about that. He'll be as pleased as punch when you've fixed it," and she turned to go.

"Wait, you ain't stayin'?"

Anxiety laced my voice and the Reverend laid a sympathetic hand on my arm.

"You'll be fine, Jordan. Hector says there are tools in the trunk. Just leave the keys on the stoop when you're finished."

"That ole fucker will shoot me rather than look at me—pardon my language, ma'am."

"I can assure you that Hector will be very grateful," she said, hesitantly.

It sounded good every time she said it about one of the townsfolk, but it didn't make it true.

She patted my arm again, and like the whipped dog I was, I set to look at the broken down Chevrolet that had been abandoned under an old oak tree.

The dust from the Reverend's tires was still swirling through the air when the door of the shack banged open, and Hector stood there pointing a twelve-bore at my favorite stomach.

"Got my eye on you, boy!" he spat. "You might have done got the preacher-lady fooled but I know you're bad to the bone. So jest you get on with what you've gotta do. One false move and I won't be ashamed to let loose a barrel of buckshot in your

14

direction. Unnerstan', boy?"

"Yes, sir. You'll have no trouble from me."

Isn't that the truth.

He waved the gun again, motioning for me to carry on, and I picked up the wrench that I'd dropped in the dirt.

I felt a cold prickle on the back of my neck. It just didn't sit right with me letting that old bastard talk to me that way, and I really wasn't happy turning my back to a man who hated my guts, and who happened to be holding a loaded shotgun.

I tried to ignore him and work out why his battered old Chevrolet sounded like a forty-a-day smoker.

The sun was getting high in the sky, and I'd worked up quite a sweat. I could feel the heat burning the back of my neck, even though I'd turned my Rangers baseball cap around to give me protection.

I looked over my shoulder, but Hector hadn't moved. He was still sitting in his rocking chair, a bottle of beer beside him, and the shotgun still unwaveringly pointed in my direction.

"Uh, Mr. Kees, could I get a cup of water, sir? It's hotter than a billy goat in a pepper patch out here."

"You think I'm dumb enough to turn my back on you, boy? My momma didn't raise no fool."

I couldn't even get a fucking glass of water in this town.

Then I remembered that I had the take-out coffee still sitting in the cup holder of my truck. It would be stone cold by now, but that was fine by me.

"Okay. I'm just gonna get somethin' from my truck."

The barrel of the shotgun followed me as I walked past him. The hairs on the back of my neck rose when I heard a double hammer being cocked. I backed out slowly, the paper cup in my raised hands.

"It's just a cup of coffee," I said, quietly.

He grunted, which could have meant anything. But at least he didn't shoot me.

The coffee tasted strong but not too bad, and went some way toward getting rid of the dust in my throat. I drank it down and went back to work.

The Chevrolet was a hunk of junk but I reckoned I could get it running again.

Half an hour later, I finished up and turned over the car's engine. It fired on the second try and a rare smile crossed over my face.

I didn't know much, but I knew cars.

I turned off the engine and the silence spilled out.

"Go on now! You skedaddle!" snapped Hector. "The preacher-lady has done gotten her good deed for the day and I don't want you on my property no more."

I nodded, expecting nothing less.

"Murderer!" he yelled after me, as I drove away.

I expected that, too.

With nothing better to do and nowhere else to be, I drove home.

Thankfully, the house was empty. Dad was at work and Momma—hell, I had no idea where she was. She hadn't been around much since I'd come back. Maybe I should have felt bad for driving her from her home, but somehow I couldn't care less.

I took a long cool shower then helped myself to the fixin's for a ham and cheese sandwich, and sat out in the shade of the porch, finishing my chow.

When I heard her car pull into the driveway, tension crept into my stomach as her footsteps sounded across the kitchen floor behind me. I didn't turn around, but I could sense that she was watching me.

"What are you doin' home at this hour?"

Her voice rasped out through the screen door.

"Finished a job for the Reverend and come back to get somethin' to eat."

She didn't reply, just walked away, leaving me alone.

That was okay. It was still a freakin' holiday to be by myself.

I went inside and lay on my bed for a while, just thinking. I could spend hours lost in my thoughts. I used to wonder what my life would have been like if I'd made a different decision that night. But thoughts like that could drive a man crazy. Instead, I tried to do what my counselor had told me, and focus on what I wanted for the future.

I'd gotten my GED and taken a couple of college courses, but nowhere near enough to get my degree. It had been hard to keep any motivation under the circumstances, but now ... Community college was a possibility, but there was no way I wanted to stay around here once my time was up. I think my folks were counting down the days as much as I was.

It was hard to make plans for what I wanted to do with my life when I didn't deserve to have any. I didn't deserve to live, but I was too much of a coward to do anything about it. I'd tried a couple of times and it just hadn't taken. I guess my punishment was to carry on living.

My mind drifted back to the preacher's daughter. That was one hot woman. I felt myself getting hard thinking about her. She was beautiful, too, but she acted like she didn't give a shit about it. She knew she was sexy, but it was part of who she was—she didn't use it as a weapon.

Thinking of her full lips had inevitably given me a boner, and I was gonna do something with it when I heard the floor creak outside my door.

I sat up right quick and made sure there was nothing obvious on show.

Momma's voice hammered through the wooden panel.

"I'm headin' out. You said you needed some jeans—I guess I'll have to drop into Goodwill. What size are you now?"

I climbed off of the bed and cracked the door to look at her.

"Thirty-two waist, 34 long."

She nodded and walked away.

The short conversation had sufficiently deflated me, so instead of going back to my room, I headed for the garage to lift some weights. Mikey had left a set in there and since I'd been back, I'd turned the space into a mini gym.

I worked out for a couple of hours until I heard Momma's

car crunch to a halt, immediately followed by Dad's truck.

I debated whether or not to go into the house but decided to stay in the garage where I'd be out of the way.

After half an hour, Momma banged on the door.

"Supper's ready."

The kitchen smelled of fried chicken. Momma had a way of using a whole load of herbs, so it was slightly spicy and tasted amazing. It was the only thing I liked about living here.

The first day I'd arrived back, she'd set three places at the table so we could all eat together. I think every single one of us had gotten indigestion staring at each other while trying to eat. Since then, she'd left my food at the kitchen table while she and Dad ate on trays in the family room.

It had become our unspoken agreement that the least time we all spent together, the better we'd get on.

I knew they didn't want me here, but for now we were all locked together with our memories—frustration and hurt on my part; hatred on theirs.

I knew the preacher-lady thought she'd done me a damn favor talking them into having me back, but I wished a dozen times a day that she hadn't.

It didn't help. Wishing was for fools.

I rinsed off my plate in the sink and stacked it in the dishwasher, before heading back to my room.

I hoped I'd be able to sleep through the night, but the nightmares had been pretty bad since I'd gotten home. The counselor had warned me about it—I just didn't think they'd be so fucking terrifying. The first night back, I thought I was having a heart attack. Dad had shaken me awake, then left without a word. Guess I'd pissed him off by spoiling his sleep.

I wasn't surprised to startle awake in a cold sweat at 3 AM, but at least I hadn't roused the house this time. Or if I had, no one cared.

I blew off some steam in the garage for an hour, then headed back to bed. It was just after dawn when I woke again.

Another fucking day in Paradise.

Chapter 2 – Trepidation

Jordan

"What are you doing here?"

I didn't need to look up to know who was speaking—I recognized her voice. It wasn't that hard. Apart from my family and the Rev, no one else spoke to me—unless it was to yell curses.

I didn't want to look at her, even though she was fucking beautiful, so I mumbled an answer.

"Workin'."

"What? You work for my mom?"

That did make me look up. I thought she knew. Wasn't that why she gave me the coffee? Because she knew who I was—the local charity case.

I made a mistake when I met her eyes. I was immediately caught in her intense gaze.

"I thought you knew."

"Nope, not till now. So you're what, like a handyman?"

I nodded, unable to speak.

"Oh, okay."

I couldn't help my eyes drifting up across her body as she spoke. I guessed she must have just woken up because her hair was all tangled and she looked like she was wearing what she'd slept in. She held a mug of coffee in her hands and the smell of those beans had my nose quivering like a coon dog. But then she crossed her legs, and my eyes were drawn to the sexy boy shorts she was wearing and tight tank top showcasing the most fan-fuck-tastic tits that...

"My eyes are up here, jerk-off!" she snapped.

I felt the heat rising in my cheeks and dropped my eyes to the ground once more. I picked up the handles of the wheelbarrow and headed toward the back of the yard.

Stupid stupid stupid.

"Hey!" she yelled after me. "You forgot your damn coffee again!"

I looked back at her, surprised. She was holding out the mug of coffee with an amused smile on her face.

"Black, no sugar—right?"

I nodded, still unsure what she meant.

"Well, I'm not carrying it across the damn yard to you!" she huffed, wiggling her bare toes at me.

She cussed a lot more than any preacher's daughter I'd ever met before. She put the coffee down on the porch step and patted the space next to her.

"It's okay, I won't bite."

God, I really hope that isn't true.

I clamped my tongue between my teeth to keep from saying something dumb like that out loud.

Gingerly, as if she might change her mind and explode with anger, I sat down next to her and picked up the mug of coffee. It smelled like heaven. I took a small sip and almost moaned with pleasure.

"The good stuff, huh?" she smiled, raising one eyebrow.

"It sure is, ma'am. I haven't tasted anythin' that good since, well … since forever."

"Ma'am?" she laughed. "Jesus, that makes me sound like I'm a hundred or something. How old are you, for crying out loud?"

"I'll be 24 at the end of the year," I answered, my head spinning like a pinball.

"Oh, me, too. I turned 24 in April."

I stared down at my coffee, unsure if I was supposed to say 'congratulations' or something. She looked like she was expecting me to speak.

"Don't get all Chatty Cathy on me!" she laughed, and nudged my shoulder.

Christ, I'm pathetic. A hot woman is talking to me, and I just sit here, dumb as a rock. I used to be good at this shit.

"You from around here? You sound like you are, but ya never know."

A jolt of surprise shocked me. *She doesn't know who I am!*

"Yes, ma'am. Born and bred."

"I told you—don't call me 'ma'am'. My name is Torrey."

Even her name was pretty.

She paused, and I realized she was waiting for me to introduce myself. I guess the last eight years had robbed me of my manners, along with everything else.

"Well, did you ever go away to college?" she went on, overlooking my silence. "I went to Boston University," she said, proudly, "and then I did law school for a couple of months. That sucked, so I did a certification class for paralegal studies instead. That was much better." She frowned. "Well, until recently."

I decided that if she really didn't know, I'd better just tell her, like ripping off a Band-Aid.

"I got my GED in juvie."

I cringed internally, waiting for the shutters to come down.

Instead she gave a small laugh. "Oh, are you a bad boy?"

I didn't answer, not having a fucking clue what to say. I couldn't even look at her.

Her voice was softer as she spoke again. "Oh, sorry. I can be really blunt sometimes. It's okay, you don't have to tell me. I take it you didn't go to college after juvie then?"

I shook my head then risked a quick look at her. Her expression was kind but not pitying. It gave me a moment of hope. False hope, in all probability, but hope nonetheless.

"I guess you could say I graduated to prison after juvie. I got out a month ago."

She was silent for a moment.

"This must be weird then. What was it like? When you got out?"

My eyes slid to hers. No one had asked me anything so direct.

"Why do you want to know that?"

She shrugged. "Just wondering. Must have been hell."

I nodded. Yup, hell. That was one of the ways I could have described it.

"Did you know that your momma convinced my folks to take me back when I got out?"

I don't know why I offered her that information. I just didn't want her to stop talking—it had been so long.

She gave a wry smile. "No, I didn't know, but it doesn't surprise me. Dear ole Mom, always trying to fix other people's problems."

I was desperately trying to think of something else to say. "So, um, you just moved here?"

Great question, genius! There's a freakin' U-haul trailer still parked in the driveway.

"Yeah, just moved down from Boston. After I quit my job, I thought I'd try small town life for a while."

I nodded, still having no clue what to say next.

"So, you're back living with your parents," she began again.

"And you."

She pulled a face. "Yeah, it's surreal."

"I wish she hadn't."

"Wish who hadn't what?"

"Your momma. I wish she hadn't told my parents to take me

back home."

"Why's that?" she asked, staring straight at me.

I struggled with what to tell her. I mean, I didn't know this woman, and certainly shouldn't go around trusting her just because she was the preacher's daughter. But it felt so good to shoot the shit with someone who wasn't judging me by what I'd done, or what they'd heard. It was addicting, and I didn't want it to stop.

"I just think it might have been easier to be a nobody in one of the halfway houses in the city. An ex-con like a thousand other guys. Here, everyone knows my story and has decided I'm trash."

"Except me," she said, still staring straight into my eyes.

It kind of hurt to have her look at me like that—like she was seeing into my soul, or some shit.

"Yeah, but that's because you don't know me."

Her eyes didn't flinch.

"You want me to leave you alone?"

The way she said it, I knew that if I said yes, she'd walk away and that would be that. Painful as it was to talk about everything, I didn't want this to be the end of it.

"No, I don't want you to leave me alone."

Her lips turned upward with this amazing smile that made her eyes sparkle, and her nose did this cute little wrinkling thing. I was hooked—and in so much trouble.

"Good," she said, simply.

We sat there in comfortable silence for several minutes. Well, I think she was comfortable—my dick was so hard, looking at those long legs of hers stretched out in front—comfortable was the last thing I was.

She seemed to be staring into the distance, but I guess she must have noticed my condition after all, because she said in a conversational tone, "If you want to use the bathroom to jack off, better do it now because I'm going to take a shower in a minute."

I nearly swallowed my tongue, and I'm sure my jaw was

pretty darn close to dropping on the floor.

"Excuse me?" I managed to cough out.

She turned an amused face toward me.

"You just look a little uncomfortable there, cowboy. I thought you might need some relief."

"Jeez! Are you always this direct?"

She hitched her shoulder in a delicate shrug.

"Pretty much. Does it bother you?"

"Um…"

"Don't worry. You don't have to answer that. It bothers most people."

She sighed and looked a little sad.

"No, I like it," I said, surprised that I was trying to reassure her.

"Really?" she said, smiling again. "That would be cool since we're going to be friends."

"We are?"

"Sure, cowboy."

"My name's Jordan. Jordan Kane."

I finally managed to stammer out my name. She studied my face and I felt my cheeks heat up. I hadn't had a woman look at me like that in a long time. Finally, she held out her hand.

"Jordan Kane," she said, thoughtfully. "Cute name for a cute guy."

When I took her soft hand in mine I was in total shock, and her words weren't doing anything to help distract the enormous fuckin' log that had planted itself in my pants.

Suddenly, the screen door opened. Torrey let go of my hand as the Reverend came out. She didn't look happy to see me talking to her daughter, and I wondered if she'd heard Torrey's last comment.

"Um, I'd better get back to work," I mumbled, hastily standing up.

"Sure thing, Jordan Kane," Torrey called out. "Nice talking to you."

I muttered something indistinct and hurried away, but not

before I heard the Reverend say, "Don't you think you should put some clothes on, rather than sitting around half dressed? Come on in, I need to talk to you about something."

I saw the Rev throw a glance in my direction. I didn't hear Torrey's answer, but she followed her momma into the house. I could guess what they'd be talking about and I was certain that the preacher's pretty daughter wouldn't be talking to me again anytime soon.

That was okay. I didn't deserve anything good to happen. Just talking to her like a normal person was the best conversation I'd had in eight years.

Torrey

"What's up, Mom?"

"I really don't think it's appropriate for you to go around dressed—undressed—like that," she said, firmly.

I couldn't restrain an eye-roll. *Really? She's trying to be a parent now that I'm 24?*

"Well, first of all, *Mom*, I don't 'go around' dressed like this. I sat on your back porch with a cup of coffee. It's hardly like I was streaking down Main Street. And second, why don't you tell me what's really bothering you?"

She huffed and dodged the issue for a while. I stood there with my arms crossed, waiting.

"Well, fine, you should know the truth."

"About?"

"Jordan Kane just got out of prison and..."

"I know. He told me."

"He did?"

"Yeah."

That seemed to take the wind out of her sails, and she

slumped down onto the sofa.

"Did he tell you *why* he was in prison?"

"I think he would have gotten around to it, but we were interrupted," I said, arching a brow.

"Come and sit down," Mom said, patting her hand on the cushion next to her.

I took the furthest seat away, sprawling in the easy chair opposite, hanging my legs over the arm.

"Go on then. Lay it on me."

"It's not something to joke about, Torrey."

"Do you see me laughing?"

"No, well … the truth is Jordan Kane is a very troubled young man. Now, I'm doing my best to help him settle back into society but…"

"But what? Get to the point, Mom."

She looked up at me sharply.

"But it won't help him if you start talking flirty to him."

I burst out laughing at that. "*Talking flirty*? Jeez. Did we just get beamed up by a spaceship and land in the 1950s? I made the guy a cup of coffee, and I kind of get the impression that I'm the only person that's tried to have a conversation with him in a while." My voice sobered. "He looked lonely. I made him coffee."

Mom shook her head.

"I heard what you said to him—you told him you thought he was cute."

"Mom, that's not flirting. That's a fact. That dude is smokin' hot."

She gasped, and I couldn't help riding her ass just a little more.

"Saying that he's cute is like saying that it's dark at night."

"I know you're trying to aggravate me, Torrey, so I'll let that pass. The *fact* is that he would have seen it as you flirting with him, no matter what you call it."

"Fine. You busted me eye-fucking the hot handyman. So sue me."

"I don't want you talking like that, Torrey!"

"Oh, jeez, Mom! I didn't hump him on the porch!"

"There's no need to be so crude!"

I was getting seriously pissed now. Did this woman not know how hypocritical she was being?

"Oh, is that right? So, talking to the handyman, whom *you* employed, and giving him a damn coffee is suddenly a cardinal sin? Why don't we talk about what's really bothering you, instead of dancing around it like a couple of queens at an Abba convention?"

"I can't talk to you when you're like this," she said, standing up suddenly.

"Yeah, well I guess we'll never have a real conversation then, because this is who I am. And if you'd stuck around instead of leaving us when I was 13, you'd know that."

"Torrey, I fully realize you've got a lot of unresolved issues about my calling…"

"Screw you, Mom! You don't get to use that as a defense! Not everything comes back to you. You don't know me, and you sure as hell don't get to judge me."

"Then stop judging *me*!" she yelled. "I'm doing the best I can here!"

I sat back, and we stared at each other for a long moment while she took several deep breaths.

"Jordan Kane isn't someone you should be associating with."

"Mom, come on! *Associating*? What does that mean? I shouldn't talk to him? Shouldn't make him a damn coffee? What?"

"I really think you could take my word for it that he's not a suitable person."

I couldn't help sighing dramatically.

"So you're not going to tell me what he was in prison for?"

Mom looked conflicted, but stayed resolutely silent.

"Fine, don't tell me. I'll ask him myself."

"Torrey," she said, grimacing, "can't you just trust me when I say he has a history of violence? I'm just trying to protect my only daughter."

Whoa! I didn't expect that.

"After being placed in a juvenile detention facility for two years, he was transferred to an adult prison for an additional six. Surely that tells you something. You're trained in the law—you know what that means. Now he's served his sentence, I'm trying to help him every way I can, but he's dangerous. I don't want to see you get hurt."

I couldn't do the math. The sweet, shy guy I'd met on two occasions just didn't fit with the image of a violent criminal that Mom was painting. Something was off, but I had no clue what it was. I mean, I could see he was a big, strong guy with abs like a washboard, but he just didn't seem the aggressive type. The only vibe I'd gotten from him was that he was lonely.

"And from what his parents have told me," she continued, "Jordan's *behavior* started a long time before that. It seems that Jordan was always the wild one, always in trouble: drinking, drugs, fighting, girls…"

Mom threw me a look. She was telegraphing a message, but all I could think was that Jordan sounded like an average 16-year-old.

"Yep, drink, drugs, fights, girls—got it. What else?"

Mom sighed and shook her head, irritated that I *wasn't* getting it.

"His older brother, Michael, was completely different. A straight-A student and a hard worker, he stayed away from strong liquor and had a nice girlfriend whom he was planning on marrying. He was a good boy."

"Yeah, and?"

Mom sighed and looked away.

"Michael … died and it destroyed the family. It was at that time that Jordan was … sent away."

"Wow. That's … awful! The poor parents."

"Yes, I know. It's a terrible story. I feel for Gloria and Paul, losing two children that way."

"Wait, what? What do you mean 'losing two children'?

Jordan is still alive!"

Mom shook her head sadly. "They lost two children in a very real way. It's a terrible thing. Michael died, and ... well ... Jordan was in prison."

"Yeah, sure, but he's home now. He told me that you persuaded his parents to take him back."

She looked puzzled.

"He told you that? You were only talking to him for five minutes!"

"Guess I have a friendly face," I said, evenly.

"Well, it's true. I did persuade his parents to take him back. They didn't want to have anything to do with him, and they hadn't seen him for seven years, so..."

"You mean they didn't visit him in prison? Not at all? Not even once?"

"Well, no. When he became an adult and was moved to the prison, they felt he was a lost cause and decided to grieve for their sons together."

"Are you kidding me?" I almost yelled at her. "They just gave up on him? So much for being good Christians!"

"You don't know the grief of losing a child," Mom snapped back.

I leaned forward in the chair. "You didn't 'lose' me, Mom. You left me behind. Your calling was more important than your family. But you know what, you made a choice—good for you. At least you didn't hang around making everyone miserable while you decided what you wanted."

She knew I was referring to the year before she left, when she'd prayed every night for God to tell her what He wanted from her. She'd been strong enough to make a tough choice. It was one of the few things I admired about her, even though it had been pretty shitty for me—and Dad.

"You don't understand," she said, quietly.

"Whatever, but you're saying that Jordan's family wouldn't have anything to do with him all that time?"

"No."

"So why the hell is he living with them now if they still hate him?"

Mom sighed.

"I thought it would help them heal—getting the family back together again. I'm sure it will, in time."

Even though she said the words, she didn't sound very sure at all, and bearing in mind what Jordan had said, I didn't think time was going to make much difference.

"He's damaged and he's vulnerable, too. So you see now why I don't want you getting involved with him."

My head jerked up at that.

"Um, not really. All you've told me is that the State says he's no longer a danger to the community, but everyone around here is treating him like a leper."

"I know," Mom conceded, at last. "It's been very difficult … for everyone. And because Michael was well liked and well respected, having Jordan back—well, it reopens a lot of wounds, reawakens a lot of bad memories." She shook her head. "I understand Michael was the school's quarterback and on his way to college with a full football scholarship. He was going to put this town on the map. You know how Texans are about football. And a lot of good people lost a friend the day he died. It damaged the whole community. Some people are still grieving."

"Yeah? Well, those 'good people' treat his brother like shit."

"You don't understand."

"That's because you won't tell me the whole story!"

She nodded slowly.

"I keep hoping that it will get easier for everyone."

"So how come he's working for you?"

"Well, he needed a job to fulfill his parole requirements…"

"Let me guess: no one around here would give him work."

She sighed again. "No, I'm afraid not. Although I'm still hopeful, of course. I've gotten him a day here and there. He has a way with car engines. I'm sure a good auto repair shop could use a person like that. I haven't given up, but in the meantime, I thought he could do something with my backyard. It's like a wilderness out there."

"I think you're fighting a losing battle trying to get him a job, Mom. I know you like to give people the benefit of the doubt, and I kind of think that's cool, but most people like to have someone to look down on, and serving them up Jordan isn't doing anything to help *him*."

She smiled. "You're more like me than you want to admit."

"What?"

"You like giving people the benefit of the doubt, too."

A reluctant smile crept across my face. "Yeah, you got me there."

It was the first real moment that we'd had between us since I arrived at the Rectory. It passed quickly.

"You'd better go take that shower," she said, her eyes amused for once. "I believe you have a job to look for today."

"Yeah, hopefully one where the people aren't so frickin' spiteful."

"Don't judge them too harshly, Torrey."

"I think they're the ones you need to say that to, Mom."

I left the room and headed for the shower. She'd laid a whole shit load of information on me, and I needed some time to process it.

I felt really bad for Jordan. Ending up in juvie when you were 16—that sucked balls. He'd been painted as this villain, but it sounded to me like he was a kid who'd made some bad mistakes. Working in the law firm, I'd come across a lot of cases where one dumb decision ruined lives. It happened more often than you might think: infidelity, fraud, theft, drinking, drugs. You think you're on one path and suddenly you're bumping down some dirt road wondering what the hell happened to your life. Believe me, I'd been there.

I wondered again what Jordan had done. Maybe one day he'd trust me enough to tell me.

I also suspected that if I hung out around town long enough, I'd probably hear the full story anyway. It was only Mom who had any reservations about spreading gossip. It was irritating as hell, but I thought it was cool of her, too.

It had been good talking to her, having a real conversation instead of tiptoeing around each other. I didn't talk to Dad that much. He'd lost interest in me after Mom left. He spent his time chasing women and living it up. I pretty much raised myself from the age of 13, and I'd always thought I was more like him, so Mom's comment had thrown me for a loop.

To my surprise, I found that I didn't mind being a little bit like her. At least she'd stuck up for Jordan and tried to show people he was more than just the ex-felon they all thought he was.

But then again, my tolerance level for her had been reached when she'd accused me of flirting with him. He was good enough to mow her lawn, but not good enough to talk to her daughter? There were some serious double-standards at work here.

I showered quickly, but it took forever to wash my hair. It was so damn thick and curly; there was so much of it. Guys liked that about me, and I liked it about myself, but it was a real bitch to take care of. Most of the time I let it do its own thing. Hairdryers were a waste of time. I'd tried to blow dry it when I was younger, but when I'd burned out my second hairdryer in a month, I'd given up. Now it just air-dried and hung mop-like from my head. The only alternative was shaving it off, and believe me, there were days when I considered it. The Texas heat and humidity didn't help, because regardless of how I styled my hair—or tried to style it—as soon as I walked into the sweltering summer heat, it just frizzed out.

I dug through my meager pile of clothing to find a reasonable pair of jeans and conservative shirt. If I was going job-hunting, I wanted to look like a responsible and sober citizen. And I had no qualms about playing the preacher-daughter card if it was going to help me find work.

I glanced out of the window as I buttoned up my blouse.

Fuck me! Hot guy alert!

Jordan had taken off his t-shirt and was wearing a pair of

cut-off jeans that looked about two sizes too big, making them hang dangerously low from his hips, showcasing the curve of a very nice ass.

The sun danced on his back muscles as he pushed Mom's beast of a mower, and I could see a tattoo on his left shoulder blade. It was a Celtic cross and had a bleeding heart motif in the center. Something was written across it, but he was too far away for me to see what it said.

Then he turned around and started mowing in my direction. His chest and stomach looked rock hard. Whatever else he did in prison, he must have worked out a lot. I guessed there wasn't much else to do.

I thought I was having a hot flash because his body was making me think all kinds of things that nice girls shouldn't have dirtying their minds. It was a good thing I'd never professed to be a nice girl.

I hoped he'd look up and see me watching him, but his eyes remained fixed on the grass he was cutting.

I enjoyed the free show a little longer before unpeeling my eyeballs from the window, and finished getting dressed.

I had a job to hunt down before my gas money ran out.

Jordan

I didn't get to see her after the Reverend took her back inside. I knew it was likely that I'd never see her again, certainly not to talk to. She'd have been warned off me by now.

I didn't blame the Rev—I wouldn't want a guy like me spending time with my daughter either.

I heard her car start. I'd have recognized that engine sound anywhere—Pontiac Firebird—one of the last of that model. It was a damn fine car. I'd spent several minutes checking it out when I arrived this morning. It seemed like an usual car for a woman to drive. Most around here went for compact Japanese cars that were easy on fuel.

But not this woman. She was different.

I figured she was going to her job at the diner. Now that I knew she truly hadn't known who I was, I questioned even more why she'd followed me with that coffee. She'd said I was cute. Maybe she'd been hitting on me, and I'd been too dumb to see it? Well, it wouldn't happen again, not after her nice little talk with her momma.

I tried to put all thoughts of the preacher's daughter out of my head and concentrate on bringing the yard back from the wilderness.

I finished the lawns then contemplated what needed doing next. It was a long list.

I started working on the rear section of the Reverend's yard, hacking back the brambles and rambling roses that had taken over the corner by the property line. I really needed work-gloves for a job like this, since both my hands and my arms were getting cut to pieces. But I didn't really mind; the pain felt good.

In prison, a lot of guys had cut. No one talked about it much, but we all knew it went on. I guess it relieved some of the pent up feelings. I thought about trying it once, but the anger and guilt were all I had left of myself, so if I lost those, there'd be nothing. That was a scary thought.

As I'd gotten toward the end of my sentence—my second sentence—I'd been assigned more of the sought after jobs, like working in the prison garden. It felt good to be outside, working with the sun on my back. I mean, yeah, we were allowed to exercise outside, but really working, growing something, it felt more meaningful.

I guessed the Rev wasn't much for tending God's garden because the place had gone wild. I wondered how long she'd lived here. There sure hadn't been any lady-preacher when I was growing up. So I figured maybe three or four years: long enough that people paid mind to her, and recent enough that she was still an outsider. Although that might have been because she was a woman preacher and a Yankee. It didn't take much to make you an outsider around here.

I worked until the sun was getting lower and a breeze was cooling the sweat on my skin. There was no one around for me to tell I was leaving, and this was no nine to fiver where I needed to punch a clock, so I just packed up and drove home. Dad and Momma had gone out, so I showered, ate my meal in a silent kitchen, and slept in a silent bed. I couldn't even hear my parents talking to each other when they came in later.

You know the phrase 'the silence was deafening'? It sounds like horse shit, right? But in prison it was never silent; there'd be people yelling and doors banging, and a thousand and one different noises echoing from the walls. Even at night, you'd hear people moaning and crying—all those nightmares from the combined crimes of two thousand inmates.

But here at night—no sounds. No one talked; no one cried out. Unless it was me, and I wasn't aware. I'd asked Momma if I could sleep in the family room and have the TV on the first night. Dad replied that it was a waste of electricity. It was three nights before I managed to sleep more than a couple of hours, and that was from sheer exhaustion. I'd lie awake, straining to hear the small sounds of the house settling at night, occasionally the hoarse bark of a dog fox, or the whine of a skeeter buzzing around. We were too far from the road to even hear another car—just a whole lot of silence. It was unnerving.

I dreamed about Mikey again. He was laughing at me this time, and pointing to something in the road, just seconds before we crashed. I saw it all happen in slow motion—the way his neck snapped, the way the glass fanned out in a shower of shards as his body flew through the windshield, the look of surprise fixed in his dead eyes.

I jerked awake, shaking and sweating. Three AM again. I knew I wouldn't be able to get back to sleep, so I headed to the garage to work out—again.

Four hours later, I stumbled out of the house and made my way to the Rectory.

I was just working up a good sweat from hacking the brambles and heaping them into a pile when I heard her voice.

"Hey, cowboy!"

I turned around and saw the preacher's pretty daughter, Torrey, sitting on the porch, just like yesterday, holding up a mug of coffee for me.

Her smile disappeared as I got nearer, and I guessed her momma's talk had had an effect.

"What the hell do you think you're doing?" she asked, her voice sharp and angry.

I froze in my tracks. What was she talking about? I looked behind me at the wilderness that I'd been hacking into and turned back to her. Her jaws were clamped together, turning her plump lips into a thin, white line. What sort of game was she playing? Was she going to make out like I'd attacked her or something? The thought caused bile to rise in my throat, and I had trouble swallowing it down.

"Ma'am, I…"

"What have you done to your arms?" she snapped, pointing at the numerous cuts and scratches that were decorating my skin where the tattoos ended.

"Are you freakin' crazy?" she went on, her voice getting louder by the second. "Why aren't you wearing gloves?"

"I don't have any."

She stared at me like I wasn't speaking English.

"Come here, you idiot!"

She grabbed my wrist and dragged me into the house.

I'd never been in the Reverend's kitchen before. It was pretty basic, not all fancy like I'd seen on TV. I guess she didn't make much money in a one-horse Texas town. Or maybe she just didn't care about cooking. I somehow thought a Boston lady would have something fancier. I knew the Rectory belonged to the church, but I guess I thought she'd have it fixed up a little more.

Torrey pushed me in front of the kitchen sink and filled it with warm water. She was mumbling and cursing to herself the whole time. Even while I was wondering what she was doing, I couldn't help thinking she was so damn cute.

Then she started washing my arms, using her hands to cup water and pour it down over the cuts. It stung plenty, but that was nothing compared to the spark I felt every time she touched me. I realized with horror that I'd gotten an instant boner.

"I can manage," I said roughly, taking over cleaning my cuts.

"Sure, big guy," she said, snidely. "You managed just fine in the yard, didn't you, cutting those brambles down to size with your bare hands. Oh yeah, you showed them who's boss. What's a little blood as long as you can look like a big strong man? God! Men can be such assholes!"

Boy, this woman was a firecracker. Just the kind I would have gone for once. Not now, of course. She was still standing behind me, and I could feel her eyes burning twin holes into the back of my neck.

"I'm going to get some bandages and Bactine. Don't move!" she ordered.

She was gone for a few minutes and I started panicking, wondering how it would look if the Rev came back to find me standing in her kitchen, looking all kinds of creepy.

I ignored what Torrey had told me and had one foot out of the door when she came back.

"I told you not to move!" she said, crossly. "Jeez, have you got attention deficit disorder?"

I shook my head slowly like a dumb dog.

"Sit!" she ordered, pointing at a wooden chair.

I sat.

She smoothed dollops of hospital-smelling cream all over my arms and put Band-Aids over the worst of the cuts.

"Don't you have a long shirt, or something you can wear to cover up your arms? And you really need some work-gloves. I'll tell Mom to buy you some. For now, you'd better use these."

She threw me a pair of pink rubber dish gloves. I stared at

them in disbelief.

"I cain't wear those!"

"Is this some macho bullshit thing about not wearing pink? You'd rather get your arms ripped all to pieces? Do you actually have two brain cells to rub together to keep your head warm?"

"Do you ever make any tips when you're waitressin', 'cause you're so damn charmin'?" I snapped back.

I could have bit off my tongue when I realized I'd said that out loud.

She sat back in her chair, and I wasn't sure if she was fixing to bawl me out or if she was fighting down a smile.

"Hey! I can be charming—when I want to be!"

And then she laughed. God it was a wonderful sound. People didn't laugh much around me, and I certainly hadn't heard my folks laugh lately. It stirred something deep inside me. I didn't know what it was, but I liked it.

Her amusement finally ended in an unladylike snort, and I could feel my lips turning up in an awkward smile.

"I can be charming," she said, again.

"Oh yeah?"

"Yeah!"

"Prove it!" I taunted her.

She blinked in surprise, and then her smile turned devilish. I wondered what wicked thoughts were hiding behind that pretty face.

"Oh, baby," she said, her voice all soft and sweet. "I can be charming! Now let me look at those cuts on your poor lil' arms. Poor you; poor baby."

And she leaned forward, giving me an eyeful straight down her tank top. She wasn't wearing a bra and I could see soft, golden mounds of flesh. I closed my eyes and bit back a moan.

I don't know what she saw in my eyes when I opened them, but her flirty words came to a sudden stop.

"Sorry," she said, quietly. "I didn't mean to tease. I was just playing."

I nodded, uncomfortably aware that if I stood up now it

would be obvious just how much her words—and lack of clothing—affected me.

"Okay, you're good to go," she said, slapping my knee and standing up. "I'll just put some more coffee on first."

She stood at the coffee maker with her back to me, allowing me to slide out of my chair. Perhaps she knew exactly what my problem was. It was humiliating, but I'd had worse things happen.

The only sound in the room was the soft burble of the coffee maker. In the end I couldn't stand it anymore.

"I'll wait outside, ma … Torrey," I mumbled.

"You don't have to, Jordan. I'm the prick here."

"I … um … I think it would be better. If your momma … if the Reverend saw me…"

She sighed.

"Sure, okay, if you feel more comfortable. I'll bring it out to you."

I nodded my thanks and walked out carrying the pink dish gloves. I studied them, appreciating the gesture more than she could imagine, but there was no way I'd be able to get my hands in those teeny tiny things.

I heard the screen door close softly and when I turned around, a mug of coffee was sitting on the porch step.

But Torrey was gone.

I picked up the mug, inhaling the delicious aroma and felt my eyes sting. The loneliness hit me hard. In prison I'd kept to myself; out here, I didn't know what the boundaries were anymore. It was a game of life where I didn't know the rules and couldn't work them out—and I was losing. Big time.

Torrey

I felt like the worst kind of cock-tease after I left Jordan. I'd been messing with his head and hadn't even realized it. When I saw the look on his face, his desire black in those expressive eyes, I knew I'd crossed a line.

I hadn't meant to. I swear I hadn't meant to. But he was so easy to talk to, and I hadn't made any other friends since I'd moved here.

Was Jordan my friend? I know I'd said we could be friends and I would try. Because I'd never met a person who needed a friend more. It was almost a shame he was so goddamn hot. It made the friendship boundary hard for me to respect objectively. Especially when all I wanted to do was jump his bones.

I shook my head. Mom had certainly been right about one thing—Jordan was vulnerable, and he didn't need me making his life any harder.

But after that scorching look of lust, his expression had turned icy—a cold, hard prison stare. For the first time, I could almost believe what Mom said about him.

Returning to my room, I decided that there still wasn't any harm in making him a coffee in the mornings and having a short conversation. That was safe territory. I kicked off my shorts and tank top, leaving them in a heap on the floor before walking down the hallway to the shower.

My priority was still to find a job, and yesterday had been a washout. Apart from anything else, I hadn't heard back from Dad, so there'd been no happy stork delivering a couple of grand to my account. Looked like I was on my own after all.

I dried myself on a random towel that was hanging in the bathroom and hurried back to my room. I ignored my tangle of hair—I definitely didn't have time to spend 20 minutes trying to drag a brush through it. So I just pulled on my best jeans and one of the dressy shirts I used to wear to the office, and applied a small amount of mascara and lipstick. It was so darn hot, that just walking to my car melted makeup.

I remembered Mom had left the local paper on the coffee table so I swiped that on my way out the door.

From the backyard I could hear the sound of some power tool, so I knew Jordan was still working. I hoped those dumb dish gloves were helping him. I decided to buy him a pair of work-gloves with long, protective cuffs. Mom could pay me back.

I got lucky when I looked at the want ads in the back of the paper. A new Starbucks was opening in the mall, a few miles out of town. I'd worked in a couple of their rival cafés when I was a student, so I was confident I had the kind of experience they were looking for.

As I spun the wheels leaving the driveway, I saw Jordan in my rearview mirror. He was watching me, a look of longing and disappointment on his lovely face.

I couldn't think about that now. I needed to get my head in the game and find a damn job.

A couple of hours later, I had a stack of applications under my arm and one interview scheduled for the next day.

Okay, so it wasn't as well paid as the paralegal job I'd walked away from in Boston, and no, it didn't exactly require a college degree to make great coffee, but it was a start.

I allowed myself to celebrate by buying a really cute skirt that whispered my name as I'd walked past from the small boutique.

Not the smartest thing I'd ever done, spending $75 that I didn't have, but it made my legs look great. And after the last few days, I really needed a pick-me-up.

When I got back to the house, Jordan had already left for the day.

Yeah, I admit I was avoiding him.

I had one other job to do: I needed to empty out the U-haul trailer. Mom had been on my case about it already.

When it came down to it, there wasn't much I wanted to keep. Somehow it all seemed tainted with bad memories. Everything could go: Goodwill, e-Bay—I didn't want any of it.

Chapter 3 – Options

Jordan

I heard her before I saw her.

She was swearing up and down, cussing worse than I'd heard in prison half the time.

"You useless piece of shit! You worn out worthless hunk o' junk! I'm going to send you to a scrap yard! Start, you motherfucker!"

Holy cow! That girl had a mouth on her.

She was sitting in her Pontiac Firebird, wrenching the ignition key and pounding on the dash. I could tell straight away that the engine was cranking but not turning over. Only two reasons why a car won't start: it's not getting gas, or it's not getting power.

"Um, Miss Torrey?"

Her cute face was red and angry when she looked at me.

"What?"

"I reckon you got a problem with your spark plugs."

"How the hell do you know that? Did you … do something to them?"

I was stung by her accusation. She must really think I was a piece of crap if she thought I'd mess with her car like that.

"No, ma'am," I said, quietly. "I just know engines."

Her face relaxed.

"Ignore me and my big mouth, Jordan. I'm just pissed because I have to be somewhere and the Princess has let me down. Now I'll have to reschedule."

I couldn't help a small smile escaping.

"You call your car Princess?"

She grinned up at me. "Sure, she acts like a total bitch most of the time. I only put up with her because she's pretty. That's a princess, right?"

An odd coughing sound came out of me, and I realized I was almost laughing. The recognition hurt my chest, and I stopped immediately. I didn't deserve to laugh.

Torrey looked at me curiously as I dropped my eyes to the ground.

"Um, I can fix it for you, if you'd like."

"What? You can fix my car?"

I hitched one shoulder and nodded. "If you'd like."

"You really know cars?"

I nodded again.

"Hell, yes! I'd like!"

"Um, you wannna pop the hood? I could take a look now…"

"Yes! God, yes!"

I examined one of the spark plugs and saw that my first guess was right. I showed it to her.

"See this, Mi… Torrey? It's dry. That means no fuel is getting through. If it was black, that would mean too much fuel."

"Can you fix it?"

"I'd need to check the in-line fuel filter, clean out the carb, and check the jets for blockages, make sure everything is sweet.

44

If that don't work, you'll need to get a new spark plug fitted, but I don't reckon you'll need to do that. Yeah, I can fix it."

"My God, you'd be a lifesaver."

Her comment punched me in the guts.

You're so wrong.

Did she know? She *must* know. I couldn't explain. I turned and started to walk away.

"Hey, wait up!"

When I didn't slow down, I heard the car door open and then Torrey grabbed my arm.

"Jordan? What the fuck? I thought you were going to fix my car, and then you just walk away!"

"Sorry, I'm sorry, I…"

She let go of my arm, and her voice softened.

"Obviously I said something to upset you … but I have no clue what it was. I do that all the time." She laughed sadly. "I'm notorious for it. Look, I'd be really grateful if you could fix my car, Jordan, and I promise I'll shut the fuck up."

I nodded again, too choked up to talk. I seemed to have turned into a freakin' emotional wreck since leaving prison. I couldn't control myself anymore. It was so fucking frustrating.

She clapped her hands together, immediately changing the energy around us, chasing away the darkness that constantly hovered around me.

"So, you can tell me what you need to do the job, but first I need you to drive me so I don't miss my job interview."

"A job interview?" I was confused. "I thought you worked at the Busy Bee in town."

She lifted one eyebrow and smirked at me. "Guess they didn't like the way I served coffee."

And then I got it. She'd been fired … because of me.

She had her hands on the passenger door before I managed to choke out another sentence.

"Miss Torrey, I…" My eyes bulged. "I cain't drive you!"

"Why the hell not? You got some 'no chicks in the truck' rule?"

45

Was she joking with me? I wasn't sure so I risked a quick glance at her. Yep, she was smiling.

"No," I choked out. "It's not that…"

"Glad to hear it," she said, with a cute wrinkle of her nose. "Have you got your keys?"

"Miss Torrey…"

"Just Torrey! Jeez! Do I have to wear a name badge for you, too?"

"Torrey … if I give you a ride to your interview, I can guarantee you won't get the job."

"Don't be such a douchebag!"

"It's true," I said, willing her to understand. "You've already gotten fired from one job because of me. Folks around here … they don't like me. In fact, they pretty much curse the ground I walk on."

I waited to see some pity on her face or an excuse to drop from those pretty lips about why it wasn't such a good idea that she got a ride with me after all.

"Are you going to tell me why?"

I stared at her.

"You … you don't … your momma didn't…"

She folded her arms and stared at me calmly.

"No. Mom didn't tell me anything really. Why don't you tell me?"

Because you'll never speak to me again.

She sighed. "You don't have to. Just give me a ride, okay?"

"People will talk, and if they see you with me…"

"Screw 'em," she said.

"Excuse me?" *Did I hear her right?*

"I said, screw 'em. If someone refuses to give me a job because of who has given me a ride, then they're not the kind of asshole I want to work for. Now, do you have your keys?"

I nodded, stunned into silence. Again. Christ, this woman rendered me mute every time I saw her. She was so fucking fearless; she'd charge hell with a bucket of iced water.

She climbed into my truck and sat waiting for me. I followed slowly, still reluctant. I didn't want to cause trouble for her; not when her momma had tried to do so much for me. Not when Torrey took the trouble to make me great coffee every day.

I didn't know how to phrase it so she'd understand what she was up against. Like I said, couldn't get the words out of my dumb mouth.

She looked completely at home in my truck. One of her long legs was hitched up so her foot rested on the dash. She'd worn a skirt today, slightly more conservative than her usual clothes, but she still looked hot whatever she had on. She wore a plain, sleeveless blouse in a pale blue that made her honey-colored skin glow. She was so fucking beautiful and she was sitting in my truck like she didn't have a care in the world. I don't know, maybe she didn't.

I climbed in next to her and slowly pulled out of the driveway.

"Where to?"

"Left. Into town."

I did as she said and drove carefully, keeping under the speed limit the whole time.

I was trying to concentrate on driving, but a million and one thoughts were spinning through my brain.

She must have sensed the glances in her direction that I just couldn't help.

"Ask me," she said.

"Ask you what?"

An amused smile pulled her lips upward as she looked across at me.

"Whatever you're busting a gut to hold in. Ask me."

I vomited out the question that had been fighting to get past my lips.

"Don't it bother you? Sittin' here with … with someone like me?"

My stomach clenched when she didn't reply immediately. I knew she was considering her answer carefully because normally she just blurted it right out, like she didn't have an edit button.

47

"Well, I'd say it bothers you more than it bothers me," she said, at last.

I wasn't sure what to make of her answer. Was it true? Did it bother me that this beautiful girl would put herself at risk by getting in my truck? No one even knew she was with me.

"Yeah, it bothers me."

"Are you going to hurt me?"

My eyes widened with shock.

"Fuck, no!"

I could *not* believe she asked me that!

"Then we're good," she said, evenly.

My mouth hung open.

"You're really not bothered?"

"Jordan, if you did something that made me uncomfortable, I'd let you know. Believe me. I have no interest in hanging out with crazies."

"I'm not normal," I stuttered out.

She looked at me appraisingly, and I felt my cheeks flush under her intense gaze.

"Sure, you've got issues. Who doesn't? You're normal, Jordan. Your past is just a bit more colorful." She arched an eyebrow. "You're not *that* special."

What a first class bitch!

Then I wondered if she was joking. I couldn't tell and that just made me more pissed—at her, at myself. I was too angry to speak. Confused, too. Luckily, she quit jabbering and gave me some peace to think.

Soon enough, we were driving through town, and I think I was holding my breath, praying that no one would see us together. They couldn't think any worse of me than they already did, but I didn't want to make life harder for Torrey or her momma.

Of course, when I braked for the stop light at the Main Street intersection, I saw Mrs. Ogden gawking at us. She'd always been the town's biggest gossip. I doubted she'd changed over the last eight years.

"People will see you with me," I spat out, thumping the steering wheel in frustration.

"Mmm, yeah," she said, her voice far away.

I turned to look at her and saw that she was staring out of the window.

Well, I couldn't do anything about it now, and it wasn't like I hadn't warned her.

"What have you got on your iPod?" she asked, after a short silence.

"Um, I don't have one."

"Really? You must be the only guy I know who doesn't."

I shrugged uncomfortably.

"Weren't you allowed one in prison?"

I was taken aback by how easily she asked the questions that most people wouldn't dare voice. My own parents never mentioned prison, and even the Reverend had tiptoed around the subject. But not Torrey. I didn't know whether that was a good thing or not.

"No, we weren't allowed electronic devices. A few people had radios—I had one for a while—but you didn't keep them for long. Those things are too easy to steal or swap for drugs."

"Oh, of course." She nodded to herself. "And you haven't gotten an iPod since?"

I shook my head, too embarrassed to tell her that I didn't have any money. Her momma paid me next to nothing to do odd jobs and keep the yard tidy, and what with paying my $40 a month to the parole service for the privilege of them checking on me, and a little to my folks for food and rent, there wasn't more than a few bucks in change left.

I was glad when she didn't ask any more questions; my brain was reeling from the ones she'd asked me already. I hadn't talked this much in, well, eight years.

I started getting twitchy when I realized that her directions were taking us out of town again. I'd soon be beyond the area I was allowed to go. If I broke my parole requirements, I'd be thrown back inside until the next millennium.

"Um, Miss Torrey, is it much further?"

"Just Torrey," she said, rolling her eyes. "Don't worry, I'll pay you for the gas—if I get the job."

"It's not that…"

"Then what?"

I stared straight ahead, feeling the burn of humiliation flare up again.

"I'm not allowed to go more than ten miles beyond the town limit. It's a requirement of my parole."

"Oh," she said, looking at me with concern. "Shit, I'm so sorry! I had no idea! Fuck! Look, you can drop me off here. It's only another mile up the road. I can walk."

"Another mile to where?" I knew this road, and there was nothing along it for miles.

"To the mall," she said. "Honestly, you can drop me here."

There's a mall?

"Since when?" I blurted out.

She looked puzzled. "Since when what?"

"Since when is there a mall here?"

I was choking the steering wheel, my knuckles turning white.

"Oh," she said, softly. "I think it's pretty new. The Starbucks where I'm going for an interview hasn't even opened to the public yet."

Shit. They'd built a whole goddamn mall since I'd been inside. I wondered what other changes had happened that I knew nothing about.

"Really, it's fine," she said again. "You can drop me here."

"I guess I can do another mile."

"I don't want to get you into trouble."

I sighed. "Don't worry about it. Trouble finds me anyhow."

I prayed that the mall was within my ten-mile limit. I didn't want to think about the consequences if I put a toe over the line. And I'd only been allowed to drive because my parole officer had argued that without transport I wouldn't be able to get work, what with living somewhere so remote.

Thankfully, the new mall soon appeared just over the hill,

and I stared at the sight. I couldn't imagine that this small town would be able to sustain anything that size. There must have been parking for over a thousand cars, and several acres of scrubby grassland were now paved and covered in gleaming steel and glass.

But the newness had a feeling of anonymity about it, and I felt more relaxed here than I had in a while.

I pulled into a spot away from other cars and waited for her to climb out. I had an old paperback on the back seat so I planned on just sitting and reading while she went for her interview.

"Aren't you coming?" she said, frowning up at me. "You're not going to just sit there, are you?"

"Well, yeah."

"You're not in jail now, Jordan, and you don't need to hide away. Live a little. Take a chance."

Anxiety spasmed through me, but I knew she was right. And being somewhere like this, where there was less chance of being recognized, well, that appealed. A lot.

My eyes were scanning the area, searching for trouble. I took a breath and tried to act something like normal. At least I hoped I didn't look crazy mad-dog scary.

Somewhat reluctantly, I climbed out of the truck and locked the doors. I nearly passed out from shock when Torrey hooked her arm through mine and started walking toward the shops.

I looked down at her, speechless.

"Is this okay?" she said, not letting go. "Dad's always telling me I don't respect people's personal boundaries."

"Um, no. It's ... fine," I stammered.

"Good," she said, her voice peaceful.

I liked the way her soft skin brushed against my forearm. I liked it a lot—too much, probably. I realized we would have been taken for a couple, walking together like that. My throat seized up, and I couldn't have said a word if my life depended on it.

She pointed out the coffee shop and let go of my arm. I

missed her touch immediately.

Then she stood in front of me, holding out her arms.

"Well? How do I look?"

Beautiful. Gorgeous. Sexy. Off limits.

"Um, fine," I managed to squeeze out.

She raised her eyebrows. "You smooth talking stud. I can see that I'm going to have to watch myself with you."

She walked away shaking her head. Then she did a little pirouette as she called out, "Wait for me here? I'll be about 20 or 30 minutes."

She didn't even stay to hear my answer, but who was I kidding? Other than hauling shit at her momma's place, I didn't have anywhere else to be—and nowhere I was wanted.

I found a bench where I could see the coffee shop entrance and sat down.

It felt weird being outside without anyone watching me—no guards, no cameras, no townsfolk judging me and finding me lacking. It was hard to believe I was free. I didn't deserve to have this, but I was so darn grateful to be out of that shithole prison, that I could have kissed the asphalt in the damn parking lot.

Even so, I didn't feel completely free. I probably never would. I would always carry the knowledge that my brother was dead because I was an asshole. There were days when I wished they'd lock me away forever, because that's what I deserved. For reasons I didn't understand, life had given me a second chance, and that was hard to deal with. I had no clue how to live anymore.

"Jordan? Jordan Kane?"

I looked up to see a woman with auburn hair looking at me. Oh shit, I could tell from the way she was staring that she knew me. And there'd been only one person at high school with hair that color.

"Allison?"

I stood up, and she immediately took a step back.

"Wow, it is you!" she said nervously, trying to force a bright smile.

I nodded and shoved my hands in my pockets.

"How've you been? I mean … I heard you were … out."

I nodded again.

Allison had been my girlfriend when I was a sophomore in high school. Although, thinking back, there had been quite a number of them. We were together the night Mikey died. We'd been making out until I was too wasted to know who I was with or what the fuck I was doing. I'd only seen her once since then and that was the day I'd been sentenced. She cried.

"I'm sorry I didn't write," she said, twisting the strap of her purse around her fingers.

"It's okay."

What else could I say? I don't think I would have written back if she had.

"I should have," she continued. "I wanted to … I just didn't know what to say."

Christ, this is awkward.

I looked over to the coffee shop but there was still no sign of Torrey.

"How are your folks?" asked Allison, tentatively.

"Yeah, they're … okay. It's hard for them, y'know?"

She nodded.

"How've you been?" I asked. "Did you go to college like you wanted?"

She smiled her first genuine smile.

"Yes, I did! I just graduated with my MBA from Texas State."

"Wow, that's great. Good for you. Um, I thought you wanted to study Dance and Theater?"

She pulled a face.

"That was just a pipe dream. I … I grew up a lot after … after what happened. I'm so sorry, Jordan. I never got to tell you that."

Her words had me all choked up, and I could see from the look on her face that she felt the same way.

"You look good," she breathed out, reaching out to touch

my arm and tracing a finger along one of my tattoos.

Her voice was filled with regret, but I didn't think it was for me.

"Thanks. You, too," I muttered.

I searched again for Torrey, but instead I saw a skinny guy with glasses walking toward us.

"Hey, there's my girl," he said, placing a possessive arm around Allison's shoulders and giving me a hard stare.

Allison's cheeks flushed, and her words collided as she struggled to introduce us.

"Oh, Henry, this is, um, this is Jordan. We were ... friends ... in high school."

He held out his hand, and after a short pause I shook it. I was surprised and sort of amused when he tried to crush my knuckles. I squeezed back a little harder than I should have and saw him wince.

"Alli didn't mention you," he said, pretending to be all jokey.

"You know that's not true," she said, quietly. "This is *Jordan*," and the way she emphasized my name, I could see the exact second that he finally got it.

His eyes widened and he tugged Allison more closely into his side.

"The ex-con?"

She elbowed him hard in the ribs.

"Yep, that's me," I said, the bitterness evident in my voice.

"Um, we should go now," said Allison, yanking on her boyfriend's jacket. "Nice seein' you again, Jordan. I hope ... it all goes well. Say hi to your folks for me."

As she walked away, they seemed to be arguing.

A moment later, Torrey came practically dancing from the coffee shop.

"That looked uncomfortable," she said, cocking her head toward Allison and the prick. "I saw them from the window. Who are they?"

I was irritated by her nosiness, so I just shrugged. "Girl I knew from high school and her boyfriend."

"Okay," she said, accepting my answer immediately.

Then *I* felt like the prick for being so defensive.

"Allison was my girlfriend at the time … at the time I was sent to juvie. I haven't seen her since. The guy was her boyfriend, I guess."

Torrey sat down next to me on the bench and patted my knee.

"Bet that sucked, seeing her again."

Hell, yeah!

"It was okay, I guess. Her boyfriend was a prick."

She laughed. "He probably didn't like the fact that his girlfriend's ex looks like a freakin' model!"

I was pretty sure I turned red, hearing her words.

"I think the whole jailbird vibe made him uncomfortable," I said, forcing out a hollow laugh. "But at least she spoke to me, which is more than most people have done. Didn't suck too bad."

"See!" she said, sounding delighted. "Things are getting better already!"

I wouldn't have gone that far, but still, it hadn't been as bad as it could have been. Maybe she was right.

"Hey! Wake up!" she yelled, poking me in the side. "Didn't you hear what I said? We have to go celebrate!"

I rubbed my ribs, and she grinned at me as she stood up.

"Celebrate what?"

"Me getting a job, doofus! Come on, I'll buy you a drink."

"Uh, that's pretty neat, Torrey, but I cain't go into a bar."

Her face fell. "Oh, that's right." Then she smiled. "Okay, well I can't buy you a coffee yet either as the only decent place isn't open, but how about pizza?"

I practically drooled when she mentioned pizza. I hadn't had one since I got out, and the ones you got in prison, well, let's just say if I'd slapped some tomato paste on the sole of my shoe it would have been tastier.

"Ha, the look on your face!" she said, pointing a finger at me. "If a guy ever looks at me that way, it'll be a first."

I stared at her in surprise.

"Seriously? But you're gorgeous!"

Her mouth dropped open. "You think I'm gorgeous? Wait, don't answer that—I don't want to give you the chance to take it back."

She smiled and linked her arm through mine again. I *really* liked the way it felt.

"You are," I said, quietly. "You are gorgeous. Any guy would be crazy not to think so."

She flashed her beautiful smile at me and leaned her head against my arm.

"Thanks! You're not so bad yourself, Auto Man."

We strolled along in the late morning sunshine, just like any of the other couples out at the new mall. It was so normal, yet it felt utterly bizarre, like someone would jump up and start yelling shit at me, saying I shouldn't be around ordinary folk. I started tensing up, my eyes darting around, waiting for the attack to begin.

Torrey tugged lightly on my arm, her expression worried. "Too much?"

"Um, just…"

I scrubbed my hands over my face hard enough to tear the skin off. I felt her grab my wrists.

"Hey, it's okay. Nothing bad is going to happen. And if it does, I'll protect you."

The idea of her protecting me was comical. She was nearly a foot shorter and probably weighed a hundred pounds soaking wet.

She smiled. "Take-out pizza?"

I nodded, relieved she'd understood.

"Yeah, that would be great. Um, but I don't have any money."

She shook her head. "I told you—my treat. Your money doesn't work here today. Besides, you're going to fix my car for me, aren't you?"

I almost smiled. "Yes, ma'am. That I am."

She poked me in the ribs again.

"Stop calling me 'ma'am'! It makes me feel about a hundred. If you do it again, next time I'll kick you in the nuts. Understand?"

I didn't think she was joking. "Yes, ma... Torrey."

"So what do you like on your pizza?"

I scanned the menu in the window and my mouth watered at the thought of a meat feast with ham, pepperoni, beef and chicken.

"I don't mind. Whatever you like."

"Stop doing that," she said, frowning. "Stop trying to please everyone all the time. Just tell me what you want on your damn pizza."

"Sorry," I mumbled, "I'm not used to ... having a choice."

"It's okay," she said, patting my shoulder. "Just tell me."

"Could I have the meat feast?"

She rolled her eyes. "You're such a guy—I should have known," and she pushed me with her shoulder.

She was so tactile, touching me the whole time. But it wasn't weird or a come on, it was just how she was.

We had to wait in the pizzeria while they put our order together. She held my hand the whole time, letting me know that she was there for me.

The waiter kept throwing worried glances at us, like he was one twitchy finger away from dialing 911.

"It's okay, Jordan," Torrey whispered. "Try to relax. You look like you're about to make a run for it, and you're making him nervous. We'll be out of here in just a few minutes, and that meat feast will be partying in your mouth."

Then she palmed her face and groaned.

"I can't *believe* I just said that. It sounded really bad. Don't ever remind me I said that!"

I didn't know what to say when she winked at me and grinned. I just took a deep breath and smiled back.

God, this woman! She just had a way of making everything okay ... bearable.

The pizzas arrived and Torrey pulled out her wallet, handing over a credit card. I picked up the boxes, desperate to get the hell out. I held the door while Torrey scooped up the two cans of soda, and then we headed back to my truck. The smell was driving me crazy and I must have been walking faster than usual because Torrey yelled at me to slow down.

"I can't keep up," she yelped. "Just because your damn legs go on forever, it doesn't mean mine do!"

"I think your legs are just fine," I said, automatically.

Yeah, like I haven't thought about them every second of every day since I met her.

"Have you been checking out my legs, Jordan Kane?"

Up until that moment, I didn't know that prison had sucked out my mental filter along with everything else I'd lost. I felt my face get hot, but Torrey just gave a quiet little laugh and let me wriggle off the hook.

We rolled down the windows in the truck so it wouldn't get all steamed up. Yeah, that had me thinking things, too. I tried to concentrate on eating. As soon as I opened the lid, the scent of melted cheese, tomatoes, spice and the meat feast had me drooling. I took a huge bite and felt my eyes roll back in my head. That shit was *good*.

"I think someone's enjoying their pizza," Torrey deadpanned.

"Sorry," I mumbled, around a second slice. "'Sfuckin' wunnerful!"

She smiled and shoved the best part of a whole slice in her mouth. *That* got me thinking stuff, too. But the lure of the pizza pulled my mind back out of the gutter.

We ate in silence, but it wasn't awkward. I was just a guy eating pizza in his truck with a pretty woman sitting next to him. It was … normal.

As soon as I had that thought, the guilt flooded back. And, as always, a huge rock sat in my stomach, sickening me.

"You've got that look again," said Torrey.

I didn't even bother to ask what she meant—I already knew.

I sighed and closed the lid on the pizza box. Maybe I'd be able to eat the rest later.

"Do you want to talk about it?"

I shook my head. "No. Won't help."

"Are you sure about that? Have you tried?"

I stared straight ahead out of the window.

"My counselor said…" I darted a sideways look, but her face showed no reaction. "My counselor said I should talk about … stuff."

"Okay…" said Torrey, carefully. "But you don't because…?"

My eyes dropped to the steering wheel. "There's no one to listen."

She rested her hand lightly on my thigh.

"There is now."

I tried to get the words out, but nothing was happening. Her fingers slid away, and I hung my head, defeated.

"Tell me about Mikey. I'd like to hear about your brother."

"He was the best," I said. "The best guy, the best son, the best brother. You'd have liked him."

Torrey

I'd thought we'd had a breakthrough with the pizza, you know, doing something ordinary, but he closed up again half way through. I could practically hear the prison doors of his mind slam shut.

I knew a guy at college who'd gone to see a friend in prison once. Just one visit had given him nightmares for weeks: the noise, the dehumanization of people, the smell.

So I figured if Jordan couldn't talk about the bad stuff,

maybe remembering the good times he'd had with his brother might be easier.

As soon as I mentioned Mikey's name, he changed again, a smile lighting his lovely face.

"He was the best," he said, sincerely. "The best guy, the best son, the best brother. You'd have liked him." He paused, "Everyone loved him, he was easy to love."

"Was he as good looking as his brother?"

He lifted an eyebrow at me and grinned—a for-real, all out, teeth-showing grin. It was just a glimpse of the cocky young kid I imagined he'd been. I didn't think it was possible for him to be any cuter. Live and learn.

"When we were younger, people thought we were twins."

"And later?"

"His hair is … was darker than mine and he kept it short." He swept a hand through his messy curls. "He was a big guy— the high school quarterback, just solid muscle, but a bit shorter than me. I was kind of skinny back then."

His smile faded. I was desperate to keep him positive and upbeat. He had a great smile and I wanted to see more of it.

"That explains it."

He glanced over. "Explains what?"

"The cut-offs you wear when you're gardening. They look like they're about to fall off." *Not that I'd mind.*

But instead of smiling again, he frowned.

"Yeah."

I waited but he didn't explain. I was about to explode with frustration. Trying to get him to talk was worse than pulling teeth.

"And? Don't just tell me 'yeah' and then go all quiet!"

"Sorry," he muttered.

"For fuck's sake, Jordan! Don't be sorry all the time—just talk to me!"

He looked at me warily.

"Am I pissing you off?"

"Hell, yeah!"

"Sorry ... I mean..." He sighed. "I didn't think anyone would mind—about the clothes. When I left prison none of my old stuff fit anymore. They don't let you leave in your TDCJ uniform."

"What the hell's that?"

He leaned back in his seat, rubbing his forehead.

"Texas Department of Criminal Justice. We all wore uniforms so prisoners can be easily identified. I think it's to depersonalize you, too, ya know, so corrections' officers don't form associations or whatever."

"Was it striped? Not that you wouldn't look good in stripes."

I wanted to bring back his lovely smile but all he managed was a wry twist of his lips.

"Ha, no stripes. No arrows, either. Nah, we had to wear these white cotton pullover shirts and white elastic pants. But those are State property. So when I was released, I got issued a pair of sweatpants and a t-shirt. It was all they had in my size. I don't know, I didn't ask. When I got home, I took some t-shirts and a couple of pairs of jeans from Mikey's room. They'd kept it all, so ... I really didn't think it would matter..."

He looked down.

"I take it that didn't go down well with your parents."

He shook his head sadly.

"You could say that. Momma screamed at me then started cryin'. Dad yelled, sayin' how I'd been home five minutes and had already upset my momma, and that I was an ungrateful bastard after they'd agreed to have me back ... that it was disrespectin' my dead brother ... I didn't mean nothin' by it. I just needed some clothes."

He sounded so upset and frustrated, I wanted to lean over and give him a big hug. But I didn't.

"So what happened?"

"They let me keep the shit I'd already taken. Momma said I'd 'defiled' them, so there was no point puttin' them back. She got me some stuff from Goodwill after that."

I was so angry with his parents. What the hell was the matter with the both of them?

"Jordan, you didn't do anything wrong. Your parents overreacted, that's all. I guess that's to be expected, but it's not your fault. If they'd thought about it for two seconds they'd have realized you needed clothes to wear."

He shook his head in silent disagreement.

I tried to think of a way to lighten the mood. "Anyway, I like the baggy shorts."

"You do?"

"Sure," I said, with an evil grin. "I keep wondering how far south they're going to go. I'm thinking of running a pool. Maybe some of the moms in the neighborhood would like in on it."

He looked taken aback for a moment, then his shy smile came out again and I think he might have been blushing. Damn, that was cute.

But, as ever, his good mood didn't last.

He glanced at the clock on the truck's dash.

"We'd better get back," he said, sadly. "Your momma is gonna be callin' the police to say I've abducted you if we stay out any longer."

"Jordan Kane, did you just crack a joke?"

He looked surprised. "Um, no?"

"Well, I thought it was funny."

He considered that for a few seconds then smiled a little, but didn't reply.

I turned on the radio as he drove, and watched him drumming his fingers to the music, lost in thought.

When we arrived back, I hopped out of the truck and threw him the plastic bag that I'd hidden in my purse.

"For you."

His surprise turned to astonishment as he pulled out a pair of long-cuffed work-gloves, size large.

"You … you bought these for me?"

"Sure! I said I would. Don't worry, I'll get the money back off of Mom."

I waved and headed for the front door.

"Torrey!" he called after me.

I turned to look at him.

"Thank you," he said.

Jordan

I couldn't believe she'd bought me a gift. Even if her momma was paying for it. I hadn't had anyone do something like that for me in so long.

I took the gloves out of their packaging and pulled them on. They fit perfectly.

I went back to work and took out some of my frustration on the Rev's overgrown rambling roses. I only got a few scratches on my upper arms. I hoped there'd be a garden emerging from the wilderness once I was done. I didn't want to think what would happen to me when I'd finished—I couldn't keep working here if there was nothing for me to do. I hoped that the Reverend was praying for a plan B.

I kept an eye open, but I didn't see Torrey again. I'd hoped to be able to thank her once more for the gloves, and for, well, everything.

When I got home, my parole officer's car was parked in the driveway.

More joy.

My parents hated having the house searched, but it was part of the agreement they'd signed as a condition of my parole, so they couldn't object. But they could resent me just a little bit more.

At least Officer Carson wasn't a complete bitch. I mean, she was *one of them*, so I didn't really trust her, but she didn't go out of her way to make things difficult either.

I saw Momma standing in the kitchen with her arms folded,

fuming as Officer Carson went through the cupboards. They both turned and saw me at the same time.

"Hello, Jordan," said Officer Carson, pleasantly. "It's good to see you. How are you?"

"Fine thank you, ma'am," I mumbled. It was my default answer for most questions.

I saw her glance at Momma who still hadn't spoken.

"How's work going?" the officer continued.

"Fine."

"Reverend Williams says she's very pleased with you."

I nodded and shoved my hands into my pockets.

She smiled congenially. "Well, I'm about done here. Thank you, Mrs. Kane. Jordan, I just need to take a look in your room now, if that's okay?"

She didn't have to ask permission, so it was kind of nice of her that she did.

"Yeah, sure."

I followed her up the stairs and along the hallway, then watched from the door as she checked under the bed, in my closet, under the mattress, and rifled carefully through my chest of drawers. She even checked under the drawers and behind the back of the unit. It was a reasonably thorough search, but if I'd wanted to hide drugs or shit, I wouldn't have been so fucking obvious. I'd probably leave them outside or in the attic, hidden behind the rafters, like Mikey and I used to do.

"How are you finding it, being home?"

"Fine."

She sighed. "You know, Jordan, part of my job is to help you with the transition. I know it's difficult, but if you talk about it, and with the support of your family, you'll have a much better chance of staying out of prison."

Yeah, right—the support of my family.

"Yes, ma'am."

She waited a moment but got nothing more from me.

"Do you have your monthly report for me?"

"Uh, yeah. I'll just get it."

I handed her the sheet of paper, covered in my usual chicken scratch writing. Along with all the other parole requirements, I had to write a 'complete and truthful' account of my month.

I passed the scrawl to her and she cast a brief eye over it.

"Thank you, Jordan. Well, this will be the last home visit I make. There'll still be the random searches, of course, but other than those, we'll continue to meet in my office. You have my card—you can call me any time if you have a problem."

I nodded.

"Okay, I'm done. I'll see you in two weeks. Don't forget to get your testing done at the police station."

"Yes, ma'am."

I walked her to the door, and she gave me a professional smile before leaving.

Momma was thumping pots and pans around in the kitchen when I shut the door behind Officer Carson. I knew she hated these inspections as much as I did; the difference being, she wasn't used to them. I headed out to the garage and threw some weights around. It helped. A bit.

I ate supper alone in the kitchen, washed my plate, and lay upstairs, praying for sleep to numb my mind.

I woke up suddenly. It wasn't a dream that had disturbed me. I was fairly sure I'd heard something.

I listened carefully and then I heard it: a car engine turning over. The twin beams of headlights split the dark. Whatever was going on, I was guessing it wasn't anything good.

I shot out of bed and ran to the front door. I was just in time to see red tail lights disappearing down our road and toward the town.

I flicked on the porch light and saw immediately what my night time visitors had done. My truck was covered in red paint, and someone had slashed each of the tires.

I swore loudly, and then I heard my dad's voice behind me.

"That's your brother's truck."

"I know, Dad. I didn't ask for this to happen."

"I should have known that lettin' you use it would end up like this. Everythin' you touch…"

I wanted to tear my hair out with frustration. Dad had been reluctant to let me use Mikey's truck, and Momma had flat out refused to even discuss it. But when Dad pointed out that she'd end up having to run me everywhere, I think that forced her to agree. Mostly, because she couldn't stand the thought of spending all that alone time with me.

Whatever.

It took a solid week of hard work getting the truck to run again. And now this.

I couldn't believe it had happened. Why did they have to violate Mikey's truck? I mean, what the fuck? How was I going to get to work now? How was I going to do anything?

My hands were shaking from the adrenalin burning through my body, and I wanted to hit something … badly.

"No, you didn't mean for any of this to happen. You just went off and got drunk and Michael died because of you."

Dad's voice was so tired, barely even angry. It sounded more like something he'd said in his head a thousand times. He turned on his heel, shutting the door in my face.

Some things didn't change.

Chapter 4 – Nascent

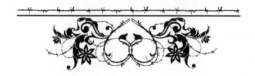

Torrey

In deference to the morality police—a.k.a. Mom—I'd set my alarm half an hour earlier than usual so I could shower and dress before Jordan arrived for work.

She'd pretty much accused me of 'leading him on' by making coffee while wearing the clothes that I slept in. I'd only changed my routine because I was a little bit worried he might think the same thing.

I'd seen the way he looked at me, and he'd told me that he thought I was attractive … well, 'gorgeous' was what he'd said. I took that comment with a grain of salt—I mean the guy was practically a virgin. Okay, probably not an *actual* virgin given what Mom had mentioned about him getting into trouble with girls, but unless he was taking it up the ass in prison, which I somehow doubted, then he hadn't had sex in eight years. A born-again virgin, maybe. Either way, I didn't want to make it harder for him. And I'd *definitely* seen how hard I was making it.

Not that I was intentionally looking, it was just very, um …
obvious and for it to be so obvious he must have had quite the
… yeah, better not think about that.

But losing half an hour's sleep made me grumpy. I was *not* a
morning person.

I staggered down to the kitchen, desperate for a shot of
caffeine before I moved an inch further.

I was listening out for the sound of Jordan's truck when I
suddenly saw him from the kitchen window. He was wearing his
too-big shorts, and it looked like he was limping.

I banged on the window, and he jumped. *Shit, I must stop doing
that to the poor guy.*

But when he turned around, I was shocked. I yanked open
the screen door and marched toward him.

"Jeez! What the hell happened to you now?"

Jordan was a mess. Blood was dripping down his leg from a
cut across his left knee; his right elbow didn't look much better,
and the palms of both hands were badly scraped.

"Fell," he said, with zero inflection in his voice.

"What? You fell in a way that managed to scrape your *left*
knee, your *right* arm, *both* hands, *and* rip across the back of your t-
shirt?"

He nodded and shrugged one shoulder.

"You're full of shit, Jordan! Get your ass over here."

He seemed reluctant to come in the house, so I grabbed a
fistful of his sweaty t-shirt and dragged him inside, pushing him
onto the couch.

"Sit there. Don't move."

He let his backpack slip off his shoulder and leaned back, his
eyes closed.

I ran upstairs to get Mom's first aid kit and a bottle of
peroxide for the second time in as many days. Then, as an
afterthought, I went to the kitchen and boiled some water, put it
in a bowl and carried it over to the couch with a clean towel and
more Bactine. It seemed likely that we were going to have to
stock up on that if Jordan was going to carry on working here.

Maybe kissing the boo-boos better would help, too—or kissing other things. *Aaagh! Mind on the job, Delaney!*

"Soak your hands in there," I ordered.

He hissed as his raw hands sank into the hot water.

"Wimp," I teased him.

He raised his eyebrows, and I thought I saw a slight smile twitch at his lips.

When he'd washed his hands thoroughly, I dried them with the towel then smeared the palms with more ointment. He needed two small Band-Aids on the worst scrapes, but otherwise his hands weren't too bad. After yesterday's tussle with the rose bushes, his arms were already a patchwork of scratches and Band-Aids. He looked like he'd been wrestling a pair of bobcats. Did people still do that? Well, we were in Texas.

"Just keep your hands clean and dry. They'll be fine. And remember to wear your work-gloves *all* the time. Now, let me see your elbow."

I repeated the process of soaking and cleaning, and then used tweezers to pull out a couple of pieces of grit from his elbow. The cut was pretty deep but not too big. I cleaned it with the peroxide and felt his body tense as I dabbed the clear liquid into the cut, but he didn't speak.

If I had to think of a word that defined Jordan, it would be 'stoic'. He took pain the way other people took coffee. Definitely stoic, along with 'hot'.

Still, this probably wasn't worse than having a tattoo. I couldn't help wondering when and where he'd got them all done. When he was 16? Possible—just.

His left knee had taken the worst of whatever had happened to him. And I didn't believe his bullshit story that he'd simply fallen over. If I had to take a guess—which seemed likely since he wasn't telling me anything anyway—I'd say that he'd been running when he fell, then rolled. Running *from* something, maybe?

It wasn't my business, but I was still curious.

I settled down between his feet and took a good look at his

knee. Several pieces of grit were stuck in there and I could see that I was going to need a magnifying glass as well as the tweezers.

"Wait here. Don't move," I snapped at him.

I thought I saw a flash of irritation, but his blank look was soon in place again. I was kind of pleased that I was getting under his skin. I wanted to know what the real Jordan was like. He was a master at keeping himself closed off. It couldn't be good for him—it wouldn't be good for anyone to keep themselves wound so tight. I imagined he'd had eight years of it. I shivered at the thought of what unraveling eight years of fear and tension might look like.

I found a scratched magnifying glass at the bottom of Mom's ancient makeup bag. Satisfied I had the tools for the job, I ran back downstairs and was pleased to find that he hadn't moved.

"How y'all doin' over there, cowboy?" I said, in my best Texas drawl.

"Waal, jest fine, ma'am," he said, hamming it up for me.

This time there was a definite smile lurking at the corners of his mouth, and it gave me hope.

I knelt down between his feet again and started pulling out pieces of grit.

I saw a muscle quiver in his thigh a couple of times, but he didn't say anything.

When I heard Mom's car outside, I felt Jordan tense up again, but I was so focused on what I was doing that I just carried on.

Mom walked in the door and I heard her shocked intake of breath.

"Oh excuse me!" she gasped, and immediately started to back out.

What the hell?

I turned to see her retreating figure.

"Mom! What are you doing?"

She turned around to meet my irritated gaze. Her face was burning with embarrassment.

"What?" I said again.

She took in the sight of Jordan's messy knee and the first aid kit, then heaved a sigh of relief.

"Oh, I'm sorry! I thought…"

I realized what she'd seen: me kneeling with my head nearly in Jordan's lap. She'd obviously sprinted to the wrong conclusion.

"Jeez, Mom, really? Did you think I was blowing him right here on your sofa?"

Her face went an even darker shade of red, and behind me Jordan sounded like he was choking.

Mom uttered a few mangled vowels then almost ran to the kitchen, mumbling about making coffee.

"I should go," Jordan said in a hoarse whisper, standing up awkwardly.

"Sit your ass down and let me finish!"

Hesitantly, he lowered himself to the couch again. I shook my head in disbelief at the weirdness of people and went back to work.

Five minutes later, I was happy that I'd gotten all of the grit. I finished cleaning him up then slapped a large Band-Aid over his knee.

"You're done."

He stood up hurriedly, his eyes fixed to the floor, as usual.

"Thanks," he said, softly.

"Yeah, yeah. I'm a regular Saint Joan."

"A warrior."

"What?"

This time he risked meeting my eyes.

"Saint Joan was a warrior. She led the French in battles against the English."

"Who died and put you in charge?" I said bitchily, still more than a little irritated with my mom.

His face froze.

"Oh, God! I'm so sorry, Jordan! That was…"

But he was already out the door.

Jeez, I wondered if there would ever a time when I didn't have my foot in my mouth.

Mom watched him through the kitchen window.

"Torrey…"

"Don't start, Mom."

"I shouldn't have assumed … but what you said—that language was uncalled for."

I whipped my head around to look at her.

"Seriously? You're that much of a hypocrite that what bothers you is *not* the fact that you leapt to a hugely wrong conclusion about both me and Jordan? But *that's* not what bothers you—oh no! The fact that I called you on it is a big fucking problem!"

"Please don't swear! You know I don't like it."

"Fine! I won't swear if you won't assume that I'm a giant slut!"

I walked out of the room, fire just about shooting from my eyeballs. By rights the house should have been alight by now.

I ran up to my room and upended my purse to try and find my car keys, causing unpaid parking tickets, lipstick and loose change to rain down on my bed.

Then I sat down heavily, bouncing slightly on the too soft mattress—I couldn't take off in a cloud of smoke and squeal of burning tires because my car was still fucked.

I looked out of the window, my eyes searching for Jordan. He was standing with his shoulders slumped, staring at the thicket of brambles and roses in front of him.

The way he was just standing there was painful to watch. He looked so defeated. I hated that I'd contributed to him feeling like that. Just because Mom had assumed I was being my usual sluttish self. Okay, so I'd hooked up with quite a number of guys in the couple of weeks I'd been here, but did she really think I'd do a guy on her sofa in the middle of the day? Scratch that, because the answer was obviously 'yes'.

I couldn't really blame her—I hadn't given her many reasons to think well of me. She didn't know that I still had boundaries;

they just weren't the same as *her* boundaries.

I heard the front door slam so I assumed she'd gone back out. She was probably as eager to get away from me as I was from her. I sighed heavily. I might not be able to fix my relationship with my mom, but I could try to make things better for Jordan.

I went back downstairs and opened the screen door leading from the kitchen.

"Hey, cowboy!"

He turned around; his face stiff with the studied blankness that seemed to be what he did to hide himself. I guess it was a necessary skill in prison.

"You going to fix my car for me or what?"

He blinked and stared at me warily.

"You still want me to try?"

"Well, duh! Of course I do!"

He nodded and limped toward me.

"Are you going to tell me what the hell happened now, or do I have to play twenty questions again?"

His eyes wouldn't meet mine when he replied.

"I fell over," he said, again.

"Fine. So don't tell me. You fell over. Whatever."

I tossed my keys to him. "Fix my car and I'll fix you something amazing for lunch. How about feta and quinoa spring rolls with roast tomato nam prik?"

His eyes widened.

"Um, I don't know what that is. The only words I recognized are spring rolls and tomato somethin' or other."

"Guess the prison wasn't too hot on Thai food, no pun intended."

He shook his head.

"I've never had Thai food. Is that, as in, Thailand?"

"Oh, baby, you're in for a treat! I make the meanest nam prik this side of Bangkok. You feeling brave?"

"Not so as you'd notice," he said, his mouth twisting down. "And I'm real, real sorry I made things tougher between you and your momma."

His voice was rough with sincerity, and he wouldn't meet my eyes.

"Ha! That was nothing to do with you. We have our own drama, so don't worry about it." I paused. "It was pretty funny though, when you think about it."

From the way his face immediately reddened I guessed he wasn't ready to make a joke of it.

"So, the Princess: why won't the bitch run?"

I followed him outside and realized immediately what was missing.

"Jordan, where's your truck?"

His eyes slid to my car and he wouldn't look at me.

"Had a problem with it this mornin'."

"So … you walked here?"

"Yes, ma… yeah, I like to run, so … um, can you pop the hood for me again and I'll take a closer look?"

He was clearly unhappy talking about whatever had happened, so I left it at that.

It was fascinating watching him work, he was so competent and in charge. It offered another glimmer of the person he used to be, and the person I hoped he could be again.

And I admit it, seeing his tight body bent under the hood of my car was a real turn on. If he'd been anyone other than who he was, I'd have jumped him by now. But knowing he was in a vulnerable place—that had me hitting the brakes hard. He needed a friend, not a casual hook up. Although, on the other hand, maybe he wouldn't be so uptight if he got laid.

"Well, you seem to know what you're doing," I said, after several minutes of enjoyable ogling, "and I feel like a spare part. I'll go whip up something exotic for lunch."

"You don't have to do that," he said, peering up at me. "I brought a sandwich."

"Pah! Sandwich, smandwich! I can do better than that. Prepare to be amazed."

I headed back to the kitchen, pleased that I'd gone grocery

shopping with Mom earlier in the week, and stocked up on the kind of things I liked to eat. I was *so* bored of pasta with spaghetti sauce, no matter how many mushrooms Mom put in it.

I lined up my ingredients like soldiers about to go into battle, which was an apt simile, because when I cooked, I always seemed to end up using every utensil in the house, and left it looking like the fridge had exploded.

Quinoa had been a go-to staple when I was a student: easy to use, you could store it forever, and it went great with whatever you threw into it. Today, I added frozen peas, onions, Greek cheese, lemon juice and foraged a bunch of dried mint leaves. Maybe when Jordan had finished on Mom's garden I'd plant some herbs for her so we could cook with fresh spices.

The nam prik needed a bit more preparation: tomatoes, olive oil, garlic, red chili, ginger, coriander, lime juice and the secret ingredient that I'd had to order from Galveston, tamarind paste.

I cheated with the filo pastry, using the ready-made frozen stuff. I was pretty sure Jordan wouldn't know the difference, unless I was dumb enough to leave the packet wrapper out.

After a lot of fiddling around, and more cursing than usual (which was saying a lot), just as the spring rolls were ready to be taken out of the pan, I heard my car start.

I ran to the window in time to see Jordan smiling from ear to ear while he revved the engine.

I screamed for joy and ran out of the front door.

"You did it! You are amazing!"

His cheeks pinked with pleasure, and I had to stop myself from hugging him.

"Thank you so much! You've saved me from selling my blood."

His expression wavered, and I could tell he wasn't sure whether or not I was joking.

"Okay, come on in and wash up. Lunch is about ready."

He nodded and cut the engine, before following me hesitantly into the house.

I got back to the kitchen just in time to stop the smoke alarm from going off. Great: ten slightly singed spring rolls. Oh well. It's the thought that counts, right?

Jordan hovered by the kitchen door with a look on his face that said he was expecting to be ordered right out again.

It broke my heart to see him looking so beaten.

"Sit," I ordered, pointing at one of the kitchen chairs.

"Um, is your momma gonna be back, because if she is, I…"

"Sit!" I said, emphatically. "You're my friend and until she says otherwise—which she won't—this is my house, too."

He smiled tentatively.

"Somethin' smells good."

"Yup, my special recipe." I laid the dishes out in front of him. "You want chopsticks?"

His eyes widened anxiously.

"That's okay. You can have a regular fork, but it's not nearly as much fun."

I grabbed a fork from the silverware drawer and placed it in front of him.

"Dig in."

He waited for me to pick up one of the spring rolls, and put some of the nam prik dip onto my plate. Then he skewered his own spring roll with a fork, dunked it in the dip and tentatively tasted it.

His eyebrows shot up and he instantly started coughing.

Darn. Perhaps I should have warned him that I'd added extra chili.

I poured him a glass of milk and sat back, watching his eyes water.

"Too hot?"

"It's … great," he wheezed.

I couldn't help laughing.

"No, really," he coughed. "I just wasn't expectin' that…"

"It's okay. I like it spicy—it's not everyone's thing."

He gulped down the milk and tried nibbling at the spring roll again. This time he stayed well away from the dip.

I guess it wasn't too bad because in the end, he chewed his

way through seven of those babies, finishing up with an apple.

I gave him a glass of green tea to take out to the porch. He sniffed it suspiciously then took a sip.

"Tastes like dirty bath water," he said, his tone slightly accusing.

"It's not supposed to," I replied, rolling my eyes. "It's a delicate after-dinner refresher—good for the digestion. At least *try* something new!" I complained.

He nodded slowly, but I don't think he was agreeing with me.

"Just because everyone in the South seems to like sweet tea! This is much better for you."

I watched him sternly until he drank most of it then took pity on him, promising to make coffee later.

"Can I do the dishes for you, seein' as I didn't cook?"

"Hell, no! You're my guest, although I might not let you off so easy next time. But seeing as you fixed my car, we're good."

"Thanks, Torrey. It's been great."

"Liar!" I laughed. "You hated it!"

"No, really," he said, earnestly.

"You are such a bad liar, Jordan Kane! But it's okay."

He looked at me sheepishly. "You're not mad?"

"Nah. I can't help it if your culinary experience is stuck at meat and potatoes." I had a brain wave. "But you know what, I can help with that. Tomorrow I'll make you a real Thai curry— just not so hot."

"Um … thanks?" he said, his expression somewhat wary.

"Make the most of it. I start work next week so you'll never see me after that."

His lips thinned and his eyes dropped to the ground.

"Okay."

Gah! I really want to slap him! I hate this subservient crap he keeps giving me. But I knew he'd had eight years of it—a couple of days with me ragging on him wasn't going to fix it.

I slapped his shoulder and went back inside, leaving him to attack the garden again.

But when I turned to look at the disaster of a kitchen, I wondered if maybe I should have taken him up on his offer to do the dishes after all.

Oh well, Mom was always saying that hard work was good for the soul. I wanted to know what sucker came up with that load of horse shit?

At 4:30 PM I banged on the kitchen window. Darn—I made him jump again. I couldn't seem to remember. Maybe I should put a sticker on the window: *Don't give the hot handyman a heart attack.*

"Quittin' time!" I yelled.

He nodded and scrubbed the back of his arm across his sweaty face.

"Come on, cowboy, I'll give you a ride home in my newly fixed car!"

He walked toward me slowly, obviously still in considerable pain from the way he was limping.

"That's okay. I can walk home. But thanks."

"Don't be such a sap. Get in the damn car."

He shuffled from foot to foot until I felt like yanking open the car door and tossing him inside. And I would have, if it weren't for the fact that he was probably 200 pounds of solid muscle.

Eventually, he grimaced and stared at a spot somewhere near my left foot.

"Uh, I kind of stink right now."

"Yeah, well, I'd let you shower here, but I can't risk giving my mom another stroke, which would certainly happen if she found a naked man in her house. I'm pretty sure it's been a while for her. So just get in the damn car, and I'll open the windows."

He mumbled something I couldn't hear and pulled open the passenger door, carefully rolling down the window first. It would have been kind of sweet, if it wasn't so sad.

I turned the radio up loud so he wouldn't feel forced to talk if he didn't want to. But it was Jordan who started a conversation.

"Why do you call me 'cowboy'?" he asked, softly.

I shrugged. "Just 'cause."

"I've never roped a cow in my life. I've probably even forgotten how to ride," he said.

"No riding, huh? What a pity!" I smirked, and saw his ears turn red. "Look, I won't call you 'cowboy' if you don't like it."

His reply was so soft I could barely hear it.

"I didn't say I didn't like it..."

"Okay fine … cowboy."

I saw a smile tugging at the corner of his mouth.

I drove out of town and took the turning for Placedo Road.

"You'll have to tell me which way because I don't know exactly where you live."

He nodded and after a mile or so, told me to hang a right.

"You can drop me here," he said, quietly.

"Don't be dumb and don't think I haven't seen you limping. I'll take you all the way."

I couldn't help noticing that the nearer he got to his home, the more rigid he became. It didn't take a genius to work out that home wasn't a very happy place.

Finally, more than three miles from the main road, we even ran out of the dirt road and were bumping over clumps of wiry grass. A small, two-story clapboard house stood among a grove of cottonwood trees. It might have been pretty once, but now it just looked sad and neglected—probably an indicator of the state of mind of the people who lived there, too.

His truck was parked in front of the house and covered by an old tarp.

"Something you couldn't fix?" I asked curiously, climbing

out of the car.

"Somethin' like that," he said, evasively.

Before he could stop me, I peeped under the tarp and immediately wished I hadn't.

The word 'murderer' had been sprayed in red paint along the side, and every tire had been slashed.

Murderer? Oh my God! A thousand questions rushed through my mind. My hands were shaking as I stared at the man next to me. I just couldn't believe it. *He was a murderer?* No, that couldn't be right. Mom would have told me. Surely? She'd said he was dangerous … but *a murderer?*

"Fuck, Jordan! What…? Who…?"

I wondered if I should be afraid of him, but he looked just the same—sad, beautiful, broken.

I couldn't believe he was a murderer. The truth was I didn't *want* to believe that, and I was too much of a chicken shit to ask him directly. Yet.

He shrugged tiredly.

"I don't know who did it. Kids."

"What did the police say?"

He threw me an incredulous look. "I didn't call them."

I shook my head at him impatiently

"You *have* to! This is serious harassment! Vandalism, Criminal Trespass, Criminal Mischief, and, of course, Graffiti."

"No," he said, firmly. "No police. Not here. No way."

It was the most definite statement I'd ever heard him make.

"And how did you get in that condition?" I asked, pointing at the bandage on his knee. "You look like someone tried to run you over."

My eyes widened when I saw the truth in his face.

"Shit! That's what happened, isn't it?"

"Please, Torrey," he said, hoarsely. "Don't tell anyone. I don't need any more trouble."

His eyes were pleading

"I think you're wrong, but it's your call," I said, quietly.

He let out the breath that he'd been holding.

"Thank you."

Then I had an idea and pulled out my cell phone, quickly snapping a photo of the damage. I figured he might need evidence of the harassment. Guess my legal training was good for something even if I couldn't force him to file a complaint.

"What's that for?" he asked, suspiciously.

I shrugged. "I don't know, but you might be grateful I've got that one day."

He didn't look like he believed me, but he didn't ask me to delete it either.

"Most people around here didn't have cell phones with cameras when I went inside."

My mouth dropped open. That small statement made me realize how much he'd missed; how much had passed him by. I didn't know what to say.

"Well, thanks for the ride," he mumbled.

"Sure. What time do you want me to pick you up in the morning?"

He shook his head quickly. "Nah, that's fine."

"Your folks going to give you a ride?"

His eyes slid away from mine, something I noticed he did when he didn't want to answer a direct question.

"I'm good."

Just then the front door banged open, making me jump. Served me right for all the times I'd scared the crap out of Jordan.

A woman I assumed was his mother stood there. She didn't look much like her son. Jordan must have gotten his looks from his dad.

She looked pissed about something.

"Hi!" I said, as cheerfully as I could manage, given her baleful expression. "I'm Torrey Delaney, Reverend Williams' daughter."

"What's he done now?" she snapped, ignoring my outstretched hand.

"Excuse me?"

She seemed to pull herself together because her demeanor changed instantly.

"Oh, I was wonderin' if there was a problem, Miss Delaney?"

"Well, apart from the wreck some asshats have made of Jordan's truck, and the fact that it looks like someone tried to run him down, no, we're all good," I said, sarcastically.

Her eyes flickered up and down me, and then she turned and went into the house without saying another word.

"Seems like a very warm person," I said, in a low voice.

"She wasn't always like that," Jordan said quietly, shaking his head. "She used to laugh all the time. Everyone wished their momma was like ours." He shrugged. "Things change."

"Is she like this all the time with you?"

He nodded and sighed.

"She hates me. They both do. But no more than I hate myself."

I could feel tears prick my eyes; I *never* cried.

"God, Jordan, I'd fix it for you if I could."

He gave a small smile. "I know you would. Thanks for the ride."

Then he turned and walked into the house.

Jordan

Everything hurt. Torrey had called it right when she'd guessed how I'd gotten injured.

After I'd seen what they'd done to the truck, I'd had no choice but to jog to the Rectory. It was only five miles, so nothing I couldn't handle. But I hadn't counted on the bastards who'd wrecked my truck waiting for me.

They'd followed me as far as the main road, yelling and

cussing at me, throwing some trash that they'd stored up in their car. I'd thought that was the extent of it, so I'd just ignored them. Maybe that made them even more pissed.

They looked like high school kids, so it wasn't as if I'd known any of them from before. But one of them had auburn hair; it reminded me so much of Allison. Then I remembered that she'd had a younger brother named Trent.

When I'd called out his name, the car sped by me, clipping my hip as it went, sending me somersaulting down the road, and leaving me sprawled out in the dirt. It sucked, but there was nothing I could do about it.

I hadn't expected Torrey to take care of me the way she had. She was just so fucking compassionate. It spun my head. I couldn't work out why she was wasting her time on me. If I was honest, I'd been expecting her to want some sort of payback. So far she'd just treated me good. I'd heard Dad and Momma talking about her so called reputation, but other than being a little flirtatious, she was just a really nice person to me.

I'd nearly had a heart attack when she'd called her momma on the whole couch thing. I was still sort of shocked that she'd found it funny, although that was later on. At the time, I was mortified. I'd been able to hear her yelling at her momma from the garden. I hoped I hadn't screwed anything up between them. I probably had. I was good at that.

I limped into my room and peeled off my disgusting, sweaty clothes. I don't know how she could have stood to be in the same car with me. You didn't really notice it that much in prison because everyone smelled like ass. But it was different now. Every time she came near me, I caught the scent of summer flowers.

The shower felt amazing. It was a real luxury to have as much hot water as I wanted, and not have to keep one eye open the whole time for who was coming into the shower block. I still couldn't get used to having so much privacy. When I first got out, I used to forget where I was and wore my boxers in the shower to wash them. In prison, everyone did that—for obvious reasons. But as I only had the one pair, oftentimes I didn't bother wearing any now that I was home.

The water stung my arms and legs. I had to admit I was looking pretty busted up. But I'd had worse in prison, and had gotten several black eyes and my nose broken once. I'd been put in solitary for 72 hours even though it had been nothing to do with me, just the wrong place at the wrong time. Shit like that happened; there was no point being a whiny bitch about it. And anyway, it had healed pretty straight.

I was surprised to see that Dad was waiting in my room after I finished in the shower.

He looked at the new holes in my body but didn't comment.

"This isn't workin'," he said, flatly. "I cain't have your momma harassed like this. She's gettin' so she's scared to leave her own home again."

I stared at the bare floorboards, pretty sure I could guess what he was going to say.

"We have our home searched by strangers; comments in the street—you don't know what that's like for us. Then last night with your brother's truck—well, that was the final straw. I'll contact your parole officer and tell her you need to move out. They have places for people like you in the city; I think it would be best for everyone if you just left."

He stood up and walked out. I didn't bother to argue because, well, he was right. And it didn't matter to me where I went—I still had to live inside my skin. But maybe it would be better if I went somewhere no one knew me. I wouldn't be leaving anything behind—except Torrey.

I felt the pain of regret in my chest. Yeah, I'd miss her.

Torrey

I didn't want to admit it, but I needed to talk to my mom.

I called her cell phone, but it went straight to voicemail. When she turned it off it usually meant she was visiting with some parishioners. I waited a while, standing in the kitchen staring into the garden as the shadows lengthened. I could see the hulking shape of the dumpster with long fingers of torn brambles hanging from it, as if they were trying to crawl out. The idea made me shiver.

I looked at the clock on the wall again, ticking away with annoying regularity.

In the end, I decided to head on down to the church in case she was caught up there.

It was close enough to walk so I didn't bother taking my car.

It was the kind of neighborhood where people walked their dogs, and kids rode their bikes and played in the street. Real small town. Nothing like where I'd grown up.

The church was in the middle of a bunch of newish houses on the intersection of one of the bigger roads. It was large, but as I stared at the outside, I was unimpressed with the bland modern exterior. It wasn't supposed to matter what a place of worship looked like, but I thought the right ambience helped, you know?

But as soon as I walked inside, I was swept into another world by the scent of beeswax polish. I hadn't smelled anything like that since my grandma's house. It brought back memories of home baking and listening to her bedtime stories.

"Torrey? What are you doing here?"

Mom's voice floated out from behind one of the rows of chairs.

"Oh, hey, Mom! What are you doing on the floor?"

She sighed.

"Both of the ladies from the cleaning roster called in to cancel. One has gone to look after her sick sister in Gainesville, and the other has an ingrown toenail so she can't walk."

"Jeez, Mom. You run this place, sit on all those fu… darn committees, set up for the parent and toddler group *and* clean the church? You should ask God for a raise."

"Don't be flippant, and hold the blasphemy," she said, but I caught the smile in her voice, too. "You could help me, you know."

I rolled my eyes. "Fine. Just so long as you know that cleaning is against my religion."

She laughed. "I've noticed. Just tell yourself it'll be good for your soul."

"Whatever. What needs doing?"

She pointed me in the direction of some rags, a can of polish and a darn large pulpit that needed to glow in honor of God's glory, or some such.

Grimacing, I slathered some polish on a cloth and got cleaning.

"So, what's so urgent that you deigned to set foot inside our church?" she asked, her voice amused.

"It's about Jordan," I replied, diving right in.

"I thought it might be," she said, quietly.

"Someone slashed the tires on his truck last night. And if that wasn't enough, they sprayed paint all over it. Also, I'm pretty sure that the same someone tried to run him down this morning. You saw how banged up he was. He wouldn't tell me about it, but it's obvious he's being victimized."

"Did he report it?"

"No, and that's part of what bothers me. He refused to involve the police. I mean, I get why he wouldn't want to—he's kind of allergic to the boys in blue—but if he doesn't do something, I'm worried it's just going to get worse."

"I'm afraid you're right," she said, tiredly. "I've been preaching about tolerance and forgiveness until I'm blue in the face: 'With all humility and gentleness, with patience, bearing with one another in love,' but it doesn't seem to have made much difference."

She sounded despondent—that wasn't like my mom.

"I was hoping you'd have some ideas," I admitted.

"Honey, Jordan's problems aren't your responsibility."

"I know that, Mom, but it's totally shit the way people around here treat him. They painted the word 'murderer' on his truck. Is it true?"

She shook her head immediately.

"Not in the eyes of the law."

"But in your eyes?"

She sighed and looked down.

"Jordan is responsible for the loss of a life. It's not for me to say more: I believe he'll be judged by a higher power when the time comes, as will we all."

Her answer was only partially satisfying.

"He's really trying, but no one will give him a chance," I said, quietly. "Even his own parents act like they hate him."

"I didn't know you'd met them."

"Well, only his mom, this afternoon when I gave Jordan a ride home. She didn't even manage to say 'hello' before she was asking me what trouble he'd gotten into now. He says himself that they hate him, and he has to live with that twenty-four/seven."

She sat down heavily on one of the chairs.

"I was afraid of that. I thought having Jordan home would help them work through their problems together, but from the sound of it, that's not happening. I don't think they've even grieved properly. They're stuck in the anger stage. They can't seem to get past that. I tried to get them to go to counseling but they refused."

"Jordan said he had a counselor in prison, but he didn't say what they talked about. It might not even have been that sort of therapy."

Mom shook her head. "As I understand it, Jordan received the kind of counseling that's designed to help a prisoner readjust into society prior to being released. He may have had some grief counseling at the time…"

She didn't sound very certain.

"Could family therapy help them?"

"I'd really like to think it could, honey, but getting them there is the problem. I've even offered to help them from the church's hardship fund, but the Kanes are proud people." She looked up at me. "Sweetheart, I know this isn't something you believe, but will you join me in a prayer?"

"Mom…"

"Just listen, you don't have to say anything."

She got on her knees and faced the altar.

"Lord, I ask for your divine help to shine on the faces of your children, Gloria, Paul and Jordan Kane. Bring peace in their hearts and light into their darkness. I also pray for my daughter, Torrey Delaney. Show her the path, Lord, and help her make the right choices. You have turned my mourning into dancing; You have put off my sackcloth and clothed me with gladness. To the end that my glory may sing praise to You and not be silent. O Lord my God, I will give thanks to You forever. I ask for these things in Jesus' name. Amen."

I didn't know what to say, so I made a joke of it.

"Hey, you're getting pretty good at this, Mom!"

She clambered off of her knees and raised an eyebrow. "Well, gee! Thanks, honey! Good to know. Do I get a sticker with that?"

Okay, so maybe I got some of my sarcasm from her. It was kind of cool to find that I didn't mind so much.

"Funny, Mom. You could do stand up."

"I do, honey, every Sunday. You should come."

"Um, no!" I shook my head vigorously, and she laughed.

My thoughts drifted back to Jordan again.

"Seriously. Do you think you could maybe talk to his parents so they don't give him such a hard time?"

She sighed. "I'll try, but I can't guarantee anything."

"Thanks, Mom."

We finished the cleaning in silence, each lost in our thoughts.

Chapter 5 – Expectation

Torrey

Mom woke me ridiculously early.

"I'm sorry, honey, but I have to head on out to a meeting with the bishop in Houston. I just wanted you to know that I'll be contacting the Kanes to see if I can meet with them. I'm going to try and do it on the way back, so I might be pretty late."

"And you couldn't put that in a note?" I asked, grumpily.

"Yes, I could, but I wanted to see your smiling face," she smirked at me.

"Okay, Mom. Drive safe."

"Will do, honey. Oh, one more thing … you said Jordan's tires were slashed?"

"Yeah?"

"Well, I remembered that there's a junkyard over toward Corpus, about eight or nine miles out of town. I left the address on the kitchen table for you. I thought you could take Jordan over there and see if there's anything he could get for his truck that wasn't too expensive."

I sat up in bed, pushing a tangle of hair out of my face.

"That's really nice of you, Mom, but I don't think he has any money at all."

"If you can get something for $50, I'll take the money from the hardship fund. That's what it's there for. Just make sure you get a receipt."

I think we were both surprised when I pulled her into a tight hug. We didn't have a touchy-feely relationship, but I thought this definitely warranted a show of affection.

"Thanks, Mom. You just keep on surprising me—I like it."

"Oh you too, honey. I'm so proud of the compassionate young woman you've become."

"Yeah, don't overdo it, Mom."

She laughed and stood up straight. "Don't wait up!" she called over her shoulder.

I was wide awake after that, so I decided to ignore what Jordan had said and go pick him up. Then we could drive straight to the junkyard and get him some new tires. I hoped.

And I wasn't sure if I'd be able to get four truck tires in the Princess, so we might have to make two trips. Better get started.

I admit that I had an excited bubbly feeling in my stomach at the thought of having a whole day to spend with Jordan. I wanted to help him, for sure, but there was more to it than that. And not just the fact that the guy was seriously hot. I wanted to *know* him, and I wanted him to have the chance to be the person he was meant to be, not just the shadow of a man he was right now.

And hell, if I had to stay in this small town another four or five months, I may as well do someone a good turn if I could. Jeez, I was turning into my mother. Was that like some kind of curse? We all end up turning into our parents no matter how much we fight it?

I took my time in the shower and pulled out my favorite jean shorts for my non-date with Jordan. I wasn't hungry, but I was desperate for coffee so I made a full pot, drank two cups and filled a thermos with the rest to give to Jordan.

I was a bit apprehensive driving to his house, especially after last night's little scene with his mom, but I struck lucky. I spotted him jogging down the road, his backpack thumping against him with every stride. I took a moment to appreciate the smooth glide of his gait despite the thick scab on his left knee, and took pleasure in watching the muscles lengthening and contracting in his strong thighs.

He looked surprised and slightly worried when he saw me. That was okay, it was his default setting—one I was determined to try and change.

"Hey, cowboy! Did ya forget your damn coffee?" I yelled out of the window, waving the thermos at him.

He cracked a smile and leaned against the car, one arm on the roof.

"Thanks! I could definitely use it. Are you headin' out for the day?"

"Sure am. Hop in."

"That's okay. I can make my way on over to your momma's place—you don't have to give me a ride."

"Get in, doofus, we're going shopping."

He was half in the seat when he honed in on the word 'shopping'.

"Um, pardon me, but what did you say?"

"You heard—shopping! There's nothing wrong with your hearing, cowboy."

He clipped his seatbelt into place and watched me as I put the car in drive.

"Why are we shoppin', Torrey?"

I liked the way my name sounded when he said it.

"Waaal," I said, drawing out the word the way I'd heard him pronounce it, "my mom is one of those Christian types who likes to do good deeds…"

"I've noticed," he said, his voice toneless.

"Yeah, and she's decided that I can be her sidekick, like…"

"SpongeBob and Patrick Star?"

"Oh, boy! You watched waaaay too many cartoons in prison. No, I was thinking something cooler like Batman and Robin."

"You think Robin is cool?"

"Fair point. Well, maybe not the Burt Ward version…"

"Not any of them."

"Okay, well Catwoman then."

"Catwoman was Batman's arch enemy."

"I know, but the outfit was cool."

"I thought it was hot," he said, raising one eyebrow.

I liked the way he looked when he did that.

"Yeah, but that's not the point…" I reminded him.

"So there is a point?" he smiled.

I loved seeing his smile, too.

"There was when I started, I'm not so sure now; I keep getting interrupted by a giant know-it-all."

"Sorry."

"Apology accepted."

"So, where we goin' again?"

"I told you: shopping."

"Shoppin' for what?"

"You'll see."

He huffed, looking irritated. *Yay! At least he didn't look anxious or scared—progress!*

I patted his leg.

"Just sit back and enjoy the ride."

"Can you go back to the bit where you were sayin' your momma liked to do good deeds?"

"I don't know, are you going to interrupt me again?"

"Nope."

"Promise?"

"Yep."

"Hmm…"

"Hmm?"

"No, I've changed my mind."

He ground his teeth with anger and frustration ,and shot me a dirty look.

I couldn't help laughing out loud and watched from the corner of my eye as he cracked another smile. If he kept this up, smiling would become a habit.

It took nearly 30 minutes to drive the nine miles to the junkyard, mostly because I took a wrong turn out of town. Then I realized I was getting near Jordan's ten-mile limit, and had to turn around and start from the beginning, turning the whole trip into a 35-mile drive.

Jordan didn't seem to mind. We chatted about random stuff—movies he'd liked as a kid, a few that he'd seen while in prison.

I should probably have asked him the way to the junkyard, seeing as he'd lived here since he was born, but I wanted to surprise him.

When I turned into the dusty lot, he was definitely surprised.

"We're at the junkyard," he said, flatly.

"Yes, Captain Obvious. We're looking for truck tires," I explained, climbing out of the car.

A look of disappointment crossed his face.

Darn. Maybe I should have told him earlier where we were going.

It was a pretty depressing place. Wounded cars and trucks littered the whole area, the aluminum and steel glittering under a layer of fine, brown dust. The dead had been heaped into pyres of crushed metal, waiting to be taken away and recycled—the *Soylent Green* of the auto world.

A mountain of rubber tires stood out darkly at the rear of the lot. It was a grim reminder of where cars came to die. I swear my Firebird quivered in terror.

"Um, good surprise?" I asked tentatively, risking a glance at Jordan's blank expression.

He frowned slightly and shook his head.

"Torrey, this is real nice of you, but I don't have money for new tires. I told you this."

"True, but you weren't thinking of God's bounty."

"You're gonna have to explain that."

"Mom gave me fifty bucks to get you some new tires. And before you argue, it didn't come out of her own pocket, so don't start bitching about it."

He crossed his arms, a move that made his biceps look lickable, I mean, likeable—whatever—and he leaned back in his seat.

"You mean the money came from the community hardship fund, don't you."

"Aw, you guessed," I said, pretending to look disappointed.

"I cain't accept it," he snapped.

"Sure you can."

"Folks around here won't…"

"Folks around here won't know. And guess what, even if they did know, it's not their call. That money is Mom's to dispense as she sees fit. Besides, don't you find it an interesting paradox that it was people from the community who slashed your tires, but that the same community will pay to replace them? Some might call that serendipity."

"Or ironic."

"Both work," I agreed, happy that he understood.

"I don't know…" he began, biting his lip.

I want to do that. Jeez, my inner monologue is a horny harlot.

"I *do* know, so get out of the darn car and help me find what we're looking for, Auto Boy."

He scowled but unclipped his seatbelt. "You sure have a lot of nicknames for me."

"I know. I'm creative like that. You should hear the ones I've got for my new step-mom."

"I didn't know you had one?"

"You don't know everything about me," I said, raising an eyebrow.

Before he could reply, we were approached by an enormously hairy guy, the size of a WWE wrestler. I was very glad that Jordan was with me, because this guy was seriously scary.

"Well, well," he bit out, in a deep baritone voice. "If it ain't the notorious Jordan Kane."

Ooh, hadn't counted on that. I hope things aren't about to get violent.

"How you doin', Hulk?" Jordan asked, quietly.

Oh wow! Winding up a 400 pound monster is not my idea of smart.

"Better than you, boy, that's for sure." Then the monster-man held out a meaty fist. "Good to see you, kid."

They shook hands in some complicated man-moves and slapped each other on the back. Jordan coughed slightly and I wouldn't have been surprised to see his spine sticking out through a lung.

Then the Hulk turned to me. "And who's the purty lady, you dawg!"

"Give me a break," Jordan muttered, looking and sounding embarrassed. "This is Torrey Delaney. She was nice enough to give me a ride."

"Was she now?"

"Hi!" I said brightly, proud that my hand didn't tremble as I held it out.

The Hulk took my fingers gingerly and gave my hand a gentle shake, as if afraid I'd disintegrate if he held on any tighter. His eyes flicked up and down me then turned back to Jordan.

"So, what are you doin' over this-aways, kid?"

"Need me some tires for Mikey's truck, Hulk."

Oh, so 'Hulk' is his name, not an insult. And Jordan has been ragging on me about nicknames.

"Yeah? How many you need?"

"Four."

Hulk looked surprised. "What the hell you do?"

Jordan didn't reply, suddenly finding the dirt at his feet utterly fascinating, so I stepped in with the answer. "Some asshat slashed them."

Hulk looked back to Jordan who was still staring at the dusty ground.

"Think I might have what you need, kid," Hulk said. "Grab ahold of that tire iron and follow me."

Hulk led the way and I trailed at the back.

"Hey!" I hissed at Jordan. "How well do you know this guy?"

"Pretty well, why?"

"Just wondering. I didn't want to end up in his car crusher."

Jordan grinned at me. He had nice teeth.

"Nah, you're safe. Hulk is a pussycat." Then his smile faded. "Me and Mikey learned all we knew about cars from him."

Hulk led us past a small mountain of mangled metal, to the truck area of the junkyard, where the maimed and three-wheeled had limped to a halt, the spare parts huddling together for comfort.

"Help yourself," he said, waving his arm at the plastic and aluminum carcasses.

He started to walk back to the office.

"Um, Mr. Hulk?" I said, a little nervously. "We only have fifty dollars…"

Hulk looked amused. "There's no charge."

"Oh, really?"

"Nope."

And he turned away again.

"In that case…?"

He looked over his shoulder, his expression patient.

"What is it now, girl?"

I don't like being called 'girl' but right now I need his help—plus I don't know if he turns green and doubles in size if he gets mad.

"I was wondering if you had any spare car paint. Jordan's truck kind of got redecorated, too."

"That right?"

His eyes flicked across to Jordan who shrugged.

"I'll see what I can find. This a-way."

I trotted behind Hulk and he led me to a shed behind his office. It was a cornucopia of metal paints. Cans of all colors and all sizes were scattered around. Some had dried to powder, but there were enough that were still usable.

"Wow! This is great! Thanks, Hulk."

He nodded then frowned at me.

"You ain't from around here."

It was a statement, not a question.

"No, I'm just passing through."

"He don't need no woman trouble."

I rolled my eyes.

"Not all women are trouble."

"Sez you."

"And your point is?"

"Jordan's not a bad kid."

"I agree. In fact I'm sort of surprised to find anyone other than me and my mom who'll actually talk to him."

Hulk studied me steadily. "You're that preacher lady's girl, ain't you?"

"Yep, that's me. Guilty as charged."

"Huh. So, Jordan is your charity case—that right?"

I stared back coldly. "There's nothing wrong with charity. But as far as I'm concerned, I'm just helping out a friend. What's your excuse?"

He barked out a loud laugh that made me jump. "Well, ain't you a lil' firecracker! I'm glad to see Jordan done got hisself a good 'un."

Then he ambled back into the office, still chuckling.

I was left alone with the paint stash, feeling a little confused.

By the time I'd sorted out which ones Jordan was most likely to want, I was very dusty and sweaty. I collected the thermos of coffee from my car and went to find him.

He was even sweatier and dirtier. I guess wrestling four truck tires would do that to a man. He'd abandoned his t-shirt and was standing in just his sneakers and those baggy cut-offs. They ought to come with a health warning, because I was sure I was going to stroke out watching him hitch them up at regular intervals.

"Hey, cowboy! You forgot your damn coffee again!" I yelled.

He turned and gave me a big smile then walked over and flopped down next to me in the shade of the building.

"Did you find what you needed?" I asked, passing him the cup of coffee.

97

"Yeah, four good tires."

"Excellent. The question is, do you think we'll be able to get them all in the Princess?"

"We should be able to get three in the trunk."

"Oh, goodie, because so many trucks run on three wheels."

"Yeah, who knew?"

I slapped his arm and he leaned away, dodging as I swung again.

"You play rough!" he said.

I raised one eyebrow and watched with vindictive pleasure as his cheeks pinked up again.

"So, cowboy. Wheel number four goes where? Or do we have to make another trip?"

"Well, we could. But if you don't mind, we could fix one on the roof."

I looked at him suspiciously. "Won't that dent it?"

"Not if we're careful. All we need is that blanket you've got in your trunk so the paintwork don't get scratched. And I'll borrow some rope from Hulk."

"Well, all right then. But if there's one single scratch or tiny dent, I can't promise that I won't get violent on your ass."

He smiled and winked at me. *He actually winked! Yay!*

About 15 minutes later, after much sweating and swearing from Hulk and Jordan, the tires were all loaded into and onto my car. I wasn't very happy about it, and the Princess looked very unhappy, but both men had promised that my car would survive unscathed.

The journey back was quicker, mainly because I let Jordan give me directions. He'd been delighted with my color selection and promised that he'd paint something memorable to cover up the ugly red mess.

Back at his house, he got to work straight away. He still hadn't commented on the wording he was painting over, although I kind of felt like he might be waiting for me to speak first. Unusually for me, I wasn't keen to start that conversation right then and there.

"Um, Jordan, I really need to use the bathroom. I've got my legs crossed, my eyes crossed and if I had a tail, that would have a knot in it, too."

"Sure, no problem. There's a key under the mat."

"That's not very secure!" I complained.

He shrugged. "They've always done it that way. Came in handy when we were kids."

"What, sneaking girls into your room?"

He smiled.

"Nope. Never had a girl in my bedroom."

"What? Not even a friend who was a girl?"

"No."

"Why not?"

He sat back on his heels, thinking about his answer.

"Well, I guess it's because I went from thinkin' girls were lame, to playin' spin the bottle over night. Momma read us the riot act, and me and Mikey were both forbidden to have girls in the house—ever."

"Oh, figures: two teenage boys. They were probably worried about becoming grandparents before their time. They did know that banning girls from the house wouldn't necessarily guard against that?"

He smiled wickedly. "I don't think they wanted to know, which was just as well as far as me and Mikey were concerned."

"Hmm, there's a story there, Jordan Kane, and I intend to find out what it is. But first I need to pee!"

After I'd finished in the bathroom, I couldn't help taking a peek into the other rooms. There were three bedrooms upstairs. One was obviously his parents' room so I didn't go in there; the next I assumed was Jordan's.

The bed was made and there were posters of various football teams tacked to the walls. It was messy, with several pairs of jeans and a couple of plaid shirts heaped up on the single chair. Paperbacks were stuffed into the narrow bookshelf, and when I looked closer I was surprised to see that most were high school textbooks.

I jumped when I heard Jordan's voice behind me.

"What are you doin' in here?"

"I couldn't help wanting to violate the 'no girls in your bedroom' rule," I said, smiling at him.

He frowned. "This is Mikey's room."

"Oh!" Color flooded my cheeks. "I'm so sorry! I just assumed…"

I looked around again, this time seeing the signs that I'd missed before: the layer of dust over everything, the slightly dated feel of the posters and pictures.

A cold tremor passed through me. This room was a shrine. Nothing had been touched. Now that I looked closely, I could see that even the sheets on the bed were covered with a film of dust. It was unbearably sad—but also a little creepy.

"You still want to see my room?" he asked, cocking his head to one side.

"You don't have to. I was just curious."

He jerked his head toward the next door, and pushed it open.

This room couldn't have been more different. In fact, if I were looking for comparisons, I'd say it looked like a cell. There were no pictures on the walls, and the bookshelf held just two books: a tattered paperback that looked like it might have come from a yard sale, and the Holy Bible.

There were no personal possessions at all.

I looked around, searching for something, but there was nothing. I stared at him, confused, wanting to ask, but dreading his answer.

"Go ahead," he said. "Ask me."

"What happened to all your stuff?"

"They burned it."

He turned and left me gaping into the empty room.

I felt horrible that I'd invaded his privacy in that way, even though he had nothing to hide. Well, he had nothing at all, which was sadder.

An overwhelming feeling of grief pressed on my body as I

followed Jordan down the stairs. What would it do to a person, living day in and day out surrounded by nothing but memories and hatred? In so many ways, his home life resembled a prison, and I began to understand the extent of the problems he faced, as well as the reasons for the walls he'd erected around himself.

But perhaps this was worse? In prison, you don't expect anyone to give a shit about you. But shouldn't he have had an expectation that he would be loved by his parents no matter what? Isn't a parent's love unconditional? I guess not.

I wondered again what Jordan had done to suffer such hatred from them. I really hoped he'd tell me.

I tiptoed down the stairs, almost afraid to breathe in that haunted house, and sat on the porch, watching him silently work to replace the slashed tires on his truck. I offered to help but he refused, saying it would go quicker if I just stayed sitting.

"Where do you think you'll go—I mean, when your parole is finished?"

He fidgeted with the tire iron.

"It's all right, you don't have to tell me," I reassured him. "We can talk about something else if you like."

"No, it's fine. I like talkin' about it with you. It's just a little strange for me. I feel like you're a dream and I'll wake up and find that my life really is totally shit after all."

My heart ached to hear him sound so unhappy.

"Jordan, you've got a few months left then you can leave this place and never look back."

He sighed and closed his eyes.

"It's not that easy."

"Sure it is. You say, 'to hell with this small town'. And then you get in your truck and drive away."

"Maybe for you it's easy…"

"No, if it's what you want—you just leave."

"I don't own anything, Torrey. Not even this broken down old truck. It … it belonged to Mikey, and there's no way my old man would let me have it. It just about kills him that I drive it— well, when folks aren't slashin' the tires. I'd have to walk outta here and beg for food like some hobo."

"But at least you'd be free."

"Free to starve? Anyway, I'm not so sure about being free. My real prison is in here," and he tapped a long finger against his head. "'Men are not prisoners of fate, but only prisoners of their own minds.' Franklin D. Roosevelt. Guy knew what he was talkin' about."

I was impressed. "How do you know this stuff? I was a History major and I don't know half the things you do."

"University of life," he said, offering a small smile. "I had eight years to do nothin' but read. Read every book in the damn library—twice."

"See! I knew you were smart!"

Jordan looked sad. "Mikey was the clever one. He had a full scholarship to go to UT at Austin. I was just his dumb little brother, draggin' my sorry ass in the mud and ruinin' the family name. Everyone said I'd amount to nothin'—guess they were right."

"You're not nothing," I said, sharply. "Say that again and I'll really hurt you."

I saw a small, painful smile twitch at his lips.

"Did you have any friends come see you in prison?"

He shook his head.

"Nah, no one wanted to know."

"And since you got out?"

"Nope. Cain't say as I blame them. I don't think I'd even recognize any of them now. Besides, Mikey was my best friend..."

"And you didn't make friends in … in prison?"

He shrugged.

"Maybe one guy in juvie, but no, not really. Some cons did— someone to watch their back, ya know. I preferred keepin' to myself."

"It must have been lonely."

"Yes and no. Do you know anything about Japan?"

"Whoa! Random, much?"

"I read a book about Japan once. It's one of the most populated countries on the planet; all those millions of people crowded onto four small islands. So they all have to live in each other's pockets, ya know? And they have those slidin' doors made from paper to divide the rooms up. There's not much privacy. So they get alone time by being inside their heads. That was what it was like for me."

Yeah, I understand that.

He turned back to focus on the truck, and we lapsed into almost comfortable silence.

By the time he finished it was late afternoon, and my stomach was rumbling, demanding food.

"I've got an idea," I announced.

"Another one?" he said, without looking up.

I smiled at his tone. I liked it when he sassed me back.

"Some people have more than one a year," I replied. "I'm a rare breed that sometimes has ideas frequently."

"Do tell. Let's hear this famous idea of yours."

"We'll go back to my place. I'll pack us up a picnic and we can take your big ole truck and find somewhere off-road to chill out by the shore."

"Chill out?"

"You remember chilling out? They invented it in the sixties."

He looked over his shoulder at me. "I should really do some work on your momma's backyard."

"Ach, leave that! It'll still be there tomorrow. Let's go for a swim."

He smiled. "You know, that sounds great!"

"I knew you'd like my idea. I have lots of good ones."

He held up his hands. "Not gonna disagree with you. I wouldn't dare!"

Before I left, I insisted that he splash some paint over the word 'murderer'. It was an ugly scar and I didn't want to have to see it again.

"Okay, pick me up in about 20 minutes!"

I raced home and threw together a picnic: cold chicken, some leftover salad, and an apple pie that I'd made the night before. Then I added a couple of sodas and a bottle of water—

good enough.

I dashed up to pull my bikini out of the closet, and stuffed it into my purse. No skinny dipping today—not that I would have minded, but I didn't think it would be fair to Jordan.

I was just about ready when I heard his truck pull up.

I staggered out of the house, carrying the enormous picnic basket. Jordan immediately leapt out of his truck and took it from my hands. *Aw, he was so sweet.* And wow, he smelled really good. *He'd* obviously taken the time to shower, unlike me.

"So, where should we go? You know this area better than I do. What's a good place for a swim?"

"I know the perfect spot," he said, with a smile.

I waited. "And? Is it a secret?"

"Yep," he said, a smug look on his face.

"Oh, very funny, Mr. Tit for Tat."

He shrugged. "I reckon what's good for the goose should be good for the gander, darlin'." And then he winked.

I loved seeing this playful side of him slowly emerge.

"Go west, young man, go west."

I got a full-on smirk for that, and another tantalizing glimpse of the cocky teenager he'd once been.

The truck radio was tuned to a local indie station, and I sang along as he drove.

After about four songs he turned to me with an amazed expression.

"You know the lyrics for all of these songs!"

"Well, yeah. I like listening to music. It's a very economical way of conveying emotion, don't you think?"

"Um, I guess. I never really thought about it."

"Besides, I like visiting new places by myself. I listen to music while I drive. It's no great mystery."

"Is that why you're in Texas?"

"Kind of. I needed to earn some traveling money and I needed somewhere to stay while I earned it. So I thought I'd come see Mom."

"You're not close with her?"

I sucked a thumbnail, considering my answer.

"We weren't. But I think it's good that we've spent time together this summer. I haven't really seen her that much since I was 13, and not at all since I turned 18. So, yeah, it's good … you know, getting to know her now that I'm an adult."

He shook his head, a grave expression on his face. "Cain't say I know what that's like."

I wasn't sure what he meant by that, but I didn't think it was the time or place to ask. Besides, it was a lovely day; I didn't want to sour the mood.

We drove in silence for several minutes before he grunted that we were nearly there.

He pulled off the road and drove over sand dunes for nearly a mile before stopping right on the water's edge, the bright blue ocean stretching out toward the sharp horizon.

"Not bad," I said, smiling at him. "This place is beautiful." I leaned over and kissed him on the cheek. "Thanks for bringing me here."

I realized immediately that I'd stepped over the invisible boundary that I'd been trying to keep in place. His eyes closed and he slowly strangled the steering wheel, his knuckles turning white with the strain.

As for me, my lips tingled from the contact with the scruff on his cheek, and my body burned for him.

Taking a deep breath, I pushed open the passenger door and jumped out. Jordan was a couple of seconds behind me, carrying the picnic basket and the blanket that he'd borrowed from my car. He insisted on carrying both as we settled just a few yards from where the ocean lapped languidly at our feet.

The shadows were beginning to lengthen already, and I was disappointed that we'd left too late to go swimming. I'd been looking forward to washing away the day's heat and dirt with a cooling swim.

I spread out the blanket and sat with my legs crossed, Indian style.

"God, I'm so hungry! You'd better dig in, cowboy, or I'll eat everything in sight!"

He nodded, but still looked distracted. So I threw a chicken wing at him, which he caught easily, bringing him back to the here and now.

He took a large bite.

"This is real good, Torrey," he said, continuing to gnaw hungrily at the meat.

"I know. I'm the perfect woman: I can cook *and* I drive a cool car."

"You are," he said, quietly. "You're perfect."

His mood was serious as I looked over at him in surprise.

"Um, thanks. I was joking actually. I'm a complete bitch most of the time and have gazillions of annoying habits."

"I wasn't jokin'," he said, holding my gaze. "I'm just so fuckin' grateful that you're here." He took a deep breath. "And I really want to kiss you right now."

Chapter 6 – Forward

Torrey

Knowing it was probably a huge mistake, I reached out and cupped his cheek with the palm of my hand.

"I'd really like to kiss you, too."

Which should have been his cue for diving on me. Instead, he sat staring at the sand covering his bare feet.

"It's okay," I said quietly, trying to reassure him. "I like that you said it to me. You don't have to do anything right now. I'm not going anywhere."

He sighed and leaned into my hand.

Tentatively he reached out and brushed gentle fingers over my hair. Then he inclined his body forward and kissed me, his lips merely whispering next to mine.

I moved my hand to the back of his head and pulled him closer, pressing my mouth firmly against his. He moaned softly, the hitch in his breath telling me how much this was affecting him.

I coaxed his lips to open and licked his bottom lip, then tugged it gently with my teeth. A sound like a whimper slipped from him, and I could tell it was taking all his strength to hold back from attacking my mouth with his own.

Cautiously, I dipped my tongue into his mouth and felt his hesitant response as he stroked against me. He became bolder, deepening the kiss and pulling me with him as he lay down on the blanket. Then he twisted so he was above me, his body pressing into mine.

I ran my hands under his t-shirt, feeling the defined muscles of his back and shoulders under my fingers, something I'd wanted to do since the first day I saw him. I pulled the soft material up his body and he paused long enough to allow me to tear it over his head.

I hadn't come to the beach with any expectation of having sex with Jordan. I mean, yeah, I'd imagined it *a lot*, but I just hadn't thought we'd get there so quickly—if ever.

I leaned up on my elbow and took a moment to appreciate the beautiful artwork of his tattoos coiling around his arms and shoulders.

Then I noticed a long scar at the base of his ribs.

"What's this from?"

He stiffened, his hands freezing on my waist.

"Knife fight," he said, at last.

I stroked the scar with my forefinger then leaned across to plant a gentle kiss on it.

"Thank you," he said, quietly. "You don't know what it means to me when you do things like that. You're just so…"

"So what?"

He thought for a moment then nodded slightly when he found the right word.

"So acceptin'."

I considered his choice of word. Was I accepting? I wasn't so sure. Most people thought I was an argumentative and contrary bitch, but if he wanted to think good things about me that way, I wasn't going to argue with him.

"You have scars on your knuckles, too," I said. "They stand out against your tan."

He spread his fingers out on my arm, gazing at the evidence of past fights as if he'd never noticed them before.

I shifted onto my back, pulling him on top of me again. His fascination with his hands disappeared instantly.

Then he was kissing my neck, nudging my shirt from my shoulder to find the bare skin beneath. I could feel how much he wanted me, but was he ready?

"Are we going to do this?" I said.

He hesitated and then lifted his head slowly to look at me.

"Do what?"

"Well, we're kind of in a compromising position here, and although I'd be interested in taking it all the way, I don't want to push you to do something you don't want to."

"Oh, I want to," he said, adamantly. "Fuck, I want to."

He kissed me harder and I felt his want and need in the way he touched me. I could tell it was almost overwhelming for him.

"You're trembling."

Jordan stopped kissing me and flopped onto his back. Not the reaction I'd intended at all.

"It … it's been a while," he said, his voice tight with emotion. "I know I'm not gonna … last."

I leaned up on one elbow and ran my fingers lightly down his chest and stomach, watching his body shiver under my touch, his erection showcased through his jeans.

"Then we'll just have to go again as soon as you're ready."

He groaned and squeezed his eyes shut. "I'm not sure if that makes it better or worse."

"Let's find out," I replied, my hands busy with his zipper.

I heard his breath catch in his throat as I pulled his dick out of his pants. It was large and long and well mannered, standing upright to greet me. It looked as good as I'd imagined and I couldn't help licking my lips.

His hard stomach contracted and quivered as I stroked him a couple of times; his breath was shallow and his heart was racing.

"Shit," he whispered, and I wasn't sure whether or not I was supposed to hear him.

I placed my lips over his tip, reveling in the clean, musky man-smell emanating from him. He had no idea how heavenly he looked, lying there under the dusky sky, waiting for me.

I sucked gently, and his hips thrust roughly into my mouth.

"Sorry," he gasped. "Sorry!"

I smiled around him and started licking and sucking in earnest.

He was right—he didn't last long.

Within seconds he was thrusting into my mouth, and I felt his hands tugging on my hair trying to lift me from him.

"I'm gonna come … I'm gonna…"

I appreciated the warning, but I had no intention of letting him go. I wanted this first time to be special for him.

He shuddered into my mouth for what seemed like forever. I thought I was going to run out of swallow before he'd finished, but finally he was done and I could sit up.

His eyes were still closed and his chest was heaving, his hands clutching the blanket on either side of him.

I lay back next to him and his arm curled around me, pulling me into his chest.

"Holy fuck!" he said.

"Well, not quite, but maybe next time. Although as I am a preacher's daughter, I guess it's close enough."

"You're an angel," he said, softly. "My guardian angel."

"If I'm an angel, we're in more trouble than we thought," I said, wiping my chin on his bare chest.

He laughed, a deep gravelly sound. I realized I'd never heard him fully laugh before. It was a good, good sound.

"Maybe we'll both have to be bad together," he whispered against my hair.

"Works for me," I said.

He pulled me in tighter, and I felt him place a gentle kiss on the top of my head.

"What's the matter?" I said, challengingly. "Don't want to

kiss my mouth now that you've come in it?"

I could see by the way his body froze that he was surprised. Maybe even shocked.

"Is that what you think? God, no! I could kiss you for hours. I think I'd be happy just doin' that."

I couldn't help the smile that spread across my face.

"Really?"

"Hell, yeah! You've got the most gorgeous lips I've ever seen. I lov… kissin' them is incredible."

"Prove it."

He moved so quickly, I didn't know what was happening until he was lying on top of me, his body weighted over mine, his lips brushing against my mouth.

The contrast of his hard body and soft lips was driving me insane.

He kissed my chest, my neck, my cheeks, my eyelids, even the tip of my nose. Then he teased my lips with his tongue until I grabbed his hair and pulled him closer. Our tongues tangled together and then he began this amazingly sensuous stroking, full of sensation and passion. I was so turned on, I thought I might come just from him kissing me. *That* had never happened before.

"Beautiful woman, I want to make love to you," he said, huskily. "God, I want you so bad right now."

True to his word, I felt his hard cock digging into my hip.

"Wow, that was quick," I commented, reaching down to stroke him.

"One of the benefits of it being a while," he answered, in between kisses. "The *only* benefit."

He pushed my t-shirt up over my breasts and tugged it off, then ran the tip of his tongue along the lace edge of my bra.

"So beautiful," he murmured.

"Only because you've got nothing to compare them to," I laughed.

"Hey, that's not true! I had game in my day, and I can tell you that your breasts are sen-fuckin'-sational. I think this bra should come off."

"Can you remember how to do that?" I laughed at him.

He cocked an eyebrow and gave me a slow, devilish smile. "I think it'll come back to me."

He slid his arm under my waist and pulled me up sharply, then reached around behind with his free arm and tugged at the elastic.

"Damn," he said, after fighting with it for a few seconds. "Where's the freakin' clasp?"

I couldn't help laughing. "It's a sports bra, genius. There is no clasp."

"Fuck! I really thought I'd lost my touch there for a moment. You're pure evil, woman."

I sat up and raised my arms over my head. "Now see if you can take it off."

With surprisingly gentle fingers, given how obviously aroused he was, he pulled the bra up my body and slid it over my arms and hands.

Then he lowered me back to the blanket and began to worship my breasts. It was the only way to describe how he kissed every inch of skin, pressing his soft lips into my flesh, and teasing my deliciously hard nipples with his tongue.

When he nipped gently with his teeth, a long breathy moan flew out of my mouth.

"You like that, Torrey?"

"God, yes! Keep doing that!"

I reached up to stroke his hair and wound my fingers into the shaggy curls at the nape of his neck.

I swear, the man purred. Just like a big old lion stretched out in the sun.

When I dragged my short fingernails down his back, his neck arched away from me and his eyes were tightly closed.

"God! Every time you touch me I think it cain't get any better, and then it just does," he muttered.

I pushed his jeans over the curve of his butt, and used my heels to push the denim down to his knees.

"Take them off," I insisted. "I want you naked."

"Yes, ma'am!" he said with a laugh, kicking his legs free.

His beautiful, bare body loomed over me and a shiver of anticipation shot through every nerve. This man was damn fine.

"I think you should be naked, too," he said, nuzzling my neck with his nose, his hands traveling across my breasts, lightly twisting the nipples.

"Go for it," I said, encouragingly.

Within a few seconds, he'd wrestled my jean shorts off of my hips, and I saw his jaw drop open.

"No panties!" he hissed. "God, woman! I swear you're gonna kill me stone dead."

"Well, if that's the case, hurry up and fuck me first!"

He groaned loudly and started making a trail of scorching kisses between my breasts and down to my stomach.

"Christ, you smell good," he said, his head dipping lower. "Can I give you some good ole southern lovin'?"

"Maybe another time," I said, a little impatiently. "Right now I want to feel that big cock of yours inside me."

"Fuck!" he whispered.

"That's the general idea," I said. "While we're still young."

Suddenly, he rolled onto his back, the palms of his hands pressing into his eyes.

"What?"

"I haven't got any fuckin' rubbers!" he cried, furiously. "I never thought … I mean, I didn't…"

"Oh, don't be such a dumbass," I said, pushing his shoulder. "Did you really think I'd come out for a ride in a hot guy's truck without a stash of condoms? You've sure lost your game, Big Boy."

He rolled onto his side. "You think I'm hot?"

"Hell, yes! Now stop teasing me and get sheathed up."

I dragged my shorts toward me and fumbled around to find the strip of condoms that I'd stashed earlier.

"We've got three," I said, throwing them to him. "Go crazy."

His eyes glittered with lust and determination. I'd say the

man liked a challenge.

He tore the packet with his teeth, a move that looked cheesy on some guys, but totally suited him.

"Don't lose the spares," I warned him.

"No freakin' way," he said, his voice tight. "I have every intention of fuckin' you to a standstill, you and that pretty mouth of yours."

"Many have tried."

His frantic hands stilled.

"Don't say stuff like that, Torrey."

"Stuff like what?"

"About … the number of guys you've fucked."

"Why not? I like guys; I like sex. I'm not ashamed of it. Am I supposed to pretend like I'm a virgin or something? It's okay for guys to behave like dogs, and you just get a pat on the back. But when a woman does it…"

"That's not what I meant!" he groaned.

"Then what the fuck did you mean?" I snapped, starting to feel pissed.

"I just don't want you thinkin' about any other guy when you're with me. I want you with *me*—all of you. It's not just fuckin'. Not for me, not with you. I know you think it's because I haven't slept with a woman in a long time, but it's not. It's because it's you, and I meant it when I said I wanted to make love to you."

I was stunned by his little speech.

"Let me make love to you, Torrey Delaney," he said, his voice tender and almost pleading.

I nodded wordlessly, and immediately his lips were on mine, soft and forceful, urgent and compliant.

His hands stroked up my body and teased my breasts, his thumbs rubbing soft circles over my nipples.

I could feel his cock pressing against my thigh now, softly massaging it as he kissed up and down my body. Then one hand slid between my legs and he rubbed gently against my clit.

"Damn, you feel so good, sweetheart. I cain't wait to be

inside you."

"Then do it!"

"So impatient," he said, a smile against my skin. "I've waited eight years, I'm not gonna rush this now."

I ceded control and decided to let him go at his own pace. It wasn't like I had anywhere else to be. Besides, it had been a while since a guy had taken his time with me. I was usually in a hurry and not looking for anything more than a quick pick-me-up, so to speak.

But if Jordan Kane wanted to take his own sweet time, who was I to argue?

He slid one of his long fingers inside me, showing me whatever else he'd gone without over the last few years, he hadn't forgotten how to touch a woman.

I was a quivering mess of melted jelly within seconds. Those were some talented fingers that he had. No wonder he was so amazing at fine-tuning an engine. Damn!

Soon, I was beyond rational thought, my body moving to his every touch like a puppet as he worked the strings, pulling sensation after sensation from me.

Just as he'd brought me to the brink, and my whole body was pulsing with desire, he pulled his fingers out. I was about ready to tear him a new one when I felt the incredible fullness of Jordan pushing his body inside mine.

He moaned softly and stilled a second when he was fully sheathed by my body, obviously trying to catch his breath and avoid blowing his load.

"I'm not gonna be able to hold back," he gasped. "Fuck, I'm so close already!"

"Then don't. Don't hold back," I whispered, my nails digging into his back. "I want it hard. I want to feel every part of you now. I want to feel you come inside me."

It was as if my words had released him, broken through some mental barrier that he'd built up, because he did exactly what I said. His hips rose and fell rapidly as he pounded into me, forcing me higher and higher up the blanket.

He reared up, taking his full weight on his forearms and the change of angle sent me wild, his pubic bone slamming roughly against my already sensitive clit.

I fell so hard I saw stars. Then I remembered we were outside and it was evening; I could still see stars when I opened my eyes again.

Jordan yelled out my name as he came. It was the sexiest thing I'd ever heard.

I'd heard guys yell a lot of things when they came—mostly other girls' names, and one guy shouted, "mother" which I found deeply disturbing—but Jordan was perfect.

His biceps trembled, and I pulled him down so my breasts squished from the weight of his chest crushing mine.

His breath roared in my ear as he fought to get his breathing under control.

After a long moment, I felt his hand drift down to where we were still connected, and he carefully pulled out.

He snapped off the used condom and tied a knot in the end. It reminded me of tying a knot in the end of party balloons and the thought made me giggle.

"What?" he asked, turning to look at me, doubt clouding his soft brown eyes.

"Oh, nothing much. Just feeling good."

"What were you laughin' about?" he insisted.

"Don't go getting all performance-oriented on me. I was just thinking that condoms remind me of party balloons, that's all."

"Really?" he said, his face creased with worry. "Because I wouldn't blame you. I know that was damn pitiful. I *know* I can do better than that and…"

I leaned up on my elbow to look him in the eyes so he'd know I meant what I said.

"Stop worrying! That was amazing. In case you're wondering, that whole yelling and thrashing around thing, that was me having a freakin' amazing orgasm."

He still looked worried. "You're not just sayin' that?"

"Jeez, Jordan! No! Have I ever said anything just to make

116

you feel better?"

He chewed his lip while he thought about that. "I guess not."

"Well, you guess right. I don't go around telling lies, even little white lies just to make people feel better. And if a guy is a two pump chump, I tell it like it is. You have nothing to worry about. On the other hand…"

"On the other hand what?" His voice was tentative.

"I'm looking forward to getting in a whole shit load more practice with you. You've got eight years to make up for. What do you say?"

His grin could have lit up Vegas.

"I say you're a very wise woman, and I'm damn lucky to have met you."

"Now you're getting it," I said, with a smile.

"I thought *I* was the one gettin' it?"

"Don't be such a guy," I said, pushing his shoulder. "I got laid good—I'm a happy camper."

We lay together and he pulled me against him, his warm and solid body close beside me.

I rested my arm on his stomach, idly tugging at the few hairs that grew up from his belly.

"How come you've got all these tats?" I asked. "I've been wondering about them. Unless you had them when you were 16, you must have gotten inked in prison."

His fingers that had been drifting up and down my arm, stilled.

"You're the only one who ever says that."

"Says what?"

"About prison. Everyone else is just embarrassed and don't know what to say. The ones who speak to me, anyway. But you—you just say it."

"Do you mind?"

"God, no. It's a relief in a way. I mean, it happened and I cain't change it. But pretendin' like it didn't—and that I'm normal like everyone else—it gets so damn wearisome."

I took a deep breath.

117

"Jordan, do you think you could tell me now? What happened to Mikey? To you?"

He shot me a panicked look.

"Torrey, I…"

"You know you can trust me. I'm not going to judge you."

"You will," he said, heavily. "Of course you will. And I won't blame you when you do."

His eyes were pleading with me.

I sighed and looked away. We lay there for several minutes, not speaking, the air growing cooler.

Eventually, I sat up and started pulling my clothes toward me. Without saying anything, I passed Jordan his t-shirt and jeans.

Guess I was good enough to fuck, but not for him to share anything important with.

We dressed in silence and I started to stand, when suddenly, I felt his hand on mine.

"I was 16," he said, his voice barely louder than a whisper.

I turned to stare at him, but his gaze was fixed on the sand at the edge of the blanket.

"We'd celebrated Mikey's eighteenth birthday with our parents the week before. That was … nice, but kinda tame."

Oh my God! He's really talking to me. He's going to tell me…

"Ryan, our buddy, he wanted to have a kegger while his folks were away. And … I said I'd drive so Mikey could have a drink. When we got to Ry's, the place was jumpin', cars everywhere, people drinkin' and dancin', kids makin' out all over the place. You know, ordinary stuff.

"Mikey hooked up with this girl Sonia that he saw sometimes. I went lookin' for Allison. When I found her, she was already pretty tanked. Seein' as Ry's folks were gone, we decided to stay the night. I started drinkin', and Allison was bein' a bitch 'cause one of her friends was hittin' on me."

He sighed.

"I wasn't discouragin' her too much, I guess. Anyway, we got into a fight and Allison was screamin' at me. I took off and found Mikey. He was wasted—been smokin' weed and shit. I said I was leavin' and he tried to talk me into stayin'. We argued some, and then he said he'd drive. Man, he was so high, he couldn't even see straight. And ... I had the keys."

Jordan took a shuddering breath.

"So Mikey got in the car with me, sayin' 'bros before ho's', and I started drivin' us home."

His body felt tense next to me, but I didn't dare reach out to touch him. He seemed so far away, lost in his memories.

Jordan

I remember it all.

I remember turning up the radio real loud to keep awake for the short drive back, but I guess I fell asleep at the wheel because the next thing I knew the car had shot off the road, flipped over and hit a tree.

I don't think I was knocked out for long because I remember crawling out of the car and seeing the wheels still spinning, around and around. I couldn't understand why Mikey wasn't in the car with me. I was stumbling all over, calling his name.

"Oh my God! What happened then?"

What the fuck?

Confused, I looked up, jolted from the painful past, and saw Torrey's beautiful blue eyes watching me. *Was I talking? Did I just say all of that aloud?*

"You don't have to tell me if it's too hard, Jordan."

We were still at the bay, still lying on that rough blanket, her arms around me.

I closed my eyes, traveling back to that night again, pulled toward the dark memories.

"Someone must have seen the car leave the road because there were people there right quick. I remember thinkin' I'd gone blind in one eye, but it was just because of all the blood. I'd cut my head open and a flap of skin was hangin' down. I didn't realize. And then my foot caught in somethin' and I fell over—I literally tripped over his body. I didn't recognize him at first."

Telling this part of the story hurts so bad. I can't breathe, my chest aches, and it's like it just happened.

"He hadn't been wearin' his seatbelt and he'd gone through the windshield. His face was … gone. But I recognized his t-shirt, and I knew it was him. I was screamin', I think. I remember that. They told me later that it was me. When I remember it, it's like someone else is tellin' me about it, you know? Like it was a movie—except I *feel* it. All of it."

Torrey held my hand so tight, my fingers started to tingle. I didn't care, because I didn't want her to let go. I didn't ever want her to let go.

"Someone pulled me away, some guy. I never knew who he was. Just an unlucky passer-by. I remember he put his coat over Mikey's face, and I was screamin' that he wouldn't be able to breathe like that; he'd suffocate. And this guy kept sayin', 'He's gone, son. He's gone.' Over and over. There was an ambulance and then the police. They took me to the hospital first and sewed me up. I think I was in shock because I kept askin' them why it was so cold, and I couldn't stop shakin'. The police wanted to interview me, and someone had to phone my parents. I remember Momma screamin' and cryin' and she collapsed on the floor, and Dad was holdin' her and cryin', too. And I was just sittin' there and everyone was lookin' at me like I was some kind of monster. I kept on at them about Mikey: 'Where's my brother? I need to see my brother.' I think I knew he was dead, but I didn't want to believe it."

Torrey ran her fingers across my cheek and kissed me gently.

"Oh my God, Jordan! I'm so sorry."

I met her eyes and was amazed to see that they were glistening with tears.

"My God," she continued, her voice dropping to a whisper, "that's just … horrible and awful and shitty—but it was an accident."

She wrapped her arms around me and it felt so good to have her there, anchoring me to the here and now.

"I can't imagine what that was like for you," she said, softly. "I mean, you were just a kid. And dealing with all of that alone."

I felt the gentle touch of her fingers on my skin and I wanted that feeling to go on forever.

"You're not alone now," she said.

And I felt it. I felt it in her words, in her voice, and in her body. I closed my eyes: I wasn't alone anymore.

I rolled onto my side to look at her.

"You're still here," I said, quietly. "I was sure you'd have headed for the hills by now."

She smiled sadly.

"Life's dealt you a shit hand and I can't imagine how it was for you losing your brother like that…"

"I didn't *lose* him!" I snapped. "I *killed* him!"

"It was an accident."

"It don't make no difference!"

"I think it does."

"He's still dead!"

"Yes, he is. And you're alive, so stop acting like you think you should have been buried with him."

What?

"I mean it, Jordan. You've got to stop torturing yourself—it was an accident!"

"Everyone around here thinks I'm a murderer."

"Jordan, no!"

"My own parents think that, Torrey. Hell, even *I* thought that … think that."

"But…"

"It's what I am. I nearly killed a man—in prison. I wanted to."

She closed her eyes briefly.

"Tell me," she said, a determined expression on her face.

I turned my head to look at her.

"You mean the town gossips haven't told you that either?"

"No, but even if they had, I'd want to hear it from you—your version."

I sighed and looked down.

"Well, what they say is mostly true anyway. I got into a fight—a guy got stabbed. I got the blame. The truth is, I was in the wrong place at the wrong time." I looked at her sideways, watching her expressions as they flowed across her face. "They charged me with attempted murder. I mean, hell, the shank—the knife—it wasn't even mine. It should have been pled down to aggravated assault, or assault with a deadly weapon at most, but … I don't know … I mean, I'm not sure how it ended up being on me. Anyway, I got seven years." I smirked, and Torrey's lips turned down. "I got nine months off for good behavior … and overcrowding. Now, I'm serving the last six months on parole…"

My voice trailed off.

"What started the fight?"

I shrugged.

"Happened all the time. It's hard not to get dragged into stuff, you know, stay neutral. There were two major gangs running juvie: the ABTs, the Aryan Brotherhood; and EPT, the El Paso Tangos. Being white, I was supposed to join the ABTs," I continued, "but I just wanted to be left alone. But wantin' and gettin'—those are different things. Two of them got me alone. I got this," I raised my t-shirt and pointed to the white scar at the base of my ribs, "and I turned the knife on one of the gang members—nearly killed the bastard."

I looked directly at her.

"I wanted to kill him. I would have if they hadn't pulled me off of him."

For the first time since I'd met her, she looked scared—scared of me. A sharp, stabbing pain threatened to split my chest open. She was scared of me. But maybe that was a good thing even though it killed me. She needed to know about the darkness inside.

I held her gaze as I carried on, my words and memories relentless.

"I'd gotten me a punctured lung, but I was almost 18 by then—my juvie record would have been sealed." I gave a humorless laugh, "I wasn't deemed fit to be let back among decent folk. They moved me straight from juvie to prison. But the gangs weren't so bad there. It was almost a relief."

I looked across at her again, but she was staring toward the city lights reflecting off the water in the distance.

"I guess you know the rest," I said.

I was trying to read her thoughts from her face, but I couldn't see her eyes, so I wasn't sure what she was thinking or feeling.

"Thank you for telling me," she said, quietly.

She didn't look scared anymore and I didn't know how to feel about that. Instead, I wanted to beg her not to leave me. I was afraid of what she'd say when she'd had time to think it all through. But Christ, I was so relieved that she was still here with me now.

I just wondered how long it would be for.

We didn't talk much after that, and Torrey was quiet on the drive back. Every time I risked looking at her, she was staring out of the side window.

I silently begged her to speak, to say anything, even if it was to yell at me. *Just say something!*

As the seconds ticked by and she still didn't speak, I felt like I'd lost her already, and it hurt so bad. I didn't think I could take losing someone else I cared about, that I loved.

I'd always known I'd have to tell her the truth at some point, I just hoped it wouldn't have been so soon. But I knew it was just a matter of time before somebody told her, maybe her own momma, so when she'd asked—again—I had to tell her.

I felt sick, reliving it all, and I realized that she was the first person I'd told about how Mikey died since that useless fucking shrink in the pen. It was a completely different experience telling Torrey, and all the old guilt and pain had flooded back. *Why* was I so stupid that night? *Why* had I gotten in the damn car? *Why* was I the one who'd survived? *Why* was it Mikey who had paid? And my parents, too. We'd paid and paid and paid, but the debt was *never* going to go away. I'd never be done paying. Never.

As I looked at the future I had, I just saw fifty empty years of trudging through each long, lonely, gray day. It seemed unbearable. And if Torrey didn't want to be with me, I wasn't sure I wanted to face that journey.

I thought telling her had been the right thing to do, but now I wondered if it only looked like she'd taken it well. Maybe she'd been in shock. Maybe she was afraid of me now. Maybe she was disgusted that she'd slept with me. Maybe she just wanted to get away from me…

When I pulled up outside the Rectory, she still hadn't spoken. I felt like my skin would split from the tension burning inside me.

"Torrey, I…"

But I didn't know what to say to make her stay.

She sighed heavily, and my heart shriveled.

"Jordan, tonight … thank you for telling me."

I nodded and swallowed down the fear. "Has it … does it … change … things?"

Of course it does.

She didn't answer immediately, and the sadness in her eyes all but killed me. I wished she would kill me. I wished she'd take a gun and shoot me in the fuckin' head, rather than gut me slowly from the inside out.

"I guess I understand … things … a little more. I just need to … let it all sink in."

Oh God…

She leaned forward and touched my cheek with the tips of her fingers, turned and wearily climbed out of the truck.

It felt like goodbye.

Words tried to force themselves out of my throat, but they turned to dust before they reached my lips.

"I'll see you, Jordan," she said, her voice distant and sad.

And then she was gone.

I sat staring at her house, willing her to change her mind, willing her to come talk to me—to notice me. But one by one, the lights went off until the house was dark and silent.

Feeling nauseated, I drove home slowly.

I dragged myself up the stairs to my room and dropped onto the bed. I could still smell her on me, although the scent was fading—wild flowers.

I rubbed the palms of my hands over my eyes, forcing them closed. But I was afraid to fall asleep, because then it would all seem like a dream, and when I woke up, I'd be alone again in a nightmare.

I sat up, staring into the dark.

One mistake.

That's all it took.

One fuckin' stupid, childish, dumb mistake. And it had torn my family apart, my brother dead. Killed. By me. I saw every day what I'd done, the grief that I'd caused. In prison, I'd been isolated, protected from the consequences of my actions. While I was the only one suffering—the only one I thought was suffering—it was fair, it was justice. *Christ, how selfish had I been even then?* But this? How was this fair? *Why am I alive?*

I pressed the tips of my fingers against my eyelids, trying to press back the images that shattered my dreams every night.

I couldn't stand it anymore. Seeing the grief and pain in Torrey's eyes as she'd looked at me. I was wrecking her life, too. I was damaged, I knew it. My broken edges cut everyone who came near me.

I found myself standing in the kitchen, reaching into the drawer where the carving knives were kept.

My hand pulled out a small, long-bladed knife. Thin. Sharp. And I held it against my wrist, watching the moonlight glint against the blade.

A long, upward stroke, that's all it needed. Not across the wrist, but following the blue lines that mapped their way across my skin.

And I stood there, poised, waiting. For something. A reason to live. A reason to die.

I stood there.

I gripped the knife so hard, my hand began to shake and sweat blurred my vision.

Do it. Do it right this time. Put yourself out of your misery. End it. Do it now.

I stood there.

And then I thought of the way Torrey had held me.

I sank to the floor, still holding the knife, still willing myself to finish it. But I couldn't do it. I remembered the way Mikey had lived and laughed and loved, and I just couldn't do it.

The knife slipped from my fingers, clattering to the floor.

I sat there, alone with my thoughts.

I'd had some long nights in my life, but that was one of the darkest and one of the longest. One of the loneliest.

An hour before dawn, I pulled myself up and replaced the knife in the drawer. It would be there when I needed it, waiting for me. But not this night.

I headed to the garage and lifted weights until my muscles burned as much as my brain. I didn't care that I had a full day's work ahead of me. I needed to feel something other than the horror.

The sky passed from black to velvet purple, to gray, as color leaked back into the world. This world. My world.

I could see her soon. Maybe.

And if I didn't? If she refused to ever look at me again?

Chapter 7 – Opportunities

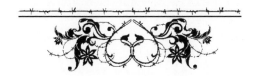

Jordan

I didn't even try to eat breakfast. I showered quickly and pulled on my work clothes. The whole time, I couldn't stop my hands from shaking.

My parents ignored my presence. I was used to that, and I was beginning to prefer it

I arrived at the Rectory far too early. The Reverend's car was already gone, but the Princess was parked in the driveway. I stared up at Torrey's window. The curtains were still closed, the window dark in the early morning sun.

I pulled on my work-gloves and started hacking at the brambles, my thoughts chaotic but caged.

It was nearly an hour before I heard the screen door creak open, and a sleepy looking Torrey plopped herself down on the porch step.

She was carrying two cups of coffee.

"Why are you here so damn early?" she grumbled, waving

me toward her.

I was so fucking grateful that she was still talking to me, that I just stared, my heart hammering painfully.

She blinked up at me, looking confused.

"Eager much?" she laughed.

"God, yes," I admitted, unable to even pretend that the sight of her didn't affect me deeply. I pulled myself free from the prison of despair and walked toward her like a sleepwalker.

She studied my face and ran her index finger across my stubbled cheek as I sat down next to her.

"You look like shit, Jordan. What's up?"

I couldn't look at her.

"Tell me," she urged, her voice suddenly gentle.

"I … I couldn't sleep. I couldn't turn my brain off. I … I wasn't sure … after what I told you … I didn't think you'd want…"

"Oh," she said, softly. "You've been worrying all night that, what…? That I wouldn't talk to you today?"

I nodded silently, and she gave an exasperated sigh.

"You're an idiot, Jordan Kane. I told you I'd see you today. Come here."

And she closed the small distance between us, leaning her head against my shoulder.

"I guess I should have said something more to you last night," she murmured. "I'm sorry. It was a shock … and I was just thinking about everything you said, everything you've been through. But I never meant for you to think that I…" she hesitated. "I'm really glad you told me. It's a lot for me to take in—for anyone to take in. That's probably why people are so shitty to you—they don't really know what to do, so they lash out."

I wasn't sure about that, but as long as Torrey was still talking to me, that was enough. I breathed out in utter relief, my desperation lanced by her words.

"You've got to tell me what you're thinking," she said, planting a kiss on my bare arm.

I nodded, but didn't speak.

"We're going to have to do something about your communication skills," she said, a quiet chuckle sending soft ripples through her body and mine.

"I think," I said, slowly, "that meeting you has been the best thing that's ever happened to me."

You don't know it, but you've saved me, Torrey Delaney.

She smiled. "I'm glad I met you, too."

Torrey

He looked haunted this morning when he saw me, like he'd seen a ghost. I felt horrible that I'd left him with the impression that I couldn't cope with what he'd told me.

I snuggled into him more, enjoying the unusual sensation of cuddling up to a guy that I'd had sex with. I was more used to the wham bam thank you ma'am variety, and waking up alone again in the morning. Although, to be fair, until now, that was pretty much all I'd wanted in a guy, especially recently. Get laid, get gone. Don't get attached.

Emotional connection had been anathema to me since Jeremy—Jem—when I was 18. I thought I'd been in love, but it wasn't a quarter of what I felt for this damaged man sitting in silence next to me. The thought scared me, but not enough that I wouldn't see where this might go.

It was real. He was real, and maybe I could stop running. Maybe.

At the same time, I had to admit to myself that he'd scared me last night. Not with his revelation of what had happened to Mikey, but with the cold certainty of having wanted to kill a man when he was in juvie.

A shiver of fear had passed through me. I knew what Jordan was trying to tell me: he believed that he was a killer.

But wasn't that inside all of us? Kill or be killed? That was the question we could each ask ourselves in our darkest hours: what would I be prepared to die for? What would I be prepared to kill for?

I couldn't answer that.

I realized, that despite everything he'd said, everything he'd told me, I'd crossed a line with Jordan, and surprisingly, I was okay with it.

I patted his thigh and stood up.

"I have some chores to do before I start this new job in a couple of days, but do you want to do something after you get off work?"

His smile was like the sun coming out.

"Maybe we could go to the bay again," I hinted, raising my eyebrows. "Get a swim in this time? Don't freak out on me—it's not a date, just two friends going swimming."

"Yes, ma'am!" he said, a grin splitting his face.

"Okay, well I'll meet you here and you can drive us. I don't want to risk taking the Princess over those dunes." I threw him a sly glance. "And if you're all sweaty from work," I said, trying not to lick my lips, "a nice cooling swim will feel even better. Don't bother about a swimsuit."

He groaned, and I winked at him.

Then I picked up the two coffee mugs and left him sitting on the step, looking stunned.

Jordan was waiting for me when I arrived back at the Rectory later that afternoon. I'd spent the day arguing on the phone with my bank, trying to extend my overdraft. I may have also treated myself to a mani-pedi, which I totally couldn't afford, but totally deserved.

Jordan's anxious look vanished as soon as he saw the Princess pulling into the driveway.

He jumped out of his truck and bent down at my window. He looked like he was about to kiss me, but then he straightened up, shoved his hands in his pockets, and gave me a shy smile instead.

I took the initiative and climbed out of the car, reaching up to brush a soft kiss on his cheek.

"Hi! You ready to go?"

"Sure am, sweetheart."

"Great. So, are you going to let me drive your truck?"

He looked surprised then shrugged his shoulders.

"I guess you can only die once."

His smile dropped immediately, and this time it was obvious that he was beating himself up for the choice of words.

"Jordan," I said, catching hold of his hand, "it's just a saying. Like me saying, 'who died and put you in charge'. People say stuff like that all the time. You've got to quit being so sensitive about it or it'll hurt you every time—and I know I don't want to do that."

He closed his eyes and breathed deeply.

"I don't know how," he admitted, quietly. "How am I supposed to *not* feel this stuff?"

It was a good question.

"Maybe you can try to forgive yourself, even just a little bit."

He shook his head. "I don't think so."

I sighed. We were going in circles.

"Okay, well, I just want you to know that I'm sorry for all the random times that I've hurt your feelings. And don't ask me to say that again because I don't make a habit of apologizing!"

That got a small smile.

He helped me up into the truck and buckled himself nervously into the passenger seat.

I swear his truck was filled with kangaroo gas, because we bumped and hopped all the way to the bay. I don't think Jordan breathed once the entire ride.

It was a beautiful day with a perfect blue sky. I decided I

could really get used to lazy afternoons like this.

I laid out the blanket and turned to find Jordan's eyes fixed on my body. I'd never had a man look at me with such intense desire.

But then he seemed to give himself a mental shake.

"I'm gonna take a swim," he said, looking out toward the clear horizon. "Join me?"

"Nah. I'm just going to sit here and ogle you for a while," I said. "You know, just enjoy the view."

He rolled his eyes but couldn't help grinning.

He pulled off his t-shirt then neatly folded it up and placed it on the blanket. He shrugged when he saw me staring at him in disbelief.

"Old habits," he said, sheepishly.

He turned away from me and dropped his shorts.

My own private strip show. Sigh. That man could have made a fortune doing that for hen parties. But this show was all for me. Life was gooood.

He smirked when he saw me staring at his ass.

"I haven't got a swimsuit, like you said."

Then he walked into the sea.

He was so graceful, cutting through the water, moving as easily as if the ocean was his natural environment. It seemed wrong that he'd been caged for so long. What did it do to a person to be limited to a 10 x 8 foot cell for years?

I sat quietly in the sunshine, wondering how free he was from the cages of his own mind. I knew they still tortured him; I just didn't know to what extent.

I lay down on my side, watching him in the distance.

I must have fallen asleep because when I woke up he was sitting next to me, water still glistening on his shoulders. And he was wearing his shorts again.

As soon as he saw that I was awake, he leaned down and kissed me. A long, slow, passionate kiss.

Strangely enough, I didn't get my swim that afternoon either, instead spending the time learning his body.

By evening, the temperature had fallen, and I shivered from the slight breeze that had sprung up. It would be time to go home soon. The thought dimmed my enjoyment of the beautiful sunset.

"Are you cold, sweetheart?"

"A little. But I have an idea about how you can warm me up again," I teased.

His lips lifted in a smile.

"Oh yeah? Maybe you could enlighten me, Miss Delaney, because I surely don't know what you mean."

"Y'all one of those smooth talkin' so'thern boys Ah heerd about?" I giggled, trying to capture his Rhett Butler meets Matthew McConaughey accent.

"That is a terrible renderin' of my accent, Miss Delaney. I might just have to kiss it off of those delicious lips of yours."

"You'll have to catch me first," I shouted, leaping to my feet and running helter-skelter toward the water.

I'd splashed up to my ankles only to realize it was a helluva lot colder than I'd expected, when Jordan caught me around my waist and we both crashed into the ocean.

"Holy shit!" I coughed. "That's freakin' cold!"

He laughed loudly. "And you were expectin' what, exactly? You were shiverin' in my nice warm arms two minutes ago and you thought the water was goin' to be warmer?

He shook his head like a wet dog, showering me with droplets.

"Damn, woman! I'm freezin' my ass off in here. Are you tryin' to end this night for good?"

I scrambled to my feet, using his firm body to lever myself up.

"Okay, I have to admit that wasn't one of my better ideas."

"Oh, hell, no!" he laughed. "Skinny dippin' with you was definitely on my to-do list."

"Why, Mr. Kane! Don't tell me you've been having improper thoughts about me."

"Since the first day I saw you, sweetheart," he said, a happy smile lighting up his beautiful eyes. "And what with havin' a room to myself for the first time in eight years, I have to say I've been chokin' the chicken pretty hard every night."

I spluttered out a laugh. "'Choking the chicken'? Really!

Because that conjures up all sorts of bizarre images of feathers and chicken skin, none of which are a turn on. I mean, generally speaking, the thought of you playing some one-handed baseball would be getting me all hot and sweaty but…"

"Wait, what? You tellin' me that *you've* been having improper thoughts about me, Miss Delaney?"

"God, yes! The day you walked into the Busy Bee Diner, I was thinking up a plan to have my wicked way with you."

His happy smile dimmed as we both thought back to that day.

"Hey! Don't let the fuckers grind you down. Like I said, a few more months and your parole will be finished, then you can get the hell away—for good."

"I don't deserve you," he said, softly. "I don't deserve to feel anythin' other than shit for what I've done."

I slapped him hard across the face, and he staggered back.

"I told you I'd hit you if you talked crap like that again. Look, I didn't know Mikey…"

"No, you didn't!" he said, harshly.

"Well, everyone keeps telling me what a great guy he was."

"That's true, he was!"

"Yeah? So you think this 'great guy'," I shouted, using bitchy air quotes with my hands, "do you think this 'great guy' who loved you would want you to be so fucking miserable every day for the rest of your life?"

"You don't understand what it's like," he muttered.

"Oh, hell. Is that the best you've got? I don't know what it's like? Well, enlighten me, shit head!"

I thought maybe I'd pushed him too far, because he splashed out of the water and stalked back up the beach.

Damn, that was a fine ass he had. I'd have to study that more later. But for now I was curious as to what answer he'd come up with, other than walking away like some sullen teenager.

But when I got back to our picnic area, he was sitting on the blanket, all hunched up.

I immediately sat next to him and put both my arms around his waist, leaning my chin on his shoulder.

"I don't know how to be anythin' else," he whispered. "I've

been the fuck up all of my life. I know it sounds dumb, but I know who I am here—the loser, the guy who killed his brother." He took a shuddering breath. "I don't know who I'll be if I leave."

"Jordan," I said, kissing his shoulder gently, "you can be whoever you want to be. You've got to take a chance on life. Yeah, you'll get shit thrown at you, but there's more to you than the sum of your history, more waiting for you than this small town. You have a good heart, and if you let people get to know you, they'll see that for themselves."

His head hung down, but when he looked up again, his icy expression was back and I shivered. This time it wasn't because of the temperature.

"Why do you even care, Torrey?" he sneered. "I'm not your problem. I'm just another in a long list of guys that you've screwed."

Ouch. I wasn't expecting that. I let my arms drop away from him and leaned back on my hands.

"Well, good to know what you think of me. Guess my blunt talking rubbed off on you after all."

Suddenly, his mood shifted again, and he looked remorseful.

"Fuck, I'm sorry. I didn't mean it like that. That came out all wrong."

"No shit, Sherlock! You know, you don't have to be a jerk about it. I just happen to like sex, and I don't think there's anything wrong with that. But people can be awfully judgmental. Frankly, I didn't think you'd be one of them."

"Oh, right, I've got it now," he said, angrily. "You thought the ex-con would have lower standards—a no-questions-asked fuck."

"You can be a real asshole. Fuck you, Jordan!"

I pulled on my shorts and tank top, not caring that my bra was buried somewhere in the sand.

Jordan watched me without moving. I resisted the urge to kick sand in his face. I knew he was lashing out at me because he was hurting and scared, but that didn't mean I had to stick around and be his patsy.

Damn, I wished I'd come in my own car. The jerk-off

asshole looked like he was going to let me walk home. And I *still* couldn't find my flip-flops. Hot tears pricked behind my eyes. *Oh, no way!* I was *not* going to let that asswipe make me cry. I promised myself a long time ago that I would not be shedding tears over some guy again.

I started walking, and when he realized I was walking straight past his stupid truck, he finally got the picture.

"Torrey, wait!"

"Go fuck yourself!"

I heard him scrabbling around behind me, so I guessed he was pulling on his pants. I stomped up the dirt road, cursing when a sharp stone dug into the soft pad of my foot. Damn, this was going to be a long walk.

I heard Jordan's voice again, begging for me to wait.

I went maybe a hundred yards across the dunes and up the dirt road, when I heard the truck's engine roar to life, and yellow headlights flooded the route ahead of me.

I briefly considered hiding behind a bush, but the thought of what creepy-crawlies and wild critters might be hiding with me nixed that idea.

The truck pulled alongside me, the engine idling.

"Get in," he snapped.

I carried on walking as the truck crept along next to me.

"Torrey, get in the damn truck, or I'll have to come down there and throw yo' ass in!" he yelled.

Without a word, I yanked the door open and sat down, refusing to look at him.

The truck didn't move.

"What now?" I bellowed. "I'm in the damn truck!"

"Put your seatbelt on," he said quietly, his voice tight with tension.

For a second, I thought about arguing with him, but then I remembered that Mikey had died when he'd been flung through the windshield of the car Jordan was driving. He hadn't been wearing a seatbelt.

I clipped it into place, and a relieved expression crossed Jordan's face, before it settled back into the more familiar impassive coolness.

We drove the couple of miles to the Rectory in silence, each too upset and angry to find words that would heal instead of hurt.

When we arrived, I unclipped the seatbelt and hurled the door open.

"I'm sorry," he said, his voice soft and tender.

"Yeah, you and the rest of the world. You know what, Jordan? I didn't fuck you out of some warped sense of pity. I did it because I liked you. But I guess you really are an asshole after all. Have a nice life."

And I slammed the door before he could say another word.

Jordan

Wow. I screwed that up big time. If I'd planned how to end our non-date in the worst possible way, that would have been it.

Could I have been more of an asshole? Well, I guess I could have let her walk home—that would have been high up on the scale of assholish behavior. But the way she looked at me, I think she would have preferred to walk home barefoot on a gravel road covered with hot coals rather than ride with me. I couldn't blame her.

I'd driven the whole way under 25, going deliberately slow just to try and give myself time to think of *something* to say to her while I still had the chance. It had just been such a fucking shock when she'd said all that heart-warming shit to me. She'd said I had a good heart. Obviously she was wrong about that, but I couldn't help liking the fact that she thought so.

And fuck! Touching her, feeling her hands on me, being inside her. I couldn't remember it ever being that good. I know it had been a long time, but I thought my black heart would explode from the raw passion rushing through me.

God! Why was I such a dumb fuck? I knew I didn't deserve her, but to go out and deliberately shoot down any chance with her. Shit.

I just couldn't find the words to tell her what the last two nights had meant to me. I tried, but I kept choking on them. After she slammed out of the truck, I drove home, using every cuss word I could think of and yelling them out as loud as I could. Ironic, huh?

I was less than three miles from home when I saw the lights of a police cruiser in my rearview mirror. He followed me for a half a mile, and I thought I might be okay, but then the siren went on and I pulled over to the side of the road.

I watched him approach me slowly, his hand on the gun at his hip. I dug my ID out of my wallet and kept my hands on the steering wheel where he could see them.

His uniform and weapon were giving me flashbacks. I could feel sweat breaking out over my entire body and my legs were trembling with the effort of not running.

"License and registration," he said.

I already had them in my hand, but I had a feeling it wouldn't be enough to placate him.

He gave them the shortest scan ever. At that point I was certain that he already knew who I was.

"Step out of the vehicle, please, Mr. Kane."

I didn't even bother to ask why I'd been stopped, although strictly speaking, he should have given me a reason.

"Have you been drinking alcohol?"

"No, sir."

He made me walk in a straight line, touch my finger to my nose, stand on one leg—all that shit—and he still breathalyzed me anyway.

When it came up negative, the other questions started: where did I live; where had I been; what had I been doing; how often did I have to report to the police station; when was the last time I got tested for drugs and alcohol; when was the last time my parole officer had visited my place of residence. On and on.

It was all designed to let me know that he was the one in control, the one with the power—and that he was watching me.

He kept me there half an hour, almost up until my curfew,

then finally let me go home.

Dad and Momma were waiting up for me. Wow, this evening really had no chance of improving.

"Where have you been?" Dad started immediately.

"Out. With a friend."

"The preacher's trashy daughter?"

My temper started to fray. I held it in tightly.

"She's not trashy." *Isn't that exactly what I just called her?*

"You stay away from her," he went on. "She's no good."

"Jesus Christ, Dad!" I exploded at him. "She's the only person around here who talks to me! How is that 'no good'?"

He pressed his lips together but didn't answer.

"Oh, I get it. Anyone who talks to me is automatically bad, is that it?"

Yep, I reckoned I'd hit the nail on the head there.

"While you're under our roof, you'll abide by our rules."

Un-fucking-believable!

"What fuckin' rules? I'm on parole! I get tested for alcohol and drugs every week. We have to have my parole officer do random searches on the damn house! I cain't go to the city to get a decent job! I have curfew! What other rules do y'all want to add to that? Y'all already said I'm bein' kicked out—well hoo-fuckin'-ray! Go for it, *Dad*, because this place is just another jail!"

"Don't you bring your foul prison language into this house!" he roared.

I gave up and headed to my room, throwing myself down onto the bed. I pressed my face into the pillow, feeling the sting on my cheek where Torrey had hit me. Fuck, I deserved more than that for the way I'd treated her.

I lay there in silence. I thought Dad might follow me, but he didn't. I heard him talking to Momma, his voice angry, but I couldn't catch the words. Probably just as well.

Then I heard the telephone ring, which was unusual this late. Whoever it was, I could tell from his tone that dad was annoyed but trying to be polite. The call ended pretty soon after and the house sank into silence.

I lay awake, listening to the night time noises, alert for any sound that meant the bastards had come back for my truck.

I thought about Torrey and what she'd said, what she'd done. And I thought about what I'd said, and what I'd done. And I thought about what I shouldn't have said, and shouldn't have done.

I didn't sleep that night either. But this time it was different. Torrey hadn't freaked when I'd told her what had happened to Mikey, or even about the attempted murder rap. No, somehow she'd accepted that. Right now I was losing sleep for being the regular kind of asshole, and treating a decent person like shit. I was pretty darn certain the irony wouldn't be lost on Torrey either.

When my old fashioned alarm clock rang the next morning, I sat up immediately and swung my legs to the edge of the bed. I felt like shit, but at least I'd decided what to say to Torrey. Well, mostly just a whole shit load of groveling. I hoped that would work.

If I could have afforded flowers, I would have bought her some. I even considered picking some wild ones that grew at the side of the road on the way to her house, but that seemed kind of lame and a bit pathetic. Which I was.

I took a quick shower and pulled on another of Mikey's t-shirts. I knew it half killed Momma when I wore his clothes, but I didn't have a whole lot of choice. She'd gotten me a couple of t-shirts from Goodwill, but they'd both been too small. I think she'd have preferred it if I'd stayed in prison uniform, like a visible mark of what I was. Jeez, I think she'd have brought back branding if she could, she hated me that much.

The kitchen was empty and the house was still silent. I thought if I hurried, I could avoid bumping into either of my parents again. I was starting to lose weight from the meals I was missing lately. Leastways, my borrowed shorts seemed even baggier.

I squished a slab of cheese between two pieces of bread and stuffed a couple of apples into my pants pockets, which left me looking deformed. It sort of matched how I felt inside.

I heard someone in the shower and knew that I didn't have time to make a thermos again. I really hoped Torrey would forgive me—again—and make me some of her damn fine coffee. But the way I'd left things last night, she'd probably toss it in my face. I wouldn't blame her.

When I reached the Rectory, I was wrong on all counts, because her car wasn't there. My first thought was that she'd found another guy to hook up with. The idea hurt so bad I thought I'd lose the small amount of breakfast I'd been able to force down.

I tapped on the door and waited, almost holding my breath.

"Good morning, Jordan," said the Reverend, opening the screen door and peering out. "If you could start by emptying out the old shed today. A second dumpster is arriving at noon, so toss anything broken. Stack the good stuff to the side and I'll take a look at it later."

"Yes, ma'am."

She started to close the door.

"Uh, excuse me, ma'am. Is Torrey home?"

Her lips thinned and I thought she'd just shut the door in my face like most people, but I guess she had her 'good guy' rep to protect.

"No, she'll be gone for a few days now." I think she must have taken pity on me because she quickly added, "She has two days' training for her new job so she's staying in the city."

I thought she was dismissing me and I turned to go. But then she spoke again.

"How are things at home, Jordan?"

"Fine, thank you, ma'am," I replied, automatically.

"Good ... that's good. Will your mother be home this morning?"

"Uh, I guess. I'm not really sure."

She nodded, offered a slight smile, then the door closed and I was alone. Again.

Shit. Torrey had really gone. If she didn't come back ... the thought was too painful to contemplate. I tried to tell myself it was just a couple of days, and then she'd be back. Then I could apologize in person. Again. If she'd let me.

I got to work in the backyard, wearing the work-gloves Torrey had bought for me. I missed her coffee. Hell, that was just so much crap—I missed *her*. I missed her smile and her sarcasm. I missed the way her hair hung in tangles around her face, and that she didn't care whether it had seen a brush or not. I missed those long legs stretched out in front of her as she sat on the step and closed her eyes, enjoying the early morning sunshine. I missed hearing her talk about her plans for the day, or the music she'd listened to, the book she'd just read. I hated to think that she was in the city where I couldn't go, and maybe meeting some slick city type, maybe going to his room.

God, that thought tortured me.

I was glad I had to throw some heavy shit around cleaning out the Rev's shed, because it was a way of venting the anger and anxiety that coursed through me. But who was I kidding? I was just an easy lay to her, and not even a particularly good one. I felt my skin flush with humiliation at the way I'd not been able to control myself with her, blowing my load like some fuckin' adolescent—again.

Ever since I'd taken an interest in girls as a kid, I'd gotten a lot of action. I was tall and considered good-looking, so even some older chicks had been interested in giving Mikey Kane's little brother a ride. Yeah, I'd been a bit of a player. Life sure had a sick sense of humor because I really wasn't anymore, and the one woman that I wanted probably hated my guts.

At lunchtime, I heard the second dumpster arrive, and the one full of garden waste was taken away. Stupidly, I kind of missed it. Seeing it getting filled, it was a way of measuring how much crap I'd cleared out of the wilderness.

I sat on the porch step and ate my sandwich. I hadn't brought anything to drink, but the Reverend had an outdoor tap in the backyard. A hose was corroded onto it, but using a wrench from Mikey's toolbox, I was able to rip it off. The first gush of water was brown with rust, but after I let it run for a minute or two, it tasted okay. A bit tangy, like when you get punched in the face and it splits your lip so you taste your own blood. It was okay.

At 4:30 PM I packed up and drove home slowly, dreading the dead hours before it was time to go to bed. Even though my body ached from the laboring I'd done, and my brain was foggy from lack of sleep, going to my parents' house was the last place

I wanted to be. I'd have liked to go for a long drive, but I wasn't allowed more than ten miles from the town limits, and I couldn't afford the gas anyway.

But when I got home, I saw the cans of paint that Torrey had found at Hulk's junkyard, and I had an idea.

I dug out some old paintbrushes from the garage and set to work. I didn't need a sketch to know what I was going to paint. I did it for Mikey, for me and for Torrey. I hoped that if I used her gift, she'd see that I was grateful, and sorry for the cruel things I'd said.

First of all, I turned the ugly red smear that covered up the word 'murderer' into a boiling blood-red sea—the way it can look when the setting sun sinks into the ocean. Then I painted a large Celtic cross onto the door, the same image I had on my shoulder blade, the same image I had seared into my brain. Then I added the bleeding heart and Mikey's name in a looping script across the whole design.

I'd probably been kneeling down for a couple of hours when I straightened up suddenly, aware that Momma was watching me. *How long had she been standing there?*

"Reverend Williams came to see me this mornin'," she said. "What have you been sayin' to her?"

I blinked in surprise.

"Nothin'. I've hardly spoken to her. Why? What did she say?"

"You must have said somethin'."

"She asked me how I was gettin' on at home. I said it was fine. That's it."

"And what about that girl of hers?"

My eyes dropped to the ground. "Yeah, I talk to Torrey."

Momma's eyes narrowed and her lips curved in a sneer.

"I knew it: that girl's trouble."

My heart started pounding. *What had Torrey told her momma? Surely nothing about us? Please God, not that!*

"I haven't done anythin'," I said, my voice entirely lacking in conviction.

"Well, the Reverend has been around here again, pokin' her nose in where it don't belong."

143

I didn't know what to say, but I got the impression that Momma didn't need me to speak either.

"Looks like we'll have to keep you," she spat out.

"What?"

"The Reverend said it was our Christian duty to keep you the whole time you're on parole. So we will. We'll do what's right, but then I want you gone. Understand?"

"Yeah, I understand."

"I don't think you do!" she said, her voice shaking with fury. "Every time I look at you it sickens me! All I can see is your brother's cold, dead body rottin' in that grave, and you're walkin' around wearin' his clothes, breathin' God's good air. It's not fair. It's just plain wrong!"

"Do you think I don't know that?" I yelled back. "Don't you think I wish a thousand times a day that it had been me and not him?"

Momma's eyes snapped to mine. "I wish that, too."

She slammed back into the house, rattling the door and frame.

I leaned over as my stomach emptied itself, splattering the open cans of paint with vomit.

Torrey

Two days in the city had been about my limit. Guess I was turning into a country girl. What a thought.

The barista training had been tedious beyond words, mainly because I didn't learn anything new, just a bunch of marketing slogans they wanted us to use as we prepared a triple soy latte chai mocha with cinnamon shit. But I liked a couple of the girls I'd met, and we made arrangements to meet up in a few weeks to hit the clubs.

I'd been given the late shift at the mall for the first month— two till midnight. It suited me. I definitely wasn't a morning person ... although some things made an early start worthwhile.

I looked out of the window when I heard Jordan's truck. I'd calmed down considerably since I'd last seen him. Thinking about it long and hard, I recognized that neither of us had a great track history with relationships. And if I was honest with myself, I knew that I'd tried to push him too hard. So I was giving him one more chance not to be a douchebag. He'd better damn well take it with both hands or I was kicking his ass.

I immediately noticed the incredible artwork he'd painted to cover up the ugly graffiti. Damn, he was some artist! I recognized the motif—it was the same as the tattoo over his back. It made sense now. It was a memorial to his brother, and it was obvious that he suffered Mikey's loss every single day.

I looked at the small box lying in a plastic bag next to my bed, wondering again about the present I'd bought him. It seemed like a good idea at the time. Now, I wasn't so sure. But as I'd already lost the receipt, he may as well have it. But getting involved with someone so ... damaged? Now *that* was a really dumb idea. Pity being smart wasn't enough to stop me jumping in with both feet.

Since I'd broken up with Jem, my first serious boyfriend when I was a college freshman, I'd made it a point of staying away from guys I liked too much. Instead, I played the field and kept it simple. Even my ex-boss was supposed to be casual. But there was something about Jordan; plus, I had a shrewd idea that the sex was only going to get better. The combination of his strength and softness, his firm fit body and kindness that he let out every now and again. Not that what we'd shared so far hadn't felt pretty damn good at the time, but I sensed he had plenty more to offer. I was looking forward to finding out, providing he did the appropriate amount of begging my forgiveness, of course.

I staggered downstairs and took the time to make some coffee. Then I carried two mugs out onto the porch step. Jordan was already shirtless, wearing just his cut-off jeans, and hauling garbage out of Mom's shed.

His smooth skin glistened with sweat, and I could appreciate again the breadth of his shoulders and his narrow waist, the fine curve of his ass, and long, strong legs. He was beautiful on the outside, but I think I was the only person who saw that there was beauty on the inside, too.

"Hey, cowboy! You forgot your damn coffee!" I shouted.

His head shot up, and I could see from the expression on his face that he hadn't expected to hear from me again. It was kind of sweet how nervous he looked. I sobered quickly when I remembered the reasons for that.

He walked up and hovered in front of me, uncertain whether to sit or make a run for it.

"Put your ass down," I said, pointing to the space beside to me. "Seeing you hopping from foot to foot is making me want to pee."

He cracked a small smile at that and sat down on the step below me so I had a grandstand view of his strong shoulders and muscled back.

"Thanks for the coffee," he said, softly.

"You're lucky I'm a forgiving person," I said.

"I am ... lucky," he agreed, nodding slowly. "I don't deserve for you to even talk to me right now."

"Oh, jeez! Not the pity party again! 'Nobody loves me, everybody hates me, think I'll go and eat worms!'"

He frowned and wrinkled his nose at the same time. "Worms?"

"I'm guessing you weren't in the Boy Scouts."

"Um, no! Not my scene."

"Oh, right—resident bad boy."

He scowled and looked down.

"You owe me an apology, you jerk," I said, insistently. "And I'm not a very patient person."

"God, I know," he said, hanging his head. "I was such a fuckin' tool."

"Yes, you were. Here…" and I dropped his present onto his lap.

"What's this?"

"For you."

"You ... you got somethin' for me?"

He seemed stunned.

"Yup."

"What is it?"

"Well, gee! Why don't you take a look-see, numb nuts!"

He opened the plastic bag and stared inside.

"You bought me a cell phone?"

"Yep. Cheapest I could find. It's pay-as-you-go so you'll have to add the minutes when you need them. I put $50 on it to get you started."

"You bought me a cell phone?" he repeated.

It really wasn't sinking in.

"Yes, Jordan, I bought you a cell phone."

"But … I don't have anyone to call."

I rolled my eyes.

"It's so you can call me to apologize when you fuck up again. I programmed my number in already. And you *still* owe me a fucking apology. So get texting."

I left him sitting on the step with his new toy. He wasn't moving, but I was pretty sure he was still breathing, so I figured he'd be okay.

I guessed he wasn't used to receiving presents.

It made me wonder what happened in prison at Christmas. I couldn't imagine they had presents from Santa, but you never know. I'd have to ask him.

When I got out of the shower, my cell phone was blinking: *1 new message*.

I grinned to see that it was from Jordan.

I'm sorry.

Well, hardly Pulitzer prize winning, but it was a start. Clearly, he was a man of few words.

I couldn't help smiling to myself as I read his message again.

I slid my new black polo-shirt out of the polythene sleeve and dressed slowly. My uniform was all black, showing that I was a barista. It was way cooler than having to wear a green apron like the rest of the staff, but not *that* cool. They'd promised me some uniform pants, too, but because they hadn't had any in my size, I was allowed to wear my own jeans for now. Yay for me.

At least they made my ass look good.

I decided to debut my new outfit to Jordan and make him another coffee before I left.

I was just about to bang on the kitchen window when I remembered that I was trying *not* to scare him to death. Instead I just took two mugs outside and waited for him to notice me. It didn't take long.

"What do you think?" I said, holding my arms out so he could see the new uniform.

His eyes swept up and down my body and he swallowed several times.

"Uh, you look good. Great. You always look great."

"Oh my God! Don't tell me my barista uniform is turning you on!"

He gave a shy smile. "Well, yeah. I guess it is."

I laughed out loud and fist-pumped the air. "Workers of the world unite!"

He sat down next to me and picked up the second mug of coffee.

"Uh, so did you get my text message?"

I smiled at him.

"Yes, Jordan. I got your effusive, heart-warming message."

His cheeks flushed and he looked down.

"I liked your message very much," I said, quietly.

"I mean it," he said, still staring at the dirt by his left foot.

"I know you do. Apology accepted. So, do you want to do something on Sunday?"

"Sunday?"

"Yes, Sunday, the day after tomorrow. I'm working Saturday but I thought it would be fun to do something on the weekend."

I paused, waiting for the penny to drop. Waiting … waiting … but … nope. No dropping pennies.

"Jordan, this is where you ask me out on a date!" I said, giving him a huge, Texas-size hint.

His eyes got big as he stared at me.

"You … you want to go on a date with me?"

"Well, jeez! You don't have to! Way to make a woman feel wanted!"

I stood up to go, feeling the raw sting of rejection.

He leapt to his feet.

"No! I mean, yeah! I do! I just … I thought I'd blown my chance with you."

"Well, you said you were sorry. I believe you, so … how about we try again?"

"God, yes!" he said, his eyes alight with hope. "Torrey Delaney, will you go on a date with me on Sunday?"

"I'll have to check my calendar."

His face fell instantly.

"I'm teasing you, Jordan. Yes, I would very much like to go on a date with you on Sunday."

He closed his eyes, a small smile curling the corners of his lips. When he looked at me again, his pupils were dark and intense.

"I really want to kiss you right now," he said, huskily.

A pulse of desire shot through me. "Go ahead."

He took a step toward me and placed his hand on my cheek, stroking it with the pad of his thumb.

Because I was still standing on the porch, we were nearly the same height. He simply leaned forward and brushed his lips against mine, sighing as he pulled away.

"So soft," he whispered.

I wanted more.

Wrapping my arms firmly around his neck, pressing his body against mine, I pulled him toward me again.

It was like striking a match, except I didn't get a chance to stand back before the flame burned. His explosion of desire awed me.

He grabbed me around the waist and took two quick steps up onto the porch, slamming my back against the wall of the house so breath rushed out of my lungs. I gasped and felt his tongue in my mouth, forceful and demanding. My legs wrapped around his waist and he ground his hips into me, a hard point of heat against my inner thighs.

His intensity was unnerving, but I was too lost in the moment to care.

"I want you so fuckin' badly," he growled, against my neck. "God, I want you!"

His grip was almost painful and I could feel his whole body trembling.

I was panting hard, mewling wordlessly.

"Please!" he begged. "Please, Torrey, please!"

Thoughts of being late for work, thoughts of any description flew out of my mind.

"Upstairs," I gasped.

Still clutching me in his arms, he shouldered his way through the screen door and into the kitchen. His eyes darted around and I pointed toward the stairs. He almost ran up them, the weight of my body insignificant against his need.

"Second door on the left!"

We crashed against the frame and fell backwards onto my bed. I felt the springs of the old mattress protest beneath me.

He bit my breasts through my shirt and started tugging at my jeans even as I fumbled with his zipper.

"Condoms are in the drawer," I rasped out.

He yanked the drawer so hard, it flew apart, showering the contents over the wooden floor. But he was a man on a mission and he found what he wanted among the debris. His hands were shaking so hard he could barely hold the packet.

I'd managed to push my jeans and panties past my knees, but they'd snagged around my sneakers. Jordan took one look at my predicament and flipped me onto my stomach, then pulled my hips up so I was on my hands and knees.

A second later, he was inside me and I cried out.

I felt his whole body hunched over me, his bare skin slapping loudly against mine. Each thrust threatened to make my arms collapse and I had to fight to keep my balance, pushing back against him.

It was hard and shocking, coarse and crude. Utterly unrefined and utterly thrilling. His roar as he came was loud and certain.

We collapsed onto the bed, his weight on top of me, his hot

breath searing my neck.

I felt his dick twitch inside me and I whimpered.

He cursed softly and pulled out, rolling onto his back.

From the moment we'd kissed on the porch, to this second must have been less than four minutes.

For a while I lay unmoving, feeling sluggish and fighting sleep. Finally, I turned so I could see him. His chest was still heaving and one arm was thrown across his eyes. I looked down to see my jeans and panties tangled around my feet and I couldn't stifle a small giggle. He froze at the sound.

"Hey," I said, "you still alive under there?"

I tried to move his arm but he wouldn't look at me.

"Jordan!"

"Christ, I'm so sorry," he mumbled, still refusing to look at me.

"Um, what for?"

"I behaved like a fuckin' animal."

"Well, yeah, you did. But I liked it."

This time he let me move his arm and he turned his head toward me, his beautiful soulful eyes filled with doubt.

"Did I hurt you?" he said, quietly. "Are you okay?"

"Hell, that was a great start to my day!" I chuckled. "It was like a shot of adrenalin followed by a coma. My body doesn't know what the fuck's going on, but damn that was good!"

"Good?" he sounded puzzled.

"Jordan, you dope! That was amazing! I haven't been fucked like that since ... well, ever. I'm slightly in shock. I think I've been missing out all these years."

I glanced at my watch.

"Oh, hell! I'm going to be late on my first day! Oh, this won't look good, turning up looking well used and smelling of sex!" I slapped his chest. "It's your fault! Look, I've got to hustle, but feel free to take your time, have a shower—whatever. Oh, and you totally have to clear up the drawer you upended."

I sat up, grabbing my pants and shuffled to the bathroom to clean up as best I could. A damp washcloth was good for soothing my throbbing lower half, and I splashed cold water on my flushed face. Hopefully, I'd look reasonably presentable by the time I got to the coffee shop.

Jordan had his shorts back on and was scrabbling around on the floor, collecting my scattered belongings.

"I like to see a man on his hands and knees," I laughed.

Jordan looked up and smiled, then pulled me forward by my hips and yanked up my shirt to plant a soft kiss on my belly.

"Sweetheart, I've been at your feet since the first day I met you."

"Glad to hear it," I said, ruffling his already unruly hair. "But I've got to run or I'll be out of a job before I start. I think it's too early in my barista career to use the hot-guy-in-my-bed defense. There's a key in the flowerpot by the front door. Lock up after yourself."

I kissed the top of his head and left him kneeling on the floor in my room, a huge smile plastered across his face.

Jordan

It took me nearly 10 minutes to gather up everything I'd dropped on the floor, fix the pieces of bedside drawer and hammer them together with my bare hands.

I didn't know what the hell had just happened. When she touched me, I completely lost my mind. The way I'd behaved was unforgivable. But the real mind fuck was that Torrey had said she'd liked it. I'd had her bent over on all fours, fucking her like a damn dog, and she *liked* it. Well, good—because I fucking *loved* it.

I didn't understand her, not for one freakin' second. I'd thought that I was just a mercy fuck. At least I'd talked myself into believing that afterward; it's not what I'd felt at the time. But when I was with her, for the first time in a long while, I didn't feel judged. I couldn't figure out why, but she seemed to accept me for who I was. Not that I knew what that meant anymore, but she made me feel alive.

Chapter 8 – Rewards

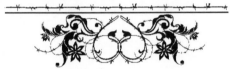

Jordan

Working in the Reverend's backyard for the rest of the day was almost relaxing. Clearing the shed tested my muscles and patience, but it gave me time to think about Torrey, too. And not just her. For the first time, I allowed myself to think about what would happen in four months and two weeks, when my parole was up. I needed a plan of some description: a job, somewhere to live … how I was going to just *be*.

My parole officer had told me repeatedly that I needed to work on having some achievable goals. I was finally beginning to understand what she meant.

I drove home stinking and dirty, and got straight into the shower. I swear I tried not to think about Torrey's tight little body pulsing around me, but the moment I had that thought, I was hard as a damn rock. It was like my libido had taken license to go crazy. I was jacking off three and four times a day like I'd just hit puberty.

In prison, there was rarely any privacy—that didn't stop everyone from beating the meat occasionally. Most guys would keep it under the covers at night. I wouldn't say it was tolerated by the guards, but I guess they understood. The only time I saw them come down heavy on anyone was when it was used to disrespect a woman corrections officer. That used to happen sometimes. One of the cons would get talking to the woman officer and keep her talking, while a guy sitting in his cell across the corridor or across the room would get himself off, staring at her ass.

It creeped me out, but a lot about prison life creeped me out. And if it didn't, you were one of the nut jobs.

But now, my damn cock wouldn't stay down. Jeez, I hoped I hadn't scared Torrey off with the way I'd behaved—all the shit I'd put her through already.

Suddenly, after the stress of the last few days, I needed to see her. I needed to be sure that I hadn't scared her off completely. She'd said she was okay but I *needed* to see her. I *needed* to know.

I finished my shower and changed into the jeans Momma had gotten from Goodwill. They fit pretty well, which was a nice change, and then I snuck into Mikey's room to get another t-shirt. I still felt guilty about being in there and using his stuff, but somehow it was getting easier. We'd always borrowed each other's shit. Half the time we never knew whose was what anyway, except for pants. I was taller and he was bigger, but everything else we'd shared. I saw his favorite Maroon 5 shirt in the drawer.

"Thanks, buddy," I whispered, as I pulled it on.

I managed to leave just as Momma was coming home. Her face was sour with disapproval as usual, glaring at me through the windshield. I wondered if I'd have to appear before the inquisition when I got back, or whether she hated me too much to care where I'd been.

The usual feelings of anxiety chased me through town and all the way to the mall. I pushed them back and reminded myself that I was doing nothing wrong by being here. I wasn't a free man, but I wanted to make the most of the liberty I had.

I studied the coffee shop carefully through the plate glass window. There were maybe a dozen people scattered around the room inside, and four or five sitting on the patio, although I got the sense it was getting busier as commuters passed by on their way home from work.

I still wasn't used to the idea of there being a mall in this piss-ant little town.

I didn't recognize anyone, which was a good start, but it was only when I saw Torrey standing behind the enormous, stainless steel coffee maker that I got up the nerve to push open the door and walk in.

I lined up behind two other guys who were buying take-out coffee, hoping that Torrey would look up and notice me. She appeared to be concentrating on the monster machine, and I couldn't help smiling as a billow of steam made her jump slightly.

I started to give my order to the cashier, but as soon as Torrey heard my voice, she looked up and grinned.

"Hey, babe!" she said, walking toward me. "Whatcha doing here? Stalker, much?"

"I missed you," I said, honestly. "So I thought I'd come see where you work."

The cashier smiled, her eyes flicking between us. "Is this your boyfriend, Torrey?"

I was painfully curious to see how she'd answer that question. It wasn't something we'd discussed. I guess technically we were still waiting for our first date.

"I don't know, Bev," she smirked. "I'm thinking about keeping this one around a while—see how he works out. He'll get his fitness report after the weekend." And she winked at me.

"Well, let me know how that goes," said the woman named Bev, "because I'll take him off your hands if you're not certain."

"Sure!" laughed Torrey. "Give me your number and I'll let you know if he's available."

"Hey!" I huffed out. "Don't I get a say in this?"

"No!" they both said in unison, and laughed.

I held up my hands in surrender. "Fine, I'll just do as I'm told. Let me know how I do, sweetheart."

"Waal," said Torrey. "I'll keep you around for now—see how you shape up."

Bev giggled. "Oh, I'd say he's in fine shape, honey. Very fine shape."

Her lascivious look was starting to make me sweat, and I glanced around, looking for a retreat.

"Take the table in the corner," Torrey said, sensing my sudden discomfort. "I'll bring you your coffee."

I smiled my thanks and turned to go, but not before I heard Bev ask, "Is he as hot in bed as he looks?"

I didn't hear Torrey's answer, and I wasn't sure I wanted to.

The place got pretty hectic after that, mostly take-out orders, so Torrey was busy. But about 10 PM she sauntered over to my table and plopped what looked like a grilled cheese and tomato sandwich in front of me, except it was made from some fancy Italian bread.

"I thought if you're going sit here all night, I'd better feed you," she smiled.

"Thanks! I am pretty hungry."

Which was an understatement. I was half starving but I couldn't afford to buy anything on the menu besides coffee.

She watched me eat for a moment, a small smile on her face.

"Are you waiting till I finish, cowboy, because I've got another two hours to go yet. God, my feet are killing me. I'd forgotten how tiring these gigs are."

I frowned slightly. "Um, actually I'm gonna have to get gone in a few minutes."

She looked disappointed. "Oh, that's fine. Don't worry about it."

"Torrey, no! I wish I could stay. I want to spend every goddamn minute of the day with you, but I..." my voice dropped to a whisper, "I have curfew."

Her mouth popped open in a small O, and a look of

157

understanding crossed her face.

"Shit! Sorry, Jordan. I completely forgot."

"It's cool. I know it's kind of pathetic that a man my age has a fuckin' curfew."

I dragged my hands through my hair, frustrated by the invisible chains that held me back, stopping me from behaving like a normal guy.

"Hey," she said softly, grabbing my wrists. "It's fine. We're fine. Go home, get some rest. I'll see you on Sunday."

I blew out a long breath. "Sunday, yeah. Should I pick you up after church?"

Her eyebrows shot upward.

"Um, no! I don't go to church, so you can pick me up any time you want."

"Oh … I just thought, what with your momma and all…"

She grinned a little. "No, we have an understanding about that. I don't do church."

"Well, I could pick you up about nine?"

"Make it ten. It's my one chance to sleep in, and I want to make the most of it."

God, I want to sleep in with her, but I don't think I can tell her that. Not yet.

"Okay, 10 AM. I'll be there."

I moved to stand up but she hung onto my arm.

"What am I supposed to wear?"

"Excuse me?" I said, my mind immediately going straight to the gutter and imagining her in a range of lingerie that was probably illegal.

"For our date, Mr. Smooth Talker—and don't think I don't know what you were just imagining. Am I supposed to dress up or what?"

Shit! I hadn't thought that far ahead.

"Oh, I'll text you," I said, with a confidence I most definitely wasn't feeling.

"Cool!" she said, and slid out of her seat.

As she passed my chair, she leaned down and pressed her

soft lips against mine.

"Sunday," she said.

But I still had 24 hours to go, and Saturday dragged endlessly. I missed Torrey. Christ, I hoped I wasn't making her my new crutch.

I thought about driving out to the mall just to catch a few minutes with her, but I didn't want to come over like a crazy obsessive stalker. I'd already pissed her off so many times. I didn't want to risk it again.

Instead, I lifted some weights in the garage, and then went for a long run. I also had to think about where I was going to take her on our date. I'd been so caught up in the sheer fucking joy of having a date to look forward to, that I'd completely forgotten to plan where we were going to go and what we were going to do.

I was as nervous as all get out. I hadn't been on a date since 2006. I assumed things were still done the same but who the hell knew? Plus, there were two fucking big hurdles: I couldn't go more than ten miles from town, and I didn't have any money.

Feeling slightly crazed, I drove to the only other place where people hadn't thrown rocks at me.

Hulk's junkyard had been a home from home when Mikey and me were growing up. The guy might look like the kind of person who'd eat your lungs with a spoon, but he was actually pretty cool. He'd taught us both about cars, although Mikey had never been as into it as I was. Still, Hulk had tolerated us hanging out there, and we'd gotten to know him pretty well.

I was disappointed to see that there were several other cars in the parking lot when I drove up. I waited a few minutes until the office had emptied out, then tapped on the door and poked my head around the frame.

"Hey, man."

Hulk was sitting behind the desk, a stack of paperwork in front of him, with a pair of what looked like kid's glasses squashed onto the end of his nose.

He looked up and grinned, waving me into the only uncluttered chair in the room. I sat down, coughing slightly when a cloud of dust billowed up around me.

"Hey yourself, kid. How'd those tires work out for you?"

"They're great. I just wanted to stop by and say thanks. I know you didn't have to do that."

He waved my gratitude away.

"Just a bunch of old rubber. No skin off of my nose, kid. So, what do you need today?"

"Uh, nothin'. Just thought I'd come hang out, if that's okay."

He gave me an appraising look. He might come over as big and slow-witted, but quite a few guys had lost their front teeth making that assumption. "Your folks giving you a bad time?"

I looked away. "I've had worse."

"Uh huh. And what about that lil' firecracker you brought by last time—she kicked your ass yet?"

"Oh, man! She kicks my ass every time she sees me."

"Heh heh! Them feisty ones are worth keepin' around. So where is she?" he said, looking over my shoulder as if Torrey might suddenly appear. *I wish.*

"Workin'. But we've got a date tomorrow."

"She's purty as a junebug, full of sass, *and* she has a job? Man, how did you get so lucky?"

I frowned. "I know I don't deserve her, Hulk…"

"You jest quit sayin' that, boy!" he growled. "I've said it over and over and even done tole your folks—what happened was an accident. A dumb luck, shitty accident. That's all. Beatin' yourself up about it ain't gonna bring Mikey back. You know that. You gotta work on findin' a way to live with yourself."

I sighed.

"That's the hard bit, Hulk. I just don't know how to."

He leaned back, making his worn out chair creak ominously.

"That purty lil' gal seems like a right good start. You tole her everythin' about you?"

"Pretty much. She hasn't run away screamin' yet."

"Knew she was a keeper. So where you takin' her on this famous date?"

I groaned and dropped my head into my hands. "I have no fuckin' clue! I'm broke; I cain't go more than ten miles from town; and I've got a fuckin' 11 PM curfew!"

"Hmm," said Hulk. "That's a tricky one, sho nuff." He scratched his balls lazily then smiled from behind his beard. "You still got them fishin' poles of Mikey's?"

"I guess. I'm fairly sure Dad wouldn't have gotten rid of them. I think I saw them in the garage."

"Well, there you go. Find a nice, quiet, *private* fishin' hole," he waggled his eyebrows suggestively to make his point, "catch a couple of big ole sea trout and there's supper."

I stared at him skeptically. "You think I should take Torrey fishin' on our date?"

"Unless you can come up with a better idea," he challenged me.

Nope. I was fresh out of ideas.

Hulk smiled proudly. "Thought not."

Just then a shadow fell across the doorway.

"What the fuck is he doin' here?" came a harsh voice.

I twisted around in my chair. Staring down at me, bristling with anger and hatred, stood a guy about my dad's age.

I stood up right quick. "I was just leavin'."

"I don't think so, boy," said the man. "I asked you a question: what are you doin' here?"

"I don't want any trouble, mister."

"You should have thought about that before you showed your face in public, you piece of shit!"

He took a step toward me, and as he stepped from the brightness into the gloom of Hulk's office, I finally recognized him: Dallas Dupont. His son, Ryan, had been on the football team with Mikey, and was one of his best friends. The three of us had hung out a lot.

I didn't know Ryan's dad that well, but there was no mistaking the hatred in his voice. I was an expert at categorizing degrees of loathing.

I tried to step past him but he blocked the doorway, pushing my shoulder roughly so that I staggered back.

Rage flooded through me and without thinking, I slipped into a defensive crouch, ready to fight back.

Hulk slammed one huge fist onto the table.

"This is my place of business," he roared, "and I'll be the one to say who is and who ain't welcome!"

"He's a freakin' murderer, Hulk!" Dallas shouted.

"You ignorant piece of crap. Get the hell outta here afore I have your damn car crushed!"

Dallas looked stunned.

"You takin' his side over mine?"

"There's no side to take," said Hulk, in a more even tone. "Jordan did his time."

"You think eight years is punishment enough for what he done? He took a life! He killed his own brother!"

Hulk stared Dallas down. "I think livin' with the knowledge of what he done is the worst punishment he could have. Now simmer down, Dallas."

"I ain't stayin' to listen to this horse shit, Hulk! You get your damn priorities straight. And you…" he stabbed a finger at me, "stay the fuck out of town if you know what's good for your worthless hide."

Then he stomped out and his truck disappeared in a cloud of dust.

"You can relax now, kid."

I stood up and blew out a breath. "Sorry, Hulk."

"You get that a lot?"

I laughed mirthlessly. "All the freakin' time."

He nodded slowly. "Cain't be easy."

I didn't answer, instead shaking out the tension in my hands.

"You gettin' into fights?"

"Nah, cain't risk it. One punch and they'd throw my ass back in jail." I knew he was referring to my reaction to Dallas' baiting. "But just 'cause he hates me, don't mean I'd let him rearrange my face."

Hulk didn't respond. Maybe I'd pissed him off, too. If word got around that I'd been here—and Dallas Dupont would probably make sure that it was well known—then Hulk's business could suffer. I was a fucking Jonah.

"I should probably get gone."

Hulk shook his head slowly.

"Don't let ignorant bastards like that chase you out, kid."

I forced a smile.

"Nah, I gotta head out. Got a hot date with a hot woman to plan."

Hulk rumbled out a laugh and heaved himself out of the chair.

"You walkin' me to my car, Hulk? 'Cause I just got through tellin' you I have a date with Torrey. You're not my type."

"I'm still fast enough to whup yo' ass, Jordan Kane!" he growled.

We stopped at my truck and he peered at the fresh paintwork.

"Very nice! You do this all yourself?"

"Yep. Made use of that paint you gave Torrey."

He looked impressed. "You want any more work like that?"

I cocked my head to one side. "What are you talkin' 'bout, Hulk?"

"Kid, this is good shit. I've got ten guys who'd bite your arm off tomorrow to get a chance at you paintin' up their trucks."

"Yeah, and all ten of them want their trucks painted by *me*?"

He scratched his beard thoughtfully. "Seven or eight wouldn't mind. You want the work?"

I couldn't believe what he was saying.

"Hell, yes!"

"Okay, you got a deal. You can use my yard—I'll take myself

a finder's fee of thirty bucks a job and supply the paint. You keep the rest. Deal?"

"Deal!"

We shook hands and I drove out of there feeling … hell, words couldn't describe how I felt. Was I happy? I'd felt something like this with Torrey but I'd assumed it was because of how I felt in the pants department whenever she was around. This was different, but the same, too. Maybe this was what happiness felt like.

But as soon as I had that thought, my mood plummeted. What kind of twisted fucker was I to feel happy when my own brother was cold in his grave because of me?

Torrey

Bev had questioned me mercilessly after Jordan left. How long had I known him? Was it serious? How far did his tattoos extend? Where had he been all her life? That kind of thing. She practically begged me on bended knee to tell her what he was like in bed.

I thought of the way he'd taken me hard and fast before I'd left for work that morning.

"Wild!" I said with a wink, leaving the rest to her imagination.

She groaned and started fanning herself.

I was hoping that Jordan might drop in again on Saturday, but I didn't see him. A couple of hours before closing and long after my feet had started killing me, he sent a text.

Dress comfy. See you soon. J.

Short and sweet. Hmm, he needed to work on his texting skills—maybe I'd have to teach him some sexting skills, too. I wondered where he was taking me. I knew his options were limited, so I was intrigued to see what he'd come up with.

I honestly didn't care what we did. I just enjoyed spending time with him, getting to know him. Of course, I hoped that sex would be somewhere in his plan ... I sort of assumed it would.

He'd said to wear comfortable clothes so I guessed it must be something outdoorsy. I wasn't big on the outdoors, so I hoped we weren't going to be hiking or riding horses or any cowboy crap like that. I'd nicknamed him 'cowboy' just to tease him about his strong, Texas accent, but he'd never mentioned anything about horses. I reminded myself I didn't know him very well. Who knew what he'd come up with?

So when Sunday morning came around, I dressed in shorts and a t-shirt and stuffed a long-sleeved shirt and a pair of jeans into a backpack. I wondered about bringing some food and drink, but thought I might hurt his feelings if it looked like I couldn't trust him to do the planning for all of that.

Mom was going to a fundraiser meeting after church today. She'd left early as usual, saying she'd be home sometime in the evening. I didn't mention that I had a date with her handyman. I couldn't face another morning of Jordan-related breakfast drama. But if it became a regular thing with him, I'd have to tell her something. Maybe she'd be okay with it. After all, she'd stuck up for him with his parents.

I wasn't going to put money on it though.

I'd just finished my second mug of coffee for breakfast when I heard his truck crunch into the driveway. I felt as giddy as a 13-year-old on her first date, but without the glitter eye shadow.

I was clambering into his truck before he'd even had a chance to turn off the engine.

"Hi," I said, leaning in for a kiss.

A huge grin stretched across his face.

"Hi," he said, cupping my neck with his hand and kissing me back.

His lips pressed against mine, softly at first, then more firmly.

I was very tempted to sit there making out for the rest of the morning, but he pulled back, his eyes glowing.

"Hi," he said, again.

"We already did that bit," I snickered.

"Reckon we did. I kinda lose track around you."

He linked his fingers through mine and placed my hand on his knee, before winking at me and putting his truck in drive.

"So, where are we going on this magical mystery tour?"

"Hush now," he said. "I'm thinkin'."

"About what?"

"Where to take you."

"You haven't freakin' worked out where you're taking me, you ass!" I snapped, snatching my hand back.

He smiled, apparently pleased with himself.

"Throttle back, firecracker, I'm just joshin' wit ya."

He reached for my hand again, and rather reluctantly I let him take it.

"I *have* got somethin' planned, but I'm kinda worried you'll think it's lame."

"That's entirely possible," I said, waspishly.

His bright smile fell a little, and I felt like a complete bitch.

"Jordan, whatever it is, I'm sure it's fine."

He was silent for a moment.

"If I could, I'd take you somewhere real upscale. There'd be a starched white cloth on the table, napkins folded into fancy shapes, and candles all around us. I'd order champagne and the best food on the menu. We'd eat and laugh and talk, and I'd take you dancin' till dawn. Then I'd lay you down on soft sheets and love you till the sun was high in the sky."

My mouth dropped open.

"Jordan … that's … that's…"

"But I cain't," he said, flatly. "I'm an ex-con on parole who hasn't got two nickels to rub together, a pot to piss in or a window to throw it out of. I cain't even take you somewhere you can have a beer, or leave the fuckin' town without gettin' arrested and my ass thrown back in prison."

His expression was bitter.

"Jordan, don't," I said quietly but insistently, kicking myself that I'd started this grim downward spiral. "I couldn't care less where we go. Just sitting on my mom's back porch drinking coffee with you has been the highlight of each day since I landed in this town."

He threw me a skeptical look.

"It's true. And besides, I'm not the kind of girl who needs swanky restaurants and fancy food. I like *you*."

He shook his head. "I don't know why."

I rolled my eyes. "Because you've got a fuck-hot body and a dick that touches parts no dick has ever touched. Give me a break on the pity party!"

A reluctant smile crossed his face and he chuckled quietly.

"You got a dirty mouth, Miss Delaney."

"Why, yes I do, Mr. Kane. You got a problem with that?"

He grinned and squeezed my fingers. "No, ma'am. Not at all."

I turned on the radio and we drove along listening to Linkin Park's 'Breaking the Habit' which seemed oddly apt.

"Mikey always liked this song," he said, his voice aching, lost in the past again.

"Tell me something else about him—something nobody else knows."

Jordan looked thoughtful, and then he suddenly smiled.

"He got his cherry popped when he was 13—on a church picnic."

I laughed out loud. "You're kidding me!"

"I swear it's true! Miss Morgan the Sunday School teacher thought he'd been drinkin' spiked punch because he couldn't stop his grin. But when we got home he told me what had happened. A mother of one of the other kids from another church. She was like thirty!"

"Are you sure he wasn't playing you?"

"Nope. He had lipstick on the inside of his t-shirt and

hickeys all over him."

"That's awesome! What a great story! And nobody ever found out?"

Jordan shook his head, still grinning.

"And there was this one time he got so high, he swore he could fly. I was pretty wasted, too, so I told him to prove it. Mikey, he climbed to the top of this ole oak tree just outside the school yard, fell out of it and broke his arm. He was so stoned, it didn't even hurt 'til the next day. We told everyone that I'd tossed a Frisbee up there and he was just gettin' it down."

I laughed as he told me story after story of the scrapes he and Mikey had gotten into. But after a while, I started to feel uneasy as a distinctive pattern emerged. I paid close attention—this didn't sound like the Saint Michael that Mom had told me about, or the guy that everyone seemed to have looked up to.

"What about his girlfriend?"

Jordan laughed. "Which one? He was a bigger player than I was! Hell, he taught me all the moves. Um, okay that sounded weird. I just meant he wasn't the kind of guy who wanted to get tied down any time soon."

That was really odd. I *definitely* remembered Mom telling me that Mikey had a steady girlfriend that he was planning on marrying. Someone had fed my mom a load of bull.

Listening to Jordan's stories, it became clear that each time it was Mikey that led them into some sort of trouble, but Jordan who'd taken the blame, while his big brother came out of it smelling of roses.

I was still pondering what it meant when Jordan announced that we'd arrived.

For the last five minutes, we'd been bumping along a dirt road, and now we'd stopped at the edge of a pretty part of the bay.

Maybe his plan was to recreate our picnic. I wouldn't have minded, although I was a little disappointed he hadn't thought of something more original.

I clambered out of the truck while he reached for something in back.

He looked nervous as he approached me. I realized he was holding a pair of fishing poles.

"Fishing? We're going fishing?"

I was nonplussed. I'd never been fishing in my life, and I wasn't entirely sure I wanted to start now.

"We don't have to," he said, his expression wary. "I just thought maybe we could catch ourselves some sea trout and cook them over a fire." He looked so earnest I didn't have the heart to tell him that the thought of fish-guts made me want to hurl. "And, um, I've brought a couple of potatoes. We could put them under a fire while we're fishin' then dig them out when they're cooked."

"Sounds fun," I said, mustering as much fake enthusiasm as could reasonably be expected.

"We can do somethin' else…" he began, worry creasing his forehead.

"Hell, no! Fishing! Lead me to it, but I'm telling you, gutting these poor suckers is *your* job, and if I don't catch anything, I'll get grumpy if you don't feed me."

"I consider myself warned," he said, relaxing instantly and throwing me a huge smile.

I sat on the same blanket, the one he'd borrowed from my car before, watching while he dug a small pit in the sand and placed the potatoes wrapped in tin foil at the bottom. Then he built a fire over the top from pieces of twig and driftwood.

"A couple of hours, give or take, and we'll have ourselves some baked potatoes," he said, happily. "Mikey and me used to come out here and do this, drink some beer, smoke some weed. It was kind of our place." He raised his eyebrows at me. "No chicks allowed."

"So right now you're breaking some sort of guy-code."

He shrugged and looked down, but didn't answer.

It seemed as if with every other sentence I was trampling over sensitive subjects, but it was preferable to walking around on eggshells all the time. Besides, he'd said he liked that I was the only one who asked him real questions. Guess I should just go on doing what I was doing.

I picked up the thermos of coffee and two mugs, while Jordan carried the fishing stuff. He led me to an old log at the side of the saltwater lake, and set up the pole for me with some icky looking bait and a bobber thingy so I'd know when a fish had gotten interested. Then we sat side by side, watching the water lap at the sand beneath our feet.

I emptied the thermos between the two mugs and passed one to Jordan.

"It's peaceful here," I said.

"Yup."

We sat for several more minutes in silence, drinking our coffee, before I felt his eyes on me.

"What?"

"I was just wonderin'," he said. "You didn't leave some guy back in Boston? When you were workin' there?"

"Yes, no. I mean … there *was* a guy." *Uh-oh, time to tell the truth. I hope he isn't going to think I was a giant slut, or an idiot, both of which would be kind of true.* "Well, I had this thing with a guy at work…"

He studied me thoughtfully but didn't speak.

"He was my boss. And engaged—to someone else. And, uh, when he broke it off with me … well, it wasn't so great. Truth is, he treated me like shit after … so I quit my job and came here."

He cleared his throat several times, and I waited for him to work himself up to his next question. I wasn't sure I wanted to hear it but fair was fair: he'd answered my questions.

"You, um, you still care about him?" he asked quietly, not meeting my eyes.

I laughed bitterly.

"Hell, no! Guy was an asshole. I'm just so mad at myself that I didn't see it before. Anyway, let's just say I got him out of my system."

Jordan looked relieved at the first part of my answer, but then his anxious look was back.

"You mean you … dated … a lot?"

I threw him a look to say that I knew *exactly* where this conversation was going.

"It depends on your definition of 'dated' and 'a lot'. I dated one guy when I was a freshman in college—Jem—for about seven months. Then he dumped me. Well, I assumed that's what it meant when I found him in bed with my roommate. Seems it had been going on a while and I was the last to know."

Jordan winced.

"Want me to find him and make him apologize? Him and your roommate?" Jordan asked.

It sounded like he was serious.

"Ha, thanks, but no. Besides, if there's any violence to be

done, I'd rather do it myself."

"He hurt you bad, didn't he?"

I looked across at him, seeing only sympathy and sadness in his beautiful eyes.

"Yes, you could definitely say that. I find … found … I find it hard to trust people—men. But not just men. My roommate—that betrayal was almost worse. So … after that … I decided: nothing serious. I was just going to have fun. And I pretty much stuck to that for the rest of college and when I started working, too. But then I met Craig, and it kind of backfired on me."

"The asshole you worked for?"

"Yes. But it was my own fault. I mean I knew he was engaged but I didn't care. I just figured it was up to her to look out for herself. I know that sounds pretty bad, but that was how I felt. It was exciting. He took me to expensive restaurants and fancy clubs…"

I saw Jordan look down.

"But it wasn't supposed to mean anything. And it didn't—to either of us. But when he got tired of me, well, he was a complete bastard. He made it intolerable at work, giving me the shittiest jobs, yelling at me in front of the other paralegals. Well, you can imagine. I wasn't going to put up with that shit, and everyone knew about us, so if I'd tried to sue him for harassment, I wouldn't have had a hope in hell of winning a case. I thought about telling his fiancée, letting her know what a prize asshole he was, but in the end, well, I'd just had enough. So I left."

"And came here?"

"Yeah, well, after that disaster I thought I'd give up on dating for a while. Instead, I just looked for hook ups, nothing too serious. And no, before you ask, I don't consider you a hook up."

He nodded slowly.

"What, um, what do you consider … us?"

Ooh, so hoping he wasn't going to ask that question.

"Honestly?" I sighed. "I don't know. I mean, strictly speaking, this is our first date, and like I said, I don't do dates in general. So I suppose it's progress. Does that answer your question?"

He didn't reply to that but answered my question with one of his own.

"That woman on Friday night at the coffee shop, Bev, she asked you if I was your boyfriend. You said you were thinkin' about it."

"That's right."

"Well, did you think about it anymore?"

"You have to know something about me, Jordan. I'm not great with the whole 'boyfriend' thing. That's probably why I get treated like shit all the time. All I can tell you is that I enjoy spending time with you, but I'm not planning to be here in town forever. When I've got some money together, I'll be gone. And if you're as smart as I think you are, you'll do the same."

He sighed and ran one hand through his hair, pushing a stray curl out of his eyes.

"I would never treat you like those other guys, Torrey, I promise. But yeah, okay, I get it."

I knew he was disappointed by my answer, but I was trying to be as honest as possible. The expression on his face told me it wasn't what he'd wanted to hear.

I tried to think of something to say to distract him.

"So, tell me about the tats," I said, running a finger along a design of barbed wire that trailed from under the sleeve of his t-shirt, down to his elbow. "They offer classes on them in prison, or what?"

He gave me a look that said he knew what I was doing, followed by a wry smile.

"Not exactly. It's illegal, for a start. You get caught, and they add 180 days to your sentence for each infraction. I guess that wouldn't make much difference when I was facing an attempted murder charge, but they sure kept it on my record when I was sent from juvie to prison." He shook his head. "One of the things they kept on my record," he repeated, quietly.

His expression darkened, and I could sense a further dive in his mood.

"So, you were a bit of a rule breaker even in juvie?" I asked, hoping to lighten the suddenly dark atmosphere.

He twitched a shoulder.

"Guess so. I did this one myself."

He held out his left arm and I saw again the word 'love'

tattooed on the back of his wrist. I remembered seeing it the first day I met him.

"Seems like an odd sort of word to have gotten while you were in prison," I said, nudging his shoulder. "Unless you're telling me you were in love with a 300 pound biker called Graham."

He tried to smile. "No, no bikers. I did this one for my brother. I loved Mikey. I mean, he was my big brother, but you don't love people just because they're your family."

I felt certain he was thinking of his parents at that moment.

"Mikey was the world to me—best guy you'd ever meet. Everyone loved Mikey."

He sighed, and I watched the dark descend again.

"He was easy to love. Not like me. So the tattoo was to remind me that no matter how angry I was at myself, at everyone, that Mikey was always full of love. I don't know— somethin' like that. My head was kind of fucked at the time. Still is," he whispered.

"The first time I saw that tat, I thought you probably had 'hate' tattooed on your other wrist or behind your knee or something. You know, like that scary preacher in *Night of the Hunter.*"

I could see him making the effort to lift his mood to match the one I was trying to create for us.

"Hey! I remember that movie," he nodded. "Yeah, that was freakin' scary when I was a kid—Robert Mitchum gave me nightmares." He threw me a teasing look. "Hey, you think your momma has tats in interestin' places?"

I slapped his arm hard.

"You *cannot* be thinking about my mom in the nude when I had your dick inside me just a few nights ago!" I half shouted.

I saw his cheeks flush immediately.

"Hell, no!" he snorted. "I never ... I mean I didn't think ... no!"

I couldn't help laughing at the look of horror on his face.

"Teasing! Boy, you're so easy."

He growled at me and pinned my wrists together with one hand, sending our coffee mugs tumbling onto the sand.

"You'll pay for that, woman!"

And then he started tickling me until tears were pouring from my eyes, and I was begging for him to stop. But he was relentless; it was only a lucky kick to his nuts that got him off.

"Oh, God, you've finished me," he groaned, holding his sack with both hands, his thighs pressed together defensively.

"You deserved that!" I coughed out, wiping the tears from my eyes.

He might have had some tears of his own at that point. Served him right.

Eventually, we calmed down enough to sit peacefully again.

He stared disconsolately at his empty coffee cup, but I was too comfortable to move. He'd have to wait for a refill.

"You were telling me about the tats?"

"I wasn't good at much in school," he admitted, at last. "But I was good at drawin' and pictures. There was this kid in juvie whose older brother was a tattoo artist and he knew some stuff. So I did the sketches and he taught me how to do the ink. It was pretty risky…"

"Why?"

"Well, like I said, it's illegal, but the other thing is, you cain't exactly order the equipment in, so we had to make it. First of all, Styx just used a sewin' needle and a magic marker pen. It wasn't exactly sterile and there was a lot of Hep C goin' around. Then he started usin' old guitar strings, lead from pencils and sometimes ash from burned paper."

"You're kidding me! You put that stuff into your *skin*?"

"Well, yeah. There's a lot of empty time when you're inside. Gotta find somethin' to do. When I got to prison, one of the guards could be bribed and he brought in colored ink. But I gave it up after a while."

"Why?"

"I didn't want to stay in for the rest of my life. I'd already had time added to my sentence, and 180 days for the first time I got caught tattooing another prisoner. Even then, I knew there was more to life—more I wanted from it."

"Tell me what they all mean," I said. "I mean, the barbed wire is kind of obvious. What's this one?" I pointed to a teardrop, weeping from one of the wire points.

"An unfilled teardrop is the death of a friend."

"Oh. And this one?"

"That's a swallow."

"It's beautiful."

"Thanks."

"What does it mean?"

He sighed. "Swallows don't fly far from land into the ocean, so when sailors saw them, it meant that land was nearby. It's a symbol of hope."

"I like that," I murmured. "And the dolphin?"

"Duality: a creature that lives in the water, but needs air to survive. I don't know—I just liked it."

"I think I can guess this one, but what does the spider's web mean?"

He smiled sadly. "Being caught in prison."

I started to say more, but then I felt a tug on my line and the bobber dipped down into the water.

"Ooh! I think I got one! What do I do?"

"Reel it in slowly, don't jerk it."

I panicked and pushed the pole into his hands. "You do it! I don't want to lose it."

I watched, enrapt, as he played the fish—reeling it in, letting it out, and reeling it in again, his arm muscles and shoulders showcasing his amazing physique. Who'd have thought fishing was so hot.

A minute later, he'd landed an ugly old fish the length of my arm, whose eyes gazed at me pitifully, while its mouth gaped.

I was mesmerized and appalled at the same time, watching it thrash out its last few minutes of life.

Jordan saw the look of horror on my face.

"Go wait by the truck, Torrey," he said. "I'll be there in a minute."

I was happy to leave him to it. I knew it was hypocritical, but I preferred my food a little less *lively*.

I mooched back to our blanket and threw myself down. I seemed to be spoiling everything today. At least the fire was still smoldering. I threw on some more of the dried wood that Jordan had found and built it up again. Even though it was a warm day, the flames were comforting.

He came back a few minutes later, with the poor fish impaled on a stick. I was relieved he'd already done the nasty bits and in deference to my squeamishness, he'd also removed the head. Thank God! I couldn't have stood having it looking at me as it slowly cooked. I'd be waiting for it to blink.

"You okay?" he asked, concerned.

"I'm fine. Sorry to be such a wimp. I've always been more of a city girl. Dad never did stuff like sleeping in tents or hiking with me. And I hated the idea of summer camp so much I made him promise never to send me. But as long as I have someone to gut my fish, it's all good."

He gave me a look like he wasn't sure he believed me, but didn't argue the point. I watched, feeling like Jane in the jungle as he arranged the fish over the fire, making a crossbeam with two longer sticks. When he finished, he stretched out on the blanket next to me and closed his eyes.

I took a moment to appreciate the view. His long legs were clad in jeans today, not the baggy shorts I'd gotten used to. His gray t-shirt stretched over his muscular chest, which at that moment was pulled up slightly, showing a strip of taut stomach with a sprinkling of light brown hairs pointing below his waistband.

His arms were thrown above his head, and I could see the beauty and simplicity of the tattoos twisting around his biceps. Long lashes fanned out over his cheeks, and his lips were slightly open, making me want to lick between them. The small frown between his eyebrows was less pronounced than usual. I leaned down to rub my finger gently over the faint lines, hoping to erase them.

He jumped slightly, and his eyes blinked open.

"Sorry I startled you. Again."

He smiled and ran a warm hand down my side. "I like it when you touch me."

"Yeah," I breathed, "works for me, too."

I was just about to lean further in to kiss those lips when he sat up suddenly.

"Shit! The fish!"

He was right: the poor creature was looking a little black

around the edges. He turned it quickly, so the other side could cook, then gave me a flirty smile.

"You are very distractin', Miss Delaney."

"Are you blaming me? You were the one lying on the blanket looking all delicious and sinful!"

He laughed out loud. "Delicious and *sinful?*"

"And you know it," I huffed out. "I practically had to stop Bev mounting you in the coffee shop when she met you."

His gaze turned hungry, his dark eyes boring into me.

"There's only one woman I'm interested in, and she's sittin' right next to me."

I gave a delighted laugh even while sweat broke out all over my body, my skin heated by the fire in his eyes.

"That's good to hear. Well, how about you feed me, and we'll see about some sin for dessert?"

He closed his eyes and groaned. "The things you say, woman!"

He shook his head as if to clear it then stood up. "I'll be right back."

He jogged over to the truck and returned carrying a couple of plates, knives and forks, and a carton of something that he wedged under a rock by the water's edge, presumably to keep it chilled. I wasn't sure how well that would work, as the water was being warmed by the late summer sun.

I watched him carefully cut the fish in half, then kick sand on the fire to put it out. He used one of the long sticks to dig out our potatoes, juggled them in his hands while he pulled off the tin foil, and set the food out on plates.

"Lunch is served, ma'am."

"Smells wonderful! You've got some sharp cooking skills there, cowboy!"

"Don't forget I'm sinful, too," he said, running his lips across my cheek.

A shiver ran through me, and it definitely wasn't from cold.

He handed me one of the paper plates and the smell of the hot food wafted up, utterly enticing. Despite my misgivings, the fish was amazing and completely distracted me from thinking about it thrashing around in the water just half an hour earlier. The baked potato was good, too, although I missed being able to slather it in butter.

"This is really great, Jordan," I mumbled greedily, through a mouthful of food.

He smiled happily. "Good!"

We ate in silence as I carefully avoided swallowing any fish bones. It would be too bad if that old trout had the last laugh, and I choked to death on one of the bones. I was pretty sure Jordan would give me mouth-to-mouth, but I had other ways of testing that theory.

Finally, I pushed my plate away and rubbed my full stomach. "Fabulous."

"It's not finished yet, sweetheart."

"There's more?"

He winked at me and headed to his truck again, reappearing seconds later with a packet of chocolate chip cookies. Perfect. Then he retrieved the carton from the lake.

I laughed out loud. "Jordan Kane, you are too smooth for your own good! You brought me milk and cookies?"

He shrugged, looking a little embarrassed. "I didn't know what you liked, but I figured girls like chocolate, right?"

"I'm sure there are some women in the world who don't like chocolate, but I've never met any of them. Thank God. I think this makes you officially perfect," I said, pulling open the packet and popping a piece of sweet, sugary goodness in my mouth.

I moaned around the chocolatey crumbs as my eyes rolled back in my head.

Jordan sat down next to me, looking uncomfortable.

"What?" I said, eyeing him with amusement.

"It's nothin'."

"Spit it out, whatever it is."

Then I noticed that he had a rather prominent erection beneath his jeans.

"Oh my God! Watching me eating cookies is turning you on? You're such a pervert!"

"I cain't help it," he complained. "You're there a-moanin' and a-groanin' and lickin' your lips. It just does things to a man!"

I threw a cookie at him. "Eat this. It'll take your mind off of that monster in your pants."

"I doubt it," he said darkly, but ate the cookie anyway.

I opened the carton of milk and chugged some of it, wiping my mouth with my arm. I stared at him and licked my lips slowly.

He growled and pulled the carton out of my hands, slopping

at least a quarter of it onto the sand.

He pressed me into the blanket and planted hot, open mouthed kisses across my chest and throat.

"Damn, woman! I cain't get enough of you."

I wanted to tell him that I felt the same, but instead, I tugged his t-shirt up his back and dragged my nails down his skin. He hissed and writhed above me, pressing his hard cock into my belly.

He grabbed his t-shirt from the back of his neck and yanked it over his head, giving me acres of smooth flesh to drool over.

My shorts went one way and his jeans another. Neither of us had underwear so it only took seconds before we were naked under the sky.

He was more patient this time, learning how my body responded to his touch, and the look of triumph on his face when I came on his fingers would have made me laugh if I wasn't panting and breathless.

"Condom!" I gasped, aching to feel him inside me. "In my shorts!"

"Shit!" he cursed. "Where the hell did you toss them?"

I was treated to the sight of his tight ass as he ran across the sand to retrieve my shorts from a nearby bush. On the way back, I could see his erect dick bobbing up and down expectantly.

"Goddamn! Remind me not to do a streak with a boner again—freakin' hurts!"

I couldn't help laughing.

"Hey, you're killin' the mood!" he said, laughing with me.

"I'll take your mind off it," I grinned, snaking my hand up his thigh.

His breath caught in his throat as he kneeled down beside me. I sat up and straddled him, then ran my tongue up his neck and bit his full lips.

"Goddamn," he breathed out.

I slid back a short distance so we had room to maneuver, then I took the condom from his nerveless fingers and rolled it on.

His whole body shuddered and he drew in a deep breath that made his nostrils flare.

"You have no idea how it feels to have your hands on me, sweetheart," he whispered. "Every touch of yours is pure gold."

My God! How did this man who had endured eight long

years of brutalizing treatment hold such love in his heart? It stunned my soul. I attacked his lips and felt the rising heat of raw passion pour from him.

I pulled myself back onto his lap and let out a long wail of pleasure as I impaled myself on him.

His breathing was fast and erratic as he tugged me forward so my chest was flush against his, then he bucked into me repeatedly.

"Torrey!" he gasped. "Goddamn, Torrey!"

I could feel him swell inside me, and he moaned louder.

Suddenly he tipped me over and my back crashed onto the blanket. Then he pulled my ankles over his shoulders so I was almost bent in half. His eyes were closed and his biceps bunched as he pumped hard. I cried out and his eyelids flew open, the intensity of his gaze thrilling me. His back arched and he shuddered as his body pulsed into mine, almost an entity of its own; a life force passing between us.

He cried out and collapsed onto me, his crushing weight forcing out the small amount of breath I had left from my lungs.

Then he rolled onto his back, tugging me with him so I was splayed across his broad chest.

It took several minutes before either of us was capable of speaking.

His dick slipped out of me, but I still couldn't move.

"You okay?" he whispered, his hands stroking up and down my spine.

"Mm-mm."

"Is that a 'mm-mm, yes' or a 'mm-mm, no'?" he asked, a smile in his voice.

"That's a 'mm-mm, shut the fuck up'," I yawned.

He laughed quietly and sat up slowly, letting me slide from his chest and onto the blanket.

I couldn't open my eyes but heard the telltale snap as he pulled off the used condom, tying a knot in the end.

He lay back down and looped his long body around mine, snuggling against me, and peppering tiny kisses over my shoulder.

I stretched out my well-exercised muscles, impressed that his vigorous love-making hadn't snapped me in two.

He wrapped his arm around my waist and pulled me in even tighter.

"Every time," he breathed into my hair, "every time I think it couldn't be better than the last time, but every time it is. You. Are. So. Special."

He paused, as if waiting for me to reply, but I was too comfortable, too replete, too entirely exhausted to speak.

He sounded hesitant when he spoke again.

"Christ, Torrey, I hate soundin' like a fuckin' juvenile, but ya gotta tell me, sweetheart, how was it for you?"

I almost snapped back some sarcastic answer, but his words exposed his vulnerability. I didn't want to hurt him that way, knowing that a word from me was all he needed.

"Well," I said, rubbing my finger in a small circle over the back of his hand, "every time I think it couldn't be better than the last time, but every time it is. Every time I think I've had the best there is, you teach my body something new. I can't get enough of you, Jordan Kane."

The breath rushed from his lungs, and I felt him tremble. He clutched me to him with painful pressure, as his body shook behind me.

I lay in his arms, my back against his chest, stroking his hands and wrists, twining my legs with his, letting him lose his tears in my hair.

After several minutes, he stilled, and I felt his body stiffen with embarrassment at his loss of control.

I twisted in his arms so I was facing him and kissed the tears from his long lashes.

"It's okay, Jordan. You're safe with me."

He took a shuddering breath. "I love you, Torrey Delaney. You don't have to say it back to me, but I love you. I didn't believe life was worth living 'til I met you. I'm so, so happy I was wrong."

Any chance of a reply dried in my throat. His arms tightened around me and I waited for the moment when I freaked, afraid of what he'd said, afraid of the intensity of his emotions.

But the panic didn't come. Instead I leaned into his strong, solid body and held him just as tightly.

Chapter 9 – Grieving

Jordan

This woman.

What she did to me. I felt as if I'd been in a dark cave for years and she was the sun exploding around me. She'd stripped away every layer of skin and poured her kindness and compassion into my body, healing me from the inside out.

I watched her lying beside me at the fishing hole, her hair tumbling across the blanket, her golden skin glowing in the sunshine, trusting me with her thoughts, and memories, and feelings—and with her body.

It scared the shit out of me to feel so much.

I'd spent eight years keeping every emotion frozen and numb, trusting no one.

In prison you're caged alongside other people like you, close but not touching and untouchable, until all the anger and rage and frustration explode in violence. Every second you have to watch your back, and if you show any weakness, you're fucked.

Sometimes literally.

Parole had come as a shock. I'd been turned down so many times, year after long year, that I'd pretty much given up any hope that I'd ever be released. I sat in that chair in my white pullover shirt, my hands cuffed, watching the indifferent faces of the review board in front of me.

My past misdemeanors were listed: fighting, wounding another prisoner, prohibited tattooing, poor attitude, disrespecting the guards. But then, apparently, I'd shown 'progression in my rehabilitation'. That was news to me, but I'd take anything I could get.

I was surprised—stunned into incomprehensibility—when I learned that my parents were going to take me back as part of my parole package plan. I hadn't expected that. In fact I'd been certain that I'd never see or hear from them again.

The day I was released was a rollercoaster ride of emotions.

I was excited, I was nervous—fucking terrified if I'm being honest. I knew how to be a good convict, but I didn't know anymore how to live *out there*. I had to find a new way of relating to ordinary people, learn to read a different set of signals. I couldn't take the prison mindset into the real world. I had no fucking clue how to behave.

Seeing my parents was the biggest mind fuck ever. For years, I'd believed that they'd washed their hands of me. There'd been no letters or cards, no phone calls, no communication whatsoever. I might as well have been dead to them.

So to find that they were willing to take me home: it raised all sorts of hope inside me. And I had questions … a lot of questions. They all started with 'why?'

I was up early on release day, mostly because I hadn't slept. I was given some crappy clothes to wear and escorted from my cell. I had a couple of paperbacks in a box and some of the sketches I'd done for tattoos, and that was it. That was my entire life for the last eight years.

The corrections officer took me into a room where a man and a woman were sitting—my parents. It was a shock. They looked older, of course, but I hadn't been expecting it. In my mind, they were frozen in time, the way I'd last seen them, at my trial, in tears.

I could see them scanning my face, searching for something they could recognize of the boy they'd known in the man before them. Dad's eyes followed the lines of tattoos on my arms, and he frowned. I could see him trying to work it out—how had I gotten them in prison?

When my eyes met Momma's, she looked away.

They didn't try to touch me. No hugs, no handshakes, no words for their son.

I was pointed toward a chair by the corrections officer, and we sat looking at each other—strangers thrown together by the sick fuck that was fate.

The corrections officer handed me a copy of my release form, and explained again the rules of my parole.

Nobody else had spoken.

I was processed and released.

It was a bizarre feeling walking into the visitors' parking lot. I don't know what I'd expected, but it all seemed so unreal. I was looking for Dad's old pickup truck, but he pressed his key fob, and lights flashed on a Toyota.

"You got a new car, Dad?"

He looked shocked that I'd spoken and nodded in reply.

"Four years now," he said.

Those were the first words he'd spoken to me since saying that I was no longer his son all those years before.

Momma just stared at me.

No one spoke on the way home. I sat in the back seat, staring out of the window while roads and houses and trees flashed by me. As the scenery gradually became more familiar, the panicky feelings started to subside, and I was excited to see places I recognized. But all the time the stone in the pit of my stomach weighed heavier the nearer we got to the place I'd called home.

We bumped down the familiar dirt road and the

cottonwoods parted. They were taller than I remembered, more luxuriant, but the house looked smaller and kind of rundown. Dad had always been insistent on cleaning out the gutters and keeping the paintwork fresh. I remembered the times Mikey and I had bitched about having to climb up ladders to fix things. It looked like nothing had been fixed in a long while. Eight years, perhaps.

Inside, the house was the same but different. A new lampshade here; a new table in the kitchen there. The family room seemed the least changed, the sofa and curtains familiar. Only the TV had been updated.

"I've made your bed."

My head snapped up, stunned that Momma had spoken.

I scanned her face for something else, but she wasn't looking at me.

"Thanks," I said at last.

I headed upstairs, pausing outside Mikey's room. I took a deep breath and pushed the door open—and stared. Nothing, *and I mean nothing* had changed. His clothes were still hanging across the chair as if he might come back at any moment and throw them on. His posters and pictures were still tacked to the walls, and his yearbook was open at the page with the football team.

I closed my eyes as my stomach coiled and rolled. I backed out and headed for my own room.

That had definitely changed. Everything had been stripped out, all the posters gone, all my books and school stuff gone, the closet and drawers empty. It hit me then—they hadn't planned on me coming back. I wondered what had changed their minds. Why was I here?

I know now it was a way of punishing me more—as if I hadn't thought about Mikey every waking hour of every day since it had happened.

Beside me, Torrey stretched and yawned.

"Did I fall asleep?"

"Only for a few minutes—twenty, maybe."

"Did you sleep?"

"Too much snortin' and snorin'," I smiled.

"I do *not* snore!" she complained, roughly pushing my shoulder.

"If you say so, sweetheart."

"You're not being very smooth, Jordan Kane. I bet Mikey wouldn't have told a woman that she snored!"

I liked to hear her talking about Mikey like he was a real person, not someone whose name had to be whispered. She had a way of helping me remember the good stuff, not just the way he died.

"I wish you could have known Mikey. He was a great guy."

"Hmm, two Kane brothers," she said, with a gentle smile. "That sounds like double trouble to me."

"Hell, yeah! We got into a lot of shit, that's for sure."

"Sounds like he led the way most of the time."

I smiled to myself.

"Well, yeah. He was the oldest by 18 months. I wanted to be just like him."

She looked thoughtful for a moment.

"That's something that's been puzzling me, Jordan. When you talk about him, I picture this wild, bad boy—a version of you. But when everyone else mentions him, it's like he was halfway between a saint and an angel."

I knew what she meant, but that's only because people wanted to remember the good stuff.

"He was real, Torrey. But special. Blessed, you know? He just had a way of drawin' people to him. Like you."

She was quiet and I didn't know what she was thinking.

"Did you ever say goodbye to him?"

"What do you mean?"

"Well, you went straight from the hospital to juvie. Did you get a chance to visit Mikey's grave since you got out?"

Her words hit me with the force of a ten-ton truck.

"No, I … I don't even know where … where they put him."

"It's not hard to find out—if you wanted to go."

Do I? The words 'final resting place' seem so unreal.

I felt her fingers flutter down my chest, and she laid her hand over my heart.

"I'll come with you, if you want to go … if you want me to."

"I don't think I can. I don't deserve…"

She slapped my chest hard and my eyes snapped to hers. She looked genuinely angry, like a bad tempered bull in a horn tossing mood.

"For God's sake, Jordan! Love isn't a life sentence! But that's how you're using it, like a punishment. You loved your brother and it sounds like he loved you. Do you think for one second he'd want you to live your life rotting away like this? Blaming yourself for being the one who survived? Blaming yourself for living? Would you have wanted that for him if it had been the other way around? Don't you see? You have to live for *both* of you!"

She jumped to her feet and started scrambling around for her clothes. My heart pounded and I felt sick.

"Are you leavin'?"

"*We're* leaving. We're going to find Mikey's grave. Right now!" Her expression softened. "So you might want to put your pants on for that."

Was I ready for this? Probably not. I didn't think I ever would be. But she was right … I needed to do this.

I dressed fast, while Torrey picked up our trash and paper plates.

"I don't even know how to go about findin' how… where … where the right place is at," I admitted, cringing at the thought.

Torrey squinted at me. "Um, I kinda already know."

I turned around to stare at her. She looked slightly nervous, but stuck out her chin defiantly.

"You do?"

"Well, yeah. Do you mind?"

I blew out a long breath. "No, I don't mind. I'm just…" I ran my hands through my hair. "It's a lot to take in."

She nodded, looking wary, as if I was about fixing to bolt—

or she was.

The thought of running had definitely crossed my mind. Stupidly, I'd even considered disappearing while I was still on parole. And the first week with my parents had been so bad, I'd seriously considered doing something to get myself sent back to prison. I guess some sense must have kicked in, because I'd stuck it out.

Part of me wanted to visit Mikey's grave, to see if I could do this, but part of me was still that 16-year-old kid, lost and hurting, the kid who just wanted his big brother.

We packed up the truck in silence. It didn't take long and Torrey didn't call me out for going slower than I needed to. Finally, we were done and I'd run out of excuses.

"So, um, where are we headin'?"

"South Trinity Street," she said calmly, measuring my reactions.

I took a deep breath and started the truck's engine. The sound reassured me, but as I drove through the town and along familiar streets, I felt sweat break out all over my body. My heart rate escalated until I was afraid I'd pass out.

I was almost hyperventilating by the time she said quietly, "We're here."

I climbed out of the truck, feeling numb, my hands shaking, the palms clammy. I thought I was going to be sick.

I walked to the entrance in a daze, and stared out across the neat turf and narrow, well kept paths.

"Fuck, I could use a drink," I admitted.

Torrey clasped my hand between both of hers. "I'm all out of booze, but I've got a hard candy you can have. That any good?"

I gave a shaky laugh. "Maybe later."

"It's this way," she said, tugging gently on my hand.

We walked past rows of ornate headstones, some of which had wilting bouquets in vases next to them.

"Was I supposed to bring flowers? I feel like I should have."

"Just yourself," she said, soothingly.

Then I saw his name and cold reality washed over me. It was real—this was real. My brother, who'd been so full of life, so full of love—this was his grave. This was his end. Because of me. The future spun out in front of me and I was alone, my brother no longer at my side.

I touched the cool stone with my hand, needing to feel it, to make that connection. I closed my eyes, trying to sense something—his presence—anything. But there was nothing, just the polished marble under my fingers.

Then I opened my eyes and it was as if someone had punched me in the gut when I read the full inscription.

> *Michael Gabriel Kane*
> *November 25, 1987—July 10, 2006*
> *Beloved Son*

> *"Do not fear those who kill the body but cannot kill the soul."*

I heard a weird, strangled sound, but it was only when Torrey wrapped her arms around my waist that I realized it had come from me.

"'Beloved Son!' Christ, they couldn't even … they didn't want … he was my brother, Torrey! My brother! It's like I never even existed. God, Mikey! I'm so, so sorry! It should have been me! I'd do anythin' to take it back!"

I fell to my knees, my head spinning, bile rising in my throat.

"It should have been me."

Torrey was on her knees next to me, the strength of her small body the only thing that kept me from falling further.

"No!" she gasped. "Don't say that! I'm glad you're alive. I'm glad you survived." I felt her fingers in my hair and her breath was warm against my neck. "You have to find the strength to be glad, too—for the rest of your life."

She tightened her grip and slowly the ground stopped shifting beneath me. I leaned against her, breathing in the scent of summer in her hair.

After a few minutes, I felt her grip relax.

"My knees are killing me, Jordan. Can we please sit down?"

Some of the tension left my body as we both collapsed onto the grass. Torrey snuggled into my side. She leaned her head on my chest and stroked my arms, as if calming a frightened child.

Her touch soothed me, and I felt an odd sense of peace, sitting there among the tombstones.

"I was wondering…" she said, after a few minutes.

"What's that, sweetheart?"

"What would you tell Mikey about me?"

I raised my eyebrows and shifted so I could look at her, but she wouldn't meet my eyes.

"You know," she went on, "guy to guy, brother to brother."

"Hmm, you want me to break the bro code?" I teased her.

"Pretend I'm not here."

I almost laughed. "That would be a fuckin' impossibility."

"Aw, go on!"

I took a deep breath and tucked her into my side again, taking strength from her slender arms around my neck.

"Hey, Mikey! It's been a while. I guess you know why I haven't been by. So, you see my girl, Torrey? She's somethin', ain't she? God, she's so fine. She's got the sweetest face, and this mess of long, curly hair the color of corn just before harvest, and it near about kills me to wind it around my fingers, it's so soft. She's a real firecracker, too. And she's one of those people that lights up the room when she walks into it, ya know? She's so full of livin', so full of laughter. And fuck, she's honest. I don't get away with shit when I'm with her. In the bedroom? Hell, yeah! She's so fuckin' hot! I cain't get enough of her. I know, I know—totally pussy whipped. But I gotta tell ya, bro, she's so worth it. When she looks at me I can see my future in her eyes— us livin' our lives together, gettin' old together, kids—the whole thing. She don't know it yet, but she's not gettin' away from me. Do I love her? It's more than that, bro. She's my reason for livin'."

I stopped talking and risked a sideways glance at Torrey. She looked stunned, her mouth hanging open. I waited nervously for her to speak. She'd asked me to say the kind of things I would have told Mikey, so that's what I'd done. I was terrified it was going to backfire on me.

Say something! I was screaming inside my head.

She cleared her throat nervously. "Uh, Jordan, that's … I mean, wow! I didn't realize … phew!"

"Too much?" I asked, afraid of her reply.

"Um, just a little overwhelming."

I shrugged. "That's how I feel. I know you're not there yet…"

She didn't answer, and a small stab of fresh pain entered my heart like a splinter.

I stood up and pulled her to her feet.

"Come on, let's get out of here. We've got a date to finish."

She nodded wordlessly and worried her bottom lip with her teeth. The longer she went without saying anything, the more nervous I became.

"Jordan, I really care about you…"

I waited in silence as ice formed in my heart.

"But I don't … I'm not…"

"It's okay, Torrey," I sighed, "I know you don't feel the same. I wouldn't expect you to. Why would you? You're beautiful and sweet and kind and so fuckin' feisty and good. You've got your whole life ahead of you. You don't need me draggin' you down." Just saying it tasted like dust and despair.

She turned angry eyes on me. "Stop putting words in my mouth, Jordan! That's not what I said and not what I was going to say. It's just a lot to get my head around. I mean, everything is in front of you now. In a few months you'll have all the choices you could want. I just happened to be the first woman you ran into. You're a great guy, and you'll be beating girls off with a stick once you get your groove back and…"

That's what she thinks? Really?

"No, you're so wrong, Torrey. It's way more than that, and I'm gettin' mighty pissed hearin' you talk this way. You think I don't know my own mind, what I want? Hell, I've had eight years of wishin' and dreamin' but I never thought I could meet someone like you. It's not just that you accept me for who I am. You make me want to be more than I thought I could ever be. And the way we connect—I've never felt anythin' like that. Look me in the eyes and tell me you don't feel it, too. Tell me!"

I was almost shouting at her by now, and I could see by the stubborn angle of her chin that I was making her mad. Well, good! This shit was important! I *had* to make her see what she meant to me.

But she surprised me again when the expression of fury morphed into a huge grin.

"You know you're pretty hot when you get mad, Jordan. You should do it more often!"

I couldn't help laughing with relief.

"Woman, you blow my mind! Are you trying to seduce me in a cemetery?"

"Hmm, the thought had occurred, but I'm fairly sure there are laws against it."

"Yeah, probably," I agreed, still smiling. "Although Mikey would have got a kick out of the idea."

She winked at me and flicked her tongue against her teeth; a move that she knew would have me adjusting my pants.

"Come on, then. Let's get out of here. Do the rest of the date thing."

I turned to Mikey's grave one last time, resting my hand on the headstone.

"Bye, Mikey. Love you, man, wherever you are."

Torrey hugged me gently, and as we stood there in the afternoon sunshine, I felt a weight that I'd been carrying around for so long slip from my shoulders.

We walked back to my truck hand in hand and I felt a new sense of purpose and a new sense of peace.

Painful as it had been, I was glad that she'd forced me to come. I hadn't realized that it was something I needed to do.

"Okay, confession time," I said, as I drove away from the

cemetery. "I don't have anythin' else planned. But we could maybe catch a movie if we can sneak in through the fire door. Mikey and me used to do that all of the time. I'd take you for a coffee, but the only place that won't kick my ass into the street is where you work, and that just don't seem right for a date. Sorry, I'm kinda out of options, unless you want to hang out at the junkyard with Hulk."

Jesus, help me! Did I really just ask a smokin' hot woman like Torrey if she wanted to hang out at a junkyard? Smooth, Kane, real smooth.

"Tempting," she said, tapping her finger against her lip as she obviously tried not to laugh. "But I prefer my idea."

I glanced across at her and caught the wicked glint in her eye.

"Are you gonna share?"

"We go back to the Rectory and fuck on every flat surface we can find."

I nearly drove off the road.

"Damn, woman!" I said, my voice choked from the rush of adrenalin as I braked hard and the truck came to a shuddering stop.

I looked down at my hands gripping the steering wheel for dear life and was aware how close we'd come to having an accident.

We were half off the side of the road, and my mind was flashing back to the night Mikey had died, my body in panic mode.

"Shit," I whispered, unable to get the shaking under control.

"God, I'm so sorry," Torrey stuttered. "I'm such a freakin' idiot. Are you okay? Do you want me to drive?"

"Uh, no, that's fine. Just … just give me a minute."

I closed my eyes and forced my body to relax, breathing in and out slowly, as my racing heart fell back into its normal rhythm. I felt Torrey's warm hand on my thigh.

"Okay now?" she asked, guilt painting her voice.

I smiled at her—well, grimaced. "Yeah, I'm good. And now that I've managed to make a complete ass of myself, I'd really like to take you up on your offer—if it's still open."

"Oh, I'm still open," she laughed with relief.

Even though I was aching to take her up on that as soon as possible, I drove even more slowly to her house. If we'd been going any slower, the truck would have been in reverse.

I pulled up outside the Rectory, pretty damn relieved that we'd made it in one piece.

"I'm hoping your momma is out," I admitted. "I don't think I'd be able to, uh, *perform*, if she was in the house. It just wouldn't seem right."

Torrey smirked at me. "You're quite an old fashioned gentleman underneath all those muscles and tats, aren't you?"

I glanced over at her.

"Well now, if your momma is out, I'll be perfectly happy to demonstrate how much I'm *not* a gentleman."

"Deal!" she laughed, leaping out of the truck.

I followed her right quick, almost tripping over my feet in my eagerness to get to her.

We fell in through the front door and she damn near attacked me, pushing me against the wall, her hungry hands roaming freely up and down my body.

"You want it here, sweetheart?"

She laughed throatily.

"Well, it *is* a flat surface."

Can't argue with that.

"Hmm, let's see what's cookin'."

I picked her up so her legs wrapped around my waist automatically and carried her into the kitchen.

"W-what are we doing in here?" she gasped.

"First horizontal surface," I breathed against the salty, damp skin of her neck.

Then I placed her onto the kitchen counter and snapped open the button on her shorts.

"Lift up for me, sweetheart."

I slid the shorts down her legs while she reached for my zipper.

I managed to grab my jeans before they fell to the floor and pulled out a rubber.

"Gonna have to stock up on these, sweetheart."

She gave a breathless laugh. "We should buy shares in the company."

I pumped myself a couple of times then rolled the condom on, tugging it to make sure it was as far up as it could go.

"God, I love seeing you do that," she said.

"What, sheath up?"

"When you touch yourself," she said, her voice low and full of need. "It turns me on."

"Does this turn you on?"

I held her knees wide apart and pushed myself inside her inch by inch. She rested her hands on my shoulders, but her eyes were focused on my dick, slowly sliding in and out.

"You like to watch, Torrey," I murmured, my eyes trained on her face.

She nodded wordlessly.

I picked up the speed, relieved that I could finally show some fucking control, and that I wasn't blowing my wad the second I entered her.

I knew this was fucking to her and not making love, but I'd take whatever she'd give me. And right now I wanted to feel her come around my cock.

I reached down to massage her, and she whimpered and tried to wrap her legs around my waist.

"No, sweetheart," and I pushed her knees even further apart, giving me room to touch her as I circled my hips.

"Oh my God, Jordan!" she shouted.

I could feel the small tremors begin building through her body, and I started moving faster, but without losing the rhythm. I was determined to make this good for her.

She leaned on her hands; her head falling back and some mangled vowels fell from her lips. I felt her sweet pussy clamp around me. I managed to hold on for another few seconds, before my vision went dark and I was pulsing inside her.

My head was buried in her neck, and I allowed her to fold

her legs around me.

"Oh my God, Jordan!" she half laughed, half groaned. "That was … I don't know *what* that was! Felt gooood!"

"Seein' as I'm just an old fashioned country boy," I said, between hard kisses, "how about we take it to your bedroom for a change. Make some lovin' in comfort?"

"Hmm, a bed," she snickered, digging her heels into my ass as she spoke, "that sounds different. I guess we could try it."

Which we did. Several times. That woman just about wore me out.

We'd been three rounds, and I wondered if I'd used up the ration of spunk that I'd been storing over the last eight years. Could that happen? I didn't know. I *did* know that if she grabbed me hard again, my dick would probably fall off or just plain give up on me.

I propped myself up on one elbow to look at her. Her hair was a soft, tangled mess like a halo around her head, and her body glistened with sweat. It made me want to lick her salty skin. My dick twitched once in appreciation before admitting defeat. Poor guy needed some time off for good behavior.

"Oh my God," Torrey moaned. "I don't think I can move."

I stroked her soft stomach, enjoying the silkiness of her skin.

"You don't have to, sweetheart. You can stay here till sun up. But I'm gonna have to get goin' soon."

"Noo," she whined.

"Sorry, darlin'. Your momma could be back any time now and my curfew will be up in an hour."

She sighed and opened her eyes.

"I've really enjoyed today, Jordan. All of it."

"Me too, sweetheart. Maybe we can do it again sometime?" I added, hopefully.

"I'd like that. Big fat yes."

She yawned and sat up. I carried on looking at her. Well, staring really, my eyes fixing to dribble out of my head. She was so peaceful in her own skin—she just fit. That was rare.

Then she wrinkled her nose.

"Ugh! My room smells of sex!"

"We have kinda been goin' some, sweetheart," I said, running a hand down her back, almost drooling when she pushed her tits out at me. "We'll have to spend a whole day in bed next time."

She arched her spine and stretched her arms above her head, ensuring that my eyeballs remained glued to her chest.

"God, yes!" she laughed. "So, will I see you tomorrow morning? Maybe we could get in a quickie before I have to go to work."

"Woman, you are insatiable! I'm just gonna have to marry you!"

The words were out of my mouth before I realized what I'd said.

Torrey froze.

"What?"

"Aw, hell. I'm sorry. It just sorta slipped out."

"So you were joking?"

Was I?

"It's crossed my mind," I answered, truthfully.

"Oh my God!" she snorted, leaping off the bed as if she'd been stung. "Do you have any idea how crazy that is? We barely know each other! Marriage is big! Huge! Until death do us part-huge! I mean, fucking shit! We'll both be leaving soon and … it's just freakin' crazy!"

"Whoa, whoa! Slow down, Torrey! It's marriage not a prison sentence!"

"Same thing!" she snapped.

"Not hardly," I said, grimly, "and I think I know what I'm talkin' about here."

She paused for just a moment before resuming her nervous babbling.

"No, but … come on! It's just … I mean, marriage is just … it drives people apart!"

"I don't think that's how it's supposed to work," I smirked, amused to see her freaking out at a few words.

"I'm serious, Jordan!" she yelped, hurling a pillow at me.

I caught it before it took my head off.

"I can see that you're serious. All I'm sayin' is that you're my dream woman. Why *wouldn't* I want to marry you?"

She stared at me, completely unaware that she was totally naked and utterly magnificent. She looked like a wild animal that had been cornered but was untamed. I wouldn't have been entirely surprised if she launched herself at me, teeth and claws flailing. Well, it wouldn't be the first time.

"You … but … we … not…"

"Just think about it. Mr. and Mrs. Ex-felon. It has a ring, don't cha think?"

"You *are* teasing me," she said, dropping back onto the bed in relief.

"No, firecracker. I'm givin' you a get-out that you can live with. I'd marry you tomorrow if you'd have me."

"I have to work tomorrow," she said, faintly.

"Why you so down on marriage, sweetheart?"

She gave me a look that said, *are you kidding me?*

"Was it that bad when you were growin' up?"

She sighed and snuggled up to me like a kitten, her claws retracted … for now.

"No, it wasn't all bad. They were happy once, I think. It's almost like it fell apart so gradually, none of us realized until it was already really bad. The year before Mom decided to leave, that was horrible. They didn't argue that much, there were just all these silences. I used to get so tense I could hardly eat. I lost so much weight, they ended up taking me to see a doctor, but I couldn't say what the problem was, not with Mom sitting there."

I pulled her into my body, stroking her back, a strong need to protect flooding through me.

"You're only a lil' bitty thing now."

"Big enough to kick your ass!" she snorted, biting my chest.

"Okay, okay, you win! Don't hurt me!" I laughed.

She smirked and pretended to bite me again, instead turning it into a soft kiss.

"When Mom finally left, I couldn't help feeling like she'd chosen God over me. I didn't get why she had to make a choice, or why God would want her to make that sort of choice. I still don't get it. But I see how hard she works and how much it means to her. And I think she's happier now. I know the choice wasn't easy. It's just that she made it, and everyone else had to face the consequences."

"Yeah," I said, quietly, "I know what that's like."

"What about your parents?" she asked, tracing a finger across my chest, and then following the lines of my armband tattoo.

It signified mourning and was the first one I designed and the first one I had my buddy Styx ink.

"They were mostly happy, I think. I mean, they had arguments like anyone else, mostly over stuff I'd gotten caught doing. I told you Mikey was the smart one—he never got caught."

That was so true—I couldn't help smiling at the memory.

"Hell, Momma was called up to the school just about every week because I'd gotten caught fightin' or smokin' or makin' out with some girl in the janitor's closet."

Torrey wrinkled her nose. "Ugh, really? That's *so* not classy!"

I shrugged and winked at her.

"I was 15 when that happened. Mikey thought it was pretty funny. 'Specially as we'd been caught, um, ya know, doin' it. The girl's father threatened to whup my ass. Momma was so embarrassed 'cause it was someone she and Dad knew from church. It was Mikey's fault. He was the one who'd told me to use that damned closet in the first place."

Torrey laughed. "I'll stay away from closets when you're around." Then her face turned thoughtful. "What would you tell him, that teenager? What would you say to him?"

"Christ, I don't know. Don't drink and drive? Don't drink."

"Do you think he would have listened?"

"Nah. I was so damn cocky … thought I knew the answer to every question, even before anyone had asked."

"Seriously, Jordan. If you met a kid like that now, how would

199

you try to get through to him?"

I thought about her question. Was there anything that could have stopped the 16-year-old me from taking the first step that led to Mikey dying?

"I guess I'd take him to juvie, show him what that's like. They did that when I was there—schools organized groups of kids who were gettin' into trouble and then they'd march 'em through. The kids would stare at us like we were animals in a zoo. I think that would have made an impression. Maybe."

She nodded slowly. "Yeah, I remember seeing a documentary about something like that in high school. *Scared Straight* I think it was called."

I didn't reply but looked out of the window again, noticing that the moon was brighter and traveling steadily across the sky.

I sighed. "I've gotta git now, Torrey. And I won't see you tomorrow mornin'."

"Why not?" she pouted.

"Gotta go see my parole officer. Usually she just talks for a while, but it can take longer if she's feelin' officious. I might have to wait. It's first come, first served. Maybe I could come by the coffee shop after work?"

She sat up, pushing her hair out of her eyes. "Well, okay, I guess. But I can't guarantee that Bev won't try something—she thinks you're pretty darn hot."

"You'll protect me," I smiled. "You're my guardian angel."

"Aw, get out of here, you sap!" she laughed, throwing my t-shirt in my face.

I tugged it over my head and found my pants under the bed, and then I leaned down to capture her soft lips one more time before I left.

"See you soon, sweetheart."

"Bye, Jordan," she said, her voice tinged with sadness.

My feet dragged as I walked down the stairs. My heart and soul wanted to be up in that small bedroom with my girl. Because no matter how much she argued it, she was mine and I was hers. She just needed a little persuading of the fact.

I was so lost in my thoughts that I didn't notice the front door was opening.

"Jordan!" said Reverend Williams, her expression darkening with every second. "What are you doing here?"

Crap.

Torrey

I was still recovering from Jordan's workout when I heard voices at the bottom of the stairs. And I knew that there was only one person he could be speaking to. Holy hell. Mom had come back early.

I glanced at the time on my cell phone. Oh. Not early. I'd just lost track of time while we'd been getting freaky between the sheets.

Damn it! I'd hoped to put off telling her about him … me … us … for a while longer.

I pulled my robe off of the hook and wrapped it around myself. I didn't have time to dress, but even if I had, my flushed face and Jordan's large presence would have painted a damn accurate picture.

"What are you doing in my house?" Mom questioned, her tone upset.

His reply was a low rumble, so I couldn't hear how he answered her.

"Torrey!" she called sharply.

"On my way," I grumbled.

They were standing about five feet apart, Mom looking angry and shocked, Jordan looking tense, his hands shoved in his pockets.

"Oh hey, Mom," I said, as casually as I could manage. "How did your meetings go?"

"Never mind that now. I'd like to know what's been going on in my home while I've been out!"

"You sure you want me to answer that, Mom?" I said, more cockily than I should have.

Her face reddened.

"I won't put up with this!" she snapped. "I have a reputation in this community! I'm supposed to provide moral guidance. And yet, my own daughter is so disrespectful as to flagrantly pursue this ... this *immoral and hedonistic* lifestyle in my own home!"

Yeah, I shouldn't have laughed.

"Mom, really? Immoral *and* hedonistic?"

"Reverend Williams..." Jordan began.

"I'm talking to my daughter right now, Jordan," Mom clipped out. "But I must say I'm very disappointed in you. I've given you every chance, offered you every olive branch, and instead you just throw it back in my face. I'm going to have to reconsider my offer of employment—under the circumstances."

Jordan paled. We all knew that finding a job was a prerequisite of his parole.

"That's low, Mom!" I barked. "He hasn't done anything wrong!"

"Jordan, I'd like you to leave now," said Mom, her voice struggling for control. "I need to talk to my daughter, and your curfew is far too close."

His face twisted with anxiety, and I thought he might argue, which would have made things worse.

"It's okay," I said, quickly touching his arm. "I'll call you later."

"Promise?"

"Promise."

He kissed me quickly on the cheek. "I love you," he said, softly.

Mom's eyes bulged, and I was pretty sure an aneurysm would be her next trick.

Jordan closed the door quietly behind him.

"Way to go, Mom," I said, coldly. "I can't believe you'd threaten him like that. He's trying *so* hard."

"Then he should have thought about that before he slept with my daughter!"

"Really? You want to play the parent card? I'm over 21, Mom. In fact I was 24 a few months back, if you remember. Yes, I drink alcohol. Yes, I've gambled in dens of iniquity. And yes, I've had sex with a really nice guy who just needs a break."

"You silly, silly girl!" she shouted. "You're the first female who's shown him any interest—the first he's seen in eight years, and you've been using him for your own gratification. I'm ashamed of you! I cannot believe you'd be so thoughtless and selfish. Now he thinks he's in love with you!"

My face flushed with anger and guilt. In one way she was right: it had started out as gratification, but it had become much more than that.

"You're so wrong!" I hissed. "We … we have something special. I don't know what it is yet, but I'm willing to find out."

She fell back against the wall. "Oh no! You … you're in love with him, too!"

"God, Mom! No! Yes! Maybe, I don't know. But what if I was? Does it really matter that much? He was a kid! He made a mistake. Yes, it was a terrible, terrible mistake, but he's paid for it now. He's trying to move on with his life. He deserves a fresh start. Surely, you of all people understand that?"

I saw her touch the crucifix she wore around her neck and take a deep breath.

"Has he told you … about himself? Everything?"

"Of course!" I snapped.

"And it doesn't bother you?"

"It bothers him, Mom. But what I want to know is why does it bother you so much? Isn't forgiveness kind of in your job description?"

"For pity sake, Torrey!" she said, beginning more calmly, but her volume increasing rapidly. "He's a criminal. Not only did he kill his own brother, but he nearly killed another prisoner in a knife fight. He's violent! You can't trust him. You'll never know when he might turn on you. No! You can't be with a man like that! No!"

I shook my head at her disbelievingly.

"Didn't you teach me that charity begins at home? Maybe this is a little too close to home, Mom. Or should I call you 'Reverend'?"

She sucked in a deep breath.

"Go to your room!"

I laughed out loud. "With pleasure. Night, Reverend."

I strode up the stairs, anger and disdain trailing in my wake. So, she was ashamed of me. Well, I was damn well ashamed of her. Fucking hypocrite!

I sighed. Everything had been going so well.

Before Jordan had left, I'd planned on taking a shower. We'd gotten plenty sweaty over the course of the afternoon. But now, I reveled in the fact that his scent was all over my skin, on the sheets of my bed, filling my pillow with the smell of his soap and sweat and sex.

I picked up my phone and called him. He answered immediately.

"Torrey! Are you okay?"

I laughed thinly. "Yeah, I'm fine."

"What did she say? Did she … will she …" he took a deep breath. "Is she going to stop you from seeing me?"

"Hell, no! Jordan, I'm an adult. She doesn't get to make that sort of decision. I mean, I'd understand it if you wanted to break it off because of your work…"

"No fuckin' way!" he said, his voice loud and clear. "I'll find somethin' else. I'm not givin' you up. No chance."

"So we're good," I said, as tension seeped from my body.

He sighed softly. "Yeah, we're good. God, I miss you already. I just want to fall asleep with you in my arms and see your beautiful smile when I wake up."

I grinned and hugged myself, his words were making my body tingle.

"Oh, you're not missing much. I'm really not a morning person. I'm usually grumpy when I wake up."

He tried to laugh, but it was forced and uneasy.

"I'm really sorry about what happened tonight, sweetheart. I didn't want you and your momma arguin', especially not because of me."

"Oh, don't worry. It would have happened sooner or later."

He sighed. "I guess. Can I see you tomorrow? I could come by the coffee shop later like we discussed?"

"Yeah, that would be good. Sleep well, Jordan."

"Night, sweetheart. Sweet dreams."

The phone felt lifeless in my hands. I threw it onto the bedside table and fell asleep with the memory of Jordan all around me.

Chapter 10 – Instincts

Jordan

I didn't want to worry Torrey, but her momma's threat was freaking me out. I *had* to have a job as a condition of my parole. Without work, I'd be on the fast train back to prison.

Hulk had said he could pass some business my way, but that was a couple of weeks' work at most. I needed to show I had a steady income. I was close to losing it all.

I'd been pacing up and down, waiting for Torrey to call, desperate to hear from her after I'd left earlier in the evening. I was praying that her momma wouldn't be able to talk her out of seeing me. I felt flayed by even the possibility of it.

The sheer relief when I heard her voice—I felt like I could breathe again. Her momma hadn't persuaded her against me, and we'd arranged to meet tomorrow. Just hearing her say the words was immense.

It had been one helluva day. My emotions were still

bouncing all over the place from everything that had happened.

Visiting Mikey's grave had been a huge step for me. The weight I'd carried around for years seemed to have finally lifted. I could even believe that Torrey was right, and that I didn't have to live under a rock for the rest of my life. I didn't think I was free and clear either, and if I had to spend the rest of my life atoning for my sins, then I'd sure as shit do it, no questions asked. But I knew Mikey had loved me. That was one constant that hadn't changed. As the river of my life flowed around me, my brother's love was the one thing I could rely on. I could still remember what that felt like—my brother had my back, no matter what. We were a team. And teammates wouldn't let the other one suffer if they could help it, right? I *owed* it to him to make something of my life. By shaking me hard enough, that's what Torrey had made me see.

I stood in front of the bathroom mirror, taking a long, hard look at myself for the first time in years. Could I really be the man she saw? Could I have the future that was so tantalizingly close? Could I live for me *and* Mikey? Maybe Torrey was right. Maybe I owed it to him to try ... to live a good life, a big life.

Yeah, I could try. But I needed to change. I needed to accept what I'd done and find a way to live with it. Something I hadn't achieved in eight years. But now ... somehow I needed to start again. I hoped it would be with Torrey, but if not ... I wanted to live.

It was a goddamn revelation.

I dug through the bathroom cupboard until I found Mikey's clippers. The charge had long since gone, but I plugged it into the wall socket until the tiny red light told me they were useable. Then I set the length to half an inch and watched my shaved hair fall into the sink. It looked a lot blonder than I'd realized. Huh, weird.

I was stunned when I saw the finished result. I looked like him. Like Mikey.

There was a shocked gasp behind me, and I turned around to see Momma staring at me in horror, her face white with anger.

"Don't you dare!" she hissed. "Don't you dare look like him!"

My heart shuddered in my chest.

"Momma, I … I didn't know. I never realized…"

"You just had to find a way to make it hurt some more, didn't you!" she shouted, shaking an accusing finger at me. "Why did you have to come back here? Why couldn't you let us all rest in peace?"

I heard my father's footsteps pounding up the stairs, and he caught her as she collapsed sobbing.

"Haven't you done enough?" he shouted. "Why do you keep on hurtin' her?"

My voice was calm and quiet when I replied.

"I hurt her by bein' alive, Dad."

He looked up and met my eyes. I think for the first time I saw some sort of acknowledgment in them. I didn't know what, but it meant something.

"Clean up the bathroom," was all he said, as he led her away.

I don't think any of us slept that night. I lay on my bed, listening to the soft hum of voices from the TV downstairs. Occasionally, I heard a chair scrape across the floor or footsteps on the stairs. Along the hallway in her room, Momma cried for hours. You'd think the tears would have run out years ago. Maybe she had a lifetime supply.

My eyes were dry, burning with tiredness, but sleep was a long way away. Before dawn, I pulled on a pair of Mikey's old running shorts that weren't too big, and headed out. It helped sometimes. A bit. The cottonwoods loomed out of the darkness and the road was a paler patch of ground ahead, leading me onward. Memories flickered behind my eyelids: me and Mikey, Mikey and Momma, Torrey, school, home, Dad, the junkyard, prison, Torrey, the trial, the grave, Torrey, spinning off the road, the upside down car, Mikey's body, blood, the hospital, Torrey, Mikey playing football, Mikey falling from the tree, getting drunk, getting stoned, making love, Torrey, Torrey, Torrey.

Daylight was filtering through the trees by the time I limped home—back to my parents' home. My body was burning, but my mind was clearer.

I took my turn in the shower and dressed more tidily than usual. I rolled up the cut-offs and stuck them under my arm. I hoped I'd need them later, assuming I still had a job.

Instead of avoiding my parents, I headed into the kitchen to get some breakfast. As soon as Momma saw me, she left the room. Dad looked up at me, almost apologetic.

"Give her some time," he said.

It was the most personal thing he'd said to me since I got back. I nodded at him, and we ate in silence. It wasn't completely uncomfortable.

After I rinsed out my cereal dish, I reminded Dad that I'd be visiting my parole officer in town. It was irritating, but better than one of the random home searches. Sometimes they could be around for a couple of hours going through every drawer, cabinet, medicine chest and storage space.

"Do you want me to go with you for that?" he asked, out of the blue.

I looked at him in surprise. "Um, that's okay, Dad. She'll just want to talk about how it's goin'. The usual."

"And how is it goin'?"

I leaned against the sink and looked at him.

"You really want to know?"

"Yes," he said, at last. "Will you tell me?"

He pointed to one of the kitchen chairs and I sat down, curious as to what had brought on his sudden interest, although it left me feeling a little on edge.

I waited for him to speak.

"You've been runnin' again," he began. "You used to do that when … before."

"Yep. It helps clear my head. It helps to be outside—away from … you know…"

"Good … that's good."

We stared at each other across the table.

"And workin' for the Reverend? How's that?"

"Well, it was okay…"

"But it's not now?"

I sighed. "I don't know what to tell you, Dad. I'm not even sure I have a job anymore."

His jaw tightened perceptibly. "What did you do?"

A pulse of anger jolted through me.

"Yeah, that's about right, Dad. What did I do. It's always what I did, isn't it?"

"You must have done somethin' for her to fire you!" he snapped back.

Rage burned my throat, but I forced myself to control it.

"She doesn't like me seein' her daughter."

He blinked a couple of times. "That's it?"

"Fuck, Dad! What? What did you think? Not as shockin' as you thought, is it? I'm datin' her daughter. Big fuckin' news! But no, Reverend Williams is not happy about her only daughter bein' with an ex-con. So last night she questioned whether or not she still wanted me to work for her. I don't know. Maybe I'm screwed. Maybe I'm on my way back to prison. *I don't fuckin' know!*"

I stood up abruptly, knocking my chair over and needing to get out of the house. I tore open the front door and headed for my truck. I was fixing to get the fuck out and go see Torrey, when I remembered I had a meeting with Officer Carson.

I couldn't help pounding the steering wheel in frustration.

I started the engine and forced myself to drive slowly. Getting in a wreck was not going to make this suck-ass day any better.

I was still wound up when I arrived at the Regional Parole Office on the edge of town. I'd just signed in when Carson came out to meet me.

She took one look at my tense expression, and the friendly smile dropped from her face.

"Calm down, Jordan," she said, her voice firm with authority.

"Shit, sorry! I just…" I took a few deep breaths, "I was just talkin' to my old man, and…"

She nodded. "Go to my office, please."

Sighing, I followed her down the corridor. She pulled open the door and pointed to a seat on the far side from her wide desk.

Her office was kind of cramped, filled with metal filing cabinets, but two large windows made it feel less like a hutch. There were some sort of framed certificates on the walls, and a small photograph of three kids on her desk. I assumed that was her family.

"Sit, please, Jordan."

Reluctantly, I sat on the edge of the plastic chair, my knees bouncing with tension.

Officer Carson frowned as she pulled my file out of the drawers.

"You look a little anxious, Jordan."

"Yeah."

"Have you taken something?"

My eyes shot up to meet hers.

"What? Fuck no! No, nothin'. I'm just … wound up right now."

I couldn't tell if she believed me or not.

"Well, after this visit is concluded, I want you to go to the police station and get tested. Okay?"

"Ah, hell! I did that three days ago!"

"I'm requesting that you go again. Do I need to make this more official?"

"No, ma'am," I said, resignedly.

She nodded and made a note in my file. Just then my cell phone beeped, and she looked at me sharply.

"You have a phone?"

"Yeah, I just got it."

"I'll need to check that."

"What? *Why?*"

"I need to see who you're talking to; what sort of messages you're sending and receiving."

I didn't want her seeing the things Torrey and I had said to each other, but I had no choice. I wasn't allowed the privacy afforded to upright citizens. I was a felon and I wasn't allowed to forget it. I had no right to the Fourth Amendment.

Reluctantly, I retrieved my cell from my hip pocket and handed it over.

"Who's Torrey?" Officer Carson asked, scrolling through it.

"My girlfriend."

"She's the only name in your contact list?"

"Yes, ma'am."

She handed my phone back with a small smile.

While she made another note in her file, I looked at Torrey's message, the one Officer Carson had already read.

How about a booty call
before you see your PO?

I looked up, my cheeks hot, and Officer Carson smiled at me.

While she was checking through her notes, I sent Torrey a quick text to tell her I was already in town.

"So," said Carson, looking up at me, "let's work through the usual questions, Jordan. Have you had any police contact since we last met?"

"Yes, ma'am. I was stopped when I was drivin' back from my girlfriend's a couple of nights ago."

"Why were you stopped?"

"I'm not sure, I wasn't told."

"Hmm … and what happened?"

"He just wanted to know where I'd been and what I was doin'. He reminded me that my curfew was gettin' near. He breathalyzed me but it came up negative."

She looked up quickly, her pen poised. "Why did he breathalyze you?"

I shrugged. "Because he could?"

"Have you consumed any alcohol since the last time I saw you?"

212

"No, ma'am."

"Have you wanted to?"

"Hell, yeah! Pretty much every freakin' day." I laughed, but it was without humor.

"You're doing very well, Jordan," she said, forcefully. "Don't let anything lead you away from that."

"No, ma'am."

"Have you taken any drugs or felt the urge to take drugs?"

"No, ma'am."

"Good. And how are you getting along with your parents?"

Seriously? She hadn't just seen the state I was in when I'd arrived?

"Okay, I guess. Well, Dad is … okay. Momma, she don't talk to me. So … it's okay."

"I see." She jotted down something else. "And you're still in work?"

"Yes, ma'am." *For now.*

"Well, that's all good. And have you thought anymore about taking some college courses, other goals?"

My voice was bitter. "Other than to get out of this shithole? No, not really."

She looked at me sympathetically.

"Jordan, the first six months when you get out of prison are tough. I know from experience that having a support system around you doubles your chances of staying out of prison. You *need* stability."

"I don't need *them*," I growled, pointing at the door, thinking of my parents.

"They can help you," she insisted.

I coughed out a laugh. "You think? Momma cain't even look at me without wantin' to throw up or burstin' into tears. Dad … isn't so bad. But I'm never gonna be allowed to start again if I stay here."

She looked at me seriously. "Jordan, you understand that parole means you are still serving part of your sentence under supervision in the community—*in the community*. But my job is also to help ease your transition from prison to that community.

I'll help with anything I can: employment, residence, finances, or any other personal problems you want to talk to me about. My goal is to ensure that you complete your parole without problems and that you *stay out of prison*. If there's something going on that is going to jeopardize that, I need to know. Work *with* me, Jordan."

"Um … I might have lost my job."

Her eyes were sharp and intelligent, and they seemed to penetrate right through me.

"You mean your work for Reverend Williams at the Rectory?"

"Yeah…"

"What happened?"

I closed my eyes, hating to admit that the Reverend didn't think I was good enough for her daughter. Hell, I already knew that.

"Torrey is her daughter. The Reverend … she isn't happy that we're seein' each other."

"Ah," said Officer Carson, "Oh, dear. Well, as you know, any other job offers will have to be approved. Do you have something else in mind?"

"Maybe some truck repair work." *I figured Hulk wouldn't mind me calling it that.* "But it's just part-time."

"Hmm, not ideal. Anything else?"

"No, ma'am. There isn't a lot of work around here. Especially for someone like me."

"Well, this is a shame, Jordan. You've been doing very well up until now. Perhaps I could have a word with Reverend Williams?"

I shrugged. "Knock yourself out, but I'm pretty sure she hates me."

"And she's definitely fired you?"

"I was just headin' over there. I'll find out as soon as I get out of here."

Officer Carson sighed. "Let me know when you have an answer. We'll have to make arrangements otherwise."

"Yes, ma'am."

She stood up and walked me to the entrance.

I was relieved that the visit hadn't been a complete disaster, and was pleased that I was on my way out, when we both heard Torrey's car roar up the street. She skidded to a halt, wide-eyed, in front of Officer Carson.

"Oh, uh, hi!" she said, as she climbed out of the Firebird, her eyes flickering nervously between my parole officer and me.

"You must be Torrey," Officer Carson said, holding out her hand. "Jordan's just been telling me about you. I'm Sandy Carson, his parole officer."

"Oh … right. Torrey Delaney. Nice to meet you."

"You, too."

They shook hands, and Officer Carson smiled at her, before turning to me.

"Don't forget the police station, Jordan. And call me later if you hear anything."

I nodded, and she walked back inside.

"Awkward much?" laughed Torrey, flinging herself into my arms.

I nuzzled her neck, reveling in the feel of her body against mine.

"Not as awkward as her readin' your text message," I chuckled.

"*What?* You're kidding me!"

"Nope. She heard your message come in and insisted on checkin' out my phone. I don't have any privacy, sweetheart. I couldn't say no."

Torrey laughed. "Oh, well! Good thing you told me, because I was going to write about some of the things I planned to do with your dick. Just as well I couldn't be bothered to type out a long message this morning."

I groaned. "You're killin' me, woman!"

She laughed. "And what the hell happened to your hair? You look like you joined the Marines or something!"

"Nah. But this hot woman I've been seein' told me that I

needed a fresh start, so … what do you think?"

"Yeah," she said, stroking the back of my head above my neck. "It's so soft. It's not hair, it's fur! I think I like it."

I kissed her throat, sucking on her pulse point, feeling the tender skin under my teeth.

"I'm happy about that."

"So," she said, running her fingers under my t-shirt. "About that booty call?"

"I'd love to take you up on that, sweetheart, but I've got to go see your momma. I don't suppose she gave any clue what she was thinkin'?"

Her demeanor shifted, and she scowled. "I'm not sure. We certainly *discussed* it last night." Her eyes turned to me. "I'm sorry, Jordan, you'll have to ask her yourself. As of last night, it wasn't looking good, but maybe she's gone all Christian and had second thoughts."

"That's okay, sweetheart. I'll call on her after I go to the police station."

Her eyes zeroed in on me.

"My PO wants me to get another drug test," I explained. "Apparently I seemed somewhat anxious when I arrived."

"How come?"

"The usual: talkin' to my old man."

"Oh," Torrey pouted. "That sucks. I'll come with you. I've got a couple of hours to kill. I'll follow you in my car."

"Um, you really want to come to the police station with me?" I confirmed, shaking my head in confusion.

"Sure, why not? I've got nothing better to do."

I raised my eyebrows. "You really know how to have fun!"

She laughed. "Well, my plans for a booty call seem to be on hold. But if the police don't take too long, you have a nice large truck ... who knows?"

"Miss Delaney, you have a wicked streak a mile wide. God, I love y… I love that about you."

"Hurry up then!" she snorted, snapping her fingers at me.

"Yes, ma'am!"

The police station was in the center of town, a couple of blocks from the Parole Office. I hated coming here; it brought back the bad memories.

Mostly, they weren't assholes, but I didn't trust them either. Too many years of being controlled by people in uniforms—it left a mark. And they had the power to put me back behind bars. Who wouldn't be freakin' unnerved by that?

Torrey was quiet as she stood next to me.

"So, um, what are they testing for?"

"Usual stuff: speed, coke, weed, opiates, PCP. No test covers everything, so they pick the most common drugs, or the cheaper tests for the lab to do, I don't know."

"Is it a blood test?"

"Nope, just have to piss in a bottle."

"And they can see from that if you've drunk a beer or something, as well?"

"There's a different test for that—the EtG. They're looking for the metabolites your body produces when you have alcohol. That stays in urine up to 80 hours. Sucks, huh."

She looked thoughtful.

"Torrey, this is what it's gonna be like for the next four months if … if you date me. This is my reality."

She poked me in the ribs.

"Really, Jordan? Is that what you think of me? Just because you have to go pee in a cup once a week, you think that will put me off?"

I pulled her into my arms and kissed her firmly.

"You are the best thing that's ever happened to me, Miss Delaney, and I am *not* lettin' you go."

"Just promise me one thing," she said.

"Name it!"

"Let me go when you pee into that cup."

I couldn't help laughing. "Trust you to say that when I'm bein' all romantic, woman!"

"Keeps it real!" she grinned.

Our light-hearted mood vanished as soon as we entered the

police station.

The guys on duty recognized me, but I could see them throwing looks at Torrey. I didn't like it.

I showed my ID, even though they knew who I was, and explained why I was here. One of them phoned the collections supervisor, while Torrey and I tried to get comfortable on the ugly plastic chairs in the waiting room. We sat there for what seemed like an age. Torrey tried to chat away, but the delay was getting to me. I was twitching like a smack addict waiting for his next fix.

"Hey, calm down," she whispered, resting her hand on my thigh. "We'll be out of here soon enough."

We were interrupted by an officer holding a stack of papers and a familiar-looking plastic bottle with a screw top.

"Mr. Kane? This way."

Torrey squeezed my hand, and then I followed the guy into the men's restrooms. He pointed me to a cubicle and left the door open. Then he snapped on a pair of rubber gloves and handed me the small plastic bottle. At least he turned around while I pissed into it.

Stuff like that didn't bother me. Eight years of having to take a shit in a restroom with no door—well, that strips away any ideas of modesty or privacy. Not saying I liked it, hell no, but I didn't let it freak me out either.

When I was finished, I handed him the bottle and washed my hands. Then I signed my name, got a copy of the form, and I was done.

I got the hell out of there as fast as I could.

"All okay?" Torrey asked anxiously, when we were back outside in the town square.

I took a deep breath and tried to shake off the tension that still filled me.

"Yep, all done. 'Til next time."

Suddenly, I was aware that we weren't alone. Three guys in baseball caps had spotted me. They were heavy looking dudes but maybe not as fit as they once were. If I could work this right,

I'd talk my way out of it. If not…

"Torrey, take your car and get out of here."

"What's going on?"

"Just do it, please, sweetheart!"

She glanced behind her and stiffened.

"No way! I'm not leaving you here with those thugs."

The men were too close now, and the window of opportunity to get her somewhere safe had slammed shut.

I stood slightly in front of her and kept my stance casual, although in my mind I was on high alert. I just hoped that they wouldn't start something since we were still directly outside the police station.

"Ain't you Jordan Kane?"

Fuck.

"Yes, sir. That's me."

"Who the hell you think you are showin' yo' face around here, boy?"

"I don't want any trouble."

"Well, trouble done found you."

One of them looked straight at Torrey, his gaze running up and down her body. I tensed immediately. Those fuckers were *not* getting their greasy hands on her, even if it meant I ended up back in the pen.

"What you doin' with a piece of shit ex-con like him, sugar? Why'nt ya come an' spend some time with a real man. Sure we c'n be right friendly."

Torrey tried to get past me, but I kept my arm out, holding her back.

"I wouldn't piss in your ear if your brain was on fire," she yelled.

"Ha ha ha! She done tole you, Eddy!" laughed the one with the mustache.

'Eddy' didn't seem very happy about that and I thought things were going to turn bad. But for once, thank you Lord, luck was on my side.

Two cops came out of the station and immediately honed in

on what was happening. While they weren't fans of mine, it was pretty damn obvious that I wasn't the instigator either.

"Y'all got a problem here?" the older cop said.

"We's just havin' some fun, officer," said Mustache, giving a creepy, snaggle-toothed grin.

"Mmm-hmm. Well, take your 'fun' someplace else. Y'all git."

Muttering to themselves, the men left. Immediately, the cops turned to me.

"It would be better all around if you didn't go showin' your face in town, Kane. Folks around here are mighty picky 'bout the company they keep."

"Oh for God's sake!" yelped Torrey. "Those rednecks were just itching to start a fight. Jordan didn't do anything! Hell, he's just reported to your damn police station!"

"It's okay, sweetheart," I said, quietly.

"Let me give you a piece of advice, Miss Delaney," said the older cop. "You get home to your momma and be careful about who you spend your time with. Some folk cain't help attractin' trouble."

Torrey looked taken aback that they knew who she was. Then she rolled her eyes. "Maybe you should look up the whole concept of 'innocent until proven guilty'," she snapped.

"Do tell," said the older cop. "Kane *was* proved guilty."

"And how long does he have to keep on paying?" she hissed.

"Torrey!" I begged, tugging on her arm. "Now's not the time, sweetheart!"

She whirled around and turned on me.

"When is the time, Jordan? When three rednecks have kicked the crap out of you for fun?"

"Watch your mouth, young lady," said the cop. "You might be the preacher's daughter, but that doesn't give you any special privileges."

I had to practically drag her out of there, still shooting sparks and spitting fire.

When I finally managed to get her back in the Firebird she hadn't calmed down much.

"You can't let them treat you like that, Jordan!" she yelled.

"Sweetheart, it doesn't matter."

"The hell it doesn't! How could you just stand there and say nothing? We have a Constitution! They can't just go trampling all over your rights!"

"And you think they apply to me as much as they apply to you?" I shot back, rapidly losing my temper. "Don't you get it? They *want* me to fuck up. They want a reason to put me back inside. They'd love to just throw away the key!"

"Then fight back! Don't let them! Don't quit!"

I ground my teeth with frustration.

"I cain't afford your fuckin' principles!" I shouted.

Her face became pale with anger, and her blue eyes were as hard as sapphires.

"Fuck you!" she yelled, and drove off in a cloud of dust and smoke.

Great.

Torrey

I was so mad at Jordan. I wanted him to stand up for himself. I hated this subservient, cowed side of him. I understood it, sort of, but I was afraid he'd sink back into the darkness and depression that he'd been stuck in when I first met him. I was certain it was better for him when he fought back.

This day was really going to hell in a handbasket.

I drove to work angry and miserable. I looked at my phone, hoping that Jordan might have sent me a message, but the only contact on there was from my bank reminding me that I'd exceeded my agreed overdraft. Yeah, thanks. And I still hadn't heard anything from Dad. I was hurt that he'd erased me from his life so easily to pursue *Ginger*.

Bev picked up on my mood immediately.

"Someone's having a bad day!"

"God, Bev, you have no idea."

"Fighting with that fine man of yours?"

I huffed out a tired laugh.

"Yeah, you could say that."

"Is he worth fighting for, hon?" she asked, seriously.

"Yes," I sighed, "he is."

"How about I make you a Caramel Frappuccino?" she said, throwing me a wink. "Caffeine and sugar all in one delicious iced drink."

Her dreamy expression made me laugh. "Better make it a light one, Bev. I think I might need several."

"You got it, hon."

It was good to have some girl time and get away from all the intensity that seemed to surround Jordan Kane. I thought again about what he'd said at the police station: mandatory drug and alcohol tests; visits and searches from his parole officer; curfews; travel limits; even his damn text messages were subject to examination. That was his reality. Did I really want to buy into all that? Hell, no sane person would *want* that.

But there was so much more to him than his past or even his present reality. He was sweet and funny and kind. He was thoughtful and caring, and even when we were just talking, I enjoyed his company. And did I mention that the sex was so hot I practically melted just looking at him?

It had been a few years since I'd let a guy get through to me like this. Why the hell did it have to be a fuck hot felon on parole? Life sure had a sick sense of humor. Or maybe I should go with Mom on this one: God has a plan for us all. Now *that* would be ironic.

I really hoped he'd stop by later.

Jordan

I wanted to rip out my own tongue for yelling at Torrey that way. Damn, that woman was frustrating. And infuriating. Even when she was being a pain in my ass, she was still on my side.

It had been so fucking humiliating to have those rednecks talk shit to her, and just have to stand there and take it. I didn't care what they said about me—I'd heard it all and worse. But to have her dragged down in the gutter with me, that definitely pushed my buttons.

I thought about texting her, but I really didn't know what to say. I was sure she wouldn't want to hear from me right now, so I decided to let her cool down.

Besides, I had to go talk to her momma. And after last night, I was beginning to see where Torrey got her firecracker spirit from.

I took a deep breath and headed on over to the Rectory.

The Reverend's car was out front, which was a start. Maybe.

I guess she heard my truck because I was just fixing to knock on the door when it swung open in front of me.

"Uh, good mornin', ma'am. I was wonderin' if I could talk to you?"

Her expression didn't give anything away.

"Very well, Jordan. Please come in."

She stood back and allowed me to walk past her. I hesitated, wondering if she'd want me to go to the living room or the kitchen.

Instead, she gestured toward a small room I hadn't been in before. It turned out to be her study—where she wrote her sermons, I guessed. A long bookshelf ran along one wall, and from what I could see, it was stocked with several Bibles and companion readers, but what really caught my attention were pictures of Torrey as a little girl: Torrey on a tricycle, Torrey sitting on a pony, Torrey in a ballet costume. So damn cute! The pictures seemed to stop when she was about 12 or 13, and I guessed that was when her parents' marriage had failed.

"Please have a seat, Jordan," the Reverend said, formally.

I lowered myself onto the edge of an armchair, anxiety shooting through me.

"Uh, I wanted to apologize for yesterday, ma'am. I didn't mean any disrespect to you. Torrey and I … we've gotten … close. She means an awful lot to me, ma'am and I'm sorry if it seemed like I was takin' advantage of you. Or her. I didn't mean it that way."

"Thank you for saying that, Jordan. Do you intend to continue seeing my daughter?"

"As long as she'll have me, ma'am," I replied, honestly.

"I see. And would you say you have her best interests at heart?"

"I want only good things for her. Torrey is … she's the best thing that's ever happened to me."

"I can see you believe that. But Jordan, are you the best thing that's ever happened to her?"

Wow, sucker-punched.

"Um no, ma'am. I guess I'm not. But I really care about her."

"So do I, Jordan. Which is why I hope you'll understand when I say I cannot condone your relationship with her. And I would be remiss in my duty as a mother and as a moral guide to the people of my parish if I encouraged it by continuing to allow you in my home. I am, however, willing to allow you to work here, but not if you continue to see my daughter. The decision is yours."

So, that was it.

I stood up to leave.

"Thank you for your time, ma'am. I appreciate you lettin' me say my piece."

"And your decision is?"

I looked her in the eye, knowing exactly what I wanted to say: "You know the 'Song of Solomon', Reverend?"

"Of course!"

"Then this is my answer: *I am my beloved's and my beloved is mine.*"

And I walked out.

Principles are great when you can afford them, but the way this day was going, I was down a girlfriend *and* a job.

Next stop, Hulk. Maybe *he* could save my ass.

The yard was pretty busy for a Monday morning. I guess in a recession folks go wherever they can to get a bargain and save money. Hulk was doing good business in car and truck parts— good enough to need some help, I hoped.

I waited until he'd finished taking payment for a manifold, muffler and catalytic converter on a Ford Bronco before I approached him.

"Thought you was gonna call me, kid? You miss me that much you gotta come by?"

"Yep, just wanted to see your smilin' face, Hulk."

"Heh heh! I'd rather look at that sweet girl of yours! Where's she at? Kicked your sorry ass out yet?"

I winced. "Uh, that's a maybe, maybe not."

"Huh, women, eh? Sorry to hear that. You two looked good together. And what's with the hair? Someone try to tar and feather you?"

"Funny! Well, I'm sure there's some as'd love to try. Hulk, I was wonderin' if you needed more full-time help around here. I need work, and a few paint jobs ain't gonna cut it."

He scratched his beard thoughtfully. "Last I heard, you was handyman for the preacher-lady."

"Well, I was."

"I guess she didn't like you sniffin' around her daughter."

"It wasn't like that," I said, testily. "Torrey, she's … special."

"Heh heh!" he coughed out another laugh. "You got it bad, ain't you, kid?"

"Ah, give me a break, Hulk! Can you use another pair of hands or not?"

"Quit yer bitchin'. I can give you a few hours, say two, three days a week, but that's all. Any use to you?"

"Hell, yeah!"

A couple of days was better than nothing, and if I could do some paint jobs on the other days, it would just about see me through. "That would be great, Hulk. But, uh, you know you'll have to be approved by the Probation Service. They'll come and ask a bunch of questions. I'm sorry, I know you won't like them crawlin' up your ass…"

He waved his arm in the air, and I nearly ducked out of habit.

Bastard laughed at me. "I'll live. Give 'em my number. Now go fix things with your girl. A woman like that is too fine to let go. G'wan, git!"

"Yessir! Thanks, Hulk! Um…"

"What now, kid?"

"I guess it would go better with the Probation Service if I don't have to tell them I want to work for a guy named Hulk."

"Yer skatin' on thin ice, kid. You go tellin' anyone else my business and look forward to singin' soprano."

"I've got no one else to tell."

He gave me a hard stare that had me itching to back off a foot or two, but I held my ground.

"Walter Winkler," he muttered, at last.

Wow. No wonder he preferred 'Hulk'.

"Um, okay. I'll tell them."

I sat in my truck and called Officer Carson. Her phone went to voicemail so I left a message, giving her Hulk's details. I really needed this to work.

Next thing I had to fix was how I'd left it with Torrey. Or rather, how she'd left it with me, being as the last thing she'd said to me was 'Fuck you'.

I drove to the mall and parked outside the coffee shop. I debated with myself whether or not to text her first. After all, she'd given me the cell in the first place so I could apologize. Either she had a crystal ball or she'd just been figurin' on me being an asshole.

In the end, I decided against sending a text, hoping that seeing me in person would win more points than trying to do anything over the phone. The worst that could happen was that she'd scream at me—maybe throw something. That wouldn't be anything new.

But Bev was the first person I saw.

"Wow, you're brave!" she said, which didn't fill me with hope. "What'd you do to her? She's acting like she's had a burr under her saddle all day!"

"Just a slight misunderstandin'," I said, trying to smile. "Is she around, Bev?"

She winked at me. "I'll go get her. Don't suppose you have a bulletproof vest in that truck of yours?"

"Oh, God! That bad?"

She laughed. "Not nearly! Good luck, handsome! I'll clear up the body parts later. By the way, the hair looks great."

She disappeared into the back and a minute later, Torrey came stomping out, looking mad enough to shit bricks.

"Well?" she snapped.

"I'm sorry I yelled at you, sweetheart." I rushed out an apology before she had time to start throwing punches. "This is all kind of new to me."

She took a deep breath, and I mentally prepared to duck.

"Yeah, okay. I'm sorry, too. I *don't* know what it's like for you, and I know you can't afford idealism. It just makes me mad to think they can get away with treating you like that."

I'm sure my whole body relaxed when she started talking to me.

227

"I know, and I really appreciate it, but you cain't fight the system. If I come within even a whisper of trouble, they'll throw me back inside so fast my head will spin. If I get into somethin', it won't matter who started it or why. Believe me, I'd love nothin' more than to have handed those yahoos their asses on a freakin' platter, but I cain't."

"Yeah, yeah, I get it. No asses. No platters. Just kiss me already!"

She wouldn't get an argument from me on that.

Her hands wound up my back under my t-shirt and her soft lips attacked my mouth, her tongue forcing its way inside.

She tasted of sweet coffee and cinnamon, and yep, I was instantly hard. I pulled away from her, vaguely aware that some of the other customers were watching us curiously.

I leaned my forehead against hers and breathed in the scent of her hair and skin—always so good.

"God, I needed that," I said, quietly.

"Me, too. I'm glad you stopped by, Jordan."

"Really?"

"Oh, yeah. I didn't get my booty call earlier. I was missing you."

"Can you take a break now, sweetheart? Got my truck parked outside…"

She pulled a face. "I wish. I took my break an hour ago. The manager will be riding my ass if I don't get back to work soon."

"Okay, well, when do you get a day off? Maybe we can do something then?"

"I could come by your place tomorrow morning—make good on that booty call!" she laughed.

"Sorry, no. I'll be at work."

She raised her eyebrows. "At my mom's?"

"Uh, no. She fired my ass all right. No, Hulk gave me two or three days a week helpin' him out. And maybe another day or so on the paintwork."

"Oh, wow! That's great. You should totally do some more artwork. What you did with your truck was awesome."

I wasn't used to being praised. I felt awkward and unsure. "Uh, thanks."

"Well, I could come by after my shift," she offered. "Can I stay the night at your place?"

Jeez, that would be every teenage fantasy I'd ever had—a hot girl in my bedroom.

"God, yes! You have to be quiet though. Dad and Momma will be asleep. I know, I know. I'm damn near 24 and still sneakin' girls into my room. It's freakin' sad!"

"How many girls you been a-sneaking?" she teased, trying to copy my accent again.

"None so far, but I'm hopin' to change that later."

"You feeling lucky?"

I could answer that honestly.

"Yes, I'm feelin' lucky."

"See you later, cowboy," she said.

Chapter 11 – Venturing

Torrey

I was glad the coffee shop was busy otherwise I'd have gone a little crazy. My brain was on overdrive when it came to Jordan and everything we'd talked about, everything he'd said. Perhaps even what he *hadn't* said.

"Happy now you've seen that hot guy of yours?" Bev asked, between customers.

I winked at her. "Got me some happy times planned later, that's for sure!"

"I hate you!" she moaned. "Just promise you'll tell me all about it. I've got to get my kicks somehow."

"You want me to kiss and tell?" I laughed.

"*Now* you're getting it!"

"Maybe some highlights, I'll think about it. Anyway, I thought you said you were seeing that guy from Corpus?"

"Yeah! We're having our *third* date tomorrow night. Hey, maybe we could do something together over the weekend when we're both off? Have a couple of drinks, go dancing? You know, you, me, Jordan and Pete—like a high school double date!" she laughed. "That would be awesome!"

"Or we could meet for a coffee…"

"Coffee!" she shrieked. "Are you insane? Don't we spend enough hours smelling java beans? No, hon, I'm talking about living it up a little: dress up, drink cocktails, you know, have some F.U.N. You got a problem with that all of a sudden?"

I didn't know Bev that well, so I wasn't sure how she'd react, but I decided to risk telling her the truth.

I stared at her challengingly. "No, I don't have a problem, but Jordan does."

Her face fell. "He got a drinking problem, hon?"

"Yes and no." I folded my arms and met her concerned gaze. "He's on parole. He got out of prison five weeks ago. He can't drink or go anywhere they sell alcohol, and he's not allowed to go more than 10 miles beyond the town limits."

I watched as her eyes got large and her voice dropped to a whisper.

"He's *on parole?*"

I nodded, my eyes still trained on her face.

"Wow. That's … what did he do?" She paused. "You don't have to tell me."

"No, it's okay. It's not a secret." I steeled my nerves. This was the first time I'd spoken to someone who didn't already know about Jordan. "He killed his brother in a drunk driving accident when he was 16."

Bev's mouth worked at spitting out some words, but her volume control seemed to be broken, because nothing was coming out.

"Oh my God!" she croaked. "That's … that's…"

"I know. It isn't easy to get your head around," I sighed. "He's been having a really hard time."

"How did you meet him? Was it like one of those love stories where you wrote each other while he was in prison, finally get to meet, and sparks fly, angels sing?"

231

"Yeah," I deadpanned. "Nothing like that."

"Oh," she said, disappointed.

I decided to put her out of her misery.

"My mom has a church over on the shore. He worked for her—handyman stuff, some gardening. That's how I met him."

She smiled. "I prefer my version—star crossed lovers with all the odds stacked against you. Families at war."

I snorted with sour amusement. "Oh, Bev, that's closer to the truth than you think. Mom fired him because we've been seeing each other, and he can barely step outside the door without someone from the town mouthing off at him or wanting to start a fight. Some kids slashed all the tires on his truck."

I looked down, the reality pressing on me, squeezing the breath out of my body.

"Oh, hon, I'm so sorry," Bev said, her warmhearted nature evident. "I didn't mean to make a joke of it. It can't be easy for either of you." She patted my arm. "You must really like him."

"Yeah, that's the problem."

"Why?"

I stared at her as if she was the one who'd lost her mind.

"Because this will follow him for the rest of his life. And if I'm with him, it means it'll follow me. I thought I could handle it, but now I'm not so sure."

"Did something else happen?"

"Well, kind of…"

"Do you want to talk about it?"

Suddenly, it all came pouring out. I really did want to talk to someone—someone who wouldn't just dive in and tell me what a horrible mistake I was making. I wanted the support of a sympathetic girlfriend.

"He has to go for mandatory drug and alcohol testing every week at the police station…" I looked at her sideways, gauging her reaction.

"And?"

"We went this morning and these asshats were waiting outside for him after. Everyone in town knows him and they all think his brother was some sort of saint. Jordan's forever getting people talking shit and blaming him for what happened. Not like he needs a reminder. He's always beating himself up about it without anyone else's help."

"So what happened with the asshats?"

"They tried to make him fight them."

"So he got in a fight?"

"No, he wouldn't do it. He's afraid of getting his parole revoked if he gets in trouble. It was horrible just standing there watching them bait him. But then some police walked by and broke it up."

Bev looked at me, puzzled.

"So you were mad with him because he *didn't* get into trouble?"

"Yes, no ... when you put it like that ... I just *hated* that he wouldn't stand up for himself!"

She looked at me thoughtfully.

"I don't know, hon, sounds to me like he was doing the smart thing. Don't forget I've met him. You can tell just by looking that he's a guy who knows how to take care of himself; it's as plain as the nose on your lil' face. He must be if he survived—however long it was in prison."

"I'm being irrational, aren't I?"

She smiled at me and patted my arm again. "Love makes you do the crazy, that's for sure."

"Hell, yeah! This is *exactly* what I've been trying to avoid. It's totally messing with my head!"

"So you do love him, then?"

Her words brought me up short. Did I? Did I love Jordan? More to the point, *could* I let myself?

"I don't know," I said, pulling out words like teeth.

She gave me a skeptical look.

"I'm not good at relationships, Bev. They have a bad habit of screwing me up. And this morning ... it scared the shit out of me. What if the police hadn't been there? What if they got to him when he was by himself? What if...?"

"Hey!" she said, softly. "What if a lot of stuff happens? None of us can know how each day is going to end. All I know is that man is head over heels for you. And looking at the way you're freaking right now, I'd say you're not far behind. That seems to be as good a place as any to start."

I was going to reply, but then we had the distraction of two families and a bunch of teenagers placing orders.

When the rush finally died down, Bev came and stood next to me.

"How's all that thinking going?" she asked.

"I just want to see him," I admitted.

She smiled at me. "Sounds like you got your answer."

It was after 1 AM when I drove through the grove of cottonwoods and down the dirt road to Jordan's house, hoping that I didn't snap an axle in the potholed road.

I should have been tired after another 10 hour shift, but I was wide awake, and it had nothing to do with the four espressos that I'd drunk in the last hour. Well, almost nothing.

The porch light was on and I'd picked up my phone to text him I'd arrived, when the door swung open and he was standing in front of me, a huge smile lighting up his face.

He was barefoot and bare chested, wearing only a pair of low slung jeans. My heart rate rocketed.

"Hey, sweetheart," he said, as he ran lightly from the porch and leaned down to open my door.

Before I'd fully stepped out, he swooped down to wrap his arms around me, and my hands automatically sought out his warm, smooth skin.

"God, I've missed you," he whispered, against my neck.

"Hi!" I said, happily. "Um, you want me to park my car around the back? I mean, are your parents going to freak when they see it in the morning?"

He shrugged. "Probably. But I don't care—unless you do?"

"No, Jordan. I don't care," I stated, clearly.

He grinned then stood up straight, leaving the top of my head about level with his chin.

"Are you hungry, sweetheart? Did you get anything to eat?"

I smiled up at him. "I just want you. Take me to bed, Jordan."

He scooped me into his arms as if he was about to carry me across the threshold, and I couldn't help yelping from surprise.

He pressed his soft lips to my mouth, and murmured against them.

"Gonna have to be quiet, my love."

"Sorry!" I whispered, trying not to laugh.

His lips found mine again and the gentle kiss turned urgent, his fingers gripping my arms and legs tightly.

We were almost through the front door when the hall light switched on and Jordan's mother stood facing us, an expression of hatred and disgust twisting her face.

"You're like a couple of dogs in heat," she sneered. "It's sickenin'. How *dare* you bring that girl into my home! How dare you behave like nothin' ever happened! You're evil! Just evil!"

To say I was stunned would be a massive understatement, but Jordan stared at her coolly as he set me on my feet.

"I love her. There's nothin' sickenin' about that. I think you're the one that needs help, Momma."

She launched herself at him, clawing at his face, rage igniting her whole body as she flailed against him.

"You killed my son!" she screamed. "You killed him!"

Jordan managed to grab her wrists, holding her away from him as she lashed out with her feet. Footsteps thundered down the stairs and Jordan's father seized hold of his wife's shoulders, tearing her from his son.

"Gloria! Stop! Just stop! For God's sake, stop! Jordan is our son, too! He's our son, too!"

"He's a murderer!" she screamed. "I cain't even look at him!

How can you bear it?"

"Because forgivin' him is the right thing to do, Gloria!" he cried out. "It's not right to punish him forever. He's all we've got left."

"Aaaagh! You're so weak! You're just like him! You're just pathetic!"

Everybody froze.

"Gloria?"

Her shoulders slumped and her hands dropped to her side, all the fight drained out of her.

"I cain't stand it anymore," she sobbed. "I won't stay in this house with *him!*"

"Momma…"

"Don't you call me that!" she hissed, turning on Jordan again. "You've brought nothin' but trouble and shame to our door. You've ruined it all. You always did! Every time somethin' happened to Michael it was because of you! He was good and decent and he had a future. You hated him for that so you took it from him! Get out! Get out!"

Jordan's face was torn with indecision. I could see that he desperately wanted to run, but his curfew forbid it.

"You know he cain't go, Gloria," said Jordan's father, his voice shaking. "He's our responsibility."

"Then *I'll* go," she screamed.

She ran up the stairs and slammed into the bedroom.

Jordan looked broken. His father gripped his shoulder for a second then he plodded up the stairs to follow his wife.

I stood there, uncertain what to do. Jordan's gaze was fixed on the floor.

"Do you want me to go?" I said, quietly.

That seemed to penetrate his despair, and he looked up at me, his beautiful brown eyes coming back into focus.

"I wouldn't blame you," he said, at last.

I touched his arm. "No, Jordan. I'm asking what *you* need. If you want me to go, I'll go; if you want me to stay, I'll stay."

His eyes were huge and dark as he stared back at me. "Stay.

Please, stay."

I nodded and took his hand in mine.

At that moment, his mom surged down the stairs, dragging a suitcase. It thundered down behind her, each thud a tolling bell.

When she reached the bottom, she glared at Jordan.

"You ruined my life," she said, coldly. "I hate you."

He stared back at her, his face oddly expressionless. "I know, Momma. I forgive you."

She gasped, almost as if he'd slapped her. Then her lips drew back in a feral snarl and she spat at him.

I watched, appalled, as the spittle ran down his bare chest.

"Murderer!" she hissed.

The front door slammed behind her and a moment later, we heard her car drive away.

I pulled out a tissue to clean him up. He didn't move

"Come on," I said, quietly. "Let's go to bed."

He nodded without speaking, and threaded his fingers through mine again.

When we entered his room, I dropped my purse on the floor and wrapped him in a tight hug.

"I think you're right about her," I said, stroking his face with the tips of my fingers. "I don't think she's well. She needs help. Where do you think she's gone?"

"She's got an old school friend who lives in Fort Worth, she might have gone there. I don't really know. Maybe she told dad."

He sat on the bed, looking exhausted.

"I have to get out of here, Torrey. I'm destroyin' my parents' marriage as well as ... I'll tell Carson; maybe she can get me into one of those half-way homes..."

I sat next to him and leaned my head against his shoulder.

"I think they're managing to fuck everything up by themselves, Jordan. But I agree about one thing, it's not good for you living here in this ... atmosphere. It must be so stressful. When your mom comes back ... well, I think you should look into finding somewhere else to live."

He nodded.

"I get so wound up sometimes that I…"

He couldn't look at me, and my eyes dropped to his hands. His long fingers were rubbing the inside of his wrist. My eyes widened as I took in the thin lines of scars for the first time.

I grabbed at his hands, but he snatched them away.

"Jordan! What did you do?"

"Old scars. Nothin' to worry about."

"Nothing to worry about? Jordan, these are … this … did you try to kill yourself?"

He looked away.

"Yeah."

"In prison?"

"Yeah … the second time."

"Oh my God! What … when was the first time?"

He took a deep breath.

"I thought about it all the time, pretty much. The first time … when I was at the hospital that night and I realized, really realized that Mikey was … gone … I thought about it then."

I squeezed his fingers again. "It's okay," I whispered. "I'm here."

He looked like he was in pain as he continued to speak.

"It must have been obvious to the hospital staff and police that I was drunk, and I admitted right away that I'd been in the driver's seat. But they had to wait for the blood test to come back. I had a blood-alcohol content of 0.24, three times the legal limit in Texas—and I was under 21. They arrested me on the spot and as soon as the hospital released me, I was taken away.

"Although the case started in the juvenile system because I was a minor, the prosecutors asked to charge me as an adult. I don't even remember if they did, maybe the request was denied—the whole trial—it's hazy. I didn't really care what happened to me by that point. As soon as it sunk in that … that I'd killed Mikey, I wanted to die too. I was on suicide watch for the first couple of weeks. I nearly managed it once." He took a deep breath. "And again in prison, but that was later on."

I was struggling to speak, but eventually I managed to ask,

"How? How did you ... try..."

He shrugged.

"You get creative. The first time I tied some sheets together and tried to hang myself. I was found..."

"And ... and the second time."

"I planned it better. I waited 'til I had the cell to myself for a few hours. I'd been grindin' down the end of my toothbrush. The plastic is hard, so you can make it pretty sharp. Some guys used them as weapons. I just wanted to hurt myself. I opened a couple of veins."

"But ... someone found you."

"After a couple of hours. Guess I had a lot of blood, or somethin'. So I didn't even manage to do that right. They made me see a shrink after that. I don't think it made much difference. He didn't really care one way or another. Nor did I."

I choked out a small sob, but the memories were pouring out of him too fast to stop.

"You have to wise up right quick, learn to feel people out when you're inside. The first guys who come up to you are the dangerous ones, the predators, but also the losers and the snitches. I learned it was safer to keep to myself. This big guy tried to punk me the first week I was there..."

"What do you mean?" I asked, afraid of his answer.

"He wanted to have sex with me. I was shocked and just beat the crap out of him. Turned out that was the best thing I could have done because the others like him left me alone after that.

"There's a lot of weird shit you have to get used to. The restrooms don't have doors on them—too many chances for people gettin' beaten up or worse. You get your own clothes taken away from you—well, I didn't have much and what I had on was covered in blood, so ... I was strip-searched and fingerprinted when I got there. And small stuff, like you only get three minutes to have your shower, and lights out is at 9:30 PM; I arrived in the summer so it was still light outside which was weird. Not that I could sleep. There were some kids who screamed all night, some of them were really young. One kid was like 13 or somethin'. There was a lot of fear, mostly because you didn't know what was gonna happen next. But because I didn't care, it made me … I don't know … like I was untouchable or somethin'. Some of the older boys tried to mess with me, but I was pretty tall for my age, so I got in a lot of fights. That didn't help when it came to sentencin', I guess."

"Did your parents come and see you much when you were inside?"

"Once when I was still in juvie; once again when I was sentenced—the first time I was sentenced."

"What happened?"

He pulled a face.

"Momma cried. Dad told me … Dad told me I was a murderer and I should change my surname because he didn't want to have me for a son."

"Wow, that's … harsh."

I felt him shrug.

"He hates me. They both hate me. But I don't blame them— I hate myself. If I'd just done one little thing different that night, Mikey might still be alive."

"He was the older brother, he could have decided at any time not to get in the car with you."

"He was protectin' me, like he always did. He said he wasn't going to let me drunk-drive my ass home. It was pretty much the last thing he said to me."

"He loved you."

Jordan didn't reply. I looked up so I could see his face. His eyes glittered, and I saw him rub moisture away with his fingertips.

"The last time I saw them was after the funeral. I'd wanted to go to the service but they wouldn't let me. I still don't know if that was like a rule or whether my parents didn't want me there. It was the day I was sentenced: Momma couldn't even look at me, and I didn't have nothin' to say to them neither. Dad just kept sayin' I should pray for Mikey. I was sent to a long-term detention facility in north Texas, and from there to prison. I didn't see them again. Not 'til eight weeks ago." I blew out a long breath. "I guess you know the rest."

"Have you ... have you thought about doing it, um, hurting yourself, since ... since you got out of prison?"

He nodded again.

"I thought about it, but I didn't ... I couldn't..."

"Jordan, promise me, *promise me* that if you ever feel ... that you won't ... that you'll come and talk to me first. *Promise me!*"

I thought he was going to refuse, but eventually he nodded slowly.

"I promise."

I rubbed my eyes tiredly.

"Okay then. Let's talk in the morning. We can think about finding you somewhere else to live. We won't solve anything when it's so late."

"I don't know why you're still here," he said, his voice aching. "But I'm so fuckin' glad you are."

I'd been shocked to the core to think that Jordan had tried to kill himself. Twice, maybe more. It broke my heart to think of a 16-year-old version of Jordan getting caught up in all of that ugliness. But I'd been even more stunned when I realized that he'd thought about it since he'd gotten out of prison.

It was too much to think about when it was so late and I was beyond tired. My brain was spinning in so many different directions, I felt dizzy. I badly needed to sleep.

"I'm glad I'm here, too," I sighed. "And I'm really sorry to have to mention this, but I'm dying to pee!"

He gave a small smile, and I saw a glimmer of light behind his eyes.

"Two doors down on the left, sweetheart. I'll be waitin'."

I grabbed my purse, glad I always carried a spare toothbrush with me, and headed to the bathroom. Soap and water would be fine for cleaning off my makeup, but I *had* to brush my teeth, whatever else I skimped on.

A few minutes later, I slipped back into his room and shut the door.

He was sitting up in bed, his jeans neatly folded and laid out on the chair, his face thoughtful. It was all too tidy in his room, too institutional, so I kicked off my boots into different corners, flung my socks over my head and dropped my pants where I stood.

He watched me, and I was happy to see amusement twitching at the corners of his mouth.

"You could do that strippin' professionally, sweetheart."

"Screw you," I sniffed.

"Works for me," he smiled.

I unhooked my bra and slid it through the sleeves of my t-shirt.

"I'm not gettin' the full show?" he queried.

"Nope. You're sitting in the cheap seats—this is the discount version."

I climbed over him, planting a kiss on his surprised lips as I passed, then scooted down under the sheet. He pulled me into his chest and I lay my head against his heart, listening to the slow, steady beat.

His muscles flexed as he bent to kiss my hair.

"Sleep now, sweetheart," he said.

It was still dark when I woke. I stretched sleepily but jumped when I felt a warm hand on my stomach.

"Sorry, sweetheart. Just remindin' you I'm here. I thought I was gonna get punched in the head for a moment there."

"Oh, God! I forgot where I was!"

I was still groggy, my throat husky from sleep.

"Good surprise?" he said, and I could hear the tense anxiety in his voice.

"Definitely."

"I'm happy about that," he breathed out, running his hand upward so it brushed the underside of my breasts.

I arched my back and hummed with pleasure.

"Do I finally get my booty call?" I asked.

"You can have anythin' you want, sweetheart."

He lifted my body from the bed with one hand and drew my t-shirt off with the other. Then he laid me down carefully, reverently, and hovered over me, his hot mouth wrapping around my nipple, sucking firmly, his other hand molding my breast and teasing the bud until both were standing upright.

"There's a lot to be said," he murmured, "for takin' our time."

I laughed softly. "We do seem to have been in one helluva hurry before."

"Fast, slow, hard, soft—I want it all with you, Torrey. I cain't imagine not wantin' you. Ever."

I ran my hands down his back, letting my nails drift along his spine. He shivered and moaned, the sound vibrating through my flesh.

His body was all hard ridges and edges, his fine cheekbones, his sharp jaw, his ass firm, with two wonderful dips where his thigh muscles met hipbone. His biceps were rigid as he held himself above me, and his strong forearms were flexed on either side, capturing my body.

My fingers rediscovered the narrow strip of raised scar tissue at the base of his ribs, and my legs hooked over his calves, my feet massaging the lean muscles.

I heard the breath catch in his throat when I wrapped one hand around his erection, stroking the hard silkiness.

"God, how that feels!" he gasped. "You don't know."

But I did know, because I felt it, too, inside my heart.

"Let me up," I said, sudden lust and need stretching my voice thin and tight. "I have to get a condom for us."

Swooping down to kiss me quickly first, he rolled onto his back and flung his arms above his head, his breathing faster now.

The downside of deciding that his room was too tidy was that I couldn't find my jeans in the gray gloom of early dawn.

"Goddamn it! Where did I throw my pants?"

"There's something so hot about you sayin' that, sweetheart," he chuckled.

"Not funny! I've already lost my favorite sports bra because of you."

"Waal," he drawled, "seein' as I cain't afford to buy you a new one, I'll just have to run behind you holdin' onto your beautiful titties."

"Yeah, that'd work," I snorted, "for about two minutes before we both get arrested for violating decency laws."

"Aw, you found the flaw in my grand plan," he said, feigning sadness.

"What can I say, I'm a lateral thinker. Goddamn it! Where are my pants?"

I was blinded when he switched on the bedside lamp.

"Better, sweetheart?"

"No, it's not better!" I said, grumpily. "I can't see a thing."

He laughed. "I can, and you sure look fine bendin' over like that. Gets a man thinkin' all sorts of things."

I threw a sock at him, but that only made him laugh harder. I *really* liked that sound.

He twisted over offering a view of his bitable backside, then scooped up my pants and threw them to me. "Touchdown!"

"Uh-uh!" I shook my head. "Pass interference!"

"How'd you figure that, sweetheart? Hope you're not a sore loser."

"Jordan, if you want to get laid, you'll stop talking now."

He didn't reply, so I looked up. He mimed locking his lips and throwing away the key.

"Oh, very good. See how long you can keep quiet for!"

He nodded and smiled.

I gripped his dick and pulled it toward me. He winced and squinted at me but didn't speak.

"Oops! I think that was a bit harder than I meant."

He nodded in agreement, his eyes opening wide.

"Don't you like it rough, cowboy?"

His mouth popped open but then he shrugged his shoulders, and a slow smile clung at the corners of his full lips.

"Don't move your hands. Leave them there, above your head."

He watched me, one corner of his mouth lifting in acknowledgement.

I slapped my hands onto his chest, and ran my nails over his pecs and down across his abs then tugged on the tufts of wiry light brown hair that covered his groin.

"So, never had a girl in your bedroom?"

He shook his head.

"In your car?"

He nodded.

"In the truck?"

He nodded.

"Because you know what, Jordan? It would be pretty gross if you and Mikey were tag-teaming some chick. I mean, I hope you at least wiped the seats down afterwards."

He grinned and shook his head. I made a mental note to ask him another time what he meant by that.

"Hmm … at school?"

He smiled and nodded again.

"On your school's football field?"

More nods, more smiles.

"After prom?"

His smile fell away and he shook his head.

"Shit, sorry! I know you didn't get to go. Sorry, I got caught up in the game."

He shrugged and looked away.

Gently, I pulled his lips back to mine and kissed him slowly, showing him my apology was real.

"Now, where were we?" I said, flinging one leg across his hips and settling back on his thighs.

"This game is called 'favorite positions'. You want to play?"

His eyes glowed, and he nodded his head jerkily several times.

"Good. Have you ever … been on top?"

He raised one eyebrow and nodded.

"Don't worry—I'm just getting warmed up. Have you ever … had the woman on top?"

Eye roll. Head nod.

"Have you ever done it doggy style from behind, other than with me?"

He nodded rapidly.

"Ah, now we're getting somewhere. You like that one?"

Vigorous head nod.

"Have you ever had someone go down on you?"

A sly smile crossed his face and he blew me a kiss, nodding slowly.

"Have you ever gone down on someone?"

The smile dropped a little but he nodded again.

I raised an eyebrow. "You've been holding out on me, cowboy. You definitely owe me that one!"

He winked and threw me a scorching smile.

"What about getting it mutual?"

He looked puzzled.

"I'm talking doing a sixty-niner."

He shook his head.

"Hmm, no, well that's okay. I'm not thrilled by the idea. I mean, unless you're the kind of person who likes having someone's ass stuck in your face."

He wrinkled his nose and shook his head.

"I'm not saying I'm averse to a little butt play…"

His eyes got really wide, and he licked his lips.

"Don't go breaking a sweat. I don't take it up the ass. I'm just saying, I like having my ass worked a little. You up for that?"

He smiled and nodded.

"Good. You want some of that back?"

He shook his head slowly.

"Never tried it, huh?"

He shook his head again.

"Okay, well we might need to experiment with that a bit. I'll put it on the list."

He smiled, raised an eyebrow then motioned writing something down.

"Oh yeah, I have a list. I might even show it to you some day."

He smiled.

"Okay, so where were we … um … what about in a hot tub?"

He nodded and held up one finger.

"Oh, just the once? Or just one girl?"

He shrugged and nodded.

"You want to do that again?"

More nodding—very fast nodding.

"In a swimming pool?"

A huge smile crossed his face.

"Oh, bringing back some good memories, huh?"

He grinned at me.

"Well, we can relive that some time. Um … sex in a public place. Not counting a swimming pool or hot tub at someone's home, like totally public—a park or something?"

He smiled. He nodded.

"Wow, Jordan! You really got around for a 16-year-old! When did you start?"

He held up both hands then four fingers on his left hand.

"Fourteen?"

He nodded then pointed at me.

"Oh, I was a good girl. I was nearly 18 before I gave it up."

He looked surprised.

"What can I say? I thought I was in love, that I was saving myself for the right guy and that it would last forever. How wrong can you be? Well, you already know how that story ended."

His sad expression came back and he reached up a hand, resting it against my cheek.

"Don't worry, I've been making up for it since."

He grinned and gave me a thumbs up.

"So, um, you like getting your balls sucked?"

He held out his hand horizontally and gave me a so-so gesture.

"But you like getting your dick sucked, obviously."

This time I got two thumbs up.

"Have you ever been handcuffed?"

A dark look passed across his face.

Oh shit.

"I meant … you know … for sex? Sorry, dumb question. I'm guessing you wouldn't like that."

He shook his head, his eyes dark with ugly secrets.

"So, um, you wouldn't want to tie me up?"

He looked like he was in pain, and he shook his head again.

"That's okay. I get it. I was just … you know … checking."

He cocked his head to one side, asking me the same question.

"It can be a turn on, but I haven't done it much. I'd have to really trust the guy. But that's okay, there's loads of other stuff we can do. Oh, I know, what about toys?"

He shook his head.

"Never tried a vibrator? They've got some really cool ones now. There's this one called a rabbit and…"

He shook his head and patted his chest. I was puzzled for a moment, then he pointed at his dick, which was still erect and twitched as I glanced down.

"Oh, right! You think a woman doesn't need a vibrator if she's got you!"

He nodded again, his smile stretching from ear to ear.

"Hmm, good point. But maybe I'll show you sometime and you might change your mind."

He pointed at me and raised his eyebrows.

"Oh sure! If I haven't been able to get a hook up, having a vibrator saves my hand getting a cramp."

He scowled and crossed his hands across his chest.

"Oh, relax! I haven't had any hook ups since I met you."

He smiled, looking relieved.

"What about you? Met any women who took a like to what they saw?"

He winked at me, and I felt ready to cut a bitch!

"Who? When? Who was it?"

He grinned and mimed drinking coffee. Relief washed through me.

"You mean Bev?"

He nodded.

"Oh, that's okay then."

He raised his eyebrows.

"That doesn't mean I'm going to share you! She knows you're off limits. But that poses another question. Ever had a threesome?"

He nodded.

"Two guys, one girl?"

He shook his head, curling his lip slightly.

"Oh, right. Two girls pleasuring you?"

He smiled.

I wasn't sure if I wanted to ask this next question but I plowed on.

"You want to try that again sometime?"

"No," he said, breaking his long silence. "I only want you."

He pulled me onto his chest and kissed me deeply, and I savored the way he tasted, completely natural, sweet and delicious.

Then he took the condom from the bedside table and handed it back to me.

"I want to make love to you, Torrey. So badly, sweetheart."

I shuffled back off his thighs and rolled the condom down his length. His hard stomach contracted as he held his breath.

When it was on securely, he tugged it experimentally.

"You're a safety boy!"

He glanced up at me. "I'm a what?"

"You like to be safe—no fuck ups, so to speak."

He grinned up at me.

"Waal, I guess you know what they said in health ed classes,

'No glove, no love'."

"Is that what they told you guys?"

"Yeah, but I always preferred the version Mikey came up with."

"Which was?"

"Wrap it in foil, before you check her oil."

"Oh my God! That got him laid?"

"Waal, I don't know if he actually said that to the girl..."

I huffed at that. "What other sayings did he have?"

"Cover that lumber before you pump her..."

"Ugh!"

"And my personal favorite, 'Wrap your bait before you mate'."

"Gross! Just as long as they do the job."

"Sweetheart, I'm cleaner than an ice cube in Alaska, but I wouldn't want to knock you up unless you wanted to be."

I choked, turning it into a cough while my eyes watered.

He rubbed my back gently.

"If you wanted kids, I'd be honored to be your baby-daddy," he said, planting a soft kiss in my hair.

"Not a good conversation to have right now," I insisted.

He gave a small smile and lay back on the pillows.

"I'm all yours, sweetheart. Do your worst."

"Is that a challenge?"

"Not really. I trust you."

For the second time in less than a minute, his words shocked me. *He trusted me.* After everything he'd been through, with all the challenges he faced, he trusted *me.*

"I won't hurt you," I said, quietly.

He smiled up at me. "I know."

I leaned down, and he tilted his face to capture my lips with his. Then he licked up my throat to behind my jaw and nipped at my earlobe, making me squirm.

He moved again, his tongue circling my nipple, and I pushed my chest into his face, begging him to take more. He ran his calloused hands over my breasts, the rough skin delicious on my overheated flesh.

Between my thighs, his dick twitched again and I ground down on him, eliciting a rough growl of desire.

I rubbed his tip over my clit and a shiver went through me.

"Sweetheart," he whispered. "Can I do some of that other stuff on your list? Because it was a real fuckin' turn on, you talkin' 'bout it."

"Which parts?"

"Hmm, I'd like to taste that sweet lil' pussy of yours— preferably before the lube from the condom makes it taste like ass. Uh, sorry, that came out wrong. Aw, hell! You know what I mean!"

"Luckily for you I do!" I said, halfway between a laugh and a porn-star moan of longing.

He rolled me over then knelt on the floor, dragging me to the edge of the bed. Then he grabbed my feet and rested them on his shoulders.

"Open wide!" he grinned devilishly, dipping his head toward me.

God! His stubbly chin over my clit set off a tidal wave of lust. Sparks of electricity started shooting down my legs, making me curl my toes.

"Oh, freakin' yes!" I yelled, forgetting his father was sleeping down the hall.

He unfurled his tongue winding it around the nub in slow, sensuous flicks. Then he pushed two of those skilled mechanic's fingers inside me, massaging my inner edge. I couldn't work out if it was all that flirty talking, or 36 hours without having him inside me, who knows, but I came harder than a freight train.

Poor guy! He had to put his palm over my mouth to try and stifle the piercing shrieks I was making. A pillow might have worked better.

My legs trembled and one foot slipped from his shoulder. He caught it before I could kick him in the nuts.

"Good so far?" he chuckled.

I grunted something monosyllabic and didn't object when he

hauled me back up the bed and flipped me over.

"Ready for more?" he asked, his voice suddenly strained.

"Uh huh," I said, eloquently.

A finger up my butt brought me around quickly, and I gasped.

"Just my finger, sweetheart, I swear. I'd never hurt you."

Then he dragged my hips back so I was on all fours, and he pushed inside gently, filling me, stretching me. Yeah, no way that dick was ever fitting up my ass. *Ever.*

He pulled out deliciously slowly and pushed back inside in a long, sensual stroke.

"Oh, fuck, this is going to be too quick," he bit out.

"Then make it hard!" I gasped.

He obliged immediately, hammering into me, the finger in my butt still dipping in and out with a different rhythm.

He shuddered suddenly, and I heard a strangled cry from the hot breath on my back. He pinched my clit, silently begging me to follow quickly. Overwhelmed by sensations, I clenched around him as frenzied waves took control of my body.

We collapsed together, dual breaths panting across the sheets.

Two doors down, I heard the toilet flush.

"I think we woke your dad," I mumbled.

"Looks like," he said, his silent laugh shaking the bed.

I fell asleep instantly. The next time I woke up, the bed beside me was cold and empty.

Instead, there was a small flower plucked from the backyard, resting on a note.

I unfolded the paper and saw an amazingly detailed pencil sketch of me sleeping. Jordan must have sat at the bottom of the bed drawing me while I slept.

And then I read the words he'd written.

'A life without love is like a sunless garden when the flowers are dead.'
I love you.
Jordan x

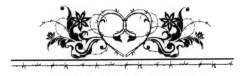

Chapter 12 – Endurance

Jordan

Life started getting good once Momma left. We all knew it was true, and that kind of sucked. She was still my momma, even though she didn't want to be. But the tension in the house left with her, and everything was calmer.

Hulk was giving me three days most weeks, and I'd had four clients ask for personal designs painted on their cars and trucks. Two more were lined up. I had a freakin' waiting list! Torrey said I should put together a portfolio. I didn't know about that, but it was a good feeling. Scratch that—it was a *great* feeling, like people saying I was good at something for a change.

Dad and Momma were talking, I think, but she still refused to come home while I was there. It hurt, but there wasn't anything I could do about it. Dad was learning to accept me again and on the rare evenings when Torrey wasn't around, we had some real conversations. We had to get to know each other again with eight years to catch up on. I'd been a boy when I was sent away; I'd grown up fast, and he didn't quite know what to make of the man who'd come home.

When I told him about the first couple of months in juvie and how I'd tried to kill myself, he broke down in tears. I think it made it real for him, how close he'd come to losing both his sons. I couldn't bring myself to tell him that the first time I tried to end my own life wasn't the last. Some things were best kept hidden even now.

From what he told me about that time, he and Momma had pretty much just shut down. He also admitted that it had been their decision to block me from coming to Mikey's funeral. That hurt a lot.

Most everyone in the high school had gone, by the sound of it, including the teachers. Even some of the football players from other high schools had turned up in their team colors as a mark of respect. Mikey's best friend Ryan Dupont gave the eulogy, and the gym had been used to host the wake after the funeral. My name wasn't mentioned.

Gradually, I began to really talk to my dad. I had a lot of trust issues and hadn't forgotten that he and Momma had basically thrown me to the wolves eight years ago, but Torrey had taught me that keeping it all inside was poison to us. Momma was the living proof of that.

So I told him about some of the crazy stunts Mikey and I had gotten up to, and I think it opened his eyes to a few things. I felt okay about telling him Mikey's secrets after all of these years. It kind of put things in perspective for both of us. I wasn't no saint, but I wasn't all sinner either. It had been a bit of a shock for him to find out how heavily into weed Mikey had been. I'd always been more of a drinker. He wanted me to promise that once my parole was over that I wouldn't go back to the booze. I couldn't do that—I was looking forward to having a beer now and again. I'd probably stay away from hard liquor, but I was done making promises I couldn't keep.

Our relationship was a work in progress but we were getting there.

As for Momma … it wasn't looking good.

Things with Torrey and me were fan-fucking-tastic. I didn't change my mind about her being the best thing that had ever happened to me. We'd been dating nearly three months and she never ceased to amaze me with her strength and beauty and love of life. And, slowly at first, we started making plans together for the future, our future. God, I loved saying that! *Our future.*

After that first night when Momma left, Torrey never really went home again—to the Rectory. The Reverend wanted her to stay there, but had refused to allow Torrey to have me in their home. That was a deal breaker as far as she was concerned. Torrey's view was that if the Rectory was truly her home, too, then her momma would allow me inside. The Rev's view was she wouldn't condone us having a physical relationship out of wedlock. Yeah right, like half her parishioners weren't shacked up together. She wasn't saying it, but the real reason was my ex-con badge. Torrey said she was a freakin' hypocrite, and didn't want anything to do with her.

I wasn't happy that they'd fallen out because of me, but Torrey insisted that she wasn't going to compromise on this. Woman was stubborn.

Despite Torrey putting her money where her mouth was, so to speak, she also admitted that she was shit scared of commitment. We talked about that a lot. In different ways, it was important to both of us. For her, it came down to having watched her parents' marriage disintegrate. It had left a mark on her, and I don't think it helped that Dad and Momma had severe problems, too. But we were working things out, kind of making it up as we went along.

Things in town were pretty much the same, maybe even a little better. Most times I visited, Torrey was with me, and folk were less likely to start something when she was around. I felt bad that she was my human shield, and frankly it sucked being such a freakin' pussy that I had to hide behind my woman.

But the day when the asshats had tried to get me to fight them had really made Torrey understand why I reacted the way I did; it had made her see that even the slightest breath of trouble, and my parole would be revoked. No way was I going back to prison. *Ever.* No fucking way. I'd rather die.

Officer Carson turned out to be pretty nice. I saw her every couple of weeks or so.

The house searches continued every five or six weeks, but we worked around them. Sometimes it was a guy called Martins. We all hated him. He threw his weight around and made it pretty damn clear that he thought I was no better than a shit stain on his shorts, and that he expected me to fuck up any moment.

Torrey hated them the most. Her shit was all over the house. I swear, she was the untidiest person I'd ever met. She only had to be home a few minutes and her shoes were in one room, her purse in another, her sweater somewhere else. She lost her cell phone ten times a day; I was tempted to put her car keys on a leash and tie them to her. The bathroom was littered with lipstick and face stuff and God-knows-what. I pretended it drove me crazy, but really, I loved it. I think she knew that.

Waking up with her in my arms every morning was officially the best part of my day. That and falling asleep with her after we'd made love. Even though I didn't think it was possible, I fell for her a little more deeply every day. I loved everything about her: the way she'd scrunch up her nose before she sneezed; the way she couldn't sit on the sofa without lying all over it so I was shoved up into the corner; the way she danced to the radio when she was cooking.

She was a God-awful cook, too, but for some reason she seemed to think she was like a freakin' chef or something. I should have been warned from that very first meal she made me when I just about melted my tongue trying her chili somethin' or other. On the days she wasn't working, she insisted on cooking 'for the menfolk' as she put it. I know Dad felt the same fear of her being in the kitchen as I did, because he'd try to insist on bringing home pizza those times so she could 'have a night off'. Sometimes it worked.

I found I enjoyed messing with food. After years of eating

overcooked gloop, tasting new things and trying out recipes was a little slice of freedom. I wasn't bad at it either—certainly better than Torrey, although she wouldn't admit it. Dad joked that I could probably get a job as a short order cook. I knew he wasn't really serious, but it felt like I had other options to earn money and that was a big thing for me.

Prison institutionalizes you. You're told when to wake up, when to go to sleep, when to eat, when to wash, and when to shit. Every second of every day is worked out for you. The only decision you get to make is whether to eat with a spoon or your fingers. Seriously.

Officer Carson said that a lot of guys didn't make it on the outside because freedom actually scares them—too many big choices to make every day; too many chances to fuck it up by picking the wrong one. Yeah, I knew what that felt like. I'd been so fucking scared when I'd first gotten released. Everything seemed like a huge, impossible challenge. Even now, meeting a stranger for the first time could have my anxiety levels shooting off of the chart, but it was getting better. Sometimes I even felt normal.

Dad and Torrey got along really well, and I was thankful for that. It had taken some adjustment all around having her living with us, but it was good. She called him 'Paul', and he called her 'Missy D' or 'Miss Take' which made her laugh. I think he would have been pretty happy for us to make it official and to have her as a daughter-in-law. I was working on that, but no way I was going to ask her to marry me while I was still on parole. That shit was just wrong.

I talked to Mikey about it. Several times a month I'd stop by the cemetery on my way home from work. I'd tell him about my day, or about some crazy thing that Torrey had done, or about how good she made me feel. I don't know why, but I felt like he was there, and that he could hear me.

It bothered me that Torrey and her momma barely spoke, and that I was the reason. She said it wasn't anything to do with me, but I called bullshit on that. I tried to talk to her about it but she said she'd speak to her momma when the Rev was ready to accept me as part of her daughter's life. I couldn't really argue it, so I had to trust that things would get worked out between them somehow.

It was real slow, but gradually I started feeling more comfortable about going out and meeting people. Not everyone in this one-horse town knew or cared who I was. Or who I'd been.

Torrey had been nudging me to get out more. The choices were pretty limited as I was still uncomfortable going into town, and had a finite catchment area and a curfew, but that didn't stop her prodding and poking at me to try stuff. Her latest plan was to double-date with Bev and her new guy Pete: a picnic at the beach. I wasn't sure about it. Bev was okay; I genuinely liked her. And Torrey said that Bev had told her guy everything about me, and she said he was nice about it. He had some high-powered job in a bank in Corpus. Just what I needed to make me feel like a total loser.

"It's just a picnic, babe!" Torrey said. "Two hot girls in bikinis, and food—what's not to like? Look, just try it. If you feel uncomfortable we can leave at any time. But I promise Pete's a really nice guy."

We were in bed at the time. She'd worked out that I couldn't refuse her anything when she was naked. She was sneaky like that. I don't think she knew that I was wise to her game. Didn't change a freakin' thing though, she had me by the balls and we both knew it.

"Fine! We'll go to the beach. But we'll take separate cars, just in case. Deal?"

She smiled and kissed my chin, happy she'd got her way.

I was feeling anxious on Sunday morning, but trying not to show it. Torrey knew me too well and sent me out to the garage to throw some weights around.

I was pretty okay with Bev, but this guy knew about me and we'd be spending several hours together. It threw me right back to how I'd been when I first got released. I didn't trust people easily and even though Torrey said he was cool, I knew she always gave people the benefit of the doubt, like she had with me.

Dad had gone to church as usual. I don't know if he talked to Torrey's momma when he was there. He didn't say and neither of us asked. I had the feeling maybe he did because sometimes when he came back, he looked like he wanted to say something. He hadn't so far; maybe he was building up to it.

After an hour, Torrey came and found me in the garage doing sit ups.

"Mmm! All hot and sweaty. I like!"

I sat up and ran a hand along the inside of her thigh. "You want to get all hot and sweaty with me, sweetheart?"

She laughed and tried to swat my hand away. "Your sexy talk isn't going to work, Jordan Kane. You're so not getting out of this beach date."

I moved my hand higher, until it was under her pajama shorts and heading toward nirvana. I wasn't the only one with a weak spot.

She moaned and bit her lip. And yep, she was wet and I was hard.

"Jordan!" she whined. "We have to get going!"

"You sure?" I said, slipping a finger inside her.

"Oh, God! Fuck it! Upstairs now!"

I would have taken her there and then but as a concession to Dad, we kept fucking around the house to a minimum.

She charged out of the garage, and I ran after her.

Two, maybe three minutes later, we were both sweaty and I had a smile on my face the size of Texas.

"You're so bad!" she gasped, kissing my chest. "My delicious bad boy. Now go throw your cute lil' ass in the shower, and I'll think about seducing you behind the dunes later."

We were going to be late. I didn't have it in me to care.

We met up with Bev and Pete right on the boundary of my 10 mile limit, just outside Matagorda Bay. Bev knew some secret spot, she said, and nobody else ever went there. I hoped she was right. Mikey and I had hiked all around here when we were kids so I'm not sure how 'secret' any part of it could be. The last thing I needed was to run into someone I knew from before.

"Hey, hon!" Bev called to Torrey as we climbed out of my truck. "Hey, Jordan!"

I waved, and Torrey ran up to hug Bev. She was leaning against a brand new Mercedes, and a guy with glasses had his arms around her.

I tensed when he gave Torrey a hug and she kissed him on the cheek as if they were best buds. I couldn't help being a possessive shit, even though I knew it meant I was acting like a prick.

I don't know what he saw on my face, but the guy looked nervous and pushed his glasses up his nose, dropping his arms from Torrey as if she'd burned him.

Torrey didn't seem to notice, or if she did, she ignored it.

"Jordan, come say hi. This is Pete—Bev's boyfriend."

We shook hands, rather reluctantly on my part.

"Hey, man," Pete said, with an open smile. "Good to meet you."

I nodded but didn't speak, wincing internally when I saw the angry glint in Torrey's eye. She'd *definitely* noticed my dumbass behavior now. I was a fucking idiot, acting like I just fell off the turnip truck. Officially. Maybe they gave out certificates.

I shoved my hands in my pockets and stared at the ground.

"So," said Bev, after an uncomfortable silence, "we standing here growing old, or what? Jordan, we'll need to go in your truck."

I shot a look at Torrey, and she shrugged unconvincingly. I'd said I'd only come if we drove separately in case I felt the need to bail. Yeah, right.

"There'll be some off-roading across the dunes," Bev continued, oblivious of the stare down Torrey and I were currently having, "and I don't think the Benz is up to that."

Pete rolled his eyes and grinned at her. "It's a piece of precision engineering, not a darn beach buggy!"

He was right about that: it was a damn nice set of wheels. I couldn't help drooling over the sleek metal and aerodynamic design. I'd never so much as seen one of these cars up close, let alone driven one. The guy must be seriously loaded. The kicker was he only looked a few years older than me.

Maybe if I'd done a degree instead of time in the State pen, I'd be driving a fancy car like that and not my dead brother's 17-year-old truck.

I may not have seen one of these cars before, but I'd sure read about them.

"You notice a difference with it being 200 pounds lighter than the steel version?"

The women stared, but Pete looked pleased.

"You bet!" he said, enthusiastically. "This is the six liter version with a seven speed automatic transmission. Flies like an eagle."

I nodded. "That sounds about right. You got the semi-active adjustable dampin', or did you go for the ABC suspension system?"

Pete started to answer, but Torrey interrupted.

"Oh my God! They're speaking in tongues. Bev, you're in the back with me, hon."

Pete shook his head sadly and smiled. "Bev doesn't appreciate beauty when she sees it."

"I appreciate you plenty, babe," she shot back.

Pete winked at her but didn't disagree.

Torrey was right—he was a nice guy. I pulled my head out of my ass and tried to act normal, whatever the fuck that was.

We transferred all their shit from his trunk to the bed of my truck, then he climbed up front with me and I started to relax as we talked cars and engines. It almost made me forget what I was.

When we got to Bev's secret spot, I recognized it at once. I'd been there a bunch of times with Mikey and some of the other guys we used to hang with. I seemed to remember it was a favorite place to go talk shit, smoke weed, whatever. Maybe that's why the memories were so hazy. Whatever—it was a long way from nowhere, so I had hopes of us being left alone.

We started unloading the food. Each of the girls had packed enough to feed a platoon. I didn't think we'd be running out of supplies anytime soon.

"Jeez!" Bev said with a grunt, as she went to lift one of the coolers. "What did you put in here, hon?"

"Just a couple of cases of beer," Pete chuckled.

I froze, and Torrey threw me an apologetic look.

Bev looked horrified. "Pete! You dumbass!" she hissed. "You can't bring *alcohol!*"

I could see that he got it immediately, his expression contrite.

"Aw fuck, man! I completely forgot. My bad. I'll leave it here."

Bev slapped his arm. "And what's he supposed to say if someone comes along and he's caught with beer in his truck? I can't believe you've been so stupid, Pete!"

I felt really bad for the guy, but it was fucking humiliating having them talk about me like that.

"I didn't think," Pete started to babble, his gaze flipping between me and Bev, who looked mad enough to tear him a new one. "Shit, man, I'm so sorry…"

I waved away his apology. "You guys should drink it. There's no law says you cain't. I think we'll be okay a ways out here."

Bev was shooting daggers at Pete, and I could see he was gutted. Torrey rubbed my back gently.

"You okay?"

"Yeah," I said, staring anywhere but at her.

She looked skeptical but didn't press me further. What was

there to say?

We carried the rest of the food to the shore in silence. I hated that my baggage was ruining everyone else's day. Still, I had a lifetime to get used to it. What a freakin' thought.

Torrey spread out a couple of blankets and sat down, patting a space beside her.

She smiled up at me. "And that t-shirt's coming off. I need something other than the ocean to look at."

"Hell, yeah!" laughed Bev. "I second that!"

"Hey!" Pete yelped. "You're supposed to be wanting to look at *my* hot body!"

Bev laughed. "I love you loads, Pete, but you sit in an office all day. Jordan is *ripped!*"

"Okay, feelin' kind of self-conscious now," I laughed uneasily, sitting down next to Torrey on the blanket.

Torrey solved the problem by tearing my t-shirt over my head.

Pete's face fell. "I think I'll leave my shirt on after all."

"Don't be such a baby," laughed Bev. "I need a view in stereo!"

"Hey, Jordan," moaned Pete, pretending to be hurt. "When did women get to be such pervs? I feel like such a piece of meat—completely objectified."

"Beats me, man. I just do what Torrey tells me."

They all laughed and Bev looked triumphant. "See! It would be so much easier if you did what I said without arguing all the time."

"You're setting a dangerous precedent," Pete muttered to me out of the corner of his mouth.

"Waal, Pete, there's two theories to arguin' with a woman. Neither one works."

He laughed, while I just shrugged and smiled. I was whipped and I didn't care who knew it.

Torrey started stripping down to her bikini, which certainly caught my attention. I kept a discreet eye on Pete, too, but he didn't even look her way. I was pleased about that. He seemed like a nice guy and I didn't want to have an issue with him leching over my woman.

When Bev finally persuaded Pete to take his shirt off, he wasn't entirely scrawny. But like she said, he worked in an office all day earning a shit load of money; I did manual labor and crushed cars. I could carry on until I was 60 and watch my body give out. He'd be sitting in a five bedroom house with a pool, and a private pension to pay for lessons to improve his golf swing.

I knew a lot of women would have picked Pete. They might want to sleep with me, but he'd be the one they married. The thought was depressing.

"By the way," said Pete, after we'd been sitting talking while the girls sipped on sodas, "what's that tat on your shoulder blade, man? It looks like it's the same as the design on your truck. What's it mean?"

Torrey sighed, throwing a despairing look at Bev.

"I guess you could say it's a memorial to my brother," I said, quietly.

Pete looked sick. "Holy hell, I'm sorry, Jordan. I can't seem to keep from making an ass of myself."

Bev snorted and folded her arms across her chest.

"It's okay," I said, sighing. "I know this is weird for you—for everyone. I really appreciate you guys doin' this. Just so you know."

Torrey held my hand, and Bev looked like she might cry.

This day was turning out great.

"Let's go for a swim," said Torrey.

I nodded and let her pull me up.

"He doesn't mean anything by it," she said, as we waded out into the sun-warmed water.

"I know, sweetheart. I'm not blamin' him or anyone other than myself. I've got to get used to this, right?"

She leaned her head against my shoulder and slid one arm around my waist.

"I just wanted this to be a nice, ordinary day, you know? It's hard not being able to do stuff like normal couples do."

I tensed up immediately. "Too hard?"

She gave my waist a squeeze. "No, it's not too hard, I don't mean that. But I just wish it were easier."

"Don't give up on me, Torrey," I said, not too proud to beg. "I've only got six-and-a-half weeks left. "God, don't leave me, sweetheart. Not now."

She twisted in my arms until she was facing me. "I won't leave you," she said.

Her beautiful blue eyes met mine and I could see the truth in their depths.

I believed her.

She kissed me softly, then rested her head above my heart, and we stood there for several minutes.

"Come on," she said, turning playful. "Let's swim."

We stayed in the water for half an hour or so, horsing around, making out a little, swimming some. Seeing her in that cute bikini did things to me.

"That is a mighty small piece of material you're callin' a bikini," I said.

She grinned and threw me a wink.

"I don't usually wear a swimsuit."

"What?"

"I normally just go skinny dipping, but since Bev and Pete are here…"

I groaned. "We are definitely comin' back here by ourselves. You, me, a blanket and nothin' else."

"Nothing else?"

"Nope."

"Not even condoms?"

She laughed at my expression and left me standing in the water while she swam back to the beach. I needed a minute.

By the time we both joined the others, Bev seemed to have forgiven Pete.

"Let's eat!" said Bev, as we sat down next to them. "I'm starving!"

The girls started laying out the chow, and I reached into the cooler and passed a beer to Pete. "Have one for me, man."

He grinned. "You got it!"

I was hungry by then, so I was pretty quiet while we ate. The girls talked about work, swapping stories of awkward customers and their bad-tempered manager, Gus.

Pete asked me if I was into football. Turned out Pete was a Dallas Cowboys fan, but I was solid with the Houston Texans. We argued about that for a while, but soon we were deep into who could bench press what, and who'd signed, and who we thought should be traded—things that bored the girls. Torrey had made it pretty damn clear to me and Dad that she wasn't interested in football. She even insisted that the TV stayed off during meals, making no never mind as to whether it was a big game or not. Dad was somewhat surprised about that but too chicken to argue. Yeah, that was pretty funny, considering it was his house and all.

Damn, she was bossy. I wasn't sure why I liked that. If a woman had tried to tell me what to do when I was 16, I was out of there faster than a bolt of lightning. Things change, I guess.

It was good talking to a guy other than my dad. Hulk was cool, but he didn't speak much and I spent most of the day working by myself.

Not one of my friends from high school had stuck around or shown any interest in getting reacquainted, and I didn't really make friends in prison, so it was good to talk to someone like a buddy.

"We should catch a game some time," said Pete.

"Sure," I said, "so long as it's not in the next six weeks."

"Why's that?"

"Oh my God," grumbled Bev. "Learning has not taken place."

"Waal, got a 11 PM curfew and a 10-mile travel limit 'til my parole's up," I reminded him.

"Oh, right," Pete said quietly. "After that then."

"Yeah, I guess maybe. Although Torrey and me might not be

stayin' around."

Bev looked up and frowned. "Why? Where are you guys going?"

Torrey shrugged. "We haven't made any definite plans, but I don't think we'll stay here. People in town are pretty shitty toward Jordan."

"You don't have to stay right here," urged Pete. "There's plenty of work in Corpus, or Galveston, or even Freeport."

"Yeah, maybe," I said, non-committal. "I don't want to make plans 'til I'm really free … until it's real."

Pete nodded slowly. "I get that. I mean, it makes sense. One of my friends joined the army straight from high school. His folks didn't have much money and he didn't want to end up with a large student debt, so he figured he'd serve in the military and get college paid for when he came out. But he didn't want to plan anything until he was done either. He said he didn't know what the future was going to bring, not when he had a tour in Afghanistan coming up. He got out this spring. But you know, man, you should think about taking some college classes. Bev says you're good with cars. You could get yourself certified as an auto mechanic at a trade school."

I threw a look at Bev, and she smiled encouragingly. I suppose I should have gotten used to people talking about me behind my back. And it wasn't like this was the usual bad shit or anything.

"Yeah, I've been thinkin' about it. I've done some of the ASE certificate, but I didn't finish…"

"ASE? What's that?" Torrey interrupted.

"Automotive Service Excellence," Pete answered. "It certifies repair and service professionals. It's a pretty big deal."

"You didn't tell me about that!" said Torrey, a beautiful smile making her eyes sparkle. "That's great! Why didn't you finish it?"

"Well, sweetheart, while the prison workshop was pretty good, they weren't really big on lettin' us out for on the job trainin'."

I raised my eyebrows at her, and she burst out laughing.

"Oh my God, Jordan! You made a joke about being in prison! That's major!"

I grinned back at her. She was right—it was some turnaround from when she'd first met me. I could tell that Pete felt much more awkward talking about it. Bev just seemed to be rather curious.

"Did you want to go to college?" she asked. "Before … before everything, I mean."

"Sure. I hadn't really decided on what I wanted to do. Mikey was gonna be pre-med…" I sighed. "But I wasn't smart enough to do anythin' like that." I looked down. "I liked art. I don't know."

"You should definitely go!" Bev insisted.

"I kind of think that ship has sailed," I said, my voice wry.

Bev shook her head. "No, really. People do college classes at all ages."

"I don't think it's for me anymore, Bev. I've spent too much of my life on hold and I don't want to go and spend time with a bunch of kids where I have nothin' in common with them."

Pete disagreed. "There are some good accounting courses at the community college. They'd be useful if you want to start your own business some day. People always need good auto mechanics."

I was beginning to feel uncomfortable with their questioning, and kind of educationally subnormal, as I was the only one of them without a college degree.

It was real nice of them to be so interested though, and I appreciated it. The accounting thing sounded like it might be helpful, but I didn't dare let myself think that far in the future. I still had six weeks of parole to get through. And a lot can happen in six weeks. A lot can happen in six seconds.

Your whole life can change in less than a heartbeat.

"They should offer more college courses in prison!" asserted Bev.

I couldn't help smiling at her. She sounded so indignant, and I knew it was on my behalf.

"Yeah, well they do. You can get online degrees from accredited colleges. But there's a lot more that are just for basic literacy and numeracy skills. The majority of the guys inside didn't get much in the way of formal schoolin'." I shrugged. "I read a lot of books—whatever they had in the library really. Wasn't much."

"What was it like?" asked Bev. "In prison?"

Pete threw her a warning look.

"It's okay. I don't mind talkin' about it. Gets easier." I glanced at Torrey and she smiled encouragingly. "I don't really know how to tell you what it was like. It's borin', mostly. Degradin', too." I laughed although the sound was off. "Just shows the shit you can get used to."

Torrey held my hand and I looked at our fingers linked together. "I know one thing: I'm never goin' back there."

I lay on the sand, eyes closed, my mind drifting to the horrors of the past.

"Prison changes you. By the time I got there, I was already a whole lot different from the kid who arrived in juvie, shit scared and in shock. I'd wised up a lot. I'd been a typical small town kid, thinkin' I was the biggest, baddest badass in the school, but then you're locked up with some really sick people. And, well, there's a lot of time to think, so maybe it's more that you change yourself, you think about the choices you made and shouldn't have made."

Torrey's hand tightened around mine and I wrapped my arm around her.

"The day starts real early, at 3:30 AM. I don't know why—maybe just to let us know we're not like ordinary folk. We go have breakfast at 4:30 AM, which is a bowl of cereal or a crappy little sandwich. The good days are when there's peanut butter. But it's never enough to fill you up. Then I'd go back to my cell. I shared, mostly, with one other guy, dependin' on how many cons they'd got in at the time. Work assignments start at 6 AM, unless it's a Sunday, then it's lockdown till 10 AM. Most guys would just go back to sleep. I'd read, do sit ups, pushups, somethin'. It helped get the stress levels down. I mean, considerin' it was so fuckin' tedious, everyone was amped up the whole time. That's what happens when you cage people up. The smallest thing and BOOM. Little things become important—like gettin' one of the good jobs such as maintenance, or workin' in the prison garden, or workin' in the kitchen so you could get extra food. The worst jobs were cleanin', laundry, and the Hoe Squad, workin' out in the fields. It was so freakin' borin', most of us wanted to work. It also meant you could save up a few cents to pay for soft toilet paper or toothpaste that don't taste like shit. Most guys spend whatever they can earn on things to make life bearable. A lot of them wanted phone privileges. But that was really expensive, like a couple of bucks for a 15 minute phone call. I didn't have anyone to call, so that helped in terms of money. Some of the guys really missed their families, especially the ones who had kids.

"By 10:30 AM you'd eaten lunch and then you get a couple of hours to wander around the pod, which is like a group of five or six cells, and talk some, play cards. Then back to the cells again for the count. After that, you'd get maybe half an hour in the rec. Sometimes an hour. There were four basketball hoops— games could get pretty rough. You could blow off some steam or get your head pounded. Whatever. Dinner is about 4 PM, then back to your cell. Maybe some TV privileges from about 7 PM, lock up at 11 PM. It was pretty regimented but the routine becomes part of you. You know down to the second and if it's like more than a minute late, shit starts goin' down. All the little stuff—it becomes real fuckin' important when it's all you've got.

"You have to watch your back the whole time, you cain't trust anyone. The gangs were bad in juvie—that's how I got this," and I pointed to my scar, "but not so bad in prison. Some people wanted to make alliances if you were strong, but there's always a price for that. I kept to myself.

"There's lots of dumb shit I could tell y'all, like there's no point havin' any good stuff because it gets stolen. Even like a spare pair of the crappy, state-issued shoes.

"The pettiness gets you after a while. You're not supposed to talk at night, so if anyone makes a noise, phone privileges are withdrawn, sometimes for days. Like I said, that wasn't a problem for me, but some guys it would push them over the edge. Or they might take the TV, and sometimes they'd take the hot water so it was just cold showers for days at a time. Believe me, that shit mattered. It wouldn't take much to cause a riot. It was all there, simmerin' under the surface. And if you're in the wrong place at the wrong time…" I blew out a breath, "your sentence is suddenly doubled—no time off for being unlucky."

I shuddered and I felt Torrey's warm hands on my chest, soothing me, stroking me.

I opened one eye to see her expression of concern.

"Wow," I said sitting up right quick, embarrassed that I was being so fucking miserable on such a beautiful day. "I should be on *Oprah*. That show's still on, right?"

"Nah, man!" Pete laughed, sounding relieved that the mope-fest was officially over. "She stopped that a couple of years back."

I stared at them in disbelief. "They cancelled *Oprah*? Wow. I've really missed out."

Torrey gave me a playful shove.

"Of all the things you could miss, you miss *Oprah*?"

"No, sweetheart. But the only thing I'd miss if I went back now would be you."

She flung her arms around me, and kissed me hard. It wasn't until I heard Bev sigh that I remembered we weren't alone.

"Aw, you guys are so sweet," she said.

Torrey unhooked herself from me and grinned at her. "I know. Sickening, isn't it?"

"Just a little," said Bev, "but I got my own syrupy goodness over here," and she winked at Pete, who was watching with amusement.

Suddenly, our peace was interrupted by the sound of a car engine, and an old military jeep crested the dune and skidded to a halt next to my truck.

I could see that there were five of them. Two men jumped out first, and I could see them looking at the artwork on the side of my truck, exchanging glances.

"Oh shit!" Torrey cussed, softly. "What do we do?"

"You don't do nothin', sweetheart," I said. "Let me go talk to them."

She grabbed hold of my hand.

"Jordan, no! There are too many of them!"

"Maybe I should go?" Pete offered, looking worried.

I shook my head.

"Chances are they don't want no trouble," I lied, shaking free of Torrey's hand.

The two guys looked right at me as I walked toward them.

"How y'all doin'?" I said, calmly.

I didn't recognize them, but that didn't mean to say they didn't know me.

"Jordan," nodded the tall one.

I studied him carefully, but he didn't seem familiar.

Three girls followed the guys out of the jeep, and I relaxed slightly. There was less chance of something going down if they had their girlfriends with them. I hoped.

"Do I know you?" I asked, keeping my expression carefully neutral.

The tall guy shrugged. "Johnny Sanger. I used to sit next to you in Chem class."

It had been a long time since I'd thought about fuckin' *Chem class*. I couldn't remember him at all.

"I've been in prison since Chem class."

The blonde girl laughed loudly.

"What did you do?" she giggled. "Blow up the science lab?"

I stared at her, unblinking.

"P-prison? He's joking, right? You were joking…" She realized no one else was laughing, and her cheeks burned. "You … you were serious?" she gasped.

There was an embarrassed silence.

"What did he do?" she hissed at Johnny.

"I'll tell you later," he whispered back.

Then the brown-haired girl spoke.

"Hey, Jordan. I'm Rachel Wheeler. We were in Math together. I sat two rows behind you."

This was getting weird.

"And you remember my second cousin, Buddy?" she continued. "He was in Mikey's homeroom…"

My throat closed up when she said his name.

I felt a warm hand in mine, and immediately knew that Torrey was with me.

"Hi," she said. "I'm Torrey Delaney. My mom's the Reverend at the Church of Christ in town. And these are our friends Bev and Pete."

"I'm Susan," said the black girl. "This is Jennifer," pointing to the blonde, "and you already know Rachel. I met these yahoos in college, and Buddy's my fiancé."

She held out her hand to Torrey and then to me.

We shook hands awkwardly, while Bev and Pete gave her a quick smile.

Jennifer started to unpack the jeep but Johnny stopped her.

"Uh, we won't be stayin' here, sugar," he said, quietly. "We'll leave them to their picnic."

"But it's so lovely here!" she frowned. "You said there wasn't a better spot for miles. Surely we can share? You guys don't mind, do you?" she asked, turning to me.

"You should probably listen to him, Jennifer," I said, seriously. "He won't want his girlfriend hangin' out with an ex-con who's just got out of prison."

She froze, a cooler slipping from her fingers and landing on the soft sand.

"Oh!" she breathed out.

"Well, nice meeting all of you," Torrey said, deliberately. "You do what you like—we're going for another swim," and she took my hand and steered me away.

"Are you okay?" she asked, when we were out of earshot of the others.

273

"Yeah, I guess. It was just … I don't know what that was. I mean, other than Allison, the first people from the old days that I meet … and it's fuckin' *Johnny from Chem class*?"

Torrey snorted out a laugh.

"Yeah, what are the chances? I can't picture you in Chem class. *Did* you blow anything up?"

"Not in class. I remember one Fourth of July, Mikey and me emptied out a whole bunch of black powder from fireworks to make one mother of a rocket."

I couldn't help smiling at the memory.

"And?" prompted Torrey.

"Scared the shit out of everyone. I got grounded for a month."

"Just you?"

"Sure. Mikey was on the football team by then. They couldn't ground him."

Torrey laughed sadly. "That sounds about right. Do you want to go swimming, or should we just sit here for a while?"

"Here's fine."

I sank down onto the sand and she sat next to me, draping her arms over my shoulder.

"It'll get easier, Jordan," she said, softly. "All these 'first times'; they're bound to be awkward, but people will get used to seeing you around again. Then they'll be talking about the next interesting subject."

I shook my head slowly. "You don't know small towns, sweetheart. Folks still gossip about things that happened two and three generations back at least. They know each other's business better'n they know their own."

Torrey sighed. "Well, I'll take your word for it. Maybe we should head back now? It seems kind of rude to leave Bev and Pete by themselves, although I expect they'll have thought of something to do."

I winced at the mental image that conjured up. I really had no interest in seeing Pete's skinny ass, or anything else.

But as we walked back, it was clear that Bev and Pete weren't alone: my former classmates were still there.

"I guess they want to be friendly," said Torrey, lightly.

Great.

The silence was slightly uncomfortable as I sat down, but Bev and the girl named Susan seemed to be doing their best to keep a conversation going.

The blonde girl stared at me as if I was about to attack someone or share anecdotes from *Prison Break*. Johnny looked bored, and Buddy was smiling at his girl like she was the most fascinating thing he'd ever seen.

I probably looked like that when I was with Torrey.

Rachel zeroed in on me as soon as I sat down.

"Do you remember when you dated my older sister, Yvonne, for like a week, when we were sophomores and she was a senior?"

I frowned, trying to remember someone named Yvonne. It didn't sound familiar, although…

Johnny laughed.

"Jordan 'dated' a lot of girls back then!" he said, waggling his eyebrows. "If even half of the locker room talk was true, you bagged most of the girls on the cheer team."

I winced, and avoided looking at Torrey.

"Ha, you were a trouble magnet, for sure," he laughed. "But even so, all the girls wanted him, and all the guys wanted to *be* him."

Not anymore.

Rachel giggled. And then I remembered her, too.

She'd chased after Mikey for a whole year before she finally gave up and started hitting on me instead. She was a nice looking girl with some good assets, but that *laugh*. It sounded like nails being dragged along a chalkboard. Yeah, I definitely remembered her.

She'd been kind of annoying then. Now, she was something else. For one thing, I didn't think that the bikini she wore could strictly speaking be called a swimsuit. It was more like a piece of string with some material attached. The minute I sat down again, she started rubbing sun lotion on her legs and chest. It was like watching the prelude to a bad porn movie. I saw Buddy cringe and Susan just rolled her eyes.

"Oh, I can't reach my back," she giggled. "Jordan, you're nearest—would you help me, sugar?"

When I was 16, I'd just brush her off. Now, I needed the cavalry.

"Oh, gee," simpered Torrey, catching my pleading look, "let me help you with that, Rachel."

And she squirted some of the lotion onto her hand and slapped it roughly onto Rachel's back.

I guess Rachel wasn't completely dumb, because she got Torrey's message loud and clear after that. I still didn't feel relaxed like when it was just Bev and Pete, but it wasn't so bad either.

"So," said Johnny, after a few minutes. "When did you get out?"

All the conversation died away and every eye turned to me.

God, I hated that.

"What?" he said. "I'm just askin' what everyone is thinkin'!"

"Four months ago," I answered, evenly. "What about you? Done anythin' interestin' since 2006?"

He coughed out a laugh.

"Funny guy! Waal, ya know: school, college, workin' in Corpus. Been datin' Jennifer for a year an' a half now. We're thinkin' of takin' the next step."

"Gettin' hitched?" I suggested.

"Hell, no!" he laughed, missing his girlfriend's angry little pout. "Puttin' a deposit on a place outside of the city. Gettin' into real estate, ya know how it is."

Guy was a jackass.

"Not really. Until recently, my 'real estate' was eight by ten feet."

Torrey snorted and Bev covered up a laugh. Even Buddy cracked a smile at that one.

"You workin', Jordan?" he asked.

"Some. Got a job at the local junkyard crushin' cars."

"And he's doing custom-made artwork on cars and trucks," Torrey added. "He did the Celtic cross and bleeding heart on the side of his truck that you were looking at earlier."

"That's some pretty neat work," said Susan. "You could make a lot of money doing that, Jordan."

I gave a short laugh.

"Not around here."

"Why not?"

"Because most folk don't want an ex-con workin' on their vehicles."

She nodded slowly.

"I understand that. I know what prejudice can be like."

"It's different for you," I said, quietly.

She immediately bristled. "How so?"

"You know you haven't done anythin' to deserve it."

There was another uncomfortable silence. They seemed to be stacking up to quite a number.

"Remember when you painted that amazin' mural along the corridor at school?" said Rachel, suddenly. "It was of the sun risin' over the ocean. It was so beautiful—always made me feel kind of peaceful."

"Oh, yeah! I remember that," said Johnny. "It was cool."

Torrey turned to me. "You did that?"

I nodded.

"I'd love to see it."

For about the millionth time, there was an awkward pause.

"Um, they painted over it after…" said Rachel, staring at the sand. "I, um, might have a photograph of it … somewhere."

I couldn't take it anymore. I got up and walked away.

"What's his problem?" I heard Johnny ask.

"Maybe not all his memories of high school are good ones," Susan replied.

I gave myself a time-out by going for a long swim. This time Torrey didn't join me. She knew when I was overwhelmed and needed some space.

277

I swam until my arms felt like lead but my mind was calmer.

Someone had gathered driftwood to make a campfire, and Bev and Susan were roasting marshmallows.

I plopped down onto the blanket next to Torrey.

"Okay?" she mouthed.

I nodded and gave her a small smile.

She passed me a marshmallow on a stick. I hadn't had one of these since I was a little kid. Sometimes it was a punch in the gut, thinking how much I'd missed out on. A third of my life I'd been locked up. I'd never get those years back.

"So," she said, "your buddies have been filling me in. I've been hearing about some of the things the Kane brothers got up to in high school. I *cannot believe* you both banged someone named Cindy O'Hara in the back of your truck."

"Not at the same time!" I defended.

She laughed. "No?"

"Hell, no!"

"And the Miller sisters," added Rachel.

"What?"

"That's what I heard," she shrugged.

"No way!" I spluttered. "Um, I *may* have had a thing with Kelsey, but I never … not with Audrey." *Although I was pretty wasted at the time…*

"That's not what Aud said," Rachel insisted, a determined glint in her eye as she slurred her words. "And she was pretty damn specific about some … details."

My head was totally spun by this conversation, hearing names from the past. It felt like they were talking about a completely different person. Hell, I *knew* I wasn't that kid anymore.

Torrey took pity on me, and swung the conversation in another direction.

I began to relax once the focus was off of me. But it didn't last.

"You still play football?" Johnny asked, obviously bored with a conversation that the girls were having, comparing chick flicks.

"Um, no!"

Jeez, this guy was dumber than dirt.

"I just wondered. 'Cause after you … left, Benson Smith took your place on the team."

Jeez, they gave my place to that loser?

Johnny laughed at the expression on my face.

"Yeah! It was a disaster! No chance of going State that year. Hell, they used to get nearly 3,000 people at the home games. Mikey was a freakin' legend. That hasn't happened in a while. Now they're lucky if they get 500 or 600 attendances."

"You didn't tell me you were on the football team, too," Torrey said, questioningly.

"That's because I wasn't. I was supposed to start as a wide receiver in my junior year, but…"

I shrugged. I didn't need to finish the sentence.

Jennifer tossed her long hair over her shoulder. "You don't look like a dangerous felon," she announced, "you're too cute. You look more like a model, an underwear model."

Bev choked on her beer, and Susan shook her head in disbelief.

Torrey murmured her reply just loud enough for me to hear. "Yeah! And who'd have thought she's as dumb as she looks."

I grinned at her, and she puckered her lips at me.

I leaned down, resting my hand on her thigh, and whispered in her ear. "You sure earned this kiss, sweetheart."

I took my time, even though it was likely that everyone was watching us. Fuck 'em. I was kissing my girl.

I only stopped when I realized that a situation was arising.

Torrey knew exactly why I pulled back, because she muttered, "Hold that thought, cowboy."

No one bothered me with more questions after that, and I didn't know if that was because they'd lost interest in me or because Torrey had said something to them while I'd been swimming. Whichever way it was, I relaxed into the evening, enjoying the unfamiliar feeling of being peaceful with a group of people.

As the last of the light faded from the sky, the conversation quieted and the group split into couples.

Soon, the old high school crowd was saying their goodbyes. Johnny invited us to meet them for drinks at a bar later. Torrey declined on my behalf, omitting to mention my parole restrictions, instead stating that she was too tired. Johnny sure was dumb, but he didn't seem to mind hanging out with me either. I couldn't imagine that we'd ever be buddies, but it had been okay seeing him and his friends.

I missed Mikey even more now that I was out of prison. I kept thinking about all the things we should be doing together—bonfires at the beach like this one, shooting the shit, hanging out. The space where he should have been left a constant dull ache. And at my parents' house, having his stuff still laid out in his room, it felt like he could walk back in any second. I sometimes felt if I called him, he'd yell from the backyard or the garage. But I also thought maybe he wouldn't have wanted me to just rot away either.

I felt Torrey's warm hand in mine, and her eyes crinkled softly as she smiled at me.

"Did you have fun?"

I wasn't there yet, but yeah, life was getting good.

Chapter 13 – Need

Jordan

It was a Friday, and Torrey had been doing the early shift at work all week. She really hated those days. Getting that woman's ass out of bed at 5 AM to be at work by seven wasn't easy. Even though I got up with her to make breakfast, she was as ornery as a mule with a toothache.

On the plus side, it meant we got to have the whole evening to spend together. Tonight we were meeting up with Bev and Pete to eat hotdogs, and see some movie at the mall that the girls had been raving about. I didn't care what we saw. The last time I'd been to a movie theater *Casino Royale* had been playing, and the girls at high school were arguing about whether Bond could be blond. I mean, really?

For pretty much the first time since my release, I had money in my pocket to take my woman out. It may not seem like much, but when it came to feeling like a man, like a regular guy, it was really fucking important.

I'd just gotten home from the junkyard and taken a quick shower when Torrey came crashing into the house. She was like a force of nature, and there was never any doubt which room in the house she was in: doors would get slammed, the TV and radio would be blaring—often at the same time. Happy noise just followed her everywhere and I loved it.

Girl was a screamer, too. I'd tried every which ways to get her to pipe down just out of a sense of decency, because it couldn't have been great for Dad to hear that every night. But short of sticking my dick in her mouth—which I have to be honest, I really liked doing—nothing worked.

Dad even made a joke about it once, saying that he hoped we never lived in an apartment with thin walls, otherwise the police would be around every night.

Yeah. That's not a conversation you want to have with your dad, like *ever*.

"Hey, handsome!" she yelled, as she barreled into the house. "Get your pants on and get your cute ass down here! We've got some celebrating to do, and not just when you've got me naked in your bed!" Then she went quiet for a moment. "Oh, hi Paul," I heard her say to Dad, sounding only a little embarrassed. "I didn't know you were home. Did you have a good day?"

I took the stairs two at a time and scooped her into my arms, kissing her soundly. Dad just raised his eyebrows and headed for the kitchen where I could hear him turning on the coffee maker.

I didn't care about showing how much I was in love; I didn't care about showing it in front of anyone. For all I cared, the whole world could know that Torrey was my girl. She was a bit more tentative about it, but here she felt at home. I was happy about that.

"What's this good news you're hollerin' about, sweetheart?"

She waved an envelope in my face and jumped up, wrapping her legs around my waist.

"Finally! I got the deposit back on my apartment in Boston, *and* Dad sent me a check for $1,000 to 'tide me over'!"

"Yeah? That's great. Did he write you, too?"

"Ha, well! I wouldn't call it a letter, but it was communication with writing. He said he and *Ginger* had a great honeymoon and that I should stop by and see them sometime. As if!"

"Maybe you should," I said, seriously. "Trust me when I say life is short and you never know if the next time you say goodbye is the last time. You don't want to live with regrets, sweetheart."

Her face twisted and she pulled her arms tighter around me.

"Oh, God. You're right. I know you're right. But if I have to spend time with *Ginger* and her surgically enhanced tits, *you* are coming with me."

Dad grinned as he walked from the kitchen to the family room carrying his coffee. He closed the door firmly behind him, obviously deciding that any conversation that included discussion of another woman's tits was one he'd duck out of. Couldn't say I blamed him. No guy was going to come out of that unscathed.

"You want me to meet your dad?" I questioned. "He's a lawyer. He's not gonna have me arrested, is he?"

I was joking. Sort of.

She rolled her eyes. "Hell no! He'll be so damn grateful that you're willing to 'take me off his hands'," she used air quotes to emphasize the sarcasm, "he'll probably put an arm around you and show you his golfing trophies." She twirled some hair around her finger. "He does that. It's a guy thing."

"I'll go anywhere with you, sweetheart, you know that. I still cain't imagine he's gonna be thrilled to see you with an ex-con who barely finished high school. But if you want to go see your old man, I'd love to be with you."

She smiled happily, and ran her hands under my t-shirt then dragged her nails down my back. Fuck, she knew that made me hard.

"Anyway," she said, pulling away and leaving me wanting, "I need to go deposit this into the bank before it closes at 5 PM, so we have to hurry. You ready?"

"I was born ready, sweetheart."

"Ugh! That's such a guy thing to say."

"True, though."

She slapped my shoulder and shouted out to Dad. "See you later, Paul!"

"Bye, darlin'. Have a good time now, y'hear! Bye, son."

"Later, Dad."

We took Torrey's car because the bed of my truck was still full of colored metal paints that Hulk had let me take from the junkyard.

We made it to the bank with just a few minutes to spare.

"Yay!" she cried happily, after depositing the check into her account. "We can have some fun spending that!"

I shook my head. "No, sweetheart. That's for you from your dad. I wouldn't feel right touchin' any of it."

She cocked her head to one side and gave me her cutest smile.

"Aw, baby, you're so freakin' sensible. We deserve to have some fun, too!" And the vixen pressed against me, discreetly running her hand over my zipper.

"Christ, sweetheart!" I mumbled into her neck. "You don't play fair!"

She gave a throaty laugh and stroked me again.

She said something else, but suddenly I was on high alert, my attention ripped away from her.

I don't know if it was some sixth sense, or just lessons learned from my years in prison, but I knew that I was being watched.

Torrey

Wow! My deposit returned *and* $1,000 from my dad. When I'd gone to Mom's place to pick up my mail, I hadn't been expecting anything that good. True, I had been hoping for $2K from Dad, but maybe he was saving for his future alimony. Still, better than a poke in the eye.

I definitely had plans for how Jordan and I could spend some of the money. I had in mind a big celebration when his parole was through in four weeks time: dinner in a fancy restaurant, dancing, a club—all the things he'd told me he wanted to do—but he was being stubborn. You know, doing that macho thing where he was refusing to touch any money that belonged to me. It was cute, especially bearing in mind some of the losers I'd hooked up with who wouldn't even spring to buy me a beer. Cute, but annoying as hell, because I wanted to celebrate the end of his parole. It was a huge deal, but Jordan seemed to want to forget about it; I thought we needed to mark it as his fresh start.

I decided he needed some persuading, and it hadn't taken me long to realize that the best way to persuade him was via his dick. He was the sweetest person, but he was such a *guy!*

"Aw, baby, we deserve to have some fun, too!" I said, pressing against him and rubbing the front of his jeans. "But ya know what, we could use the rest to put a deposit down on getting our own place, just you and me. What do you think?"

I knew from experience that by now he would be aching to go somewhere we could have privacy and let his snake loose in my lady garden.

But then I felt him tense up, not in a good way, and he didn't respond to my come-on. I realized pretty quickly that I didn't have his undivided attention because he pushed my hands away and stood in front of me protectively.

"Jordan fuckin' Kane," said a slurred voice.

Four men in their late twenties were standing in a half circle around us. My heart started racing frantically and I gripped onto Jordan's arm, peeking around his shoulder.

"Hello, Ryan," Jordan said, quietly.

I swallowed a gasp. I knew that name. Jordan had mentioned it often enough during the last couple of months. Ryan Dupont had been Mikey's best friend. The three of them had hung out together, and it had been at Ryan's party where Jordan had gotten drunk that night—the night where his old life ended, the night he'd killed his brother.

I didn't know who the other guys were and I'm not sure Jordan did either, but tension radiated from him, and his body was rigid.

I glanced around desperately, but no one was coming to our aid. Not this time.

My mouth had gone dry and I tried to swallow but I couldn't even work up enough saliva to spit.

"Why the fuck did you have to come back?" snarled Ryan. "Isn't it enough that you killed my best goddamn friend? You have to come back here and rub our noses in it?"

Jordan spoke calmly and reasonably, but his muscles were bunched under his t-shirt, and his voice was tight.

"I'm on parole, Ryan. I have to stay in the area."

"You piss on his grave every time you fuckin' breathe! You don't deserve to live!"

I gasped and my grip on Jordan's arm tightened, but he didn't move.

"I know," Jordan said, a quaver in his voice that tore at my heart. "I don't deserve to live. But I *am* livin'. For some reason I'm still here, and all I can do is try to deserve that gift and…"

"Bullshit!" Ryan shouted. "He was the best, you piece of shit! You're a fuck up and a murderer! And here you are, struttin' around on our streets with your ho!"

"You don't get to badmouth my girlfriend," said Jordan, his voice dangerously quiet. "Say what you like about me, but leave her out of it."

"Come on, Ry," said one of the other men who seemed slightly more sober. "We don't disrespect women. Let's just clean up the trash."

"Shut the fuck up!" shrieked Ryan, his eyes bulging with anger. "You don't tell me what to do! No one tells me what to do!"

I had a bad feeling about this—a really bad feeling. This guy was totally amped and it didn't sound like anything or anyone was going to talk him down.

He looked directly at Jordan. "You've got a debt to pay, you fuck!"

Jordan didn't blink. "I'm not gonna fight you, Ryan."

"You fuckin' pussy! I'm not givin' you a choice! You've been hidin' all summer and you're gonna pay for what you did!"

"I'm not hidin' from anyone," Jordan said, thickly. "I'm right here. Fuck's sake, man! You and me were *friends!* You think I don't miss him? Christ! He was my *brother!*"

Ryan shook his head. "You're walkin' the streets like nothin' ever happened. You haven't even *started* to pay."

I couldn't stand by and listen to that shit anymore.

"He pays! God, he pays! Every day!" I yelled. "You have *no idea* what he's been through. He even tried to kill himse-"

"Torrey, that's enough!" Jordan snapped.

The second he was distracted, Ryan swung. He was a big guy, built like a linebacker, and his punch was solid. At the moment he raised his hand, I saw sunlight glinting off of a large ring—a class ring. I cried out as his fist connected with the side of Jordan's face, knocking him from his feet.

"Stop it!" I shrieked, but my words had no effect.

Ryan launched a kick at Jordan's ribs as he lay on the ground, but he managed to roll away. Then the second guy, the one wearing cowboy boots, started on him and all Jordan could do was curl into a ball and try to protect his head. I heard him grunt as kicks and punches rained down on his back, but he never spoke.

I threw myself at the guy with the boots and hooked an arm around his neck, scoring my fingernails across one cheek.

He squealed like a pig and cursed, crashing backwards against the wall of the bank, winding me so I was gasping for breath and forced to let go.

I was screaming and crying, and I could see people start to approach us, but they were too slow, too wary, and too far away.

Jordan was on his feet, and I could see the anguish on his

face as he tried to get to me. Blood was pouring from a cut on his cheek caused by the ring, and the side of his face was masked in scarlet. He held one arm across his ribs, and it seemed like he was having trouble breathing.

He was still staring at me when Ryan hit him again. He hadn't even tried to defend himself. I screamed as Jordan stumbled over the curb and flailed his arms to get his balance. Boots and Baseball Cap punched him to the ground. I tried to reach him but the fourth guy, the one with the leather jacket, grabbed me by my waist and hauled me off bodily.

Jordan had managed to stand, and I could hear him calling my name, concern coloring his voice.

I think I screamed again and struggled to get free, but Leather Jacket pinned my arms and twisted his legs to the side so I couldn't kick him.

The crowd was getting nearer, but still no one tried to stop the murderous assault.

Ryan hit Jordan again and he went down.

I was begging them to stop but they wouldn't. I don't even know if they heard me, they were so crazed with bloodlust, anger and booze.

Boots and Baseball Cap held Jordan up by his arms while Ryan hit him again and again: ribs, stomach, face, ribs, stomach, face, in a sickening tattoo of knuckles on skin.

"Stop! Please, stop!" I begged, tears and snot and spittle covering my face.

More people were coming out of the shops and café to watch; a few were slowing down in their cars, but no one came to help us. No one came to help him.

A blow to Jordan's head stunned him, and he sagged to his knees. The two guys holding his arms let him drop, and Jordan toppled sideways.

All I could hear was the sound of Ryan's labored breathing.

I tried to get to Jordan again, but Leather Jacket wouldn't let me go.

Jordan's face was unrecognizable. One eye was swollen shut,

his lips were smashed, and more blood poured from his cheek and nose. His shirt was ripped and hung open, and his chest and ribs were covered in angry wheals. Ryan's ring had done its job.

Still on his hands and knees, Jordan's head hung down like a beaten dog. I watched the muscles in his arms bunch as he staggered to his feet.

Ryan hit him again before he was even fully standing, and Jordan crashed to the ground.

I held my breath, my voice shredded from screaming. My lungs burned as I sagged in the arms of the man who held me.

Stay down! I begged silently. *Stay down!*

A rumble started in the crowd as slowly, painfully, Jordan pushed himself to his feet again, and stood swaying, his arms at his sides.

"Look'ee there!" whispered one man excitedly, pointing toward us.

"I'm not gonna fight you, Ry," Jordan coughed out, the breath heaving painfully in his chest.

Ryan stared at him, panting and furious. He swung again. Jordan crashed backwards.

"Fight back you chicken bastard!" he raged. "Fight back!"

I thought this time Jordan would stay down, but he rolled slowly onto his side, his fingers scrabbling at the dirt on the ground, his hands swollen from where he'd been kicked and stamped on. Once again he forced himself to his knees. Once again he staggered to his feet.

"Oh God, no!" I moaned.

Seconds later he was down again, barely moving.

Ryan turned to me, his face furious and frustrated.

"Why isn't he fightin' back?" he roared.

"Because he won't!" I screamed. "He won't fight back because he thinks you're right! He won't fight you because he can't!" I took a shuddering breath, my words coming out faintly. "Because he believes he *deserves* this."

"Bastard!" shouted Ryan, pushed past endurance.

Jordan was on his hands and knees when Ryan punched him

in the head.

I watched as my love lay sprawled on the ground unmoving, his blood pooling darkly.

I tried to say his name but my voice was gone.

I don't know who spoke, but there was a voice in the crowd as hushed whispers began to ripple among them.

"Someone call an ambulance!"

The man holding my arms let me go and I crawled across the sidewalk toward Jordan. I wanted to hold him but somebody stopped me.

"Best you don't move him, miss," said a man's voice, a kind voice. "The ambulance will be here soon."

I reached out for Jordan's hand and held it gently in mine.

"Jordan," I gasped. "Jordan, I love you. I love you so much."

I heard sirens in the distance, coming closer each second, and a moment later the crowd parted. Somebody tried to pull me away from him but I wouldn't let go.

"Let them help him," said the kind voice again. "You have to let go now."

A woman I didn't know pulled me into her arms and stroked my hair like a child. My hands and knees, my shirt and my jeans, even the ends of my long hair were painted with Jordan's blood.

I watched as they fastened a brace around his neck, and carefully lifted him onto a stretcher. His eyes were closed, his limbs heavy and unresponsive.

I tried to go with him but they slammed shut the doors of the ambulance, and he was taken away from me.

"I think she's in a shock," a voice said beside me.

"Miss, are you hurt? Did you hit your head?"

An authoritative voice was talking to me.

I had just enough presence of mind left to realize that if I said yes, they'd take me to the hospital, too.

"Yes, it hurts," I whispered.

And then they whisked me into a second ambulance and I was taken away.

I couldn't believe what had happened. Had it lasted minutes

or just seconds? It seemed to have gone on and on, a lifetime of watching Jordan beaten into the ground. *Why wouldn't he stay down?* I knew why.

At the hospital they cleaned me up and checked me over. I had a few scrapes to my hands and knees, but nothing more serious. Even so, I couldn't stop shaking. My skin was cold and clammy, and I felt sick. Someone gave me a blanket. But whenever I asked about Jordan, it was as if I was speaking ancient Greek. No one heard me. *No one answered me!* I felt ready to scream. I wanted to scream.

I screamed.

Several people jumped, and a porter pushing an empty wheelchair stumbled.

"WHERE'S JORDAN? WHAT'S HAPPENING? SOMEBODY TELL ME SOMETHING! NOW!"

A nurse came hurrying toward me, spouting the usual inanities, the trite words that are supposed to soothe but just incense: *they're doing everything they can; you can help him most by staying calm; the doctor's with him now.*

I got their attention but I still didn't get any answers. Perhaps there weren't any to give. The thought was horrifying.

Hospitals lie. They give us hope of certainties; the solid buildings and wide, calm corridors make us want to believe it'll be okay. It isn't okay. People die in hospitals all the time. Our bodies are just fragile sacks of blood and pus and bones.

A nurse approached me with a clipboard.

"I don't have time for this!" I yelled at her. "You don't understand! I *need* to see Jordan. They hurt him so badly!"

"Dr. Manoz is with him now," she said, her voice too calm and collected. "Let her do her job. You can help your friend by helping us fill out this form.

I took the clipboard from her, and she gave me a professional smile. *See, I got the crazy woman to stop screaming. I am a great nurse.*

She passed me the pen, waited a second to make sure I was compliant, then marched away. There were more important things to do than talk to a woman who was dying on the inside.

I stared at the form then started to scratch out my answers. My handwriting was barely legible, my hands were shaking so badly.

Name of patient:	JORDAN JOSEPH KANE
Age:	24
Date of birth:	

Shit! Shit! When was his birthday? December 7th. No 8th. Or was it 9th? Shit, 8th, definitely 8th. It was late August now. That made him still 23. I think.

Address:	Buttwipe, Nowheresville, Tx

Relation to patient: Everything. No, they wouldn't like that answer, so I lied. I wrote, 'Fiancée'.

Social Security number:	

Who the hell cares? Other than the vultures who make money out of people who need help.

Is the patient on any medication?	No.
Does the patient have any allergies?	

I couldn't think of any. Jordan had never mentioned anything. Could I risk answering that? What if he was allergic to penicillin? I didn't know.

Then my phone vibrated in my pocket, and I pulled it out, my fingers trembling over the screen.

If you're late cause you're screwing that fine man of yours,
I'm going to be pissed! Bev x

Her message grounded me, and I knew I had to start pulling myself together.

Ignoring the hospital sign that said cell phones must be switched off, I called Jordan's dad.

"Paul, it's Torrey. Jordan's been hurt. He's been attacked and badly beaten. You have to come to the hospital *now*."

He tried to get me to explain what had happened but I couldn't bring myself to do it over the phone. His voice shook, but he said he'd come at once.

Then I phoned Bev.

"Where the fuck are you guys?" she yelled, on the first ring.

The only reply she got was the sound of me sniffing.

"Torrey? Are you there? Are you okay? What's going on?"

"They got him!" I sobbed. "They finally got him!"

I heard her gasp. I'd confided to her that my greatest fear was that someone would deliberately hurt Jordan. So she instantly understood what I'd said.

"Where are you? We're coming to get you!"

I leaned back in my chair, the form falling from my numb fingers. I was too stunned to cry anymore.

Minutes later, Paul was scooping me into his arms.

"What happened, darlin'? Where's Jordan?"

"They beat him up, Paul. Really bad. Four of them. They won't tell my anything! They say they're working on him but *I don't know anything!*"

My words ended in a piercing wail.

Paul's face was ashen.

He stood up angrily, and I grabbed his arm.

"I … I told them … I said I was his fiancée. I thought … just to find out … I mean I'm not … we're not…"

He kissed my hair quickly and marched straight up to the nurse's desk.

"My son, Jordan Kane. Where is he?"

"If you'll take a seat, sir," said the nurse, blandly.

"Not until I get some information. My son's fiancée tells me you refuse to talk to her. I want some answers *now* or the hospital administration will be talking to my lawyer."

I was so glad he was here. I was so glad to hear his kind-hearted bullshit. I wasn't his son's fiancée and he didn't have a lawyer. God, I loved that man. I'd only known him a few months, but he'd become a second father to me. A better father than my own maybe.

We were reassured. *Every effort ... The doctor is working on him now ... If you'll just wait ... If you could just complete the form.*

We sat.

We waited.

Paul picked up the form.

Does the patient have any allergies?	*No*, he wrote.

Jordan didn't have any allergies. I should have known that. Why didn't I know that?

Has the patient been admitted to hospital before?	Yes.
Admittance Date:	August 2006, attempted suicide by hanging, damage to trachea. November 2008, punctured lung.

"I need the pen," I said.

"What for?"

I took it from Paul's hand and added a line.

Admittance date:	January 2009, attempted suicide, severed radial arteries.

Paul was stunned and his eyes became glassy with tears. I handed him back the pen, and with a shaking hand, he filled in the last line, signed and dated it.

Next of kin:	Torrey Delaney (fiancée); Paul Kane (father).

I looked up into Paul's kind eyes, so much like Jordan's, and I thanked him without words.

We hugged each other tightly.

"I've phoned his mother," Paul said, gently. "She'd want to know."

"Are you sure about that?" I said, abruptly pulling away from him.

"Yes, I'm sure," he replied, his voice firm with conviction.

We stared at each other, each with secrets in our eyes. I wanted to argue but I didn't have the energy. I sat in angry silence for several minutes.

Paul's head dropped into his hands.

"I never wanted to see this hospital ever again," he said, his voice broken and husky.

Oh God. This hospital. The place he lost both sons, in a very real sense.

"I'm so sorry, Paul," I whispered.

He held my hand between his.

"I know," he replied.

There was a flurry of noise as Bev and Pete flew down the corridor. She stumbled to a stop when she saw us.

"Oh no! Is he…?"

Pete grabbed her as she began to sway.

"He's holding his own," said Paul.

I didn't know why he was able to say that with such certainty, but I found myself believing him. Jordan was strong. He could take a beating.

I closed my eyes, hearing again the sound of his head thudding onto the concrete sidewalk; bile burned my throat.

Bev sat down next to me and took my other hand.

"Is there anything we can do?" she whispered.

I shook my head.

"They've told us we have to be patient."

I laughed an empty laugh. It wasn't funny. It was painful. It was ridiculous. Who can be patient when you're waiting to hear how your world has changed, maybe forever?

We waited. And we waited. The slow seconds wound their way toward minutes, and the minutes lethargically stretched toward hours.

We'd been there long enough for Bev to have drunk three horrible coffees, and two each for the rest of us, when a tired looking Mexican woman in green scrubs walked toward us.

"Mr. Kane?" she asked, looking to Paul for confirmation.

"Yes. Is he…?"

She gave a tight smile. "I'm Dr. Manoz. I've been treating your son. He's pretty knocked up, but he's going to be fine."

My heart leapt and shuddered, and I learned to breathe again.

"We were worried about a head injury, but he started to come around a few minutes ago. The injury of most concern now is a detached retina. We need to take him into surgery immediately. There's a good chance he won't have any permanent loss of sight in that eye. He's lucid now, if you want to see him. But only for a minute."

If? If we wanted to see him? Why would we be wearing our hearts in plain view if we didn't? Why would we be gray with fear? I controlled my irrational anger, knowing that this doctor didn't weigh or calculate the impact of every word she spoke. She should have. She should have realized. They ought to teach doctors to do that, because it matters. Every syllable that leaves their lips wounds or heals—they have that power.

"Just two of you," she said. "He's tired, a little confused, and in a lot of pain."

Paul nodded; I just stared at her.

Bev gave my hand a quick squeeze and assured me they'd wait for us.

The doctor led us down a corridor, noisy with visitors, to a room that contained a dozen hospital beds. Most were empty, but the area at the bottom had a curtain pulled across.

She gestured toward the curtained bed.

"He has a number of injuries in addition to the detached retina and head laceration," she said. "He has a fractured cheekbone, five broken ribs, his index finger on his right hand is crushed, and he has a sprained wrist, as well as a number of cuts and contusions."

She pulled back the curtain with a quick jerk, and I swallowed hard. Jordan's face was partially covered in gauze, and a large pad covered his left eye. His lips were swollen and his chest and arms were stained with vivid purples, blues and reds.

I sat beside the bed and took his good hand in mine.

"Hey, cowboy," I choked out.

His right eye fluttered open, and I think he tried to smile.

"I'm so mad at you," I said, as tears began to fall. "And you look like shit."

"Don't cry, sweetheart," he mumbled from between his bruised lips. "Just payin' a debt."

Paul stood wordless next to me, his hand resting on my shoulder. Jordan's gaze flickered upward.

"Hey, Dad."

"Your girl's right," he said, laughing to stop himself from crying. "You look like hell, son."

"Feel like it," he mumbled, his eyelid fluttering closed again.

Dr. Manoz bustled back into the room.

"We have to take him now," she said. "It's a standard procedure and is normally performed under local anesthetic. Because of his other injuries, the surgeon, Dr. Linden, has decided to use a general. The procedure usually takes about an hour but Jordan will feel sleepy for six to 12 hours afterward. If you have any questions, Dr. Linden will be happy to answer them."

"I've got to go now," I said to Jordan, quietly. "Places to be, things to do."

I think he tried to smile but I couldn't be sure. I leaned down, hoping to find somewhere undamaged to place a soft kiss.

He even had blood in his hair.

The doctor hustled us out of the room immediately, and abandoned us in the corridor. Bev pulled me into a tight hug.

"He's goin' to be okay," Paul said.

He went on to list Jordan's injuries while Bev and Pete looked on appalled.

"You guys should go on home now," I said, quietly. "He won't be awake until tomorrow morning now. You should get some sleep."

"Come with us," Bev pleaded. "You need to rest. We'll bring you back in the morning."

I shook my head.

"No, I'm staying."

She sighed and made me promise to text her the moment we knew anything.

The echo of their footsteps followed them down the corridor.

A nurse came to move us from the ER to a surgical waiting area. Maybe she just wanted us out of the way. Maybe another family would be coming in, desperate to hear whether their special someone was going to make it. The hospital machine had to keep on grinding away.

A few minutes later, a cheerful man of about fifty wearing the now familiar green scrubs of a doctor, entered the room.

Dr. Linden had a professional warmth, and a calm, kind expression. It was the sort of face that you instantly trusted even if you didn't want to.

"We've caught the damage early," he said. "There's still a 10-15% chance that Jordan will need a further operation, but I'm hopeful that won't be the case. It'll be very uncomfortable for him for a couple of days, particularly because the area around the eye is already badly swollen. Healing takes two to six weeks, but because of insertion of gas into the eye during the procedure, Jordan will eventually develop a cataract in his left eye. This is easily treated when the cataract matures in two or three years. With luck, there'll be no permanent loss of vision."

He nodded. We nodded.

Paul signed the consent papers and we were left alone.

I didn't feel like talking, but Paul asked me to explain what had happened. He was raw with grief by the time I'd finished.

"Ryan Dupont," he said, over and over. "I cain't believe it. They were friends." He shook his head.

I didn't have any comfort left to offer him.

Just for something to do, Paul went to find food and drink. I couldn't stand any more of that foul coffee, so he promised to hunt for a soda machine.

I made a promise, too. I promised myself that as soon as Jordan was well enough to travel, as soon as his parole had ended, we were getting the hell out of this poisonous little town. We'd face forward and never look back. We'd find somewhere we could both start again. I'd find a job as a paralegal, and Jordan could finish his ASE training. We'd get our own place and start to build a future together. Maybe Paul could come visit. Maybe we…

"What are you doin' here?"

I looked up and saw Jordan's mother staring at me, dislike distorting her face.

"Don't start with me, lady!"

She'd just challenged the wrong fucking woman.

Chapter 14 – Exorcism

Torrey

"Don't start with me, lady!" I snarled. I stared back at Jordan's mother, my anger molten, becoming volcanic by the second. "I love him. What's your excuse?"

She sucked in a sharp breath, ready to reply, but the door swung open and Paul returned carrying the sodas and sandwiches. His eyes shuttled between us, taking in my rigid posture, clenched fists, and Gloria's ugly, accusing glare.

Without speaking, he handed me the cello-wrapped food and one of the cans, then he looked at his wife.

"He's goin' to be okay, Gloria."

I swear, if she looks disappointed for one second I won't be responsible for my actions.

She nodded jerkily, acknowledging Paul's words.

"He's in surgery now…"

"I thought you said he was goin' to be okay," she interrupted, and for a moment I thought a saw of flash of something other than hatred, but it was gone too quickly for me to be sure.

"He is," Paul replied, quietly, "but they have to repair a detached retina. He also has some broken ribs, a fractured cheekbone, cuts and bruises."

She snorted and settled herself onto a chair, looking irritated.

"You called me here for that? I thought … never mind."

I was on my feet again, glaring down at her.

"What? What! That wasn't enough for you? What the fuck is the matter with you? He was beaten unconscious by four thugs. He could have been killed!"

She seemed stunned by my attack, but not the words I'd spoken.

"Are you goin' to let her talk to me like that?" she gasped outraged, staring at her husband with righteous indignation.

"If she hadn't said it, I would," he snapped, his voice becoming sharper.

"I've driven all this way…" she began.

"And why's that?" I snarled. "Why are you here? Why did you even bother?"

Her eyes narrowed and she looked at me like I was shit on her shoe.

"I don't answer to you!"

"I don't think you know why you're here," I said, venomously. "Probably trying to look like you're doing the right thing again."

"He's my son," she shot back, furiously. "I'm here to take care of him."

Seriously? I laughed out loud, a hard, bitter sound.

"Like you 'took care' of him for the last eight years?"

Her hands twitched and a muscle beside her eye jumped.

We were practically nose to nose, ready to slug it out, when we were interrupted by a knock at the door. Without waiting for any of us to reply, a nurse marched into the room, escorting two men in suits.

They took in Gloria's furious stare and my angry stance

301

without comment. The nurse just raised her eyebrows. Fighting families—nothing she hadn't seen before. Hospitals bring out raw emotions, it's inevitable, like death and taxes.

"I'm sorry to intrude at this difficult time," said the taller man, without sounding the least bit sarcastic. I wondered if he'd practiced that tone. "My name is Detective Lopez and this is my colleague Detective Sanders. I wonder if you could take a few minutes to answer some questions."

Paul nodded and waved them to a pair of plastic seats.

I took a deep breath and turned my back on Gloria. If I didn't look at her, I might be able to calm down slightly. I slumped into a seat and popped the tab on my soda, taking a long drink.

The police officers took our names and carefully noted our relationships to Jordan. I could see his mother quiver in her seat when Paul described me as Jordan's fiancée.

"And this isn't the first time he's been targeted," I snapped, rubbed the wrong way by the slow progression of the interview. "He's been threatened before and I have a photo of what they did to his truck a couple of months back."

I scrolled through the many pictures of me and Jordan on my phone to find the image of his mutilated truck.

"And before you ask, no he didn't report it. He was too … he prefers staying away from you guys, for obvious reasons."

They looked at the photo, made a note of it and asked me to forward it to them, but otherwise didn't comment. Then I had to describe again what had happened in the town square outside the bank.

My voice broke several times while I was retelling the story yet again, and Paul held my hand. Gloria's eyes nearly leapt out of her head.

When I'd finished, the detectives looked incredulous.

"You're saying he never threw a single punch? Even though four men were beating on him and his girlfriend?"

I lifted my chin at the insinuation that I was lying.

"None of them hit me. One restrained me." I slipped off my

cardigan and showed them the bruises on the tops of my arms where Leather Jacket had grabbed me. "I couldn't get to him ... I couldn't ... while the others ... while the others brutalized Jordan." I swallowed back the too fresh fear as the memory fought to swamp me. "And if you look at Jordan's hands you'll see that the only bruises are where the one with the cowboy boots stamped on them."

Lopez raised his eyebrows and exchanged a look with his colleague.

Jordan's mom snorted in disgust and I turned on her, ready to slap that sanctimonious bitch into next week, police or no police.

"My son is a coward, Detective," she said, her voice ringing with disgust. "That's the simple truth."

"Gloria!" shouted Paul.

I was on my feet, shaking with anger.

"Every time they knocked him down he stood right back up and faced them ... every time ... until he couldn't stand up anymore. That's the bravest thing I've ever seen, other than facing your hatred every day."

Silence settled around us, until Lopez cleared his throat and announced that he'd be in touch.

The officers stood up to leave.

"Wait!" I snapped. "What about the men who attacked Jordan? Have you found them? Jordan knew one of them— Ryan Dupont. Will you go after them, too? What happens to them?"

"We have one man in custody," Lopez confirmed.

"Just one? There were four of them!"

Sanders gave me an even look. "Ryan Dupont turned himself in, but he refuses to name the others involved. We need to speak to your fiancé to see if he wants to press charges."

My lips thinned until I was sure they were a white, bloodless slash across my face. I knew that would never happen. Jordan would never press charges. He'd said he was 'paying a debt' earlier. God, I hoped that debt was finally paid up in full because

I didn't know if I could take much more of this.

Outrage was still pulsing through me, and Gloria was sitting there, the whiff of sulfur foul in the air.

Lopez nodded again, handed me his card in case I 'remembered anything else'. As if I could ever forget it: every blow, every kick was imprinted on my brain, burned behind my eyelids.

As soon as it was just the three of us, I turned to Gloria.

"Tell me again why you're here?" I growled at her.

"Don't speak to me! I don't answer to you," she sneered.

"Gloria, that's enough!" barked Paul. "Either you're here for our son or you're not. I know that Torrey is."

Gloria ground her teeth together.

"Are you takin' her side now? The preacher's trashy daughter, that's what you called her."

My eyes flicked to Paul, and his dull skin reddened, revealing the truth of her hateful words.

"I was mistaken," he said. "I'm sorry, Torrey. Sorry about a lot of things. Look, we're all tired. It's been a bad, bad day. I think we should go home. Then in the mornin', we can be back here for Jordan. He's the important one right now."

I thought Gloria was going to argue, but instead she picked up her purse and abruptly left the room.

Paul offered me a sheepish smile. I didn't feel like returning it.

"You go," I said. "I'm staying."

He nodded slowly, but sank back into his seat to wait with me.

In silence, we watched the hands of the clock shuffle forward. We were joined by a woman who was weeping quietly, her eyes swollen with tears. I glanced at her tiredly, but didn't have anything to say that could make it better for her. No one could. We could only wait.

Finally, as the night stretched toward a new day, Dr. Linden reappeared.

"Everything went as well as can be expected, given the level of swelling around the eye. But there's a good chance that your son won't require a further operation."

"Can we see him?" I asked.

"He's in recovery so I can only let you look through the window, but I'd really suggest that you go home and get some rest yourselves. Come back tomorrow."

I wondered why he'd bother to say that.

We shook hands, and he wished us goodnight. He was probably going home to have dinner with his family. No, it was way too late for that. He'd probably take a snack from the fridge that his wife had left for him, shower, and slip between clean sheets, with a clean conscience and no bad dreams to trouble him. Maybe. We never really know the troubles that haunt the lives of others.

A nurse showed us to the recovery room, and I stood on tiptoe to look through the window.

Jordan's face was turned away from us, so I couldn't see much. He was hooked up to lots of machines, but he was breathing on his own.

My throat tightened, and I fought back the tears of relief that threatened to fall.

Paul touched my arm.

"We should go home now, get some sleep, like the doc said. Then we can be here for him later."

I nodded, and let him lead me from the hospital.

At the parking lot, I finally spoke.

"Could you please drive me to the bank in town?"

Paul looked surprised.

"The bank? At this hour?"

"I want to get my car. I'll be coming to the hospital as soon as I can in the morning."

He cleared his throat.

"Well, I can do that, darlin', but I'd be happy to give you a ride to the hospital in the mornin'."

"No, thank you."

He shook his head sadly but didn't reply, and we drove home

in silence. I ignored the glances he threw my way every couple of minutes. I knew it had taken him a while to warm up to me, but hearing what he'd said, what he'd accused me of—it hurt.

Once we reached the bank, I slipped out of the car.

"Thanks," I said, without looking in his direction.

I heard him sigh, and then the car pulled away.

When I arrived back, lights were shining from every window like beacons, or warning lights. Gloria hadn't drawn the curtains and I could see her going from room to room, observing the changes wrought on her home. It seemed like a violation of my makeshift family, and I had to remind myself it was still her home and not mine, despite everything that had happened in the last couple of months. I wasn't sure I'd be able to stay with her in the house, her spite and hatred seeping into the air.

I climbed out of the car wearily, feeling the ache in my arms and ribs where Leather Jacket had manhandled me.

I walked in to find Paul hovering in the hallway.

Then Gloria was suddenly standing in front of me.

"So you live here now," she said.

Her voice carried no inflection, which seemed odd after the way she'd spoken to me at the hospital.

I nodded, and started to walk around her and up the stairs to Jordan's room, to *our* room.

"Why?" she called after me.

"What?"

"Why do you live here?"

I didn't know what to make of her question.

"Because Jordan lives here," I said, tired and irritated by this bizarre Q&A.

"It looks like you have *all* your things here."

I locked my eyes on hers. "You've been in our bedroom."

She seemed almost nervous. "I didn't know you'd moved in. Paul didn't tell me…"

I nodded slowly. "Well, now you know. Stay out of our room."

I turned to carry on walking up the stairs.

"Why aren't you at the Rectory?" she asked, her tone insistent.

I stared at her tiredly. "Because my mother made me choose and I chose Jordan. Don't worry, Gloria, as soon as his parole is done, we'll be gone. Long gone, nothing but a cloud of dust behind us."

She didn't reply and neither did Paul. I hadn't spoken to him since the hospital. Maybe Gloria had got the result she'd wanted when she unleashed her forked tongue.

I was about to leave them at the bottom of the stairs, when I turned to face her once more.

"You know what your problem is? You've turned Mikey's death into a life sentence for all of you—for Paul, for Jordan. You turned them into lifers. That's what you're doing here—and that's what you want for Jordan. But I'm not going to let it happen. I'm not going to let him suffer anymore. What you do with your lives is up to you, but Jordan deserves better than that. And I'll spend the rest of my life with him, making sure he knows he's loved and forgiven."

I didn't wait to hear any reply. I trudged up the stairs and into our room. I flipped the light switch on and stared around. Jordan had made the bed. That didn't surprise me, he was so tidy. He felt like he was breaking a law if he left a wrinkle in the sheets.

His towel was still damp from showering before we'd gone out, and it was hanging neatly over the back of the chair. I picked it up and held it to my face, breathing deeply. I managed to get to the bathroom before the tears came. I peeled off my clothes and crawled into the shower, my stomach heaving as I washed Jordan's blood from my hair.

I was too tired to dry it, so I wrapped myself in Jordan's towel and fell onto the bed, my wet hair falling around me like tears.

The sheets smelled of Jordan, too. He didn't wear cologne but I could smell the soap he used and his sweet, spicy, natural scent.

It felt wrong sleeping in our bed without him. I hated it. There hadn't been a night since we'd been together when we hadn't made love. Even when I got home from work and it was after one in the morning, his warm body would wake and stretch as I slid in next to him. And even if we were both bone weary, we needed that connection at the end of our day.

I'd learned a lot about Jordan in the last couple of months. I'd learned how his body responded to my touch. I'd learned the little tells he had that told me when he was desperate to come but wanted me to get there first. He'd bite his lip and stare into the corner of the room. I teased him about that and asked him what he was thinking. He never did tell me. For all I knew, he was going over baseball stats. But ya know, that wasn't really something I was desperate to hear. I just appreciated that he cared about my satisfaction.

He went crazy when I dragged my fingernails down his back, even when we weren't in bed. He didn't really have a favorite position but I'd learned that he loved fast, rough sex followed by slow, gentle, sensuous love-making. Through and through, Jordan was an intriguing mix of contradictions: his hard body, his soft lips; his serious, sensible nature; his wild and passionate side; the scary, prison demeanor he could switch on; his gentle soul.

I don't think Jordan realized half of these things. It seemed as if he was rediscovering himself, the person he was going to become since prison. He had no idea that all the other women at Starbucks drooled over him, and quite a few of the girls who worked in the mall would suddenly come in for coffee when they saw his truck in the parking lot. Or maybe he noticed but just wasn't interested. Either way, it was one of the things that I'd grown to love about him.

And he definitely had no clue how intimidating he could be. He'd scared the crap out of my manager one day. Gus had been yelling at me and the rest of the staff about some supposed misdemeanor, when Jordan had made one of his after work visits to the coffee shop. Gus saw this tall, tattooed guy with rippling muscles and cold stare, and had totally abandoned trying to ream us out. I knew that Jordan had switched to his defensive, prison mode, because he was meeting a guy he didn't know. But Gus, the little jerk, had just about shit his shorts when I introduced them and he realized that Jordan was my boyfriend. Things at work eased up a lot after that.

And then there were all the little things Jordan did that showed me he loved me.

He didn't think I noticed, but I did. Making me breakfast at 5 AM even though he didn't have to be up for work himself; starting the shower before I got in it so the water would be warm; turning over the Princess' engine so she started first time for me; putting my shoes away and hanging up my jacket so it didn't get wrinkled; making sure he recorded my favorite TV shows when I was working.

Small things, for sure, but gestures that told me more than words how much he loved me.

I pulled the cold sheets closer around me. I knew I no longer had a choice. I was with Jordan Kane and always would be. He was my life, my forever, 'til death us do part. And maybe not even then.

I woke up suddenly. There was no sleepy confusion, no sense of quietly slipping between the dream world and the waking world. I knew instantly where I was and what had happened. I knew I had to be at the hospital.

Not normally a morning person, today I moved quickly and with purpose.

Today I marched to the shower, uncaring who I met or what they might say to me. I felt like a gladiator about to go into battle.

I showered quickly and tugged my hair into a damp clump at the back of my head.

I wondered whether it would be worth phoning the hospital, but then I figured it would be easier to just get there. I contemplated going straight to my car, but my stomach growled and I decided that Gloria wasn't chasing me out of the place that had become my home with Jordan. If she wanted to avoid me, *she* could leave.

Paul and Gloria were sitting with plates of scrambled eggs and toast in front of them. Paul was distractedly pushing the eggs around his plate, and neither seemed to be eating. He looked up when he saw me.

"How are you, Torrey?"

"Tired, sore, pissed. You?"

He winced at my blunt tone. Gloria didn't say anything.

I put some bread in the toaster and helped myself to coffee.

"There's eggs. If you want them."

I nearly dropped my mug and managed to splash hot coffee over my jeans.

"What?"

I turned and stared at Gloria.

"I've made plenty," she said. "I thought you might be hungry."

"Why are you talking to me?" I asked, suspicion making my words snap and crackle.

Paul coughed, obviously ill at ease with the duel starting up in front of him.

"I phoned the hospital," he said, cutting off my anger at Gloria. "They say Jordan had a good night."

I gave a staccato nod. I knew it was irrational, but I felt jealous that Paul had done something that I'd wanted to do, that I should have done.

"The nurse said he was askin' for you," Paul added.

I couldn't help the smile that tugged at the corners of my mouth. "He was?"

Paul nodded. "Of course. He loves you."

My eyes flickered toward Gloria, wondering what expression of hatred and distaste I'd see on her face. But instead she was staring at her untouched food.

A tiny bud of hope planted itself in my stomach. I tried to ignore it, but it was definitely there.

The popping of the toaster called for my attention and I slathered two slices thickly with butter. As an afterthought, I heaped three spoonfuls of eggs onto the plate, as well.

"Do you want to ride to the hospital with us?" Paul asked, tentatively.

"No thanks. I'll make my own way."

"Okay," he said, quietly. "We'll see you there."

I nodded and occupied myself with eating.

I finished before them and cleaned off my plate in the sink. Paul called after me as I left the room.

"Torrey, wait up."

"What is it, Paul? I want to get going."

He pursed his lips. "I am sorry that I said that about you. I didn't mean it. I never did."

I sighed. "Fine. Whatever. Apology accepted. I have to go."

"Darlin', please?"

"I can't deal with this now, Paul. Yeah, what you said hurt, but I can't, I just can't!"

"You're not the only one who cares about him, Torrey."

I met his eyes at last.

"I know."

I broke a few speed limits getting to the hospital. Jordan would have been pissed. He was always such a careful driver, which given the reason, wasn't surprising.

It took several frustrating minutes before I could locate him. They'd moved him from post-op recovery to a unit on the far side of the hospital. I clip-clopped my way along the overly polished corridors, becoming irritated when slow moving patients blocked my path. Why the hell didn't everyone stick to the right hand side? I had to bite my tongue to stop myself from yelling at a woman strolling along with a portable drip on wheels.

Out of my way! I'm in a hurry here!

She smiled at me pleasantly and I grimaced in return.

When I found Jordan, he was alone in a small room. His left eye was heavily bandaged, and although it barely seemed possible, he looked even worse than the day before. His entire face was swollen beyond recognition and his chest and arms were mottled green, purple, and black.

I thought he was sleeping and I tried to hold back a sob, but his good eye fluttered open.

"Hey, sweetheart," he mumbled, his voice thick with tiredness and pain. "I've been waitin' for you."

"Yeah, well, I was going to get a manicure this morning, but the hospital was on the way, so … here I am."

He managed a weak smile, although the effort seemed to tire him, and he turned his hand palm up on the bed, silently asking me to hold him.

He was right: I felt better being able to touch him and feel his warm, calloused skin. I leaned over and brushed a soft kiss over his forehead. It was about the only part of him that wasn't damaged.

"So, how they treating you in here?"

"'Sbetter than prison," he chuckled, hoarsely.

"Nah, you just have low standards," I quipped.

He started to shake his head then winced.

"Not anymore, sweetheart. I have you. Pure gold."

I tried to laugh it off, even though his words made my heart tremble.

"You may look like you've been run over by a truck, Jordan Kane, but you are one smooth talker!"

He tugged weakly on my hand. "Not smooth," he mumbled. "I love you."

"I know," I said, quietly. "I love you, too."

His good eye blinked open again. "You … you love me?"

"I told you last night, but you were too busy being unconscious."

His eyelid fluttered closed and his face contorted with the

effort of holding in the emotions that churned inside him. I saw a single tear roll down his cheek.

"Jordan," I said, slowly, "we have to talk about this. About what you let those men do to you. It's got to stop. You know that, right? Enough is enough. I won't stand by and watch that again. I can't."

He looked up, watching me, measuring my expression. "Parole's nearly over," he murmured.

"Don't tell me that was the only thing stopping you from fighting back. You told me last night that you were paying a debt!"

His brow wrinkled in confusion. "I said that?"

"Yes. Because it was Ryan Dupont?"

"Oh, yeah. I remember," he said, thickly.

"The police were here last night," I added, as his fingers tightened around my hand. "They'll want to talk to you. They told us that Ryan turned himself in. He's refusing to say who the other guys were, though. The cops are waiting to speak to you to see if you want to press charges."

He shook his head minutely. "No charges."

Which was pretty much what I'd imagined he'd say.

My voice took on a frustrated edge. "If you refuse to press charges then you have to *promise* me that this is where it ends. Because I'm telling you, Jordan, I don't ever want to see you like this again. Ever. I won't stand by and let you self destruct out of some twisted sense of … justice … or atonement. If you can't move on, I don't see that we can have a future."

God, I didn't mean those words but I needed to shock him, to make him see sense.

His fingers squeezed around mine more tightly.

"I'll never forget what I did, Torrey."

"And I don't expect you to. But you have to *live*, not exist in some twilight half-world. I want to share a future with you, Jordan, but not like this." My voice shook. "I can't."

He tried to take a deep breath but the pain from his broken ribs drained the blood from his face.

"No more," he whispered. "Together. Us together."

"The debt is paid?"

He hesitated.

"I'll pay 'til my dyin' day, sweetheart, but by livin', not wastin' my life."

"You promise?"

"Promise."

He lay quietly while I drew slow circles over his wrist, rubbing my finger over his tattoo. Relief warmed my whole body, and I felt a glow of love for the man lying next to me.

Jordan had drifted back into a drug-aided sleep when his primary physician arrived for the morning rounds.

He ignored me completely, flipping through the chart on the end of Jordan's bed then barking out some instructions to the minions following him.

When he turned to leave, still without speaking to me, I was fuming. I'd had a really bad 24 hours and I'd just reached my limit.

"Hey!" I barked. "I am sitting here! I do exist!"

"Excuse me?" he said, haughtily.

"Doctor…?"

"Dr. Markov."

"Well, Dr. Markov, as it has clearly escaped your attention, I would point out that your patient has a relation sitting by his bed, waiting somewhat anxiously to hear a report of how he's progressing after both a surgical procedure and a severe beating." I was just getting into my stride. "May I remind you of your duty *primum non nocere*, and right now that includes not raising my blood pressure above its very comfortable base level of 120/80. So, please, be so good as to tell me how the hell my fiancé is doing!"

He blinked several times as my voice became louder, and several of the students accompanying him looked nervous. Yeah, well, they could learn a lesson in manners just as much as Dr. Jerk-off.

"Ahem. Mr. Kane's blood pressure is stable; his blood work

looks good. I believe the retina reattachment was successful and that Dr. Linden was pleased with the surgery. There's no blood in his urine, which is a good sign, especially after receiving blows to the kidneys. In short, he's doing well."

"Thank you so much," I snapped back. "Next time you might like to offer up information without having to have it surgically extracted from your anus!"

His mouth dropped open then closed with a click. He swept out of the room, but not before I glimpsed a smile on the faces of some of the students.

Jordan opened his good eye. "I think you scared him, firecracker."

"Oh, you're awake!"

"Didn't have much choice what with all the hollerin'."

"I'm sorry. It's just, he pissed me off so badly!"

Jordan gave a soft chuckle. "Yeah, I noticed. You sounded real lawyer-like right up until the part where you told him he had his head up his ass. But even that sounded classy."

I smiled and stroked his arm, happy that he felt up to making jokes.

"Well, I was a paralegal for three years; I picked up a few tricks."

He looked at me thoughtfully.

"You want to go back to doin' that, sweetheart?"

I nodded my head emphatically.

"Yes, I do. More than ever."

He frowned at me. "Why's that?"

"Well, lawyers see paralegals as pretty low ranking—'glorified secretary' I've been called, when the lawyer is an asshole—but we're the ones who can talk to the clients in plain English. I can't advise anyone, but I can explain the advice they've been given in words they understand. People find lawyers intimidating. I'm not like that."

Jordan laughed quietly and took my hand in his.

"Sweetheart, you just intimidated the shit out of that doctor. You intimidated me the first time I met you, and just about every day since."

I was taken aback. "I didn't! Did I?"

"In a good way," he said, soothingly. "You're just so fearless, a real straight shooter. You don't take shit from no one, and you say it like it is. I love that about you. I think you'd be a great paralegal. Hell, you'd be a great lawyer if you wanted to be."

I wrinkled my nose. "Nah, I tried law school. Couldn't stick with it. I like my job, or I will when I get another one. I was thinking maybe I'd look into getting a Masters degree. Maybe."

He was silent for a moment. "You know I'll support whatever you want to do, right? If you want to go back to school. Whatever you want, we'll make it happen."

"That goes for you, too, Jordan."

He closed his good eye, a peaceful expression on his bruised face.

"Kinda sounds like we're plannin' a future, sweetheart."

I smiled to myself. "Doesn't it just," I agreed.

I looked up when the door to Jordan's room opened quietly, and his parents stepped inside.

"Your dad's here," I whispered, running one finger down his neck. "And your mom."

Jordan glanced up as Paul came into his vision.

"How're you doin', son?"

I think Jordan meant to shrug, but he winced instead.

"Been better. Okay, I think."

"Momma's here."

Jordan didn't reply as Gloria stepped forward.

"I hear you got engaged," she said.

Jordan blinked a couple of times and flicked his gaze to me, then started to smile.

"Is that what you heard?"

I squeezed his hand. "Sure, goes a long way with the hospital staff."

He looked confused for a moment and some of his bright smile faded. He gazed coolly at his mother.

"Why are you here, Momma?"

Gloria swallowed a couple of times. "Well, your father telephoned to tell me what happened. Despite … all the … despite everything … I wanted to make sure you were … all right."

Jordan gave a short, cynical laugh that ended with a gasp of pain.

"Yeah, I'm fine, Momma. Nothin' to worry about."

There was an awkward silence and Jordan turned his head away.

"Right," I said. "I think we should let him rest now."

"Of course," Paul agreed, quickly.

Gloria just nodded and left the room.

"Stay with me, sweetheart," Jordan mumbled, his voice slurring with sleep.

"Always," I whispered.

Jordan had been sleeping for over an hour. All that time, he hadn't let go of my hand. I sat next to him, watching his chest rise and fall steadily.

When the door opened, I was surprised to see we had a new visitor.

"Hello, Torrey."

I froze and eyed her warily as she hovered by the door.

"What are you doing here?"

"I came to see Jordan. And you."

"Really, Mom?" I said, snidely.

"Yes really, Torrey. To be honest, I've been trying to think of what to say to you for a while now. When this happened to Jordan, I realized that I've been so…"

"Hypocritical? Judgmental? Sanctimonious?"

She gave a small smile.

"Yes, all of those. Can I come in?"

"He's sleeping."

"I'd like to talk to you, if I may?"

I nodded tiredly, and she pushed the door fully open and walked inside.

As soon as she saw Jordan's battered body, she gasped.

"Oh no!"

I stared at her.

"Oh yes, Mom. That's what they did to him. They beat him to the ground, kicked him while he was there then beat him some more. When he was unconscious, they stopped. He didn't fight back. He didn't even try to defend himself."

"But why?"

"Seriously? You can ask that question with a straight face?"

Her expression was confused and full of pain.

"Since he got out of prison and came back here, everyone's been treating him like he's trash, like he deserved this to happen. So guess what? He believed them. He believed people like you who thought he deserved to be punished. Congratulations, Mom. Jordan agrees with you. He thinks he's a piece of shit."

"No! I never … Torrey, no! I never said that!"

"Oh, come on, Mom! Your big speech to him about your 'moral obligations'? He chose love, the same as me. And these people," I waved at Jordan's bruised face, "they chose hate."

She swallowed several times.

"You love him?"

"Yes, Mom, I do. I didn't choose an ex-con just to piss you off, no matter what you think. Jordan is a good person, a kind person, and he makes me happy when he's not getting the shit kicked out of him because of some twisted sense of honor. And believe me, we've already had words about that. Before him, it was just a string of faceless guys. He made me believe in myself, Mom. Because he loves me."

"Oh, Torrey! I'm so very sorry. I like Jordan, I do. But I *love* you. All I cared about was your well-being."

I stared at her coldly.

"Well, that's just not true, Mom, is it? You cared more about your reputation as the community's moral guardian. Couldn't have your daughter screwing the local leper."

Her face flushed, and she looked down.

"I've tried to do the right thing by you as well as by my conscience. But I'm not perfect, and I don't always get it right. I really am sorry about what I said, Torrey. About you, about Jordan. You're right, it was a bad case of double standards. But I hope you'll believe me when I say I was worried about my daughter. I was behaving like a mom, not like a priest. I've had time to examine my conscience, you might say. I've prayed a lot."

I rolled my eyes. "Great. Did ya get any really good advice this time?"

"I'm here, aren't I?" she shot back.

I had to smile at that. "Yeah, I guess."

"So," she said, slowly. "How are things with you and Jordan?"

"It was getting really good. We were making plans for the future."

"And now?"

"Honestly, Mom, I want to say we'll be fine…"

"But?"

"But I need him to stop blaming himself for Mikey's death. I mean, he just let those guys beat the shit out of him. He just stood there. And you know what he said to me? That he was 'paying a debt'. When does he stop paying? When does he start living his life? For us?"

Mom sighed heavily and shook her head.

"Guilt is a terrible burden," she said quietly, looking up at me. "Believe me, I know."

I understood what she was saying. I appreciated it, but it didn't really help either.

She didn't stay long after that. But just before she left, she bent down and whispered something to Jordan. I couldn't hear what she said, but it felt like she'd made her peace with him. With us.

Chapter 15 – Souls

Torrey

"A whole month without sex? Are you fuckin' kiddin' me?" Jordan whisper-yelled, his face disbelieving, his eyes hurt.

I folded my arms.

"Nope. No sex. Doctors' orders."

I picked up the leaflet we'd been given when he'd been discharged after four days in the hospital, and waved it in his face: *What to expect after your retinal surgery.* When he ignored me, I pulled the leaflet open and read the relevant section out loud.

"'*The first week after surgery should be reserved for rest with slow, careful movements only,*'" I enunciated carefully. "'*Activity may be resumed after one month, but heavy lifting, for example objects over 20 pounds, as well as strenuous activities should be avoided while the eye continues to heal.*' So basically, Jordan, if your eye isn't healing properly, you won't get laid even *after* a whole month is up. We are *not* risking your eyesight. You went without sex for eight years—you can manage a couple of months."

He'd been home from the hospital for less than half an hour and had already begged me to get naked with him.

"I mean, jeez! Look at you!" I hissed, not wanting his parents to overhear our intimate discussion. "You're all banged up, broken ribs and shit! Other than blowing you, there's not much we can do anyway."

His uninjured eye widened and he licked his lips. "Uh, that sounds real good, sweetheart."

"No. Freakin'. Way," I said shaking my head, annoyed with myself for giving him false hope. "God knows what damage you'd do! Having an orgasm is like sneezing. Your ribs would just about kill you, let alone what it could do your eye. Ask me again in a month."

His face fell and it was quite a job to keep from laughing.

He bit his lip, thinking hard.

"Well, how about I get you off?" he asked, hopefully.

I hadn't thought of that. Huh, I had to admit I liked the way his mind worked.

"That's a definite maybe, but right now you need to rest."

Despite his objections, he was obviously exhausted. I helped him pull off his pants and shirt, trying not to wince when I saw again the mottling of yellow bruises that covered his chest, hips and back. At least the swelling on his face had gone down, but he had to wear a protective guard over his eye for another day, and for the next two weeks at night to prevent him rolling on it or damaging it in his sleep.

I'd just pulled up the sheets around him when there was a knock on the door.

"Everything okay?"

Gloria's voice was hesitant on the other side, but Jordan frowned.

"What does she want?" he snapped, not bothering to keep his voice down.

I shrugged.

Gloria had started trying to make some more effort toward Jordan since visiting him in the hospital, but I was afraid it was too little, too late. I hoped I was wrong. Hell, Jordan was the most forgiving person I'd ever met, but his temper was worn thin right about now, especially with his parents. Ironically, it was because of Gloria's previous attitude to me, rather than what she'd put him through over the last eight years.

His relationship with Paul was more tenuous, too. He seemed to think his dad had chosen sides by having Gloria back in the house. One way or another, Paul was between a rock and a hard place. I felt sorry for him, but my priority was Jordan.

I opened the door and found Gloria waiting outside with two mugs of herbal tea.

"I thought you might be thirsty," she said. "It's herbal tea … you mentioned that he shouldn't have caffeine, so…"

"Oh, right. Thanks," I said, accepting the drinks. "Jordan's going to take a nap now."

Her face crumpled.

"But I'm sure he'll want to drink this first. Thank you, Gloria. That was very thoughtful of you."

Behind the door, Jordan was pulling a face and shaking his head.

I closed the door again and tried to give him the mug with the thin brew. He wrinkled his nose.

"I hate this shit."

"Shut up and drink it. You're not getting coffee. Not while you're trying to rest."

He crossed his arms over his chest and looked mutinous.

"She's trying, Jordan," I said, softly.

He shot me a bitter look. "When did you join her cheer team?"

"Don't be a jerk. She knows we're going to be out of here as soon as your parole is up. She wants to make her peace with you. At last."

He sighed heavily. "I know. I just don't care, and I'm not sure I want that anymore."

"Maybe it's not about what you want," I hinted. "Maybe it's about helping *her* to come to terms with Mikey's death and everything that's happened. She knows she's been a shitty mom for the last eight years, but you said she wasn't always like that. If all she can manage is to make you a lousy herbal tea, then fine—it's better than nothing." I looked at him directly. "It's better than her hating you."

"Yeah, yeah. Okay, I get it. Still fuckin' hate this. It tastes like piss," he moaned, taking the mug.

I smiled, because I knew that meant he'd let her in, eventually.

The next day my words came back to bite me in the ass. Of course.

I'd been up long enough to get Jordan some juice and a plate of scrambled eggs courtesy of Gloria. Then I shoved some more pain pills at him and helped to take care of his eye. Just doing all that wore him out, so I left him to go back to sleep while I showered and dressed.

Paul had headed out to work and Gloria left a note saying she'd gone to the store. I was left to wander around the house by myself.

I ended up in Mikey's room. It was less of a mausoleum than it had been, but it still looked as if they were waiting for him to come home. It made me sad.

I picked up his yearbook and started going through it. I flicked through the photographs, seeing pictures of Mikey on every other page: the football team, the senior prom, prizes for the best smile, the best body and the guy most likely to succeed. He'd also won biggest flirt and biggest party animal. I felt like putting stickers on those pages and making Gloria look at them. But what would be the point.

Then I saw a photograph that made me pause: Mikey, Ryan

and Jordan. Mikey was in the middle and they were all standing with their arms around each other's shoulders, grinning at the camera. You could see that Mikey and Jordan were brothers. Jordan was the taller, but slighter than he was now. He looked very much a kid. That picture must have been taken just a few months before the accident. The caption said, *Best Buddies, 2006*.

My thoughts were interrupted by a knock at the front door. God, I hoped it wasn't a surprise parole inspection. That was the last thing that Jordan needed. Or me, for that matter.

But when I yanked it open, it wasn't anyone from the parole team.

"Hello, Torrey. May I come in?"

"What are you doing here, Mom?"

"Well, after our talk, I felt I wanted to speak to Jordan, too, if that's all right. I wanted to apologize to him personally."

I opened the door wider. "He's sleeping at the moment. He gets pretty tired."

"Perhaps I could wait?"

I sighed and waved her inside.

"Yeah, fine. He'll probably be awake shortly. You want a coffee or something? I can't drink it in front of Jordan because he's supposed to be off caffeine for now."

She smiled.

"That sounds wonderful. You always make the best coffee."

"Yup, almost a professional," I said, snippily.

She followed me into the kitchen while I made a fresh pot.

"I bet you're glad to have him … home."

I threw a look over my shoulder.

"I don't think this is much of a home for him, Mom. For either of us."

She hesitated a moment.

"You could always come to me, to the Rectory."

"I'm not leaving him here!" I snapped.

"I didn't mean that—I meant you could both come, if you like."

I blinked at her in surprise.

"Really?"

"Yes, of course. You're my daughter … and I hear Jordan is going to be my son-in-law—although I can't see a ring." She paused when I didn't say anything. "Is it true?"

"Maybe, yeah. I just said it to the hospital staff because they weren't telling me anything, but yeah, he has mentioned it to me."

"And?"

"And I don't have the highest opinion of marriage."

"Oh, I see."

I shrugged.

"I don't know, Mom. I think Jordan plans on wearing me down until I cave in and say yes."

She smiled and her eyes sparkled with amusement.

"I think he'll make you a very good husband, Torrey. You need someone to stand up to you."

Her optimism was making me uncomfortable.

I finished my coffee and stood up. "Come on then. Just … don't upset him, Mom. He's been through enough."

She shook her head. "I just want to talk to him, that's all."

"Yeah well, words can hurt as much as fists," I pointed out.

She nodded her agreement, and we made our way up the stairs.

"Just give me a second while I wake him. If you walk in on him now, he might think he's getting the last rites."

Mom rolled her eyes. "Very funny, Torrey."

Yeah, except I wasn't joking.

I pushed open the door and walked in. Even though I was used to seeing the bruises, it still hurt to look at him.

He opened his good eye as I sat on the bed next to him, and he smiled.

"I sure like this dream," he said. "Who are you, beautiful?"

"Ha-ha. If this were a dream, you wouldn't be all banged up."

"And you'd be naked," he added, winking at me.

"Rein it in, cowboy. My mom's right outside—she wants to

come in and see you."

He looked confused for a second, then his anxious look was back.

"She wants to see me?"

"Specifically, she wants to apologize to you."

"What for?"

Mom's head peered around the door. "A few things, Jordan. Quite a few things."

She winced as she walked into the room, shocked again as she took in his bruised and battered body, and the eye guard taped in place.

He mumbled something under his breath and struggled to sit up.

"How are you, Jordan?" she said.

"Fine," he answered, automatically.

Mom paused. "Well, I'm glad you're out of the hospital. I was … worried when I heard what had happened."

I bit back the remark that was on the tip of my tongue to spit at her. She said she'd come to apologize. I knew I should let her do it.

Jordan simply stared at her, his face slipping into that cold, unreadable mask.

Mom sat in the wooden chair next to the bed.

"I owe you an apology, Jordan. As my daughter has so rightly pointed out on several occasions, I have been guilty of double standards. I preached tolerance and forgiveness but didn't practice it. For that, I'm sorry. What's happened to you, and I don't just mean this," she waved toward his damaged body, "life has been very harsh. I hope you can forgive me for adding to your burden."

Jordan looked uncomfortable and glanced at me. I shrugged. Forgiving her was his decision. I already had. Sort of.

"Yeah, sure," he said, at last.

"Thank you," she said, quietly. "Would you mind if I prayed for you? For both of you?" She glanced at me and smiled. "I'll make it a short one."

"Go for it, Mom."

She took Jordan's hand in hers, and he threw me a panicked look. I shook my head slightly, smiling at his expression.

"Lord, you are loving and kind and merciful. Create in us today new, clean hearts that can forgive those who have transgressed against us and against you. Restore us all to the joy of your salvation, this day and evermore. Amen."

She looked up. "Short, sweet, says it all, don't you think?"

"Um, yeah?" Jordan agreed, tentatively.

I gave her a small smile. "Nice one, Rev."

She stayed a few more minutes, asking about our plans for the future. She looked sad when I said we'd be heading out as soon as Jordan's parole had finished and he was cleared to travel.

"Will you stay in touch, Torrey?" she asked, her expression resigned.

"Sure, Mom," I answered, quickly.

She nodded but didn't push it any further.

After she left, I headed back up to see Jordan.

"Not so bad, huh?" he smiled at me. "I'm glad you and your momma are speakin' again. It didn't set right with me that you were fightin'."

I chewed my lip for a while but nodded.

"Yeah, life's too short to stay angry at people, isn't it?"

We sat in silence, each lost in our separate thoughts.

The next day Officer Carson came to visit.

Jordan had only just woken up, so I made her wait in the family room while I helped him get dressed. It was too painful for him to try and get a t-shirt over his head, so he was wearing one of Mikey's old button down shirts. Gloria hadn't objected when I'd raided the closet in Mikey's room; she'd even helped me to wash the clothes I'd taken so they were freshened up after eight years of collecting dust.

I left Jordan to zip up his own pants, despite his insistence that me helping with that was the best part of getting dressed.

I headed back down to have a little heart-to-heart with Officer Carson.

"I hope you're not going to make him take a test for drugs," I said, quickly, "because half the time he's high as a freakin' kite on all the pain meds, and I've been using alcohol wipes around his eye, so he'll fail the EtG test, too."

"No, that's fine," she smiled. "Don't worry, Torrey. In fact, we won't worry about that anymore at all."

I didn't know what she meant, but let it go when she looked up as Jordan walked slowly into the room, holding his ribs.

"Hello, Jordan," she said, standing up to shake his hand. "How are you?"

"Fine," he said, automatically.

We both stared at him, taking in the multicolored bruises, the eye patch, his painful stance, then at the same time we both burst out laughing, Jordan joining in reluctantly.

"Oh, crap!" he gasped, his laughter ending abruptly. "That hurt!"

"Of course, you idiot!" I chuckled. "Sit down before you fall down and I have to scrape you up off the carpet."

"Well," said Officer Carson when we were all seated. "I have good news. I came to tell you, Jordan, that you've been exempted from further drug and alcohol tests. It seemed appropriate, under the circumstances."

"That's great!" I said, brightly. "Thanks! We didn't want to have to traipse into town."

Jordan was silent, so I elbowed him in the ribs. He yelped and threw me a wounded look.

"Oops, sorry! That was harder than I meant, but you're supposed to thank Sandy!"

Officer Carson smiled. "Don't worry, Torrey, that's fine. I'm sure it's a lot to take in. But I do have a couple more pieces of good news: firstly, you don't have to write your report this month, Jordan, and…" she paused for effect, "your parole officially finishes at midnight tonight. I pulled some strings."

We were both silent.

"So that's it," she said kindly, correctly interpreting our silence as astonished shock. "You're a free man, Jordan. Society believes you have paid your debt in full. It's up to you now."

"Oh my God!" I said, flinging my arms around Sandy's neck as tears pricked my eyes. "Thank you so, so much!"

Jordan looked stunned.

"That's it? I'm … I'm free?"

Officer Carson smiled and coughed a little, sounding choked up. I swear she was wiping a tear from her eye, too.

"Yes, Jordan. You're a free man. Congratulations."

She stood up and offered him her hand.

My heart cried out as he stood on trembling legs. Then they shook hands briefly.

"My job here is done," she said, softly. "Good luck to both of you."

She smiled again, then I showed her to the door and waved as she drove away.

Jordan was seated on the couch when I walked back in, his expression still stunned.

"Wow!" I said.

He seemed frozen to the spot.

"Jordan, this is immense! You're free!"

I sat down next to him and wrapped my arms carefully around his neck, gently folding myself around his trembling body.

He buried his face into my hair as sobs shook his body.

"Free!" he said.

Jordan

It was impossible to take in.

I knew I should feel like celebrating, but I just felt empty. For so long I'd been identified as someone outside of society: first as a convict, then as a parolee. But now...

"It's okay," said Torrey reassuringly, later that afternoon.

We were lying on the sofa together, Torrey curled up carefully next to me. Normally when we were like this, she'd be lying all over me. I missed having her head on my chest, and that soft, soft hair falling across my body. But it was too fucking painful to take her weight on me. Not only that, but just breathing hurt, I had a king-size headache, and my left eye was throbbing like a bastard. I was trying to ignore it all and concentrate on the TV. Torrey loved sci-fi programs and we were currently watching reruns of *Star Trek: Next Generation.* Well, she was. My mind was a million miles away. Yeah, ironic much.

She looked across at me. "I can only imagine how surreal this is for you."

I nodded but didn't answer. Honestly, I wouldn't have known what to say.

"It's going to be okay," she said, again. "As soon as you're well, we can do anything we like, go anywhere we want."

"Yeah, I know."

I didn't.

"Don't worry, we'll work it out." She hesitated. "When are you going to tell your folks?"

Dad had been out at work and Momma had been—who knows where she'd been. She stayed out of our way.

Officer Carson had left three hours ago. I could have called

Dad at his office but I'd held off.

"I'm not sure I'm gonna tell them yet," I said, at last.

Torrey was puzzled. "Why wouldn't you?"

I shifted uncomfortably, trying to find a piece of couch that didn't hurt like a bitch.

"I just don't want to feel ... I don't know. It's like they'll be expectin' somethin' else from me. I don't want the pressure right now. Can we just leave it for a while?"

She held up her hands. "Hey, it's totally your call! I'm just happy and proud of you. I want to shout it out so everyone knows. But if you're not ready for that, it's fine by me. But, um, I did send a text to Bev."

"Yeah? What did she say?"

Torrey laughed. "Well, her first text was just one word, at least I think it was a word. The message said 'amazeballs!'"

"Um, okay?"

"And her second message said she wanted to come over with a bottle of champagne. Don't worry. I told her no. Or rather, I told her not yet."

"I've never had champagne."

She stared at me.

"Just beer and, um, vodka, some whiskey. Ryan had ... there was red wine at his party. I remember that. But I don't think I had any. So nope, no champagne."

"We totally have to put that right!" Torrey laughed. "You'll love it. And it goes really well with sex. I think it's the bubbles."

I started to laugh then my ribs reminded me that wasn't a great idea.

"Sorry, hon," she giggled. "Oh, by the way. I talked to Hulk. He'd already heard, of course. He says the job's there when you want it and that I should kick your ass some. Not sure why he said that but I think it was a term of affection."

I grunted, not wanting to think about Hulk and 'affection' in the same sentence. It was just too strange.

"What about your work, sweetheart?" I asked, dreading the answer. "You cain't stay at home playin' nurse with me forever."

She sighed. "No, that's true. But Gus gave me the rest of the week off."

"That sure was generous of him."

"Yeah, well it might have something to do with the fact that he's shit scared of my boyfriend!"

I grimaced. "I wouldn't have thought he'd be afraid of someone who don't fight back."

My tone was bitter, and Torrey threw me a look that showed she was still kind of mad at me.

"Yes, but those days are over, aren't they?"

I guess they were.

"Yeah," I said, nodding slowly. "No free passes for anyone. Next time, I'm comin' out swingin'."

Torrey smiled, satisfied with my answer.

And I wasn't lying to her. I wasn't a parolee anymore: I had the same rights as anyone else. Well, almost. I wasn't dumb enough to think that if I got into something my record wouldn't be held against me, but it wouldn't automatically mean going back to prison either. And as for Ryan and anyone else who wanted a piece of me, next time *they* would be the ones paying. I finally believed what Torrey had been telling me—my debts were paid. There was just one outstanding, and that was a debt to Mikey—the one where I'd promised him to live my life the best way I could. It would take a lifetime to pay, but I was good with that thought.

The next day, we were visited by the detective from the hospital. Torrey said it was the same guy, Detective Lopez, but I didn't remember. I was probably out of it at the time.

Torrey offered him coffee. She was being thoughtful, but the idea of acting like I was fucking socializing with a police officer had me twitching and just about ready to leap out of my skin. I probably would have, if breathing didn't hurt so damn much.

"Hello, Mr. Kane. My name is Detective Lopez. I've already had the pleasure of meeting your fiancée."

I had trouble replying anything sensible. A police detective was calling me *mister*, that was just plain freaky. Plus, Torrey and me hadn't exactly discussed the whole 'fiancée' thing. Truthfully, I was kind of hurt that she'd just used it to get information at the hospital. Maybe it didn't mean that much to her, bearing in mind her views on marriage. Hearing the word should have made me happy, but instead I just felt a jolt of pain.

The detective was still staring at me but my mouth refused to work; thankfully, Torrey took over.

"Thanks for coming, detective. I'm assuming you have some news for us?"

He sat on one of the armchairs and leaned back. "Well, yes and no. Ryan Dupont has admitted to the assault, as you are aware, but refuses to name his accomplices. I want to know if you'll be pressing charges—either of you."

I glanced at Torrey. I'd seen the bruises on her arms, and that had made me madder than hell, and I felt guilty that she'd gotten hurt because of me. She folded her arms and stared back. She knew how I felt about this and we'd discussed what I was going to do. Or rather, not do.

"No," I said, quietly. "I won't be pressin' charges."

"Miss Delaney?"

"No, no charges."

There was a short silence.

"I see," said Detective Lopez. "May I ask why?"

I let out a long, painful breath.

"He was my brother's best friend."

In the end, out of all the things I could have said, out of all the explanations I could have given, that was the simplest answer for a stranger to comprehend.

Lopez nodded.

"Well, in that case I won't be taking up anymore of your

time. Mr. Kane, Miss Delaney."

He stood up and offered his hand. I stared at it, nonplussed, until Torrey cleared her throat. I stood up, too, and tentatively shook the guy's hand.

Torrey saw him to the door and when she came back, she brushed a soft kiss over my lips.

"What's that for?"

"Do I need a reason?"

"No, sweetheart, never."

She smiled. "I think it's because this means it's over, so I sealed it with a kiss."

"I love you, Torrey Delaney."

"I know," she said, and threw me a wink.

The next three weeks were boring as all hell, if you discounted the fact that it was pretty tense in the house having Momma and Torrey in the same building, even when they weren't in the same room. They were civil to each other, but there was no warmth there. Torrey was kind of distant toward my dad, too, which was a shame because they'd been getting along so well before. I thought it was probably because I was mad at him for letting Momma come home, but if there was another reason, I wanted to know why.

After being uncharacteristically evasive, Torrey finally told me I was right, but it was also because she'd found out that he'd called her 'trashy'. She was really hurt by that, and I was furious that Momma had taken pleasure in telling her. I already knew what he'd said, of course, but of all the things that Momma had hurt me over, telling Torrey, that was one of the hardest to forgive. If she'd just aimed her spite at me, I could have taken it, but not when she hurt the woman I loved.

I knew that Dad was ashamed of what he'd said, and

Momma had been trying to make it up to me—to us—but somehow it had cut the final cords that bound us together. I had a new family now with Torrey.

She had to go back to work in the end. One of us needed to be earning an income, and I was as useful as a suntan in Siberia. I missed her like crazy and sent a million texts to her each day. I spent the rest of my time reading some, although that was tiring with just one good eye. I listened to the radio, occasionally watched TV. Other than that, I slept a lot.

Momma didn't try and force her company on me, although she shopped for food, made sure I got meals at regular intervals, and just kind of kept things ticking over. But I'd lost my appetite since being in hospital, and chewing with a fractured cheekbone wasn't the most fun thing ever. I had a lot of soup, and mac and cheese.

Momma drove me around for those few weeks. It was awkward. We didn't talk much. I don't think either of us knew how to. I guess we tried.

One afternoon, she was driving me to my appointment with the eye surgeon guy at his office, but stopping off at the junkyard first.

"How are you feeling?" she asked, tentatively.

"Fine."

There was a long pause.

"Good," she said, at last. "Torrey seems…"

When she didn't finish the sentence, I glanced across expectantly.

"She seems good for you."

I don't know if it meant to sound like she was choking on the words, but it did.

"She is," I replied, shortly.

End of conversation.

She turned into the junkyard's entrance and parked near the office.

I needed to see Hulk and tell him I wouldn't be coming back to work for him. I could have phoned, but the guy had done a lot for me and I owed him.

Momma waited in the car while I went to talk to him. He was sitting behind his child sized desk, dwarfing it as usual.

He stood up when he saw me, shoving his chair into the wall. Then without speaking, he wrapped his massive arms around me and squeezed tightly.

"Don't break my damn ribs again!" I yelped.

Hulk released me with a snort of amusement. I didn't think it was that funny. I was healing well, but it was still a work in progress.

"Good to see you, kid!" he said. "Heard yer still kickin'. Guess it was the truth."

"Yep. Cain't kill weeds, man."

He looked at me appraisingly.

"I figured you'd be along. I'm guessin' ya come to say your goodbyes."

"Yeah. Me and Torrey will be headin' out in a couple of days. Fresh start, ya know."

He nodded, staring at me from behind his bushy eyebrows.

"I just wanted to thank you, man," I said, feeling a little awkward at doing the emoting thing with Hulk. "If you hadn't given me a job, hell, I'd probably be coolin' my heels back in prison right about now."

"You gettin' soft on me, kid?" he asked, rumbling out a laugh.

"Maybe."

He chuckled to himself.

"That's the effect of women for ya. Gotta say, your girl's fine. She can ride a horse in my string anytime. Look after that lil' firecracker—got yesself a good 'un there, kid."

"I know. Thanks, Hulk. I won't forget you."

He cleared this throat a couple of times, and then he handed me an envelope.

"A little travelin' money, kid. And a reference, jest in case ya get another job as good as this 'un."

We shook hands, and he clapped me on the back again.

"Vaya con Dios, kid.

He didn't come out to the car, but I could see his massive silhouette framed in the doorway. As Momma drove away, he raised one hand in a salute.

I looked in the envelope to read his reference, but was amazed when I counted $1,000 in hundred dollar bills. I hadn't expected that, but I knew exactly what I wanted to spend it on. It wouldn't go for gas money, but I thought Hulk would approve the way I was planning on spending it.

In his own way, Hulk had done more for me than my own parents.

I was still thinking about some of the good times I'd had at the junkyard, when we arrived at the doctor's office for the last of my weekly checkups.

I was suddenly aware that I hadn't spoken a word to Momma since we left Hulk's. Maybe she thought I was punishing her, but I wasn't.

I appreciated her doing stuff for me, but I realized that there was too much water under the bridge for us to have a real close relationship ever again. I was okay with that, and I think she was, too. But at least she didn't act like she hated me anymore, and I didn't act like I needed her to. We were good, sort of.

Two weeks after Carson had come to see me, I'd finally admitted to my parents that I was no longer on parole. They'd been quiet, not saying much. Dad said 'congratulations' and shook my hand. Momma looked like she was going to cry, but I didn't ask the reason.

I climbed out of the car and turned to look at her. She was staring straight ahead and didn't seem inclined to move.

"I guess I'll be about 30 minutes or so, Momma."

She gave a staccato nod, and I left her sitting there, still gripping the steering wheel.

I didn't have to wait too long to see the doc.

It was a month after the eye op now, and he did all the usual checks and seemed pleased with the way it was all going. Better still, he gave me the go-ahead to drive, but only for short distances. I still wasn't allowed to fly because of the altitude, but even that would probably be okay in a couple of months, and it wasn't like I was planning on vacationing in Hawaii anyway.

I seemed to be a little more sensitive to light in that eye, which kind of sucked, living in a real sunny part of the country. Maybe I'd have to go live in Alaska after all. Or maybe not, I didn't think I could handle the glare off of the snow. Torrey bought me some Aviator Ray Bans. I nearly bust a gut when I found out how much they cost. She just laughed.

But as far as I was concerned, the most important question hadn't been covered yet. So during that final appointment, I made it my priority question once I knew I wasn't going blind.

"So, um, doc, you know that bit in the leaflet about 'strenuous activity'?"

"Yes, and even now we advise no heavy lifting. No weightlifting for example," he said, eyeing me closely, and looking pointedly at my biceps. At least I still had some muscle tone after being a complete freakin' couch potato for a month.

"Nah, that's okay. I haven't lifted any weights. I've just been doing a few sit ups and push-ups this last week to stop myself completely veggin' out."

"Do you run, Mr. Kane?"

I really couldn't get used to all this mistering.

"I did. I haven't started again." I pointed to my chest. "Busted ribs, too."

"Ah, of course. Even so, I wouldn't recommend you start running again just yet. Maybe in a couple of months when things have settled down."

I sighed.

"What about sex, doc?"

"Excuse me?"

"Please tell me I'm good to go. I'm about going crazy here!"

"Ah, I see. Well, it depends on how, um, vigorous the intercourse is. Ideally, I'd recommend against that."

"Aw, hell! For how much longer?"

"Well, *gentle* activity will be fine."

What the hell does that mean?

"In English, doc?"

"Ah, let your partner take most of the, uh, strain."

"You mean let her be on top?"

"That would be one way of looking at it."

Okay, I could live with that.

"For how long? When can we … do other stuff?"

He smiled. "Mr. Kane, frustrating as this may seem, it's really only in your best interests to let nature take its course and allow your eye to heal completely. Within two or three months, you'll be pretty much back to living a normal life. We'll have to look out for cataract development, as you know. But other than that, just try to take things easy for now."

Yep, clear as mud.

I stood up.

"Thanks for everythin', doc. I appreciate it."

"Not at all. I'll make a follow up appointment for you in…"

"Actually, doc, we're not plannin' on stayin' around here. We're gonna start again somewhere new."

He looked surprised.

"So, if I could get a copy of my chart to take with me, that would be mighty handy."

"I'll certainly do that for you, Mr. Kane." He reached over to shake my hand. "Good luck with everything."

As I walked out of the door, he said, "Remember, nothing vigorous."

Bastard.

But still, it was a green light as far as I was concerned.

Of course, organizing a night of romance wasn't so simple bearing in mind I still lived with my parents, and my woman was a screamer.

I considered the options: even the cheapest motel would have wrecked my finances. I'd got a couple of month's wages from Hulk saved up—a few hundred bucks—but the bonus he'd given me was earmarked for something real important. Money was in damn short supply and now I couldn't work, and what with planning to start fresh I needed to save what I had.

In the end, I had to resort to begging. I phoned Dad at his office.

"Dad, any chance you could take Momma out somewhere tonight?"

He sounded puzzled.

"Out?"

I rolled my eyes. "Yeah, Dad, out. I'd just like to cook Torrey a nice meal and spend some alone time with her."

Alone time, Dad! Take the freakin' hint!

"Well," he said, hesitantly. "Perhaps I could take your mother out to dinner. It might be good for us, too. Fine, I'll do it. We'll be home by 9 PM."

"You could take in a movie after," I suggested.

He sighed. "I'll ask her. I'm not promisin'."

"Thanks, Dad."

Momma left the house soon after five, which gave me just half an hour to get everything ready.

My culinary skills were still limited by my budget, but I'd had an idea. I'd stopped at Krogers to buy a couple of pieces of trout, baking potatoes, and a bag of salad. I hoped the menu would remind Torrey of our first date.

Because I was short on time, I started off the potatoes in the microwave, then slung them in the oven to crisp up, grilled the fish, and cursed myself for not buying candles.

Jeez, I used to have game.

I dug around in the garage and found an old hurricane lamp and a couple of stubs of emergency candles. That would have to do. I ran around like a crazy person, putting finishing touches to my plan. At the last minute I remembered that we needed music. I'd lived without it for so long, it just wasn't usually something I thought about. I'd saved up to buy a radio in prison once, but it was broken the first week I got it when my asswipe of a cell mate got into a fight with someone he owed money to. I didn't bother again after that.

Torrey had taken her iPod to work so I found an old CD in

Mikey's room, *Smashing Pumpkins*, and stuck that on. I'd heard Torrey play it so I hoped that would be a good start in setting the mood.

It didn't work, of course.

She came crashing in through the door at a quarter before six, late enough to have me pacing up and down.

"Jordan Kane, you're up to something!" she yelled as soon as she set a foot through the door.

How the hell did she know? Damn woman was psychic.

"Hey, sweetheart," I said, sweeping her into a tight hug. "How was your day?"

"Groovy. Now why don't you tell me what the hell's going on? Where are Paul and Gloria? Their cars are missing."

"Out. We've got the whole place to ourselves. I've cooked for us. Come through and make yourself comfortable."

She threw me a suspicious look.

"What did the doc say at your appointment? You were supposed to text me!"

"Sorry, sweetheart, I wanted to tell you in person. It's all good. And I got a copy of my chart to take … well, wherever we go."

She smiled and relaxed. "Aw, that's great, honey. Come and get some sugar!"

She pouted her pretty lips at me, and I didn't need a second invitation.

I dropped pecks across the corners of her mouth and then tugged at her lower lip with my teeth.

When she opened, I kissed her deeply, sliding my tongue against hers, utterly caught up in the way it felt: her sweet, coffee flavor; the sensation of being joined with her, tasting her.

We'd avoided doing this for a whole goddamn month because it was just impossible for us to keep from getting carried away.

"Jordan," she murmured against my lips, "stop tempting me! We can't!"

"Actually, sweetheart, we surely can. Got the all clear from the doc."

She gave a little gasp and attacked my throat with her hot, wet mouth, making me groan loudly. But then she pushed away.

"Wait just a darn minute!" she snapped. "I'm not sure I believe you! Tell me *exactly* what he said."

Busted.

I couldn't lie to her. I just couldn't do it.

"Okay, fine. He said we could go ahead so long as we didn't do anythin' 'vigorous'. But I'm beggin' you, sweetheart, I've missed this, us, so badly…"

She laughed and raised her eyebrows. "You can have sex but it can't be 'vigorous'? Is that even possible?"

Nope, I didn't think so either.

She wrinkled her nose, suddenly distracted. "Are you cooking something?"

I smiled. "Yep, trout and baked potatoes."

She grinned at me and let her fingers trail down my back, over my t-shirt.

"Are you trying to seduce me again, Jordan Kane?"

"God, yes! How am I doin'?"

She smirked at me. "Not bad, although did he really say that we can't do anything 'vigorous'?"

I nodded mutinously.

"Hmm, well, I guess we might just have to get creative." She smiled. "Let's eat first, I'm starving."

Even though dinner had been part of the plan, I couldn't help feeling frustrated that food was getting in the way of taking my woman to bed. That and the thought of trying to force food into my stomach when my cock was throbbing in my pants. Fuckin' luck.

Distraction. Food.

I served up the fish onto warmed plates and slid a potato off of the skewer for her.

"And, um, there's salad, too," I said, pushing a bowl of leaves and green shit in front of her.

"Thanks, cowboy," she smirked.

She knew I hated salad. I just didn't see the point of it.

"And, um, there's this," I said, taking a bottle of champagne from the fridge.

Torrey clapped her hands together and watched as I popped the cork. I poured two glasses and handed one to her.

"To us, sweetheart."

"To us."

I sipped slowly, surprised by the way the bubbles felt on my tongue. It seemed strange to me. Truthfully, I'd forgotten what alcohol tasted like. I hadn't even had a beer in the last month. Despite not being on parole any longer, Torrey had banned it on the grounds that I was taking way too many drugs to mix and match. It didn't bother me.

I was nervous about drinking again, but I'd wanted tonight to be special.

The champagne was kind of sweet, kind of sharp, and the bubbles made my tongue tingle—all things that reminded me of Torrey.

"So," she said, slowly. "I guess we really are free to take off now."

"I guess we are."

"Well, where do you want to go?"

I shook my head. "I don't care, just so long as it's with you."

"No plans at all?"

"Sweetheart, I've had every minute of every day planned for me for the last eight years. So let's travel, see stuff, go wherever. I spoke to Hulk and he wrote me a reference so I should be able to get a job. If you get one from Gus, we'll be able to pick up casual work whenever we run out of money. If we find somewhere we like, I guess we just stop drivin'. How does that sound?"

She grinned. "I like that non-plan. What's for dessert?"

"I was really hopin' you'd ask that."

"Were you now?"

"Dessert is upstairs."

She curled her lips in a smile. "I thought it might be."

We cleared the plates from the table and stacked everything into the dishwasher. Torrey picked up the champagne bottle, which was still half full, and I carried the glasses.

I swayed slightly. I was definitely getting a buzz from the booze. I decided not to drink anymore; I didn't want to spoil tonight.

I let Torrey lead the way up the stairs, not just to appreciate the view of her ass, but to hear her gasp of surprise as she opened our bedroom door.

"Oh! You … you did all this?"

I nodded, watching the glow of happiness on her face as she looked around. The hurricane lamp threw a gauze of soft shadows around the room, and the two candles flickered in the breeze from the open window. I'd filled the room with flowers that I'd picked in the fields beyond the cottonwoods. I could name some of them. I used to pick them with Momma when I was a little kid. There were cowpen daisies, flame vines, Mexican heather, butterfly milkweed, and some pink things that I had no idea what they were called. I thought Torrey would like them. They were wild and natural, just like her.

"Jordan, it's beautiful! You are definitely getting laid tonight, cowboy."

"Thank fuck for that! My balls aren't even blue anymore, they're freakin' purple after lyin' next to you night after night and not bein' able to do anythin' about it."

She laughed. "On the bed now! Oh wait, take your clothes off first!"

It was my turn to laugh. "Did you forget how this works?"

She raised an eyebrow. "Like you and I haven't had sex with most of our clothes on before now because *you* were too impatient to get me naked!"

That was true.

I toed off my tennis shoes and lined them up under the chair. I knew that Torrey was trying not to laugh at me, but I couldn't help being tidy. Besides, I knew she'd be messy enough for both of us.

I'd gotten out of the habit of wearing socks. Mostly because the first couple of weeks I'd been home from the hospital, I couldn't bend down to put them on. And I didn't want Torrey dressing me like I was a damned invalid.

She watched while I undid my shirt buttons one at a time, and licked her lips. Yeah, my woman liked to watch.

Soon I was standing there in just my jeans. I was so turned on, I knew I wouldn't last as long as I wanted. It reminded me so much of the first time we'd been together, except now I knew how she felt about me.

I unbuckled my belt and pulled down the zipper.

"You want to do the rest, sweetheart? I'm all yours."

"Oh, I want!" she said.

She yanked my jeans over my ass and palmed my dick as it leapt out toward her. I was seconds away from coming and she'd barely touched me.

She knelt down in front of me and ran her tongue over and around the head of my cock, and my whole body responded. I grabbed her shoulders to keep from falling.

"Torrey, I…"

"Shh," she murmured.

"Please, sweetheart," I begged her. "I'm gonna…"

But she was in charge. Oh boy, was she in charge.

I came so freakin' hard, I saw stars. It was unbelievable pleasure after a month-long ban, and off the chart pain as my ribs protested at the way I was gasping for breath.

She smiled up at me, licking her lips, as I fought to control my body, trembling from eyeballs to toes.

"That was some dessert, cowboy," she laughed. "You look like you need to lie down."

She was still in charge. God, I loved that, but one thing I knew for sure, another few weeks from now and I was going to be the one calling the shots.

"Enjoy it while you can, sweetheart," I gasped out. "Payback's a bitch."

She arched one eyebrow as she smiled at me, stripping her

clothes from her beautiful, perfect body.

"I'm counting on it. But for now, I'm in charge. On the bed."

I didn't want to disrespect a lady, especially one who had me by the balls—literally—so I lay down.

I tried to run my hands along her body but she flicked them away.

"Uh-uh!" she smirked, wagging her finger at me. "And remember, nothing too vigorous."

I rolled my eyes. She was *never* going to let me forget that.

"You know," she said, thoughtfully, "the first day I saw you, I thought, now *that's* a long, cold drink of water on a hot day."

"You did?"

"Why do you think I followed you out with that darned coffee?"

I frowned in concentration, recalling every detail of that day.

"At first, I thought it was because you felt sorry for me, because … you know."

"And later?"

"I was confused. I couldn't work out why you'd done it if it wasn't … charity. I guess I just thought you were being nice."

She laughed out loud. "I was!"

"So, you'd have followed me out to the truck if I'd been toothless, bow-legged and with a gut that reached my knees?"

"Oh, especially then!" she smiled. "Honestly, Jordan, I think I would have taken a coffee to anyone just to make dismal Doreen pissed. But you…" and she licked her lips again, "you were definitely a special case. In fact, just looking at you makes me thirsty all over again."

She reached over to the bedside cabinet and took a long drink from her champagne glass.

"You want some?"

"No, sweetheart. I reckon I've had enough for tonight."

"Pity," she said, a wicked look in her eye.

Then she dribbled champagne from her mouth onto my chest and down toward my belly button. It wasn't cold, but it still made me jump. The movement drew a curse from me as my ribs protested.

"Oops, sorry!" she giggled. "Let me make it up to you."

And she licked down my whole body. My *whole* body.

"It's nice having you back in one piece," she said, with the air of someone at an art gallery. "You're so pretty."

"Pretty?" I scoffed.

"Yep. Very pretty. I mean, for fuck's sake! You've got better skin than me, longer eyelashes, and cheekbones that could slice cheese. I have acne once a month and blow up like a beach ball."

I couldn't help laughing.

"Crazy woman! Come here and kiss me. I'd come to you, but that might be too vigorous."

Her lips were warm against mine and sweet with champagne. Just kissing her was the Fourth of July, Christmas and every birthday rolled into one. My hands roamed across her narrow shoulders and down her arms, then back up to toy with her pretty little tits and rose-crested nipples.

I circled them with my thumbs, inhaling her gasps of pleasure.

I slipped one hand down to tease her clit, working her around, sliding my index finger in and out.

"Sweetheart," I whispered, "bring that perfect lil' pussy up here so I can taste you."

She opened one eye and squinted at me.

"You want that?"

"Hell, yeah! Climb on up."

She crawled up my body, careful to avoid my ribs. They were much better, but I don't think I could have taken her clamping her thighs down on me. We'd have to work up to that.

I gripped her hips and pulled her body down to my face, breathing in her musky scent deeply. I loved the way she smelled, most of all when she'd been working all day and hadn't showered. She was less sure, but damn, the way she tasted, it made me crazy.

I flicked my tongue up, and I heard the palms of her hands

slap against the wall above the headboard.

"Jordan," she groaned.

God, hearing her say my name like that.

I circled her, around and around, feeling her body shiver and tremble, touching, teasing, tasting.

When I flicked my tongue again, two, three, four times, she shuddered and moaned, her volume increasing with every thrust of my tongue. Seven, eight, nine times…

Yup, girl was a screamer.

Panting and glowing, she shook her hair from her face and slowly moved back down the bed, until her sweet ass was level with my hips.

"Your turn," she said. "And my turn again."

I grabbed a condom from the bedside cabinet and passed it to her.

"I'm going to miss these," she said, looking down at the small, foil packet. "I think it's the anticipation."

"Miss what, sweetheart?"

She tossed the condom back onto the table.

"We don't need them anymore, baby."

My heart skipped a beat.

"What are you tellin' me?"

"While you were … off limits. I got tested and got the all-clear for everything. I'm on the pill so … no more condoms."

Then she lowered herself onto me, smiling as I cried out softly.

I could feel so much more. I'd never, *never* gone bare before. There was so much sensation, and the heat around me nearly tipped me over the edge. I had to grit my teeth and concentrate. She felt so soft and tight and silky, and it was like every detail was more intense.

I could tell she was feeling it, and the increased friction was working for her, too.

She continued her sweet torture for another hour, taking her pleasure out of my body as she rode me again and again, until we were both satisfied. Every part of me hurt bad, and it was so fucking worth it.

As the sweat cooled on our bodies, we lay together, listening to the sound of each other breathing, listening to the music playing softly in the background, listening to the crickets outside our window.

"You okay?" she asked, her voice languid and soft with love.

"Yeah. Really good."

She sighed happily. "I can't think of one single, solitary thing that would make this moment better right now."

I trailed my fingers across the soft skin of her stomach. "Just one thing, sweetheart—the day you say yes when I ask you to marry me."

She stilled for a second, but she didn't argue. I smiled to myself.

Life was good.

Chapter 16 – Spinnaker

Torrey

I was soooo looking forward to tonight. Jordan wasn't.

He'd tried every possible reason to beg off, but I wasn't taking no for an answer. I'd been looking forward to this for a long, long time.

I looked at the new clothes I'd bought for him, still lying untouched on the bed where I'd laid them out an hour ago.

I'd never seen Jordan wear anything other than Mikey's old shirts, or the secondhand clothes Gloria had found at Goodwill. But tonight was our special night, and he deserved something new.

I may have also splurged on a dress in a dark sapphire. I knew he liked that color on me. He said it matched my eyes. It was rather demure at the front, having a high sweetheart neckline, cap sleeves and a skirt that rested just above my knees. But the back was something else, slashed to the waist, hardly there at all really, and revealing a lot of bare back. Which meant, of course, that I couldn't wear a bra with it. Yep, he'd go insane. I was counting on it.

I'd also gone to town on the makeup; smoky eye shadow that made my eyes look huge, lashings of mascara, and dark cherry lipstick that I planned for Jordan to kiss off of me later.

I stared down at the black jeans and plain v-neck t-shirt, also black, that I'd bought for him. My man always looked hot, but tonight he was going to look smokin'.

Although right now he was pissing me the hell off.

I marched down hall to the bathroom and banged on the door.

"Get your ass out here *now!* You're not getting out of this so just suck it up. You've got one minute before I come in there and kick your ass."

He grumbled something that I couldn't hear, probably just as well.

I'd counted to 47 when the bathroom door swung open and he walked out, his skin sparkling from the drops of water dewing across his body.

My eyes were drawn automatically to his broad chest, ridged stomach and low hanging towel, before traveling back up his tatted arms and shoulders, across his chest again, to his freshly shaven cheeks, where I finally met his amused gaze.

He raised one eyebrow, his lips curling in a devilish smile.

"Like what you see, sweetheart?"

Oh yeah, I really did.

I narrowed my eyes at him.

"I know what you're doing, and standing there looking as tasty as prime rib isn't going to work. We're going out to have F.U.N!"

"You sure about that, sweetheart?" he asked, dropping his left hand to the front of the towel and cupping himself.

I bit back a groan. He was just one big slice of wickedness.

"Jordan!" I whined. "I want to go *out!* It's been so long. Please do this for me, for us."

He sighed and looked down. "I know. I'm sorry."

I stepped forward to hold his face gently. "Don't be sorry, baby. It'll be okay. We're going to have a lovely meal, go dancing, and make love 'til dawn. Just like you said you wanted to. Besides, Bev and Pete are going to be there ... well, not for the last bit, obviously."

He managed a small smile.

"Yeah, I'm being a total pussy. Just cain't help bein' a lil' nervous, ya know?"

I smiled and planted a kiss on his soft lips.

"The worst that can happen is that you see that I've got two left feet and leave me for a woman who dances like Cheryl Burke."

He shook his head.

"I have no idea who that is, sweetheart, but there's no way she could be more beautiful than you."

"Good answer, cowboy. Now get your cute ass into the bedroom and *get dressed!*"

He smiled and winked, then strolled down the hallway dropping his towel just before he turned into the bedroom.

Ooh, maybe just a quick... No! No! No! Food... Dancing... Sex later.

God, I hoped I was making the right decision.

He emerged a few minutes later fully dressed. The t-shirt molded to his chest and the jeans advertised his fabulous, taut, toned ass.

"Um, I think you bought a size too small, Torrey," he said, looking desperately uncomfortable. "The shirt and pants are great but ... kind of tight. I really appreciate what you're tryin' to do for me but maybe I'd better change and..."

"Don't you dare change a thing, Jordan Kane!" I barked. "The clothes are a perfect fit. Every woman within a ten mile radius will be unable to keep her hands to herself."

"I don't know..." he mumbled.

"Luckily, I do." I walked forward and ran my fingers freely over his chest and waist, before finally pushing my hands into his back pockets. "See? Just perfect."

He blew out a breath. "Just so long as you think so," he said.

I kissed him quickly. "Come on. I can't wait to show you off."

I led the way down the stairs and heard the breath hitch in his throat when he got an eyeful of my backless dress.

"Christ, Torrey!"

"You like?" I asked, grinning at him over my shoulder.

"Um, yeah?" he said, hesitantly.

My smile fell. "What's wrong? Don't you like it?"

His voice was choked when he replied.

"Hell, yeah, but sweetheart I really don't want to get into a fight tonight."

"We're not fighting," I said, sucking my teeth in irritation. "You're just being a grump."

He smirked back at me. "Not fightin' with *you!* Some guy is gonna look at you wrong and I'll have to rearrange his face, that's all."

"Oh, if that's all, no problem. I'll protect you, cowboy."

He shook his head, holding back a grin. "I'll keep you to that."

Gloria and Paul were sitting watching TV in the family room as we left.

"Have fun, you two," Paul said, and Gloria offered a small smile.

Jordan just nodded at them so it was left to me to do the civility thing again.

"Thanks! See you."

I'd already loaded an overnight bag into the trunk without telling Jordan, so there was nothing else to delay us. I heard my phone beep in my purse.

"That's probably Bev making sure that we're on our way," I laughed.

"Damn," he muttered, "she's worse than you."

The drive to Corpus took about 40 minutes. Jordan was twitching and shifting around, part excited to be leaving the town limits, and part anxious about going to the city.

By the time we crossed the Copano Bay Bridge he was practically climbing out of the damn seat. The bridge floated over the warm blue waters of the bay, almost skimming the surface. I'd swear that anyone traveling underneath it in a boat would lose their hat. Jordan was straining to stare out of the window, his eyes clouded with memories.

Another 10 miles and Corpus was spread out in the distance, heralded by the elegant Harbor Bridge.

His expression seemed tense.

"Everything okay?" I asked, a little nervously.

"I remember … we came here for Mikey's eighteenth birthday."

Oh crap.

"I didn't know, Jordan. I'm so sorry! We can go back. We don't have to…"

He turned and smiled, although his eyes were sad.

"No, sweetheart. I'm done hidin' from the past. Time to start makin' some new memories."

I reached out to take his hand. I was so proud of him. He'd grown so strong, changed so much since the damaged man I'd met all those months ago.

"I love you," I said. "What we have, you and me, it's what I thought love should be, but I'd stopped believing it existed."

He smiled warmly. "Love you, too, Torrey Delaney."

The restaurant that Bev and Pete had chosen was right on the harbor, with views of yachts moored in the bay. Jordan tugged nervously at the neck of his t-shirt while I parked the Princess in a cloud of exhaust fumes.

"Stop that!" I said, making a grab for his hand. "You look gorgeous!"

His eyes shifted nervously toward the upscale restaurant.

"I don't know, Torrey…"

I cut off his protest with a kiss.

"You're a free man, Jordan. You can go wherever you want. Do you trust me?"

He nodded and took a deep breath. "Yeah, I do."

We walked slowly toward the restaurant and before we even got there, I spotted two women in their thirties checking him out. They even stopped and pretended to be interested in an ugly dress displayed in a shop window, just so they could get a look at him from the rear as we passed by. *Tramps.* Having a hot boyfriend definitely had some disadvantages. The benefits, however... Yeah, I'd be looking forward to those later.

He put his arm around me protectively when a group of students walked past, smelling like they'd been swimming in a brewery. One of them made the mistake of whistling at me.

Jordan all but growled at the guy, and I swear each one of them became a little paler at the sight of him. The ice cold expression that he'd perfected in prison was masking his face. I knew what lay behind it, but they took him at face value.

One of the kids held up his hands.

"Just enjoyin' the scenery, man. No harm, no foul."

Ooh, he really shouldn't have tried talking his way out of it.

"Back off, jerk off!" snarled Jordan, "Or you'll be wearin' your teeth as a decoration."

I had to make a grab for his arm before he tried to follow them.

"Reel it in a bit, honey," I said, as calmly as possible.

To my surprise, when he turned to face me he was grinning widely.

"What are you playing at?" I asked, exasperation heating my voice.

He shook his head, still smiling.

"What?" I insisted.

He winked at me. "Felt good!"

I slapped his arm.

"You scared the shit out of me! I thought you were about to go postal and take that guy's head off."

He chuckled lightly. "Not sayin' I wouldn't," and he wrapped his arm more tightly around me as we entered the restaurant.

The hostess perked up considerably, beaming at Jordan. He

looked puzzled, glancing at me for an explanation. I rolled my eyes—the first of many times that evening, I suspected.

"May I show you to a table for two, sir? Somewhere a lil' private, perhaps?" and she giggled.

So unprofessional! I didn't go giggling all over customers when I was making them their damn coffee! Then an annoying little memory reminded me I'd made a play for Jordan the very first day he'd walked into the Busy Bee diner. But he'd been by himself, so fair game. I seemed to have become suddenly invisible to the hostess.

"No, that's all right," I said, a little briskly. "We're meeting friends. In fact, I see them now."

I steered Jordan into safer waters, but when I glanced over my shoulder, that slut of a hostess was *still* checking him out. Yeah, she'd just cost her colleagues a tip.

"Wow, look at you!" said Bev, staring at him with obvious appreciation.

Jordan looked a little pink when she jumped up and hugged him tightly. He was definitely more comfortable with Pete's handshake. Guess he was what they called a 'man's man'. Mmm-hmm, I liked the way that sounded. A lot.

They'd already started on the wine but Jordan shook his head when Pete offered it to him.

"No thanks, man."

Pete looked surprised but Bev grinned.

"You haven't told him, have you?"

Jordan turned to look at me, a question in his eyes.

"Nope. It's your gift," I said to Bev, "yours and Pete's. Why don't you tell him?"

"Tell me what?" Jordan asked, impatiently. "What's on that tricky lil' Boston brain?"

"Well," Bev answered for me excitedly, "Torrey said how you'd been wishin' and a-hopin' to go upscale, and we know that y'all will be moving on soon, so this is kind of a farewell present. We're all staying in a hotel in town tonight—our treat. So, we'll all be drinking and dancing and lovin' till dawn!"

She squealed and clapped her hands together, then high-fived me.

Jordan looked stunned.

"What do you think, baby?" I asked, gently.

"Wow. Just wow, you guys," he said.

He stared at his hands, obviously overwhelmed.

Pete tapped him lightly on the arm and poured an extra glass of wine for him.

"Here's to getting laid tonight, buddy!"

Bev scowled but Pete's comment made Jordan smile. "I'll drink to that," he said. "Thanks, guys." Then he turned to me. "Thank you for makin' tonight so special, sweetheart."

He kissed me softly, and I was starting to respond when the freakin' server came up to take our orders.

Jordan's eyes got a little wide when he saw the size of the menu—and the prices—but other than raising his eyebrows at me, he didn't question it further.

We had a fabulous meal, gazing out at the sun setting over the harbor. The ocean turned from blue to a blaze of orange, then to silver as the evening slipped quietly into night.

I felt a frisson of sadness knowing that we'd be leaving real friends behind when we headed out. It had surprised me to find that there were lots of things that I was going to miss about small town Texas. Sure, we could come back and visit, but I also knew we were never going to live here again. It was for the best.

"So, what have you two planned for the rest of the evening?" I asked as we left the restaurant, well fed and super relaxed.

"There's a great live music place that Pete's taken me to before," Bev said, excitedly. "They have a lot of blues and Texas country, but quite a few indie bands play there, too."

We were nearly outside Dr. Rockit's when Jordan suddenly came to a halt, his body stiff and unresponsive.

I saw immediately what had caught his attention.

Ryan Dupont.

I couldn't believe that this would be the one person we'd run into, 30 miles from home.

"Jordan, no!" I gasped.

I couldn't tell if he'd heard me or not; he didn't respond.

Ryan's eyes flicked to me, back to Jordan, then across to Pete and Bev, who weren't sure what was going on, but knew it was nothing good.

Jordan spoke first.

"You gonna take at swing at me again, Ry? Because I'm tellin' you, I'm done payin' my debt and I'll be swingin' back this time."

I don't think Pete had ever gotten into a fist fight in his life because he looked as helpless as me and Bev. Even so, he took a step forward, ready and willing to take a stand.

Ryan didn't even look in our direction; his eyes were fixed on Jordan. He shook his head slowly, his expression questioning.

"You didn't press charges?" he said, quietly.

Jordan looked at him coldly. "Why would I?"

"Because…"

Ryan couldn't finish the sentence, but Jordan just watched him, unblinking, unnerving.

"We were friends," Jordan answered, at last.

Ryan swallowed several times. "I still hate you for what you did."

Jordan didn't move a muscle.

"I know."

Ryan nodded, then spoke again.

"But I'll always hate myself, too … for not stoppin' you and Mikey gettin' in the car that night."

The two men continued to stare at each other, and I held my breath. Eventually, Ryan dropped his gaze and stepped around us, walking away, his shoulders hunched and his head down.

My heart was still racing from fear as I looked up at Jordan. His expression was distant but not angry or upset.

"Are you okay?" I asked, rubbing his arm to remind him I was there.

He gave a small smile and brushed a soft kiss over my lips.

"I'm havin' a night out with my woman, so yeah, I'm good."

"Jesus! That was intense!" Bev burst out. "I near about peed myself!" Pete rolled his eyes, and she pinched his cheeks. "Aw, you love me because I make you look classy, hon!"

I couldn't help laughing and was relieved to see that Jordan was amused, too.

The bouncer at Dr. Rockit's frowned when he saw Jordan, clearly assessing how much back up would be required if he needed to get drastic on his ass, but it wasn't necessary.

We laughed and danced, and Jordan learned that I really did have two left feet, and he told me he loved me anyway. Then we danced some more, made a whole load of good memories, and drank until the place closed.

At the end of a wonderful evening, we walked to our hotel with its views over the harbor, and Jordan loved me until dawn.

Just like he wanted.

Jordan

"Are you sure you've got everything?" Torrey asked me for the ninth or tenth time.

I smiled and raised an eyebrow.

"Waal, let me see … I've got my toothbrush, a change of underwear, my cell phone but I'm sure there's somethin' … uh, wait, there's my ornery girlfriend who's incredibly hot. Yup, I've got it all."

She slapped my arm and pulled a face.

"Really, Jordan? You don't wear underwear. There's nothing else you want to bring?"

I shook my head. "There's nothin' for me here, sweetheart."

That was true in so many ways.

I had a picture of Mikey in my wallet, but I didn't need it to remember everything about him. He'd always be with me, in my quiet heart.

"I'd like to stop by Mikey's grave, just to say goodbye," I said, seriously. "I haven't been since…"

She knew what I meant without me having to finish the sentence.

"Of course," Torrey said, with a smile. "I always thought we would."

I turned to look at the house, the place I'd grown up, and the place where I'd learned to live again. I knew that it wasn't the house that had done that, it was this amazing woman at my side. But still, the house had been my home once—it had been happy.

I wondered if I'd ever see it again.

I wondered if I'd ever see my parents again, as well. I'd stay in touch from time to time, for sure, but I didn't feel particularly close to them. We'd tried to rebuild bridges, talked some about prison and about Mikey, but I was itchin' to leave. My future was with Torrey and I wanted to look ahead, not back. It was time to move on.

They'd left early for church, knowing that by the time they got back, I'd be long gone. The goodbyes had been awkward and brief. I'd given vague promises about keeping in contact. I suspected Torrey would make me keep them.

I ran my eyes over the tall cottonwoods that Mikey and I had challenged each other to climb, the paint peeling on the house's weatherboards, the gutters full of leaves, taking it all in.

I was leaving Mikey's truck behind, too. I'd meant it when I said there was nothing here for me. My parents could do what they wanted with it—it wasn't mine. Dad had implied I could have it, but I'd got over wanting anything from them. I turned him down.

I laid a hand on the fresh paintwork, the image of the bleeding heart with Mikey's name across it, then slid into the passenger seat of Torrey's Firebird.

"Ready?" she asked.

"I'm ready."

I glanced in the side mirrors as she drove down the dirt road, seeing the house sinking back into the shadow of the trees. I was saying goodbye.

Torrey reached over to take my hand, squeezing it lightly, then she rested it on her knee.

It was fall, but the sun was still warm as we arrived at the cemetery. I could smell salt on the breeze drifting in from the ocean.

We made our way along the familiar paths to Mikey's grave.

But as we approached, all the breath in my lungs left in a painful rush when I took in his tombstone.

Michael Gabriel Kane
November 25 1988—July 10 2006
Beloved Son
& Brother
"Do not fear those who kill the body but cannot kill the soul."

"Oh my God," Torrey whispered. "'And brother' … they … your parents … they've had the inscription changed!"

I nodded, unable to find the words.

I was there, memorialized with Mikey forever. With my parents. Our love for him recorded together.

After so many years of being erased, I was finally visible. It was nearly impossible to take in.

For the first time, I felt it inside, I felt forgiven.

"They'll be at church now," Torrey said, softly. "Do you want to go find them? Say goodbye properly? We can still do that if you like…"

"Yes," I managed to say. "I'd like that."

I rested my hand on the sun-warmed stone.

"Bye, Mikey. Got to get gone now. Torrey and me are leavin' town and I don't know if we'll be back. I'll never forget you." My eyes drifted once more over the fresh inscription. "I love you, brother."

Torrey took my hand as we walked back to the car.

"Are you okay?" she asked, anxiously.

I turned to smile. "Yeah, I'm good."

The cemetery wasn't far from the church. I could hear the sound of singing as soon as I opened the car door.

I knew Dad and Momma usually sat at the back, so I hoped we'd be able to see them without disturbing the service too much.

But that wasn't what happened.

The singing finished the second I pushed open the heavy wooden door. It creaked loudly and everyone—the whole freakin' congregation—turned to look.

Murmuring broke out everywhere. I saw the faces of my parents. They looked stunned. Then Dad waved at us, asking us to join them. I hesitated for a moment, but felt Torrey's warm hand in mine and she smiled.

We walked up the aisle, and I couldn't help feeling the weight of that symbolism with Torrey at my side.

As we sat down next to my parents, the murmuring grew louder. I thought we were seconds away from a walkout when Reverend Williams cleared her throat.

"The theme of my sermon today is forgiveness." She looked right at me as she said it. "I want you to think about the words spoken by Our Lord in Matthew: *Then Peter came up and said to him, 'Lord, how often will my brother sin against me, and I forgive him? As many as seven times?' Jesus said to him, 'I do not say to you seven times, but seventy times seven'.*"

I was still sort of waiting for people to get up and walk out despite the Rev's pretty speech, but they didn't.

"I've been guilty myself," the Rev continued. "Guilty of not doing as I preach. That changes today. I'd like to thank my daughter Torrey Delaney for joining us, and I'd like you all to welcome the son of Gloria and Paul. It's good to see you, Jordan."

There was a muttering of discontent but it was muted.

"Holy shit!" giggled Torrey, behind her raised hand.

It was all I could do to keep from laughing.

The Reverend talked a whole lot more words, but I didn't

hear her.

I glanced across at Torrey—her eyes were glowing with love and pride. She squeezed my hand tightly and I saw her blink back tears.

Somehow my life had come full circle and I was again surrounded by my family, and felt love in my heart. The future was the road ahead.

"And I'd like to finish," said the Reverend, "by reminding you of the words in Ezekiel: *'For I have no pleasure in the death of anyone, declares the Lord God; so turn, and live'.*"

I'd never been much for the Bible. Even so, I'd read it a ton of times in prison when the state pen library had nothing else to offer. But I liked those words, the ones about turning and living, because that was what Torrey had been trying to teach me. I'd finally learned the lesson, and it was what I intended to do.

At the end of the service, the congregation stood up to leave. Several people came to speak to Dad and Momma—a couple even thanked me for coming and shook my hand. I was so surprised, I didn't know what to say. Torrey nudged my elbow and grinned at me.

Then I saw the Reverend walking toward us.

"Looks like your momma has somethin' to say," I whispered, nodding in the Rev's direction.

Torrey pursed her lips and folded her arms.

"Don't be too hard on her, sweetheart. What she said today was real nice."

Torrey scowled. "Took her long enough to say it in public!"

"Yeah, well I seem to remember someone telling me that late was better than never," I reminded her.

"Hello, Torrey, Jordan."

"Reverend," I said, holding out my hand.

She took it with a smile. "I hear you're leaving us?"

I shrugged. "Yeah, fresh start. It seemed best."

"Are you sure?" she questioned. "You have friends here in the community. It's taken us a while, I know, but it's true."

I shook my head. "I'm not sure it's true, but we appreciate you sayin' it. Don't we, sweetheart?"

I threw a look at Torrey who'd remained uncharacteristically silent.

"I'm glad I got to see you before you left," the Reverend said to her daughter. "And in my church, too. That was a wonderful surprise."

Torrey cracked a smile at her mother's tone.

"Yeah, I'm glad, too. Good sermon, by the way, Mom. I liked the theme."

The Rev smiled sadly. "But you're leaving anyway."

"Yes. Like Jordan said—a fresh start for both of us."

"Where will you go?"

"We've got a few ideas but nothing definite. Maybe swing by and see Dad ... and *Ginger*."

The Reverend smiled and raised an eyebrow.

"I have a new motto: *Judge not lest ye be judged'*. What do you think?"

Torrey laughed. "I think it's going to catch on."

"Well..." the Reverend paused for a moment. "Say hello to your father for me—and Ginger. Travel safe. And Torrey, I know these past few months have been ... difficult, but please know that if you ever need it, you'll always have a home with me. Both of you."

Torrey's eyes filled with tears and she flung her arms around her mother.

"Thanks, Mom," she choked out.

"I love you, honey. So much."

Then to my amazement, the Rev pulled me into a tight hug.

"Good luck to you, Jordan. You deserve it, you really do. I believe you deserve my daughter's love, too. And being her mother, I don't say that lightly." She smiled. "And one more thing: 'For I know the plans I have for you, declares the Lord, plans for welfare and not for evil, to give you a future and a hope'. Look after my little girl, Jordan. She's very special to me."

"And to me, ma'am. I promise I'll take care of her. You have my word."

The Rev swiped at a couple of her own tears and managed a small smile.

"Thank you, Jordan. God bless."

Outside the church we said our final goodbyes to my dad and Momma.

It was still stilted and awkward, but I thanked them for the new inscription on Mikey's tombstone.

"I'm sorry it took so long, son," said Dad. "It was your momma's idea."

I looked at both of them, seriously surprised. "Really? Well, um, thanks."

I shoved my hands into my pockets and we stood there uncomfortably before Torrey kissed each of them, and grabbed my arm.

"We'll be in touch, Paul, Gloria," she said.

We climbed into the Firebird, and Torrey waved as she accelerated away. I didn't look back.

Torrey

I waved out of the window as I drove away. Jordan neither waved nor turned around. He looked straight ahead, his face set, but his eyes calm.

I reached over and took his hand. He looked down at our entwined fingers, then raised my hand to his lips, placing a small kiss on each knuckle. My heart skipped, and I was grinning from ear to ear.

"So, where are we going, Jordan?"

He turned and smiled at me.

"Anywhere you want, sweetheart." He waved his arm toward the horizon. "Anywhere you want."

Epilogue – Ten Months Later

Jordan

It had been some road trip.

From Texas, we'd driven east, taking in most of the southern states, stopping at Graceland so Torrey could get some souvenirs for her friends in Boston. That's what she said, but I'm pretty sure she was a closet Elvis fan.

We took our time on the journey, enjoying being together. Talking, always talking, and laughing a lot, planning for the future, daring to dream.

We stayed in cheap motels as we made the long trip north, but woke each morning to a world that seemed full of possibilities. Three or four times we slept outside, laying out blankets on the ground. Torrey wasn't keen on camping, but after years of being in small rooms, I breathed easier outside, the sky limitless above us. She tolerated it, but the further north we drove, the colder it became, and the more she insisted on staying somewhere with a roof.

Fall in New England was just as pretty as everyone said it would be, but I was shocked by the change in temperature. Torrey said that was nothing, and that if we stayed another month, we'd need to get snow tires and chains.

I liked Boston more than I expected, despite not being big on cities in general. Seeing history in the buildings around me every day was new, and Torrey gave me a full tour of the Freedom Trail, including Paul Revere's House. East Coast people were more chill than I'd been expecting, although crowds could still freak me out a little. I didn't think I'd ever be able to get used to being around so many people. But wrapped up in a heavy sweater, my prison tattoos hidden, I didn't feel like people were staring at me all the time anymore.

I liked South Boston—Southie, as Torrey called it—with the converted distilleries where a bunch of artistic types seemed to live, small galleries dotted around, and every café displaying paintings. I'd never been anywhere like that before. Hell, I'd never left Texas before. It made me want to start sketching again, something I hadn't done since I was a kid, other than the picture I'd made of Torrey when she was sleeping. Of course, that meant Torrey turned up with a sketchpad and a box of drawing pencils. She was always trying to help me think big. It wasn't easy, and I knew that if I got stressed, I'd shut down on her, but I was trying.

I hadn't been looking forward to meeting her old man, but he'd been surprisingly okay, for a lawyer. At least, he hadn't had me arrested. Yeah, I knew that was irrational, but I couldn't help it. And Torrey said if I kept acting so suspiciously whenever I saw a cop, I'd get my ass arrested. Her exact words were, 'Chill the fuck out!'

As Torrey had predicted, her dad had taken me up to his den to show me a cabinet full of golfing trophies. He cared less about the fact that I was an ex-con than that I'd never played golf. He offered to take me onto the fairway with him, but Torrey said we wouldn't be staying that long. Thank God.

His new wife, Ginger, was something else. She sure didn't

seem like the kind of woman a lawyer would marry, but they seemed happy enough, I guess. And Torrey was right about her tits—they were freakin' huge: with the emphasis on 'freak'. Ginger said she used to be a singer on cruise ships going back and forth to the Caribbean before she got hitched. After hearing her version of *Big Spender*, I thought my ears would melt, and I couldn't help wondering how much work she could have gotten from yowlin' like a bobcat. Torrey's dad applauded like he meant it, and I wondered if love was deaf as well as blind.

Ginger was friendly enough. Maybe even a little *too* friendly, and after the first evening we stayed with them, I begged Torrey never to leave me alone with her stepmom again. Torrey kept trying to find out what had happened, but I was taking that secret to the grave.

Torrey's Boston friends had been less than friendly, which I could tell was a huge disappointment to her. They didn't seem to be able to get over the fact that she'd given up her paralegal job because of her asshole ex-boss, to go and 'lick her wounds in Whogivesashit-ville', as one sharp faced woman in a suit had put it. And it was clear that they thought she was scraping the bottom of the barrel by hooking up with me. It wasn't just about having been in prison, which Torrey was pretty open about, but surrounded by people with degrees from Harvard and MIT, they seemed to think I was just a dumb hick—all muscle and no brain, with straw in my hair.

I even heard one of them telling Torrey that I was the kind of guy that she should sleep with and forget. Except she didn't say 'sleep with'. Fucking bitch.

We didn't stay long in Boston after that.

We celebrated my 24th birthday in a wood cabin in Moose Brook State Park, eating pizza out of cardboard boxes, and drinking beer out of cans. It might not sound like much, but to me it was perfect. And I got to fall asleep in my woman's arms.

We carried on north aways, almost to the border, then wintering in Vermont. We ended up living in a farmhouse with an old couple who needed someone to do the grunt work while their son was laid up with a broken leg. I knew some about cattle ranching, but that had all been big scale stuff. This was a small, organic farm that raised dairy cattle. I didn't mind the work, but getting up at 4 AM to milk a cow who was more interested in wrapping a cold, wet tail around my face—well, it wasn't for me.

But I saw snow for the first time, and Torrey helped me build my first snowman, too. I wanted to make love to her in the snow, but she'd nixed that idea, staring at me like I was crazy. Yeah, crazy for her.

Torrey had bought herself a laptop and was showing me all the amazing stuff I'd missed in the last eight years. I couldn't get my head around some of the cool shit that had been invented. She'd even tried to get me one of those smartphones, but I argued that I didn't need it, since the only person I ever wanted to call was her.

She set up Skype so we could talk to Bev and Pete. They had their own news: Bev had got a good job in Corpus working at something in finance, and they'd moved in together. They looked happy. We promised we'd meet up again, although none of us knew when that might be.

Our first Christmas together was perfect. We shared a huge roast dinner sitting with the old couple and their son in front of a real fire, watched *It's a Wonderful Life*, and phoned our parents in the evening. My conversation was short, but I was kind of glad that I did it.

We'd even borrowed a toboggan from the barn and made ourselves a run behind the farmhouse. Then we went to bed, ate pumpkin pie, getting crumbs on the sheets and on each other.

With the Spring thaw, we headed west, following an old wagon train route across an unending landscape of flat, featureless horizons. We ran out of money in South Dakota so I had to take another job on a farm, while Torrey worked in the office. This farm was huge, with over 2,000 head of dairy cattle, and everything was automated. Neither of us liked it much, so we stayed just long enough to put money in the bank and gas in the car. We were driving a 12-year-old Toyota Prius these days.

The Princess had died just outside of Iowa City. I was sad to see her go, but the whole engine block needed replacing and we just didn't have the money. Torrey shed tears for that hunk of metal, but the Toyota was much lighter on gas. She said it was an old folks' car but it got 42mpg, so I guess she didn't mind too much in the end.

After South Dakota, we pushed on west, heading through Wyoming and Utah. By then, I think we both had a destination in mind, although neither of us said anything to confirm or deny it.

It was getting late by the time I saw the lights up ahead, the neon glow of the city throwing an orange halo into the night time sky.

Torrey was fast asleep, her head leaning against the window, my coat providing a makeshift pillow.

I felt excitement bloom in my belly. It was springtime, and we'd driven past miles of yellow, pink and purple flowers painting the desert with vibrant colors. We'd seen so much and been so many places, and yet we'd ended up here. Maybe it was fate, maybe it was inevitable. I liked to think that. From the very first day I'd seen her in the Busy Bee diner—it was all pointing to here.

I rested my hand on Torrey's knee and gently shook her awake.

"Hey, sweetheart, we're nearly there. You don't want to miss this."

Her eyes opened and she blinked a couple of times.

"Wow! We're really here! Las Vegas!"

I grinned at her. "You know what this means, sweetheart?"

She gave me an innocent smile, feigning ignorance.

"And what would that be, cowboy?"

"Weddin' capital of the world. Guess you'll have to marry me after all."

She stared for a moment, then wrinkled her nose.

"Jordan Kane! That is the least romantic proposal I've *ever* heard!" she huffed.

"How many proposals you heard then?" I teased her.

"None, but it's still the worst!"

I couldn't help laughing at her. "Is that a no then, sweetheart?"

We drove past a sign that announced, *'Little White Wedding Chapel'*.

"Are you certain I cain't tempt you?"

"Huh," she pouted. "You haven't even got a darned ring!"

"Sure I do."

"What?"

"Sweetheart, I've had a ring since before we left Texas."

Her jaw dropped open.

"What … you … but … I…"

Her face was a picture—until she yelled at me.

"Turn the car around, Jordan!"

Not the reaction I'd been hoping for.

"Sweetheart…"

"Turn the damn car around!"

I made an illegal U-turn, my heart pounding, wondering how the hell I was going to fix this. But when we saw the sign for the wedding chapel again, she yelled, "Pull in!"

"What?"

"*Now*, Jordan Kane. But you'd better do it right this time!"

A slow grin stretched across my face.

"You mean you'll do it? You'll marry me?"

Her eyes narrowed dangerously. "What part of 'do it right' did you not understand?"

I drove into the parking lot and turned off the engine. She was still staring straight ahead, but I could tell she was trying not to crack a smile. I knew that look by now.

I ran around the SUV and yanked open her door. I offered her my hand and she took it, daintily stepping out of the car.

"Um, I need the ring, sweetheart," I said.

"Well, I don't have it!" she snorted.

"Yeah, actually you do. It's in the pocket of my jacket."

She stared at me in disbelief.

"I've been sleeping on it all this time?"

I smiled at her and winked.

"I'm so mad at you right now!" she hissed.

"No, you're not, firecracker," I said, calmly.

She passed me my jacket without comment, and I fished around for the small velvet box.

I took a deep breath, trying to make sure I had enough oxygen in my lungs to say what needed to be said, and I dropped down on one knee.

"Torrey Delaney, you give me hope. From the first time I saw your beautiful face, you showed me your beautiful heart, too. I didn't expect to find happiness in this world, but it's a gift you give me every single day. I love you, and I want to spend my whole life lovin' you. Will your crazy heart beat for me? Will you become my wife?"

I offered her the small velvet box and she opened it slowly. When her eyes met mine, they were shining with tears.

"Sapphires?"

"Like your beautiful eyes, sweetheart." I took the ring from the box, and slipped it onto her finger. "Looks good there."

She nodded, blinking back tears.

"You'd better get up off of your knees, cowboy," she said, at last. "We've got a wedding to get to."

"So that's a yes?" I asked, hopefully.

She smiled. "It was never going to be a no."

I stood up, not caring that I was covered in dust and dirt from a long drive. I gathered her into my arms and promised myself I'd never let her go. Through thick and thin, this woman was it for me.

"I guess we'd better see if this wedding chapel lives up to its reputation and really is 24/7," she said, giggling into my neck.

I pulled away slightly so I could see her face.

"You okay with this, sweetheart? You don't want to ask your momma to marry us or anythin'? I can wait."

I really didn't want to, but I'd do it if that's what she wanted. She shook her head and smiled.

"That's not us, Jordan. Anyway, we're already blessed."

I walked into that wedding chapel, the happiest man in the whole freakin' world. My day began and ended with her. And it always would.

THE END

HARVEY BERRICK
PUBLISHING

Don't forget to look for bonus chapters **www.janeharveyberrick.com**

The Education of Sebastian

A friendship between the lost and lonely Caroline, and the unhappy Sebastian, leads to an illicit love that threatens them both.

"This book made my heart RACE. It was a captivating story of forbidden love. I'm still recovering from the huge cliffhanger ending and most definitely planning to go straight on to book #2." Aestas Bookblog

The Education of Caroline

Ten years after their first affair, Sebastian and Caroline meet again: this time in very different circumstances, against the background of the war in Afghanistan. Now a successful journalist, Caroline meets US Marine Sebastian Hunter—can old passions be rekindled?

The concluding story of 'The Education of Sebastian'.

*"Ohhh I had so much anticipation going into this one!! After the brutal cliffhanger at the end of **book one** that had my heart in knots and my heart in my throat I just NEEDED more!"* Aestas Bookblog

Coming Soon!

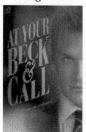

At Your Beck & Call

Hallen Jansen has it all. At 28, he has a flashy car, a great apartment, and a job he's good at and that he loves—as an escort—working at your beck and call.

His life is easy, with no emotions or attachments slowing him down—choosing to keep moving, always running from the past.

But when a new client awakens unfamiliar feelings, all bets are off. Can he convince a recently divorced woman twenty years older to trust men again—to trust him? Can Hallen trust himself not to screw things up?

Surrounded by people who choose to judge them, will they make their relationship a reality, or is it heartbreak for both?

Not all services are professional.

Dazzled

Miles Stevens is a jobbing actor in London when he stumbles into the role of a lifetime.

Hollywood claims him as one of their own and so begins his journey through the parties, premieres, agents and leading ladies—and everyone wants something from him. His best friend Clare is determined that they'll have to go through her to get it.

Will appeal to readers of 'Wallbanger' and 'Love Unscripted'.

Dangerous to Know & Love
Nineteen year old Daniel Colton is the man on campus all the guys want to be, and the bad boy all the girls want to be with. His hot, tatted up body screams sex, while his eyebrow piercing enhances his beautiful face. There are rumors he has piercings in other places, too. This walking one night stand is sullen, mysterious and moody, with an explosive temper. Is he really mad, bad and dangerous to know?

Daniel lives with his older brother, Zeb, a well-known drug dealer with ties to a local gang. Their home has become party central in the months following their parents' tragic death. You want to party non-stop, drugs, alcohol, no questions asked? The Colton house is the place to go.

Lisanne Maclaine is a good girl. She's lived a sheltered life, and is looking forward to the independence starting college will bring her. She's a music major and dreams of making a living singing the blues.

When Daniel and Lisanne have to work together, Lisanne is less than thrilled. She never wanted to be in this class in the first place. She is only minoring in business to pacify her parents, and now she is stuck working with him: Mr. Cocky-and-arrogant. Daniel's bad boy reputation precedes him, and he is the epitome of what Lisanne despises. He's rude, obnoxious and has a chip on his shoulder; she just wants to get this assignment over with. She knows he's nothing but trouble and she should stay away, but there is something about Daniel that draws her in.

Slowly, she builds a friendship with Daniel and discovers there is a lot more to this college bad boy than his reputation. But he's got a secret. Once she discovers it, she finally sees Daniel for who he really is. It explains why he's so closed off to everyone, and determined to keep people at arms' length. But being his secret-keeper is harder than she ever dreamed.

Can Lisanne keep Daniel's secret? What will it cost her? Can she help falling for the notorious ladies' man? Who else will be vying for his attention and affections? Can Lisanne follow her dreams and have it all? Or will she decide that Daniel is just too Dangerous to Know?

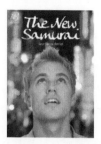

The New Samurai
Teaching in an inner city school in London is hard enough, but when Sam loses his job and his domineering girlfriend dumps him on Valentine's Day, he decides to start again somewhere new … in Japan. It's not long before his 'no women' rule is under attack.

Sexy and funny, this book will appeal to fans of 'One Day'.

Expo$ure
What would you do if you found out a really, really important secret? What would you do if people were prepared to kill to stop you revealing this secret? And what would you do if the secret was held by the US government?

A thriller that will appeal to readers of 'The Ghost'.

The Dark Detective: Venator
At 20 years old, Max Darke finds himself in sole charge of the Metropolitan Police Demon Division in London. It's not a job for the faint hearted and some days, work is Hell.

For fantasy readers.

Printed in Great Britain
by Amazon.co.uk, Ltd.,
Marston Gate.